Praise for *A Soldier*

"This gripping thriller pulls you in regardless of [...] thing about the U.S. military. Readers familiar [...] ognize it here. Those who aren't will learn something important on every page."

—W.E.B. GRIFFIN, bestselling author of the Corps, Badge of Honor, Brotherhood of War, and Men at War series

"Fast, sharp, and tight: a winner." —*Kirkus Reviews*

"An unusually thoughtful military thriller." —*Publishers Weekly*

"Military officers will bestow on this novel the attention once reserved for Anton Myrer's [novel] *Once an Eagle,* required reading for captains and majors." —*St. Louis Post-Dispatch* (Best Books of 2001)

"An engaging and thoughtful look into military-civilian relations and the moral dilemma they may present." —*Army Times*

"Smart [and] thoughtful . . . A book of intelligent ideas and prophetic warning." —*The Seattle Times*

"A first-rate novel about the contemporary American military and its response to social, political, and technological change." —*The Weekly Standard*

"Tom Ricks brings the information warfare and new weapons technology of today's military into the human conflict that confronts officers and NCOs dealing with the meanings of duty, honor, and country. This novel, *A Soldier's Duty,* has an important message for today's leaders of all ranks and services."

—GENERAL (ret.) EDWARD C. MEYER, Chief of Staff, U.S. Army, 1979–1983

"Thomas E. Ricks has written a fast-paced, disturbing, and believable story about the fragile moral fiber that binds our armed forces. Personal ambition confused with duty, information warfare manipulating loyalties, political influence degrading readiness—*A Soldier's Duty* will seem very real to those who have served."

—MAJOR GENERAL DAVID GRANGE (U.S Army, ret.), former commander, 1st Infantry Division

"In *A Soldier's Duty,* Tom Ricks weaves timeless themes of soldiering—duty, loyalty, honor—with today's-headline concerns about technology, the post–Cold War world, and our national squeamishness about the *Pax Americana* we created and cannot now let go. Lots of people write about technology; Ricks writes about how technology changes the way real people think and live. Lots of people write about military hardware and uniforms and doctrine; Tom Ricks does all that, but wraps it in a great story that gets to what is in the soldier's heart. This book will do more than entertain; it will make readers question their most basic assumptions about what holds the Republic together."

—ED RUGGERO, author of *Duty First: West Point and the Making of American Leaders*

"The author's remarkable inside knowledge of today's military is evident on every page. . . . This provocative novel is bound to be widely popular."

—LIEUTENANT COLONEL RALPH PETERS (U.S. Army, ret.), bestselling author

"In the spirit of *Seven Days in May, Washington Post* reporter Tom Ricks applies his formidable writing talents and familiarity with today's military to a conspiratorial page-turner that highlights the military's hotly debated role in contemporary American politics."

—COLONEL RICHARD HART SINNREICH (U.S. Army, ret.)

Pulitzer Prize–winning *Washington Post* Pentagon
correspondent THOMAS E. RICKS has covered the
U.S. military for more than a decade, reporting on
operations in Afghanistan, Somalia, Haiti, Bosnia,
Kosovo, Korea, and the Persian Gulf. He is the
author of the bestselling book *Making the Corps*.
He lives outside Washington, D.C., with his
wife and children.

A SOLDIER'S DUTY

A SOLDIER'S DUTY

A

NOVEL

THOMAS E. RICKS

RANDOM HOUSE
TRADE PAPERBACKS
NEW YORK

This work was originally published in hardcover by Random House, Inc., in 2001.

Grateful acknowledgment is made to the following for permission to reprint
previously published material:

Hal Leonard Publishing Corporation: For permission to reprint a lyric excerpt from "War,"
words and music by Norman Whitfield and Barrett Strong. Copyright © 1970 (renewed 1998)
by Jobete Music Co., Inc. All rights controlled and administered by EMI Blackwood Music, Inc.,
on behalf of Stone Agate Music (a division of Jobete Music Co., Inc.). All rights reserved.
International copyright secured. Used by permission.

A. P. Watt Ltd.: Excerpt from "The Young British Soldier" from *Barrack Room Ballads*
by Rudyard Kipling. Reprinted by permission of A. P. Watt Ltd. on behalf of
The National Trust for Places of Historic Interest or Natural Beauty.

Library of Congress Cataloging-in-Publication Data

Ricks, Thomas E.
A soldier's duty : a novel / Thomas E. Ricks.
p.   cm.
ISBN 0-375-76020-2
1. Washington (D.C.)—Fiction.   2. Military policy—Fiction.   3. Conspiracies—Fiction.
4. Generals—Fiction.   5. Soldiers—Fiction.   I. Title.
PS3618.I38 S65 2000
813'.54—dc21   2001018601

Random House website address: www.atrandom.com
Printed in the United States of America
2   4   6   8   9   7   5   3
First Trade Paperback Edition
Book design by Jo Anne Metsch

Dedicated with love and thanks to
Mary Catherine Ricks, again,
and to my parents
and my children.

And for Sam and Courtney.

This is a work of fiction, and the events and people portrayed here are entirely products of the author's imagination. Any similarity to actual events or real individuals, living or dead, is coincidental.

A Note on Language

I have tried in this novel to render the English language as it is spoken in today's U.S. Army. To help the nonmilitary reader, a glossary can be found at the end of the text.

I, (state your name), do solemnly swear, that I will support and defend the Constitution of the United States, against all enemies, foreign and domestic, and that I will bear true faith and allegiance to the same. . . .

—U.S. Military Officers' Oath of Office,
Public Law 89-554

You must remember that when we enter the army we do so with the full knowledge that our first duty is toward the government, entirely regardless of our own views under any given circumstances. We are at liberty to express our personal views only when called upon to do so or else confidentially to our friends, but always confidentially and with the complete understanding that they are in no sense to govern our actions.

—Major General John J. Pershing
to First Lieutenant George S. Patton Jr.,
October 16, 1916

Generals and admirals are the most undisciplined of men. They have succeeded ever since their junior years by bending orders.

—Arthur Hadley, *The Straw Giant*

Cast of Characters

INSIDE THE PENTAGON

General John Shillingsworth—chief of staff, U.S. Army
Army General B. Z. Ames—vice chairman, Joint Chiefs of Staff
Army Major Lucinda "Cindy" Sherman—aide to General Shillingsworth
Army Major Buddy Lewis—aide to General Ames
General Warren "Wimpy" Wilson—vice chief of staff, U.S. Army
Air Force Colonel Underhill—Ames's executive officer
Army Sergeant First Class Jack Stout—Ames's bodyguard and driver
Admiral Turner J. Maddox—chairman, Joint Chiefs of Staff
General Ricardo Blades—commandant, Marine Corps
Brigadier General Moe—chief, commandant's staff group, Marine Corps
   headquarters
Secretary of Defense Trent Johnson
Lieutenant General William Still—chief of Army logistics
Army Captain Robert "Bobby" Byrnes—aide to Lieutenant General Still
Marine Captain Dewayne Decamp—staff, Crisis Action Center

OUTSIDE THE PENTAGON

President Jim Shick
National Security Adviser Willy Pitch
Air Force Captain Cisco—offensive information operations, CIA
Walter Schultz—Pentagon correspondent, *The New York Financial*
Senate Armed Services Committee Chairman Feaver
Chief Warrant Officer 4 Augustino Ojeda—investigator, Army Criminal
   Investigation Division
Army Major Winston Bray—court-martial prosecutor
Army Captain E. C. Walker—defense counsel
Judge (Army Colonel) Homer Trice—court-martial judge
Army Lieutenant Colonel Jimmy Ryan—member of court-martial panel

OUTSIDE WASHINGTON

Army Major Roland Bolton—Afghanistan and Fort Bragg, North Carolina

Army Captain Diego "Rocky" Gibraltar—Fort Drum, New York

Army Staff Sergeant Sam Cumberbatch—Fort Drum, New York

Specialist Fourth Class Belsky—radioman for Army Reserve unit

Marine Colonel (ret.) "Pistol" Pete Petrosky—Shenandoah Valley, Virginia

Prologue

Pacet Hills
Java, Indonesia
July 6, 1995
2 A.M.

All the lights went out at once, those inside the American ambassador's weekend house south of Jakarta as well as the huge floodlights that illuminated it from outside and filled the humid air with a locustlike sizzling.

The sudden silence lasted just a few beats before a huge U.S. MH-53 Special Operations helicopter began descending toward the house, shaking the thick black tropical night with its revving engines, the roar clattering against the red roof tiles two hundred feet below as the pilots followed their orders to make as much noise as possible. The assault wouldn't come from the air—that was risky and unnecessary—but Brigadier General B. Z. Ames wanted the hostage takers inside craning their necks upward.

Cutting the lights was the go signal. The Special Forces hostage team walked easily to their assigned spots. There were no shouts, not even urgent whispers. Nice and easy was Ames's philosophy. There were just six of them. In SWAT team terms, Ames was an adherent of the East Coast approach: Keep it small and simple. This was a minority view—even in Special Forces, most hostage-situation specialists preferred the West Coast approach, with its swarm of as many as twenty-four rescuers hitting a target simultaneously along three or four axes.

The team's breacher slapped a twelve-foot line of sticky plastic explosive rope in a rough square on the side of the house. Never use a door when you can blow a hole in the side of your target building. All too often, doors are booby-trapped.

Watching from the ridge above them, Ames pointed a long index finger at his waiting sniper team, crouched just below him on the top level of the terraced orchid garden. He whispered "Go" into his radio. The sniper peered into the soft green light of the thermal imager atop his .50-caliber

Barrett. In it he could see, inside the house, the fuzzy warm outline of a man crouched just below the windowsill in the living room. The sniper exhaled and slowly squeezed the trigger. The huge round blasted through the wooden wall of the house and shoved the hostage taker across the marble of the living room floor as it excavated his chest.

Ames told the rescue team waiting just outside the house to be ready to go in at the count of five. The team members buried their heads in the rich lawn, more to guard their night vision against the flash than for protection, which they had from face shields and light Kevlar body armor. The boomer rope detonated, the small explosion rolled over them and they rose into running crouches.

The first three tumbled through the smoking gap and formed a rolling T—one first scanning from right to left and then pointing left with his Heckler & Koch MP5 nine-millimeter submachine gun, the other pointing right, the third behind and between them, looking up the middle. They knew the ambassador was dead from the heart attack that had hit him as he came into his house exhausted from a full day of hosting the embassy's Independence Day reception and was surrounded by terrorists lifting his wife's chin with the barrel of an AK-47.

The Special Forces team suspected that the wife was also dead. They knew that as the stunned hostage takers had lowered the dying ambassador to the floor, she had sprinted up the stairs toward her baby's nursery. One round from a warning burst from the AK had hit her in the shoulder, and she had gone into shock, or so the hostage takers had reported by telephone. She was now their leverage: No medical care until they had word that their comrades held by the Indonesian military had been released. She had lain bleeding on the couch, and neither the acoustic sensors nor the infrared imagers had detected any movement there for more than twelve hours.

The team leader rolled across the living room floor and reached up to feel her hand. Cold and stiff. "Item Two is gone," he whispered into his headset.

The team's three shooters moved up the staircase toward the nursery. One called almost conversationally into his headset for two flash-bang grenades into the nursery at the count of two.

On the ridge, the sniper launched his first XM-84 flash-bang grenade through the plate glass of the nursery. The device exploded at 155 decibels, like a freight train bursting into the room. The shock wave of noise shook awake the baby, the last surviving member of the ambassador's family. The grenade then flared to two million candlepower, temporarily blinding and deafening the baby and her three surviving captors. Outside the room the team could hear the child's terrified wail.

One of the disoriented hostage takers stood up and fumbled toward the fresh air wafting in through the smashed window. The second flash-bang hit him on the shoulder and tumbled sideways into the corner, where it dropped onto the chest of the screaming baby and detonated, first with sound and then with bright white light. The child stopped screaming, then gave one dry cough as she was seized by cardiac arrest.

The waiting shooters saw the second white flash under the closed door and burst into the room in a three-man stack, Kevlar shields in their left hands, the short-barreled Heckler & Kochs in their right. Each fired two controlled pairs of ceramic bullets—*pop-pop,* pause, *pop-pop*—into their targets. One of the hostage takers, holding his weapon by the trigger, fired a burst across the floor as he died. Three bullets smashed the right foot of one of the shooters, who continued to crawl toward his target. When he got there he kicked away the AK-47, then fired a round into the dead man's temple.

The other two shooters did the same with their targets, sending their opponents' weapons sliding under the baby's crib. The lead shooter then switched magazines from ceramic to wall-penetrating steel jackets and fired three pairs of rounds into the closet door—two low, two high, two in the middle. "Opening the door on three," he shouted, back flat against the wall next to it. The other two lay on the floor, Kevlar shields over the backs of their heads. On his shout of "Two!" he opened the door. The old ruse sometimes caught a hiding gunman still frantically loading a pistol, but on this day the closet was empty. "Room clear," the soldier said quietly, and turned to deal with the injured shooter's foot.

The team leader came into the room. "Medic for Shooter Two, noncritical," he said into his headset. He reached into the crib and felt the side of the baby's neck. "And urgent for Item Three." He began mouth-to-mouth resuscitation.

The lights came back on in the house. Ames followed the two medics into the nursery, surveying the scene: three dead men sprawled on the floor; one medic working on Black; the other members of the team slumped down around him; the second medic at the crib, leaning over the limp baby, mournfully applying salve on the reddened depression where the "nonlethal" grenade had sledgehammered the infant's body. Ames tapped the second medic on the shoulder inquiringly.

"She's going," the medic said without looking up.

Ames stared at the baby's face, now tranquil with approaching death. His black eyebrows angled downward and his thin lips tightened as he measured the situation. There was a small chance that if they helicoptered her down to Jakarta a hospital there could shock her heart back to life. But by then she would have sustained severe brain damage. And the flash-bang likely had inflicted internal damage as it detonated on her chest. What favor would he be doing this kid by bringing her back into this world, orphaned and brain damaged, perhaps with severe, debilitating medical problems as well?

"Rick, give me a fast comms check," he said into his headphone to his executive officer back in his command post at the top of the hill. The XO flipped the "Radio Silence" switch on the comms console. He knew the code: Until further notice, Ames didn't want any of the headsets in that nursery to be transmitting. The tape machine in the command post that recorded all operations would not capture whatever it was that was about to happen.

Ames gently lifted the infant and held her tight against his chest, his left hand across her tiny nose and mouth. Tears came to his eyes. When he felt her heart stop, he waited a minute more, then gently put the corpse back into the crib. He drew the pink blanket in the crib over the child's face and turned to the team. "You didn't kill this child," he said to them. "These dead fools did."

He walked out of the room and down the stairs, head down and haggard. The team leader watched him, then turned to the other five members of the team. "General Ames takes care of his people," said Staff Sergeant Jack Stout. It was said both in admiration and admonition: What happened in this room would stay in this room, or you'd have lethal Jack Stout on your case.

PART

ONE

SPRING

"WAR! What is it GOOD for?"

Major Cindy Sherman leaned forward on the hood of the shiny red pickup, her combat boots on the front bumper, watching the OPFOR officers singing along to the tune blasting from speakers in the bed of the pickup on the far side of the bonfire. Their sweaty faces looked even redder in the light cast by the flames. The two-week-long exercise had ended hours earlier, in midafternoon, and most were still in their dusty OPFOR uniforms—tan desert fatigues with big enameled red stars on their belt buckles, a remnant of the early days of OPFOR, back in the 1980s, when Fort Irwin's crack "Opposition Force" was purely a facsimile of the Red Army.

Their faces bore the reverse-raccoon look of the veteran desert officer—sunburned cheeks and foreheads, with big white circles around their eyes where tanker's goggles had kept off the sun and dust. Sherman watched them and sipped some of her cold, hoppy draft beer.

"Absolutely nothing! Huh!" the men shouted out the answer in the song. On the *Huh,* some flung their hands forward, splashing one another with gobs of foam and beer from big one-pint plastic cups. They were very loose. Unusually, for this woman's Army, she thought, DUI charges clearly didn't seem to be a concern—they knew they could sneak back down to their houses on the post by taking the unpatrolled dirt road that had led them up to this little bowl canyon in the brown hills overlooking Fort Irwin, sprawled in the rocky wastelands of the Mojave Desert, closer to Las Vegas than to Los Angeles. They'd roll down the road with lights and engines off, park when they reached the pavement, then walk or crawl the two or three blocks back to their tidy on-base houses, with their odd lawns of pebbles instead of grass. No risk of a career-ending run-in with the military police, the real-life OPFOR.

"Say it again! Good God!" Sherman savored the irony of the boys from OPFOR, the U.S. Army's premier training force, bellowing out the words of an antiwar pop song. They were in fact the masters of war, the best of the best. For probably the first time in its history, the United States possessed the world's most effective military. It had frayed some since its peak at the time of the Gulf War, but it was still very good. OPFOR's job, day in and day out, was to test that military by running visiting brigades ragged under the desert sun.

"WAR!" Sherman watched Lewis in the middle of the seven-man line, the flames illuminating the grin on his face, throwing his shadow up the wall of the canyon bowl behind him. It was his crowd, his turf, his party. She was the S-2, or intelligence officer, of the visiting brigade—she'd acquitted herself well in the last round, finding the OPFOR scout platoon with her little Hummingbird UAV drone reconnaissance planes, then calling in devastating "time on target" simulated artillery fire. Major Buddy Lewis, OPFOR's S-3, or operations officer, had come to her brigade's tactical operations center for the after-action review and had stopped by her intelligence cell to compliment her. "Not many gringos trash the OPFOR scouts, Major Sherman."

And so here she was, having accepted his invitation to the OPFOR officers' beer blast here in Punchbowl Canyon, a location of unusual convenience. It was off Fort Irwin, and so outside the jurisdiction of the MPs, yet because it was a box canyon that jutted out from the post, it was accessible only from Army land—an ideal spot for the beer blasts frowned on by the post–Cold War "no fun allowed" Army. With the end of this exercise, many of the OPFOR officers were PCSing out, so it was a particularly big occasion, Lewis had said. She herself was moving to a new billet, she told him. And when they learned that each had orders to report to the Pentagon for tours as generals' aides, he said she just had to come to the party so they could compare notes.

Sherman had been surprised by the invitation. At West Point thirteen years earlier, Lewis had been skittish around her, politely sidestepping her company. She knew the problem: Male cadets never knew whether to compete with the female cadets or try to sleep with them. And she hadn't been the easiest cadet to figure out. She hadn't gone either of the stereotypical routes for female cadets, neither ultrafeminine nor aggressively butch. Growing up an only child in a military family and moving every two or three years, she had learned how to be alone, and lonely. But that had given her a reserved air that struck many of her Army peers as aloofness. By West Point's rigid social reckoning, she was a flake. That status was confirmed by her hobby of painting, which, as far as she could tell, she alone among four thousand cadets pursued. She leaned on it especially as a cow and a firstie, when she knew she could make it to graduation if she could just tolerate the place for those last two years.

Sherman watched Lewis as the song ended and the officers migrated over to the aluminum keg in the bed of another pickup. The bulging keg's shiny curved metal caught, bent and amplified the bonfire's flames. The color, she thought, was almost exactly Indian Yellow-Orange Lake Extra, a pigment manufactured by Old Holland, the oil-paint company that had supplied Rembrandt. It was a better paint than she was a painter, but buying it at cocainelike prices per ounce was one of her few indulgences. If I painted that beer keg realistically, capturing its actual colors, she thought, people would say it was surreal. Good training for an intell officer—you need to consider not just the reality you are portraying, but also the perceptions of your audience.

She watched Lewis jive with his buddies standing around the keg. Lewis seemed utterly at home with OPFOR, with the combative spirit of the armored cavalry. She knew their mantras: If it isn't tied down, you can take it. A group of attractive women was "a target-rich environment." Infantrymen were "crunchies," for the sound they made under the treads of your tank. A good operations order was "move north and kill everything." The best way to handle a fuel spill was to kick dust over it and move out before anyone noticed. And you could never have too much ammunition, beer or sex.

Lewis came over to her perch on the hood of his truck. At six feet, four inches, his face was almost level with hers. He was deceptively slight, she thought, carrying his weight lightly. He tilted his big square face up at her. "It's going to be tough leaving this to be a staff weenie at the Pentagon." He grinned, showing perfect white teeth in a slightly oversized jaw. He was from Riverside, California, and had always seemed to her to be a true son of Southern California, a favored son of the promised land. He looked as she expected a Californian to look, with the untroubled demeanor of an unquestioning conscience. Except for his black hair.

"Oh, yeah," she said. "Like you're going to miss living out here in the rocks and sand dunes of the Mojave Desert, a hundred and fifty miles from civilization."

"I don't know if I'd call either L.A. or Las Vegas 'civilization.'" He smiled. "But, seriously, I did try to get out of the Pentagon assignment. Guys here were like, 'I don't believe you're turning this down, Lewis.' But Ames's office wouldn't let me get out of it."

Cindy was surprised herself. Lewis had been tapped for just about the hottest job a major could have in the U.S. military—assistant aide de camp to General B. Z. Ames, the vice chairman of the Joint Chiefs of Staff. Some people said that the fast-rising general's initials stood for "Below the Zone," as his promotions had almost always preceded those of his peer group. In fact, they stood for Byron Zechariah, but nobody ever called him that. Even now, as a full four-star general, Ames still had the aura of an exciting newcomer destined for bigger things.

"I had to fight to get my new job," Sherman confessed.

"Yeah, and look where it got you," Lewis said. "Everyone I know says Shillingsworth is kind of clueless." Her new boss, General John Shillingsworth, the reserved, unassuming Army chief of staff, came from an entirely different era—he had graduated from college in 1969 and been drafted into the Army seven months later.

"People say he's a decent man and a good infantryman," Sherman said loyally. But privately she knew that was damnation with faint praise, with its subtle suggestion that he was an old soldier mired in the drying mud of the post-Vietnam era. While Ames would razzle-dazzle adversaries, friends of hers in the Pentagon said, the guileless Shillingsworth was a general Woody Hayes could understand: three yards and a cloud of dust. Army reformers were drawn to General Ames and dismissed Shillingsworth as an industrial-era attritionist. He did little to respond to that view. His personal style was classic Old Army—keep your mouth shut and your head down, move on and be inarticulate and bland. It was a recipe more effective at Fort Hood or Fort Bragg than in the Washington of 2004, with its appetite for sharp sound bites and flashy shows of "genuine" emotion. He was the kind of officer anyone would want in his brigade, but not many younger officers thought he was the man to lead the U.S. Army.

Or the entire U.S. military. Just about the only thing the two Army generals had in common was that they were considered the leading contenders to become the next chairman of the Joint Chiefs. Shillingsworth was the favorite of the steady-as-she-goes crowd. If selected, he would be the last chairman to have served in Vietnam. There were only a handful of people left in the U.S. military with Vietnam experience, and most of them were sergeant majors serving in command billets with flag officers. There were hardly any other general officers who had spent time in Vietnam—Shillingsworth had served in the Southeast Asian war as a draftee fresh out of college in Uniontown, Pennsylvania. He'd found to his surprise that he liked Army life and had gone to officer candidates' school after his combat tour.

"What's the difference between *Jurassic Park* and the Army staff?" Lewis asked her.

"You tell me, Lewis," Sherman said, bracing for the jibe.

"One is an amusement park dominated by dinosaurs"—he grinned— "and the other was just a movie."

"Spare me the OPFOR joke book. Got any encouraging words for me? Or do you just want me to pour this beer over your head?"

"Seriously, you know what amazes me?" Lewis continued, holding up a hand to fend off her moving cup. "The fact that Ames is just four years younger than Shillingsworth. They've both been out to watch rotations here, and they seem like men from different generations to me."

Sherman was faintly suspicious of the way Lewis and many of their West Point classmates had made Ames their great hope. "You'd best be careful with General Ames," she said. "I hear he's real ambitious."

Lewis shrugged. "Name me a general who isn't?"

"Fair enough." She pressed on. "When I was in the Building for my interviews, I also heard he burns people up." She had picked up the odd Army habit of referring to the Pentagon as "the Building," as if it were the only one in the world. To those who dwelled overmuch on their career prospects, it was.

Lewis shrugged again. "That's why they want me, I think," he said. "I mean, people couldn't keep up with him. His aides were getting divorces because of the hours. My qualifications are, you know, that I'm single and smart enough not to trip over my bootlaces. Word is, you don't keep up with him, he treats you like a Cat Four."

Without pausing, he came right back at her: "Why do you think Shillingsworth took you?"

Sherman smiled to herself. Lewis was following basic Army doctrine with her: The best defense is a good offense.

"Shillingsworth's XO told me during my interview that the chief always makes sure he has a smart female aide on his staff to keep him sensitized to gender integration issues." What the executive officer hadn't told her was the reasoning behind that policy. Recognizing that he was emotionally out of step with the president's new policy on opening all combat roles to women, and not wanting to trip over gender issues as his predecessors had, Shillingsworth made sure there was someone around to double-check his judgment. Integration of women into all combat branches, including infantry and armor, was now the law, and despite his qualms—intellectual, cultural, personal, professional, historical—he was determined to carry out the law as best he could, and do his best by the Army at the same time.

"The XO also said they liked that I'd served with distinction as the S-2 of a mechanized infantry brigade," she added. Sherman was part of the first generation of women to be allowed to specialize in tactical intelligence—that is, battlefield work. To her, coming from the Title IX generation of women's soccer teams, it had seemed only natural. Her private motto was "Knowledge beats gender." The closer she got to the battlefield, the truer that became: During high-intensity combat exercises, at least, male officers cared more about what was between her ears than between her legs. So far only six women had served as the S-2s of infantry brigades, and she was the first to do it exceptionally well, well enough to work as acting S-3—the second most important job in the unit—on one rotation. That tour had given her a coveted "above center of mass" rating on her efficiency report. It had led to additional tests, when for several months she had been the brigade's premier exhibit for visiting general officers and congressional delegations, who forced her into becoming a spokeswoman for females in the military, not a position she desired. She wanted to be part of the military, not a commentator on it. She'd also written a well-received article for *Military Review* on how field-grade commanders could better exploit satellite imagery.

She didn't tell Lewis about the third issue the executive officer had raised in that interview. "You have a reputation of being, uh, short-fused—a little quick on the draw with your temper," he had said, testing her.

Her first impulse was to parry and say, "You tell me: Does having leadership qualities make me a dominating bitch?" But recognizing the question for what it was, she smiled and said, "Sir, you and I both know that's what the Army calls women who are decisive and stand up for themselves." The XO had dropped the subject.

Lewis jabbed again. "With this 'Honorable Service for All' shit, Shillingsworth might like it even more if you were in a wheelchair," he snorted. "I guess they just couldn't find any gay lesbian cripples." Lewis was hardly alone in his disapproval of the president's public service initiatives that had encouraged volunteerism and had opened the military to the disabled and the openly gay. The officer corps was wounded and angry, tired of presidents who neither understood nor appreciated the military life.

As the words came out of his mouth it occurred to him a little too late that he had no idea of Sherman's sexual orientation. He looked up at her on the hood of the pickup. At the Academy he'd thought of her as a kind of female porcupine—short hair, small nose and chin and a remote personality to match. Back then, he had been attracted to women more conventional in looks and personality. Now, thirteen years later, he was struck by her challenging, angular appeal. Life had left a few nicks on her. She was more interesting-looking than conventionally pretty, he thought. The older he got, the more that appealed to him.

Were the beer and the fatigue catching up with him? He'd never thought of going after her before. Without thinking, he looked down at her left hand to see if she wore a wedding ring. She didn't.

Sherman caught the glance down at her bare left hand but ignored it. She hadn't come out to Fort Irwin to sleep with OPFOR—especially after he'd had six or seven beers—she had come out to kick OPFOR's butt. Lewis was a nice guy, and smart enough, but too unformed, too complacent, too unquestioning of the Army and the world around him. Plus, she was dog tired.

"Lew-is! Ma-jor Lew-is!" His OPFOR buddies chanted, beckoning him with their beer cups back to the bonfire, now burning down to embers. Lewis and Sherman looked over. Outside the semicircle of happy drunks, one OPFOR officer remained alone at the beer keg, balefully glaring at Lewis and Sherman.

"What's his problem?" Sherman asked, lifting her sharp chin slightly in the direction of the officer.

"He's the leader of the scouts you whacked," Lewis said. "You should have seen our AAR this afternoon. The colonel chewed on him pretty hard about how you spoofed him with the decoy UAVs. I think he just realized his Three is talking to their Two." What Lewis really meant, she knew, was: *The thought just came to him that his operations officer is sleep-*

*ing with Blue Force's intelligence officer, and he is replaying his defeats with
that in mind.*

"I'm bushed, Lewis," she said with a smile. "I'm going to catch the next
ride back to post."

"OK," he said, smiling back. He gave her a "no hard feelings" wave of
the hand. "I'll see you in a month at the Pentagon."

She watched Lewis rejoin the group as the opening notes of another
OPFOR theme song began blaring from the speakers. She recognized the
weak, wavering guitar line—that old Nirvana song that had been big
when they were second lieutenants. The group at the bonfire sang it more
aggressively than Kurt Cobain had, transforming it from an adolescent
grunge whine into a warrior's challenge: *"Here we are now, entertain us / I
feel stupid, and contagious!"*

There was a reason, Sherman thought, that the word "infantry" came
from *fanti,* Italian for "the boys." They would all tell you that they love the
Army, but they wouldn't be able to tell you why.

The cold of the high-desert night seeped in as the flames burned down.
She reclined across the hood of the pickup, picking up some of the engine's residual heat through the back of her sweater. She joined her hands
on her stomach and looked up at the stars of the high desert. This sky
wasn't really black, she thought, more a rich Grumbacher dioxazine purple. It was one of her favorite shades.

Above Fort Bragg, North Carolina
Friday, April 22
10:30 A.M.

General B. Z. Ames stood in the aisle at the back end of the unmarked Air
Force 727, hands possessively grasping the seat backs on either side. He
was dressed in full paratrooper's regalia, from tall black jump boots to
chutes on his back and chest, which some congressional staffers found a
bit excessive for a passenger aircraft, even a Special Operations jet used
to fly along commercial air routes overseas and clandestinely insert Special Forces troops by parachute.

With good reason Ames was the favorite Army general of most Hill staffers who dealt with military affairs. Most generals seemed to think a good briefing was a lieutenant colonel reading aloud PowerPoint slides on an IBM laptop for forty-five minutes. Ames, by contrast, briefed in style. If you all want to know about the state of the U.S. military, he said to congressional staffers, fine, come with me to Bragg for a day. On the way down he would gather them around and give them his views, his sentences marching forward in well-ordered paragraphs.

"And that concludes the official bullshit portion of our briefing." He grinned. Now he wanted to go off the record. "Agreed?" He looked each of the fifteen members of his audience in the eye, from Senator Feaver's dour chief legislative counsel to a fresh-faced kid at the back of the group, probably an intern for an obscure investigatory subcommittee, but still someone who could play a role in the Ames network. He could see the anticipation in their bright eyes.

The services were troubled, more than they knew. The president's "Honorable Service for All" initiative was hurting morale among junior officers, and a lot of the best were getting out. Across the military, there was a distrust of the motives of the president, an uneasy sense that this White House neither understood nor liked the military and would not use it wisely.

"Not an easy time to be a military leader," Senator Feaver's counsel responded. "Why do you stick with it?"

"Because I love this military, and I love this country," Ames responded grimly. "And because I owe it to these young kids. My father lost his legs in Task Force Smith, part of an undertrained, undergunned, ill-equipped force sent in during the first days of the Korean War and demolished by the invading Communists. I grew up looking at that proud, shattered man, a reminder every day of the consequences of unreadiness and lack of vision.

"So I'm determined not to leave the military to some of our, uh, lesser generals. We have a lot of managers, but not so many leaders." The plane began its final descent toward Bragg.

The savvier staffers nodded. It was Washington's worst-kept secret that Ames had precious little respect for either General Shillingsworth, the Army chief of staff, or Admiral Maddox, the chairman of the Joint Chiefs.

As Ames spoke, the stairs at the back of the 727 began yawning downward, opening a widening swath of clear blue Carolina sky behind him. A breeze swept through the aircraft. Horrified, the military construction expert from the House Armed Services Committee reached out to Ames. The general waved him off with a broad grin and stepped backward down the stairs. He took one more step back into the air. The delighted staffers watched his descent from the windows, and as his green Army parachute blossomed out some even applauded.

When the jet landed several minutes later, Ames met them on the tarmac. "Follow me," he said as he turned to lead them toward the urban-warfare complex called Diceville. In the distance, .50-caliber practice rounds provided a thumping, heavy bass line to the Egyptian pop music wailing from metal loudspeakers inside the trash-strewn cinder-block complex, adding a sound track to the smoke and confusion of the realistic Third World slum training environment.

Maimaneh Valley, Afghanistan
Saturday, April 23
4:30 P.M.

Every soldier came to the Ames network in his own way. Major Roland Bolton's route took twelve days to traverse and began on the far side of the world, at the narrow end of a dry valley high in the unforgiving mountains of northern Afghanistan.

Bolton stared down the valley toward the plain where northern Afghanistan melted into the Central Asian steppe. A small voice in the back of his mind told him to run, that the situation was hopeless. But the point of more than a decade of training as a military professional was to overcome certain instincts, such as the one urging him to flee.

From his refuge in a grove of poplar trees at the edge of the little village, he looked down the valley toward the north, where the Uzbek military had established a firebase in recent weeks. His task was to figure out how to help these villagers respond when the Uzbeks came up the valley, which was likely to be soon.

Officially he wasn't even in Afghanistan. The U.S. government had quietly sent in him and a dozen other Special Forces advisers undercover to help bolster the Afghan response to the Uzbek incursions across the Amu Darya River. Normally the U.S. would have nothing to do with Afghanistan's Taliban-led regime, which supported radical Islam both at home and, some said, in terrorist organizations beyond its borders. But the Americans were worried by the regional destabilization that the Uzbek government, now dominated by Islamic extremists, could wreak by annexing northern Afghanistan and the natural gas field that lay under the border between the two countries. From regional greed could come global disaster. If Afghanistan broke up, with the north going to Uzbekistan, that would leave a Pashtun rump in its south. The people of western Pakistan and southern Afghanistan were ethnic cousins, even brothers, from Pashtun tribes. Their natural inclination would be to combine, which would make Pakistan a far greater power—and also chockablock with Islamic guerrillas. That would make Pakistan far more militarily threatening to India. If it looked like Pakistan might go that way, India might move preemptively. And if Pakistan thought India might act against it, then it might feel that its only military option was to go nuclear first.

And so hatchet-faced Roland Bolton, a restless son of the fir and spruce forests of northern Maine, gazed down this nearly treeless mountain valley. Snowbound for weeks at a time, he had come to know and admire the valley's inhabitants, proud Pashtuns whose ancestors had left the Panjshir Valley and crossed over to the northwest slopes of the Hindu Kush. When his beard had come out red, they had admiringly called him "haj." They seemed to him, he told his wife back at Fort Bragg in the diary-letter he wrote in every night, the most honest people he'd ever met. They might kill you if they disliked you, but you'd never die from a knife in the back. They would look you in the eye and plant it in your chest.

But knife fighting wouldn't get them far against the Uzbeks, who had MiG-29s, Hind attack helicopters, transport helicopters, tanks and other armored vehicles, and a reinforced brigade of perhaps six thousand troops to wield it all. All these four hundred outgunned, outnumbered fighters of this cluster of mountain villages possessed was handheld stuff—mainly AK-47 assault rifles, a good number of mortars, a dozen antitank missiles and five Stinger antiaircraft missiles. The villagers were tough, smart and patient, but as a military realist, Bolton knew those noble qualities usually lost out to mobile firepower backed by aircraft.

The villagers couldn't run even if they wanted to. Their backs were up against the wall of the Hindu Kush, where the major passes that were kept open were patrolled daily by attack helicopters and the minor ones were still closed by snow. The women and children could hide farther up the valley, but the men would have to find a way to fight when the Uzbeks came. The shepherds watching the firebase thirty miles to the north, out where the Central Asian steppe met the base of the mountains, reported that the Uzbeks were frantic with activity. Every evening truck convoys brought troops and supplies across the river that marked the border.

The Uzbeks were coming in two or three days, Bolton figured, probably in brigade size to maximize their firepower and compensate for their lack of imagination. Obaid's youngest son brought Bolton a glass of black tea—half sugar, half hot liquid—and a fresh loaf of bread, the long flat loaf the Pashtuns favored, not the shiny round bread customary north of the Hindu Kush.

Bolton unfolded his one-inch map on the stony ground and studied it as he sipped his tea. The Uzbeks would do here what they'd done in other valleys: use transport helicopters to land about three thousand air-assault infantrymen at three or four landing zones—all the flat space the high end of the valley offered. Attack helicopters would hover over each LZ. The Stingers might blunt the initial assault by knocking down a few before their handlers were swept by helicopter fire, but the response would be overwhelming and the attack would continue. We'd be fighting their fight, Bolton thought, our people under their aircraft, slugging it out with their greater numbers.

It would only get worse: As the LZs were established, Bolton knew, the Uzbeks would send a column of mechanized infantry crawling up the valley, forcing the Pashtuns to watch their backs. He traced a finger up the map, looking at how their hammer and anvil would come together against the cluster of villages.

Obaid, the villagers' chief tactician, joined him over the map. "If we can't keep them out," Bolton said to him, "we must let them in."

Obaid nodded. "Every military strength carries its own weakness."

Bolton looked up. "That doesn't sound like one of your ancient proverbs." Obaid had a Pashtun proverb for every occasion. Bolton's favorite was "I waited one hundred years before I took my revenge, and afterward I cursed myself for my impatience." You had to admire the spirit of people like that.

Obaid smiled. "No, I learned that from listening to my uncles talk about fighting the Soviets." He had been raised by his father's brothers after his father died in the fighting.

Together Obaid and Bolton planned the trap. They would do nothing but watch from hiding spots as the first transport helicopters arrived at each landing zone. Let them get out, begin to establish their perimeters. Then, as the second wave began to land, the villagers would open up with the mortars. They could register the eighty-two-millimeter mortars on all the likely landing zones and be ready to concentrate fire on whichever ones the Uzbeks chose.

Obaid wagged his black beard in appreciation of the plan. He saw the next step: When the Uzbeks sent in medevac helicopters and reinforcements, when their landing zones were confused pits of noise, smoke and blood—that was the opportune time to bring out the Stingers. Then you stood a good chance of getting off a good shot and even surviving. Drop three or four helicopters down into that mess, and keep lobbing in ten or so mortar rounds a minute, so that no one in the zone had a chance to organize a response and the dust and smoke and frantic radio traffic masked you from the attack helicopters.

That left the mechanized column. The two men talked about this for half an hour as the shadows reached up the valley at them. There was no good answer, they finally agreed. The best the villagers could do was send about forty fighters down the valley with all the antitank missiles. Ask them to delay the column for as long as possible, firing from ambush positions and then falling back to the next one. With luck, night would fall before the column could reach the LZs. Then the villagers could use the darkness to move into the LZs and fight their own Afghan fight, with rifles, knives and rocks. It was a plan, at least, and Bolton was grimly cheerful at finding a way to do his duty.

Bolton's mood was shattered the next morning by a radio message from Kabul. A helicopter would pick him up that night and take him to the capital. That was impossible, Bolton said in an urgent tone. To abandon the villagers now, at their moment of need, when he had earned their trust, cut against everything he was. The colonel commanding the advisers came on the radio. Usually more a mentor than a superior, today he was curt: "This isn't a debating club, Major. This is an order."

A few hours later, Bolton heard the helicopter coming through the sunset. One last time, Obaid invited him to stay and live in the village. They would find him a fine Pashtun wife, and he would lead a warrior's life. But now the invitation was halfhearted: Obaid knew that Bolton would do his duty. Bolton embraced him, then climbed into the unmarked MH-60ER.

Back in Kabul that night, the colonel patiently explained to Bolton that the order had come directly from "Mr. Pitch at the White House." The Uzbek government had learned of the presence of the American advisers and had made their withdrawal from Afghanistan a precondition of its entering into peace talks.

Eight days later Bolton, back at home in Fort Bragg and just released from six days of "debriefing and deworming," learned in a back-channel e-mail from the defense attaché in Kabul that the flatlander Uzbeks had attacked exactly as expected. The unfamiliar mountains scared them into predictability. Always a gambler, Obaid had held back his mortars until one transport helicopter landed on the flat irrigated land above the village and two were in its central square. One big mortar had been all but hidden above the village in the cleft in the rock known as the Muj Gate, along the path into the mountains. Another was secreted in a draw behind a hillock, not even visible from the main valley. Both mortars lobbed rounds into the LZs for hours, heaping body parts and broken machines into fiery piles. Other fighters enjoyed line-of-sight fields of fire from their foxholes up the sides of the valley. One managed to put a rocket-propelled grenade into the cockpit of the Uzbek command-and-control helicopter, sending it spinning down into the mess below.

Obaid's mortars, RPGs and Stingers pummeled the air-assault troops for a full day, inflicting estimated casualty rates of as high as 60 percent on some of the Uzbek infantry units. Over the course of two days, some eight helicopters were confirmed down.

When the armored column pushed through to the LZs after dawn on the second day of fighting, Obaid led his surviving fighters up into the hills where the women and children were waiting. When the last fighter was through the Muj Gate at the cliffs, they dynamited the ancient defile. Then they began to cut southwest, moving out of range of the Uzbeks and looking for a secondary pass where the snows were melting.

After reading the e-mail Bolton walked slowly out to his backyard and sat for hours staring bleakly at the descending moon. He felt like a hollow man, an accomplice to betrayal. Duty had required him to abandon friends in need. He had cut and run—under orders, yes, but he had still done it. Why couldn't doing the right thing also be the honorable thing?

After the crescent moon dropped below the pines, he walked back into his house and began writing an e-mail.

Dear General Ames, he wrote. *I know you by reputation. I would like to share with you my concerns about American policy in Afghanistan, about which I know something . . .*

Office of the National Security Adviser
The White House
Wednesday, May 4
8:45 A.M.

"Afghanistan, gentlemen," said Willy Pitch, the national security adviser.

Inspired by Pitch's pyramidal bulk, White House staffers referred to him behind his back as "Jabba." The resemblance was behavioral as well as physical. Pitch, a former Harvard professor of government, had the habit in meetings of lifting his chin and closing his eyes, showing that his thinking was so strenuous, so exquisite, that it required all his concentration. It was also a quiet but effective control mechanism, because it cut off those who would impatiently interrupt him. Only when he had finished saying his piece would he lift his heavy eyelids.

General John Shillingsworth arrived at Pitch's office, down the hall from the Oval Office, just as the meeting of senior White House and military officials was getting under way. Not everyone in the room seemed equally engaged. Listening to Pitch intently was the J-5 from the Joint Staff, a powerfully intelligent Marine general named H. R. Gates. Following the military rule of the clichéd nickname, in which a Sawyer is always "Buzz," a Newton is "Fig" and a Rhodes "Dusty," Gates long had been nicknamed "Golden," partly in tribute to his standing as first in his class at Annapolis, his subsequent Rhodes scholarship and his Stanford Ph.D. in Japanese politics.

On the other hand, Admiral Turner J. Maddox, the chairman of the Joint Chiefs of Staff, was catatonically staring out the window at the White House lawn, slowly tapping a pen against a legal pad. Maddox sensed what was coming in this meeting and didn't like it at all. First there had been the incident off the Algerian coast in 2002 in which the

USS *Kuwait City*, a big amphibious assault ship aiding the French in the evacuation of U.S. and French nationals, had been hit by a passenger plane loaded with C-4, killing 350 sailors, Marines and civilians. Another three hundred had been wounded, including Maddox's son, blinded by shrapnel and burned by exploding aircraft fuel. And now the president was getting them involved in Afghanistan.

His big head turbaned in a cloud of tobacco smoke, Pitch gestured to Shillingsworth to sit and then continued to explain why the president was serious about the possible Afghan mission. The skirmishing among their deputies in "premeetings" was finished. Now he was in lecture mode, telling the principals what they were going to do, and why. "Afghanistan has been falling apart for months—for decades, truth be told—but now Iran, Pakistan, Turkmenistan and Uzbekistan are all making their moves, looking to stake their claims and support their cousins across their borders. All hell looks to break loose when those competing claims smack into each other in the middle of Afghanistan."

Pitch opened his eyes and looked at the hardening faces of Shillingsworth and Gates. "It's already beginning. Overhead imagery shows some Uzbek tank units hitting concentrations of ethnic Pashtuns, trying to push them south of the Hindu Kush to establish an ethnic claim on Afghanistan north of the mountains.

"But this isn't just the usual round of worries about refugees, land mines and humanitarian disasters. No, the potential for trouble is a lot bigger here, which is why we need to get involved.

"Play the chess game backward here, gentlemen. Breaking up Afghanistan wouldn't normally worry me except that it's only three or four moves from there to the first nuclear exchange in history." Pitch leaned forward as much as his belly allowed. "I assure you, that isn't an idle worry. The other day I had the Pak ambassador in here. He said they have only three deliverable warheads that they can count on working. Then he shrugged and said, 'But how many really large Indian cities are there?' And he counted four—starting with Delhi, Bombay and Calcutta. He said their F-16s can't reach Madras. 'Our nuclear doctrine is very different from yours,' he said. I said, 'Give me a fucking break, Mr. Ambassador, I wrote the book on Third World nuclear proliferation. The chief of your strategic rocket forces did a master's degree under me. Got a B-plus on his final paper, as I recall.' The Pak ambassador sat right where you are sitting, General, and basically threatened the deaths of perhaps ten million people."

Maddox stood, shook his head and then walked over to the window and back. Pitch ignored him and looked at Gates and Shillingsworth.

"And that is where you all come in. Pakistan is on the brink, and the breakup of Afghanistan will push it over the edge. To head that off, the president wants you all to plan a possible preventive deployment of American troops." Shillingsworth began to wince, but thought he stopped it in time. He didn't. Pitch turned to look directly at him. "Look, John, this is the realist position. Afghan women and children are already dying on the TV every day. And we're not asking you to break the bank here. This would just be a small mission, a short, symbolic peacekeeping presence that would tell everyone to calm down."

Admiral Maddox began to speak but Pitch impatiently put up a hand. He knew the Pentagon would object to this, just as they had balked at most missions assigned them since the Gulf War. "Look, Turner, I don't need you to tell me why we shouldn't do this. I need you to tell me how we can do it.

"Put yourself in the president's shoes," the national security adviser concluded. "If by sending a few thousand American troops the president can prevent one hundred thousand deaths, or possibly ten million, how can he not?"

Afterward, as they waited just southwest of the White House for their sedans to pull up, Maddox turned to Shillingsworth. "John, these things never go as smoothly as the White House predicts," the subdued Joint Chiefs chairman said softly. "I fear Afghanistan is going to wind up a heavy load on the shoulders of the Army, just like Algeria with the Navy."

Shillingsworth understood: Maddox was asking for help. He said he had to travel down to Fort Belvoir but would be at the Pentagon the next morning.

Newburgh Hall
Fort Belvoir, Virginia
2:30 P.M.

The knot of Marine officers in khaki and olive at the back were the first to notice General Shillingsworth's entrance into the Newburgh Hall auditorium from the rear doors. One major, the senior Marine present, had both arms sprawled back over his classroom chair, his left leg flung over its arm. They all snapped upright the moment Shillingsworth entered the auditorium, like Marine recruits when they first see their drill instructor's black shoes stride into their barracks. They were already at attention, hands slightly curled, feet pointed slightly outward, by the time the colonel in command of the School of Joint Operations for Small Unit Commanders shouted, "Gentlemen, the chief of staff of the United States Army!"

The small group of Air Force officers, clad in baby blues, were a little slower and less synchronized in their rise, General Shillingsworth noticed. Air Force pilots, not so accustomed to command, more focused on the requirements of solo flight, were less tethered to military life. They were almost corporate, a bit soft-looking to his infantryman's eye. He felt they generally would benefit from some time on the ground—literally on it, waking rolled in a poncho and opening their eyes first thing to the ice crystals in the black soil next to their heads, eating a predawn breakfast of cold macaroni and ground beef from a brown plastic pouch, trying to spoon it out faster than the rain filled the pouch.

Army officers were spread throughout the middle of the auditorium, bunched by branches—infantry, armor, artillery, aviation, intelligence and so on. Down in front were the Navy officers, some already showing a slight paunch in khaki-colored polyesters. He understood that: Every time he'd been on a Navy ship, they'd shoveled cookies at him. He could imagine long hours between midnight and dawn on watch on the bridge, a mug of black coffee in one hand, a chocolate chip cookie in the other.

From the lip of the stage, Shillingsworth looked up the rise of the auditorium, across the audience of five hundred military officers. They all looked so young, he thought. This was not his generation, or even the one after. Were they even his people?

His talk didn't go well. He wasn't a captivating speaker. He didn't tell jokes, hold the audience in the palm of his hand, entice them, tease them, entertain them. He outranked them, dammit, and he wasn't going to plead for their attention. Standing still, his uniform hanging straight down his lanky frame, he gave them his official views about the state of the U.S. military today.

In the question-and-answer period, the free-floating resentment of the junior officers poured out. It wasn't directed at him personally, he sensed, but at anyone wearing stars on his shoulder. They were sour in mood, angry at both their civilian and uniformed leaders. He was just today's target of opportunity, just a general who had wandered into range. The first six questions were about the president's "Honorable Service for All" initiative. All were openly hostile. The first, from one of the Marine captains in the back, was couched fairly respectfully. "Sir, no one I know—not in uniform, not in my family, not among my friends   supports the 'Honorable Service' policy, because the disruption it has caused clearly is eroding military effectiveness. So, sir, my question is: Why do we still have it?"

Shillingsworth tried to respond in a straightforward, neutral tone: "We still have that policy because it is the policy of this government, initiated by the executive branch and approved by the legislative." Who teaches these kids these days? he wondered to himself. He tried to voice that thought a bit more politely. "It is not the role of the Joint Chiefs to dictate policy. You should know that's not the way this country works."

That last line came out more pointed than he'd intended. He saw his audience shifting in their seats, mentally taking the gloves off.

Another Marine stood up at the back. "Sir: Why should I serve with openly gay people?" As he heard the ripple of muttered approval of the question, the Marine rolled his shoulders with pleasure.

"Because you have to," Shillingsworth said. "If you don't want to—if you feel you can't—then you are free to resign your commission." From the middle of the auditorium, where most of the Army officers were seated, there came a few hisses and boos. In the front row, the school's commandant, a colonel who until now had assumed he would someday be a general, turned in his seat and glared back up the room at his students. Shillingsworth was astonished. In thirty-four years in the military, he had never heard of a general officer being booed in public by Army officers.

"Look," he said, slicing his hand down as if to cut off the booing, "say you could kill all the homosexuals at birth—"

He was cut off by a powerful wave of applause that began with the Army groups and then surged across the room. The young officers grinned in delight: They had shown this old coot. The school's commandant stood up in alarm, turned around, glared at his young charges. Up on the stage, Shillingsworth's long face turned red, and his jaw set. He abandoned any attempt to use a conversational tone and adopted the harsher, choppier phrasing of a command address.

"Let me finish," he ordered, and the room went silent. "If you killed all the homosexuals, you wouldn't have the Sistine Chapel, you wouldn't have Ian McKellen reading aloud *The Odyssey,* one of the best things you could ever read about recovering from combat." (In fact, it was his favorite audiotape, something he listened to on long flights when he was too fatigued to read—Ricardo Blades, the Marine commandant, had given it to him.) "And you wouldn't have some of your friends. I know. I've been a garrison commander. I've seen what a provost marshal nets some nights. Let me tell you: You wouldn't have some damn fine commanders if you got rid of all the homosexuals." There were no openly gay battalion or brigade commanders yet, but he knew it was only a matter of time. There was a gay drill sergeant at Fort Jackson, and he appeared to be doing OK. Shillingsworth thought the Army was taking that in stride, but wondered how the Marines would handle that one when it got to Parris Island. Marine drill instructors weren't just trainers, they were the keepers of that service's culture.

He strode to the lip of the stage. "Plain and simple, I judge the person on their service to the mission. One, does he or she accept the unlimited liability of military service? And, two, can he or she put steel on target? If both answers are yes, then I don't give a damn about what your religion is, your ethnicity, your gender or your sexual orientation."

He looked around the room. "Any questions?"

A red-faced Air Force officer stood up, barely able to contain himself, chin lifted in a challenge. "Yes, sir. I'm Captain Williams, out of Whiteman Air Force Base, B-2 Block 55 pilot, one of the new babies. So you're saying I either quit or serve alongside and even under immoral people?" Scattered applause and a few approving, low, mooing "hoo-ahs" greeted the question. The pilot looked around him with a surprised grin: *Hey, look at me, I just threw a fastball at a member of the Joint Chiefs.*

Shillingsworth paused. He warned himself not to lose patience. Nor should he let out the chilly disdain he felt for this Air Force officer. Little smart-ass, he thought, type of guy who flew "close air support" from ten thousand feet in Vietnam, rocketed us without knowing it and went back to an air-conditioned base for a frosty beer thinking he'd put in a solid day's work. "Look, you want to stay away from those judgments," he warned. "You're a bomber pilot. A lot of people think that what you do for a living, bombing people, is immoral. Back in my Vietnam days, you would have been despised by many of the American people, maybe even shouted at, spat on, if you wore your uniform out in public. So I think you need to judge people on whether they get the mission done, not on your personal assessment of their morality, whether they live in accordance with your current personal views. That's a slippery slope."

He dropped his tone and volume. "So let's be careful about 'immoral.' Let's stick to what is legal. We have a law of war. We are a nation of laws. And we have a system in this country that says you don't get to choose which orders you obey. 'Nuff said."

He nodded down at the school's commandant in the front row to indicate that the session was over, then took two steps back and looked over the rowdy crowd of young officers. The ashen-faced colonel slowly walked to the microphone at the front of the stage. He had just seen his students boo the chief of staff of the United States Army. It was time to start thinking about his post-Army career.

"Thank you, General Shillingsworth, for a most enlightening talk on today's military professional," the colonel said, head cocked sideways so he could keep the chief in his view while speaking into the microphone.

He shifted his gaze and surveyed the auditorium. Without any forethought, he barked out an unexpected order: "We will form here tomorrow morning at 0500 to continue this most interesting discussion. In PT gear." When the troops get frisky, he'd always said as a battalion commander, begin their day three hours earlier than usual—and sweat it out of them with a five-mile run. Maybe seven tomorrow.

Quarters Two
Fort McNair, Washington, D.C.
11:05 P.M.

The only light in General B. Z. Ames's study came from the screen of his laptop, which exaggerated his sharp, hawklike nose and sweeping black eyebrows.

There were two laptops on his desk. He was typing on the second, less used one. Like its twin, it tied into the SIPRNET and other more classified military networks. But unlike the other computer, it wasn't officially signed out to him. He used it for his more personal communications, the ones he wouldn't want to be traced directly back to him.

Most nights he used the secret laptop for an hour or two. Lately that had stretched to three or four as he responded to his informal network of former subordinates, former commanders, friends of theirs, a few congressional staffers, an occasional journalist he thought might be useful at some point. The one group that didn't appear often in his personal e-mails was his peers, who tended to regard him with suspicion as overly ambitious. He knew that. No matter, he had decided long ago at West Point. They were by and large go-along, get-along conformists who tended to peak as battalion commanders. In the military profession, he told his subordinate commanders, one is required constantly to examine one's own assumptions—and also those of one's commanders. "The first duty of an officer is to challenge whatever seems illusory," he instructed. To do anything less was to give less than your best, and your best was what you owed your people and your nation. If doing your duty sometimes meant stepping on toes, so be it.

He looked up at his reflection in the dark window of his study. Just a few feet beyond it, in the darkness, lay the thick waters of the sluggish, tidal Potomac. Across the river, up the dark hill of the Arlington Cemetery, he could see the trees around the house where Shillingsworth lived. He knew he had stepped on Shillingsworth's toes lately and was glad of it. The U.S. Army was in crisis, and if the growing flood of worried e-mails was any indication, Shillingsworth just wasn't up to the task.

And so Ames typed away. One of the best officers he had ever known—like himself a rare combination of armored cavalry and Special Forces, which usually drew from light infantry—was punching out at sixteen years, which was unheard of, when he could collect full retirement benefits by just hanging around for another four years. But he was too hard a charger to just sleepwalk away forty-eight months of the prime of his life. Likewise, a former company commander of Ames's, now going into brigade command at Fort Campbell, reported that two of his own captains were leaving. *They felt they were spending too much time on stuff like COO programs and not enough time on teaching how to set up interlocking fields of fire,* the colonel wrote.

Also, the colonel continued, there was a third young captain, Byrnes, whose talents were being frittered away by the stick-in-the-mud Army. Byrnes had just received orders to transfer to the Pentagon but was heading for a backwater deep in the Army staff. *Sir, a pat on the back from you would do wonders for young Byrnes,* the colonel requested.

Ames wrote back that he would invite this Captain Byrnes in for a cup of coffee. Always good to maintain multiple lines of communication with the Army staff, he thought.

Ames clicked on the next e-mail. A lieutenant colonel stationed on the V Corps staff in Germany wrote, *The higher I rise, the less I trust the White House, State and the Congress. That doesn't surprise me so much. What worries me is that I am also losing my faith in my own military leaders, except you and a few others. Why don't they tell the truth?*

Ames looked again into the night. All this energy, all these impulses to do good were being frittered away by the policy flailing of the White House and the sheer fecklessness of men such as Shillingsworth. There had to be some way to channel this frustration into helping the military and steering the White House away from its own profligate tendencies.

Need to think on that, he decided. In the meantime, he would do the best he could to help the network, and so help retain some of the best officers the Army had. *Butch,* he wrote to a former brigade commander of his, now the commanding general of the 82nd Airborne at Fort Bragg, *I need you to keep an eye out for a major-promotable named Bolton. Good man who has had some rough handling lately.*

Quarters One
Fort Myer, Virginia
11:30 P.M.

Across the river and up the hill, General Shillingsworth sat in a wicker rocking chair on the side veranda of Quarters One at Fort Myer, Virginia, looking down at the black Potomac, the bone-white monuments beyond it, and the crescent moon above them hanging over the Capitol. He was alone except for his Labrador retriever, Ranger, lying asleep below his left hand. On the table next to his right hand sat a glass of bourbon. He was drinking too much nowadays, he knew. His wife had gone to bed hours before. One night, driving back from a friend's funeral in Pennsylvania, she had broken an hour's silence and asked why he didn't talk to her any-more about his burdens. He had promised to better communicate his emotions and fears, fighting decades of training against doing just that.

How to reconcile this White House with this officer corps? he asked himself. I've become the clutch plate between those two opposing forces.

This spot is really where the White House should be, he thought. From this veranda he possessed the best view in the area of Washington, D.C. His house, the official residence of the chief of staff of the Army, was on the front of the ridge immediately above the Potomac River. In his home, as in his work, he occupied the military crest, just below the actual topo-graphical summit, a dangerous spot where the unwary could be "skylined" by an enemy at the base with a rifle. This is where he would place his front trenches if he were besieging the city. Directly in front of him, at the bottom of the hill, was Arlington Cemetery, on the land taken away from Robert E. Lee by Montgomery Meigs as Lee's punishment for violat-ing his oath as an officer of the United States Army and presiding over the killing of those wearing that uniform, including some of the boys he had taught at West Point. The historians talked about Grant as cold-blooded, but Grant never killed his former students while defending slav-ery, Shillingsworth thought.

The best of the view lay beyond that confiscated ground, on the far side of the river. This was his second-favorite vista in the entire nation, just after the walk along the high western bluff of the Missouri River at Fort Leavenworth, his spiritual home after thirty-four years in the Army.

The moon hanging over the Capitol threw pale light down on the gar-den of white stone below him. On this cloudless night it provided suffi-cient illumination for a complex night movement, he thought reflexively. At his feet was the gleaming white block of the Lincoln Memorial, hon-oring America's best president. Just beyond Lincoln's roof was the coun-terpoint of the bright white giant tent peg of the Washington Monument, commemorating America's founding general. Down to the right of Wash-ington was the white pate of the Jefferson Memorial, marking America's best thinker. And on the hill in the distance, rising above those markers for individuals, was the Capitol building, the shrine of America's best gift to the world—government of the people, by the people and for the peo-ple. Even over the past year, when the questions had become especially sharp for reasons he didn't understand, when he was being flogged in a hearing by a gaggle of congressmen scoring points off him for base political purposes, even when the House seemed to overflow with blow-dried ex-anchormen, he never lost hold of that—Congress was the best thing this country had going for it.

And then, completing and troubling his view, there was the White House, off to the left, beyond the American flag sticking up out of the hidden crypt of the Vietnam War Memorial. The White House— America's best what? He reached for his glass of bourbon. "The White House wants"—there was no phrase he hated to hear more than that, passed along by some prematurely aged eager beaver from the Office of the Secretary of Defense who clearly thought it the domestic equivalent of the word of God. Those White House people are killing me, he thought.

The problem, Shillingsworth mused as he sipped his whiskey and gazed down at the black waters of the Potomac, was that he sympathized with much of what that unhappy crowd of young officers at Fort Belvoir had been feeling. It really boiled down to the worry that they and their troops would be used capriciously, could die in some Third World hellhole for no better reason than it had seemed like a good idea to some inattentive White House yuppie. If they had to die, they wanted it to be for a reason, he knew.

This president was trouble—worse than Clinton, in some ways. At least Clinton had vulnerabilities like draft dodging, he thought, that had enabled the military to push back a bit. The Pentagon had been able to hit up Clinton for more money, had been able to make the policy makers trim their sails on how aggressively to go after war criminals in Bosnia and had utterly defeated him on gays in the military.

But President Shick didn't have those chinks in his armor. This guy, a conservative Republican with a goddamn Beatle haircut, didn't know much more about the military than Clinton did, despite spending five years as an Air Force intelligence officer specializing in nuclear weapons during the midseventies after Oxford and before going to law school. But because of his conservatism, he was able to do it more damage. After running to the right in the primaries and then breaking toward the middle in the general election, he had come into office and done a Nixon-going-to-China on the defense budget, cutting the Democrats' planned defense budgets by $20 billion a year. This will break the rice bowls, the new national security adviser, Willy Pitch, smugly had told the Chiefs in their first meeting with him, on a bleak January morning when the postinaugural hangovers still hung from the faces of White House staffers. Make you guys finally move into the twenty-first century, Pitch said, his fat jowls jiggling as he lit his fourth cigarette of the meeting, make the hard decisions on force structure that have been deferred for a decade. Shick had found military reform too difficult and soon had dropped it—but had kept the cuts in the budgets, and kept throwing Third World missions at his military.

Pitch seemed entirely alien to the military ethos, Shillingsworth thought. He sat in meetings with his tie loosened. He displayed his anxieties as if they were virtues. He had no fingernails protruding beyond the flesh. Pitch had made his name in nuclear weapons control studies, but after the Cold War ended had nimbly shifted to peacekeeping issues. It hadn't hurt that he had been a Rhodes scholar at Oxford with the president.

What the new crowd really had done was blow up the military and groove on the rubble, Shillingsworth thought. In those first few months of the Shick administration he had decided that the only thing worse than a liberal formed by the sixties was a conservative formed in reaction to that decade. The budget cuts imposed by Shick and Pitch had turned the Tank into a shark pool as the Chiefs fought each other for the money required by their always-hungry services to execute the missions being thrown at them.

It was a dangerous time for the U.S. military. They were dealing with an unseasoned president and an unsteady foreign policy, a combination that had become especially clear with the Algerian incident during the president's second month in office. The terms of military service, the way the armed services thought about who they were and what they did, were changing and unclear. They were operating all the time, but not operating against people as sharp as them—so they almost never got the tests they needed at the upper end of combat capability, that ace-in-the-hole knowledge that you probably still can take the other guy even after two or three things have gone wrong, Shillingsworth thought. They were performing in an environment intolerant of risk and casualty. And in their deployments they were doing it all on real-time satellite television transmissions, before an audience of reporters, policy makers and citizens who rarely had military experience but still felt free to second-guess every move.

Shillingsworth shifted his gaze toward the fields of tombstones in Arlington National Cemetery. A hell of a thing for a whiskey general to stare at every night from his front porch.

What do you do when your duty to your superiors is at odds with your duty to your subordinates, when your lawful orders are bad for the people you lead? That question hung in the air there each evening as he drank and gazed at the white crosses. "Resign," he would have said when he was a smart young colonel on the Joint Staff. Enticing prospect. Put his stars on the table, head out to the cabin near Moab, Utah, that he and his wife had bought two decades ago. During the winter, hike the low canyons, get lost in the irrational rocks of Arches and then figure your way out, Ranger-style. Come fall, climb the slopes of the La Sal Mountains, shoot an elk, live off it for a few days, smoke the rest. Spring, bike to Aspen and back. Live on his pension: no defense consulting. Just resign and get out of Dodge.

Keep it positive and uncomplicated. That was the Army attitude, and it still worked inside the Army. It had gotten him this far. But lately it felt like that formula no longer worked. It wasn't clear to him whether this was because of the nature of the times or the nature of his job at the top of the hierarchy. A high-profile resignation—no, there was something un-palatable about that. It was not the Army way. If I were to remove myself from the situation, would the situation then be better or worse for my people, for the Army? When I took this job, I knew who Shick was. I knew the mission. I'm not going to slap the president of the United States in the face.

And do I expect the next guy to resign, until there isn't a general left in the Army, except the ones—like Ames—who are too ambitious to resign on principle? B. Z. Ames reminded him of some lines of poetry that had come up during his last visit to West Point. *The best lack all conviction, while the worst are full of passionate intensity.* All the best West Point poetry professors came out of infantry, the superintendent told him over dinner. Probably, he had said, from being out in a listening post at night, straining to hear every sound, see every movement. It was a very different approach to combat from operating in a seventy-ton tank with a bunch of guys farting, peeing into bottles, playing heavy metal and rap music on a tape machine, two other monster tanks grinding away on your flanks.

I never trusted that passionate intensity, Shillingsworth thought. The good commander keeps himself and his soldiers cool and calm.

That night he dreamed his danger dream, the one that came to him when he felt vaguely threatened. In it he was a common soldier at Gettysburg, serving under Pettigrew in what would half-mistakenly be re-

membered as Pickett's Charge. Shillingsworth found it odd that he, born
and educated just outside Uniontown, Pennsylvania, would have a recur-
ring dream that he was serving in the Confederate Army in its attack on
his home state. The charge was just getting under way—they'd left the
tree line of Seminary Ridge, passed the twelve-pounders and were just
coming out of the first swale. Clouds of smoke hung in the July haze. He
focused on the back of the man in front of him. All he could hear were
shouts, screams and the company sergeant's Blue Ridge tenor nervously
singing out orders—"A-lign to the right. Co-ver. Close it up. Dress that
rank."

The Pentagon
Thursday, May 5
6:27 A.M.

Cindy Sherman waited at the top of the steps at the Pentagon's Mall entrance. It was an unusually bright, cool early May morning, the rising
spring sun casting sharp, dry Hopperesque shadows across the knots of
colonels and lieutenant colonels waiting for shuttle buses to run them to
the office buildings around northern Virginia where the services, out-
growing the office space in the Pentagon, now housed most of their procurement and support programs. It was her second day at the Pentagon.
The scene faintly dismayed her—every time she had been in the Pentagon during her Army career, there always had been colonels and lieutenant colonels perched like pigeons at the Pentagon's entrances, no
matter what the season.

And there were so many of them. Moving to her new billet in Washington, she had begun to read the *Washington Herald*'s Metro section
every morning. She was surprised to see that day in, day out, the obituary
columns at the back of Metro carried news of the deaths of at least two
or three old colonels and generals. On top of that there was frequently an
obit for a CIA official. She had never realized how many thousands of retired Cold Warriors were warehoused in the Washington suburbs. Now
the first wave—those who had saved Iran and Greece and Berlin and

come home at night to raise the baby boomers, coach Little League and help out at PTA meetings—was dying off and filling the obit pages. What would be in the obits of today's colonels, she wondered—that they had managed the downsizing, or kept the peace in places that no one cared about anymore, where there was no peace as soon as the Americans left?

The chief's executive officer had sent her downstairs at 6:20 to meet the chief as he arrived. "Look for the cranky old guy getting out of the black sedan with a red face and four stars on his shoulders," advised Miss Turley, the ageless secretary-dominatrix who ran the chief's front office and terrorized even lieutenant generals.

Sherman had to double-check her watch. As the hard-charging commander of the III Corps's TENCAP company at Fort Hood, she had gotten into the habit of keeping both her watch and her office clock running ten minutes fast. It had driven her first sergeant crazy: "Ma'am," he would exclaim, when he glanced up at the clock, "we're gonna be late for formation!" But now that she again worked for others, she had been forced to slow down and live on everyone else's time. Major was the worst rank—a staff job, no command. "When you make major, they take away your tongue," a friend at Hood had laughingly said to her on the night she was promoted. "When you make lieutenant colonel, they take your balls. When you make colonel, they take your brain. And when you make general, they give back your tongue."

Shillingsworth's sedan arrived a minute early, at 6:29. He began striding up the steps of the Mall entrance. Sherman waited for him at the top. An Air Force colonel strolled by her down the steps, looking to his left for the Bolling shuttle. He neither saw nor saluted General Shillingsworth as he walked directly toward him. The general, fighting through the haze of last night's bourbon, was in no mood for casual disrespect. *"Good morning!"* he bellowed at the distracted officer.

The colonel focused on the general and smiled: "Oh, uh, good morning, sir." He still did not salute.

Shillingsworth lit him up. "No salute, Colonel?" he snarled, inches from the Air Force officer's shrinking face. "I hate this place, and do you know why? Because of people like you."

He wheeled and continued up the steps, leaving the colonel looking frozen and stupefied. Who *was* that Army general?

Sherman met him at the top of the stairs with the crispest salute of her career. It was the first time she had actually met General Shillingsworth.

She was surprised to see the deep vertical lines that ran down each side of his jaw, generally the sign of a man either on a crash diet or struggling under enormous stress. "Sir, I'm Major Lucinda Sherman, your new assistant ADC. I'm to tell you that Admiral Maddox would like to see you right away."

Shillingsworth winced. Maddox wanted to talk about Afghanistan. He shook her hand and welcomed her to his staff. But it was clear to her that the summons from the chairman of the Joint Chiefs had distracted, even startled him.

Shillingsworth left Sherman and began the walk toward Admiral Maddox's office, around the long arc of the E ring, the Pentagon's outermost circle, past the stiff paintings of his predecessors as Army chief, from the competent professionals of the post-Vietnam era back through time to the intensely political pre–World War II chiefs, MacArthur and Leonard Wood.

Turner Joy Maddox had been a quiet mess ever since the Algerian foul-up, early in his term as chairman of the Joint Chiefs of Staff. "That plane came at us under your rules of engagement, Dad," his blinded son had spat at him. Until they were both named to the Joint Chiefs, Shillingsworth had known Maddox only by reputation, and even that was kind of hazy—a career naval aviator, a man of good intentions who seemed to lack depth. Throughout his career Maddox had unconsciously figured out where the consensus would wind up and then been first to adopt that view as his own and express it with vigor, acting as if it were a bold, controversial stance that he would defend despite the risk to his career. It wasn't done cynically. He genuinely thought that this method of being the first to find the consensus was the best form of leadership. And apparently his superiors had agreed, promoting him steadily throughout the late eighties and early nineties.

But when real controversy had hit, meaning that there was no consensus, Maddox had proved ill-equipped to deal with it, Shillingsworth thought. Shillingsworth harbored a suspicion of all naval aviators, not just Maddox. Naval aviation was, he suspected, a calling that had shaped the admiral—the only military specialty whose defining task, landing on an aircraft carrier, was routinely performed before an audience, the admiring deckhands and the officers up on the bridge and the air station. By contrast, the defining task of his own career as a light infantryman was more than anything else to be persistent when no one was watching, to keep going and hold together ground troops burdened by fear, fatigue and disorientation. Do your job well, and the enemy wouldn't know where you were or in what strength.

Turner J. Maddox had made his name in Operation Desert Storm, which in Shillingsworth's view wasn't long enough to be called a war, which is why he and his peers quietly declined to refer to it as the Gulf War. Maddox had commanded the VF-143 "Pukin' Dogs," named after their emblem, a griffin with its head down and mouth open. Under his command, a fleet F-14 Tomcat squadron had actually dropped bombs for the first time. He also had begun the utilization of TARPS—the Tactical Reconnaissance Pod System, which enabled the F-14s to do a lot of their own targeting work. Neither innovation was his, but because they occurred on his watch, he received much of the credit. Just as he had later shouldered much of the blame when the USS *Kuwait City* was hit.

Maddox was listening to someone on the STU phone in his inner office. He lifted his chin in greeting and waved Shillingsworth toward the easy chair in front of his desk. It was just the two of them, which put Shillingsworth on alert—the lack of an aide in the room to take notes indicated that Maddox was up to something he wanted kept off the books.

Someone who knew Shillingsworth's nocturnal drinking habits clearly had expected him this morning: When he sat down he saw the golden plastic pot of hot coffee and the pitcher of ice water on the lowboy at his elbow. He sipped ice water and watched Maddox talk on the phone. The chairman had moved into the beginnings of old age since the Algerian incident, Shillingsworth thought.

Admiral Maddox had been in mourning since then for his broken son and for his own diminished sense of self. After visiting his son, still undergoing rehabilitation in the burn ward at Fort Sam Houston in San Antonio, he had confided in Shillingsworth one night on his porch—he lived just two doors down at Fort Myer—that he had considered stepping down but had decided not to. "You and I are old warhorses," he said over his iced tea. "We know there is only one way you leave your battle station." Shillingsworth thought that Maddox meant he had contemplated suicide. It was a Roman warrior's death, not a terrible way to go, except for the damage it did to your family, Shillingsworth had thought. He didn't know Maddox well enough to go down that road with him. Hard to figure out Navy guys. Since Algeria, Maddox had given up golf and alcohol. "It just

doesn't seem right to enjoy myself anymore," he had explained to Shillingsworth.

But the chairman also had withdrawn from a lot of the hard decisions,
Shillingsworth thought. The result was that power was flowing from
Maddox to Ames. The vice chairman seemed to be taking over the building lately. That worried Shillingsworth even more. He had known Ames
for two decades and hadn't trusted him for one day.

Maddox hung up the phone and made sure Shillingsworth had seen the
coffee and water. "Still determined to donate your liver to the cause, I
see," he said, not accusingly but in sympathy, one troubled man speaking
honestly to another. "I've made appointments for you tomorrow morning to see each of the Chiefs separately on Afghanistan," he continued. "I
want you to line them up and take them all to the White House, show
Pitch and the president that our military advice is unanimously against
this." As he spoke he unconsciously whacked his pen on the edge of his
desk with a small, flickering gesture. Looking at the pen, Shillingsworth
was distracted to see that Maddox had nervously scratched holes into the
skin on the inside of each wrist.

"But isn't that the role of the chairman—for you to give your best military advice to the president?" Shillingsworth asked. But even as he said it
he felt embarrassed to be legalistically ducking behind the letter of the
law. "And what about the CinC—where is Centcom on this?"

"He's brand-new in that job, and he's thrown up his hands. And you're
not. You're seasoned in Washington. You can do better than that, John,"
Maddox said a bit tartly. "And you damn well better, for the sake of your
service."

He leaned back and returned to imploring Shillingsworth. "Look, I'm a
naval aviator. What do I know about Afghanistan? For that matter, what
do I know about ground troops? My best military advice is that the president should listen to you, dammit."

"You are putting me in a difficult position," Shillingsworth said. He
sipped some ice water.

"Welcome to the club." Maddox shrugged.

"If I somehow head off the president on this, he will see me as a political enemy," Shillingsworth said. "And if I fail to persuade him—then we
are in for one hell of a weird mission."

"Look, I'm not ordering you, John," Maddox finally said. "You know I
can't. I'm begging you. We are in trouble here, and you are the best man
to take on a difficult job."

Maddox stood up, came around his desk and sat in the armchair facing Shillingsworth. "I'm asking you as a comrade to step in, take point on this," he concluded.

The infantry metaphor struck close to Shillingsworth's heart. He had walked point on patrols in Vietnam. He had learned by himself how to look beyond the leaves for the horizontal lines of bodies and rifle barrels, for the unusual, oval shape of the human head, to sniff the air for the distinctive odors of onions or fresh equipment.

In Vietnam he actually had served under a brigade sergeant major who as a young man had served with World War I vets. That crowd in turn had been trained by Indian fighters and Civil War vets. Hell, the Bundy boys, who helped send his generation to Vietnam, dined as youths with Oliver Wendell Holmes, who had fought in the Civil War and as a young man had talked with a man who had fought in the Revolutionary War. The U.S. really was still a surprisingly young country. And Afghanistan was a very old place.

He would take on Maddox's assignment.

In the vice chairman's suite across the hall, Major Lewis arrived for his second day as assistant aide de camp to General B. Z. Ames. He walked into the suite carrying the *Joint Staff Officers' Manual*, which was the *Whole Earth Catalog* of the good Joint Staff officer. It was the size of the Washington, D.C., telephone book.

General Ames was already there, visible through the doorway of his inner office, standing and flipping through the morning intelligence briefing, stamped on its binder cover with the security incantations of the spooks—"Top Secret/UMBRA/TALENT/KEYHOLE/NIGHTLIGHT/ ZARF"—each referring to the various origins of the information, in this case, audio eavesdropping, human intelligence, satellite imagery, infrared imagery, and signals intercepts from computers. Ames knew from experience that despite the intell mumbo jumbo, the briefing's supposed revelations usually trailed CNN's reporting. He generally just read the headings to see what the intelligence crowd was trying to put on the day's agenda.

Ames looked up, spotted Lewis through his open door and glided out to greet him in the outer office. He was a surprisingly small, compact man with a razor-sharp look to him—in his nose, his hawklike eyes, his precise movements. There was a sleekness to him that was almost un-Army. One of Lewis's girlfriends once had told him that people could be divided into cats and dogs. Most Army generals, she said, were dogs—big, loyal and friendly breeds, such as Labradors, with a few smart terriers mixed in. But Ames was a cat—albeit still a hunter.

Even at Fort Irwin, Lewis had heard the talk that with a Joint Chiefs chairman who was all but dead in the water and a defense secretary who was a burned-out party hack, B. Z. Ames was the one really running the show at the Pentagon. Ames was a dynamic, even dashing leader, the great hope of many younger officers, someone who actually might initiate the military reforms the president had talked about and then dropped as too hard. Ames might get the Army's head out of the Fulda Gap and adjust it to the new realities of the post–Cold War world. "General Ames knows more about the twenty-first-century expeditionary strike force than any other officer in the United States Army," the colonel commanding OPFOR had told his staff before the vice chairman came to Irwin the previous fall, his admiration evident in every word.

Lewis had first met Ames during that visit. Unusually for a four-star general, but typical of Ames's operating style, he had requested a separate lunch with OFPOR's majors, captains and lieutenants—"O-4 and below only," his aide had informed the commanding general and the regimental colonel—and had left his ham and cheese sandwich untouched as he peppered them with questions, asking them for the straight word, telling his aide to turn off the cellular telephone and bestowing upon each young officer who spoke his complete attention, his narrow, tense face inclined toward the speaker. He'd won them over immediately.

He had talked about the need for reform, conveying somehow to them without ever explicitly saying it that he was on their side, that it was time to clear out the cobwebs at the top of the Army. When Lewis made a comment about how spending time in OPFOR would convert any fan of fires into a maneuverist, Ames smiled and almost imperceptibly nodded to his aide, a major, who made a note in his pad. Lewis hadn't realized at the time that Ames also used these meetings where he reached down several echelons as a way of scouting for fresh young talent for his staff. Nor had he comprehended that Ames always left these meetings having enlisted several new supporters in his quiet campaign to change the Army.

Ames strode across the office, his hand extended. "Lewis, is that right?" the general said. "From OPFOR? Good man. Welcome aboard." He took the big purple manual from under Lewis's arm. "You won't be needing that here." He let go of it over a wastebasket. "We stay out in front of the manuals here—any tactic that has been codified is probably outdated. You just follow the Ames way and you'll be ahead of the game here in the five-sided building. You want some useful reading, try Sun Tzu, *The Art of War*. That's the Ames office manual."

An Air Force colonel came into the room silently and stood as Ames talked. Lewis recognized him as Underhill, Ames's blandly disagreeable executive officer, the one who had interviewed him for this job. The XO wouldn't sit as long as Ames was speaking.

"If you succeed," Ames said, fixing his black eyes on Lewis, "I succeed. And if I succeed, the U.S. military succeeds. And if we succeed, I guarantee you that I will find you a good command billet when you leave here, with a good battalion.

"Now, you've got to realize what we do in this office. We're the Pony Express of the national security establishment. We carry the word between the national command authority—SecDef, National Security Council, State, CIA, the CinCs, the service chiefs when they're in the ball game, of course." He picked up from Underhill's desktop a thick white file marked "UMBRA/TACIT SHADOW." He opened it and showed Lewis the multicolored tinfoil-like strip running along the inside of its spine. "That's a microtransmitter, sending a signal that's coded by office," he said. "Joint Staff is purple. OSD is yellow. State's is red. NSC is white. CIA is blue. There are days when you can go down to the Defense Security Office, where they track all these on a real-time basis, and their electronic display map makes this town look polka-dotted. And every one of those agencies will claim every time that they're the one doing what the president really wants.

"Here in this office, you all help me get the message through. Sometimes someone tries to shoot the messenger, so it can get lively. We'll work you hard—the colonel here will see to that." For the first time since Underhill had entered the room, Ames acknowledged his presence, nodding to him. The bald Air Force officer remained blank-faced. He would let Ames do his stuff, then take over and do his when it was his turn.

"My last assistant aide de camp was an armored cav guy, like you," Ames said. "At his going-away party he said that working in this office was like shooting moving targets from his Bradley at night in haze while wearing MOPP gear and using the auxiliary sight." That was familiar stuff to Lewis—that kind of handicapped shooting was near impossible, and sweaty work to boot. Ames fixed him again with his liquid coal-black eyes: "I could have gotten any one of the twenty-five hottest majors in the United States Army for this job. They all have credentials just as good as yours." He stared at Lewis. "Do you know why I picked you?"

"Because I didn't want to come here?"

"Bingo. You really wanted to stay in the field—you didn't just say it. That's the kind of officer I want around me. Think of this as a combat assignment and you'll do all right here."

Ames turned to the colonel. "He's all yours." He walked out to begin the round of meetings that took most of his mornings.

The XO took over the orientation. "First issue, Major: You're my action officer for toilet paper." He explained: The Defense Supply Agency had let a new contract for toilet paper. But the new, low-bid paper didn't fit the old holders. They were being replaced, slowly, corridor by corridor around the building. But because it was built when Virginia was still legally segregated, the Pentagon had twice as many toilets per capita as more modern structures—284 public rooms, plus private latrines in the offices of all three-star and four-star officers and their civilian equivalents at the DASD level and above, with the result that "the upgrade," as he called it, was taking months. And in the interim, the big, wheel-sized rolls were being left on the floor of the latrines. "I assure you: You care about this, Major," the XO said. It was an order, not a question. "Because your job as the office cherry includes buying some Charmin at the supermarket, bringing it to the building with you and making sure the general's private toilet is stocked."

A week ago, thought Lewis, I was figuring out new ways to conduct land warfare. Now I'm a general's ass-wiper.

"Sir, were you ordered to do this by General Ames?" Lewis found himself asking impertinently. He still possessed the OPFOR habit of questioning superiors, of thinking of colonels especially as people to be attacked, kicked around and tormented, rather than blindly obeyed. And he thought that B. Z. Ames was too much of a warrior to be so finicky.

"No, quite frankly, I wasn't," Colonel Underhill said with surprising equanimity. "You'll learn here, if you haven't already, that a good XO never has to be ordered to do anything for his principal. Quite frankly, my job is to anticipate his desires. Your job is to anticipate mine. And I hate these huge new rolls on the floor."

Lewis looked crestfallen. The XO realized he might have pushed his special orientation a bit hard. "Sit down, Lewis," Underhill said. "I know: You didn't sign up for this." He went on to explain his own transition to the ways of the Pentagon. In his last job, he had been a wing commander at the new NATO base in southern Hungary. "I was king of that base. My name was painted right there on the first parking space next to my head-quarters. When I wanted to shortcut to the other side of the base, drive my POV across the runway, air traffic would put all incoming aircraft into holding patterns.

"Then I came here, to this job. And at the end of my first day at the Pentagon I was serving hors d'oeuvres to reporters at a reception Admiral Maddox threw for them, to try to get them off his back after the *Kuwait City* got hit." He paused. "To be candid with you, we call this the humility tour." He wasn't kidding.

After his meeting on Afghanistan with Maddox, General Shillingsworth walked slowly up the stairs and around the third floor of the E ring to his office. He prided himself on mentoring his staff officers, and also wanted to stew on this Afghanistan thing before making the next move, so he asked his new aide, Major Sherman, into his inner office for coffee. He sat in the big armchair in his sitting area. She sat down deep into the couch, her legs pushing up in front of her. She had been in enough Pentagon generals' offices to know that this humbling seat was the unspoken listening position.

"Major Sherman, I know you probably think I just need a smart female aide to warn me when I say something stupid, to keep me from being a macho pig," Shillingsworth had begun. "Well, that's absolutely true. I do need that. It is part of your job—a big part. I need you to keep me from fouling up in that area. There are any number of congressmen who would like to score a few points off me on gender issues. So when I oink, kick me in the shins, OK?"

Shillingsworth leaned forward in his armchair, hands held together. "I know a lot of the younger officers think I'm a dinosaur. I may be. But that leads me to another thing I like about field-grade females: They've put up with a lot of crap in this United States Army. You, Major Sherman, have got to really like something about the Army to have stayed in. I know there must have been times when there was gossip about you because you got along so well with your big, strong platoon sergeant, or when you were a lieutenant finishing a rotation at the NTC and after it was all over your battalion commander took you out in his Humvee for a quiet drink and then parked in an arroyo and began confessing his undying love for you as he pawed your BDUs." She was surprised both by his candor and his accurate sense of her experience as a female Army officer.

Shillingsworth had decided privately that being a woman in the Army of the nineties resembled his experience as a junior officer in the ill-disciplined, demoralized Army of the seventies: You had to really love the Army to put up with all the shit it hurled at you. He would never have put it this way, even to himself, but what he meant was that he was a principled man, and the first thing he looked for in other people was principle: Does this person believe in something bigger than his or her self? He worried that there were fewer such people among the junior officers—and intrigued by how many of those who did care were women.

"But you're going to have a lot more on your plate than just gender issues," Shillingsworth told her. Her background in intelligence also qualified her to be his strategic scout on information warfare issues. "I need to get my mind into this," he said, turning to pull his current infowar file from the top drawer in his secure files.

"Sir, I'm already in the picture on infowar issues," she protested. She was a little taken aback that he presumed she wasn't. "Sir, I've taken the Leavenworth orientation, and then last year the full Huachuca course for branch-qualified officers. And when I came here I got the offensive IW read-in from the J-383 cell." The Joint Staff had a "secret" offensive information warfare unit tucked away in its current operations directorate.

"No," General Shillingsworth said patiently but emphatically, "exhibition season is over. You're playing in the NFL now, Major Sherman. I need to get you read in on some of the black programs. Here are your clearances, and some of the things I want you to get me up to speed on." He handed her a folder. Opening it, she saw a series of three-digit codes and realized she was being given unusual admittance to a series of SAPs, the closely held Special Access Programs that even as a tactical intelligence officer she had only heard rumors about.

Shillingsworth saw the look on her face. "DepSecDef personally approved your being read into these," he told her. "I especially want you to check out the system the NSA is developing," Shillingsworth said. "They call it the Digger. This old infantryman doesn't know whether they're blowing smoke because they need to start procurement or whether they've truly developed a real-time invasive capacity."

The Pass of Jam, Western Afghanistan
11 A.M.

The dirty little secret of modern militaries is that most are far better at attacking civilians than at confronting other armed forces.

The Uzbek brigade had been no match for Obaid's four hundred men when Obaid was leading the defense of his valley. But now Obaid's column of about fifteen hundred men, women and children was out in the open, in the high, bare ground of the Jam Pass, the last hurdle before they could finally descend to the warmer, lower ground of the Obeh Valley, east of Herat.

The Uzbeks had been tracking them remotely for days, using observation aircraft to monitor the column's progress as it moved toward its point of maximum vulnerability, the windswept summit of the Pass of Jam. Two attack helicopters were sufficient to do the job. They were silent, shark-like KA-50s, the double-rotored successor to the Mi-24 Hind.

The Uzbeks were calculating that Obaid's fighters had used all their Stingers. The two helicopters came in at an almost leisurely pace, flying up the column to examine it before opening fire. Then the lead helicopter swung around to come directly down the column, front to back, sweeping it with its machine-gun pod.

Obaid crouched until the helicopter shot by him, watching the black wolf's head painted on its tail, its mouth open, its eyes closed. It was a good emblem for these unimaginative Russian-trained Uzbek pilots, he thought—all bite, no brains. He ran to take one of the last two Stingers off the back of his donkey. The second KA-50, flying overwatch to protect against exactly such a move, saw him and wheeled in. A burst from its thirty-millimeter gun blew his body parts in several directions.

The two helicopters flew away, bullets from the fighters harmlessly bouncing off their bellies.

The villagers buried their dead under a pile of rocks. They marked Obaid's final resting place with a white pennant atop a tent pole, marking the grave of a righteous fighter. Then they continued on to the southwest, toward the Minaret of Jam and the safety that lay beyond.

CIA Headquarters
Langley, Virginia
12:30 P.M.

As a mere major at the low end of the field-grade totem pole, Sherman assumed she would have to wait for days to get the CIA brief. She quickly learned that one of the perks of working directly for a senior four-star was that the system responded with alacrity. She'd had coffee with Shillingsworth at 0715. By lunchtime she was on her way to a briefing on the Digger at Langley, a fifteen-minute drive up the Potomac from the Pentagon.

She signed in and parked inside the security gate and walked up the long leafy driveway to the Agency's main building. CIA employees' automobiles were parked along one side, all declaring their anonymity—all were a year or two old, midrange Japanese four-door sedans or their American equivalent. None bore any distinguishing characteristics—not a single car displayed a bumper sticker, a canoe rack or even a college decal.

She signed in again at the guardpost in the big, cold, marbled lobby of the headquarters building, then waited for her briefer to come out and retrieve her. She looked at the quotation from John 8:32 carved into the stone of the lobby wall: ". . . And the truth shall make you free." What an oddly optimistic but accurate mission statement, she thought, carrying one meaning early in the Cold War when they were quietly fighting the Soviets, and another decades later when revelations about the Agency's misdeeds and excesses sent many officers out into the world. On the eastern wall, to her right, were eighty-two metal stars commemorating the line-of-duty deaths of CIA officers.

A young man who looked to be in his midtwenties, the rumpled powder-blue uniform shirt of an Air Force captain fluttering on his lanky frame, bounded up to her. "Major Sherman?" he said.

She eyed the unshaven chin, the stringy black hair that was more Silicon Valley than Pentagon. "Yes," she said, an edge of wariness in her voice. "Captain Cisco?"

"You got him." He smiled. If he were Army, she thought, I'd brace him for disrespect: How about a "Yes, ma'am"? The Air Force was different, she knew. And Cisco was from the far edge of the Air Force, an infowar specialist seconded from the Air Intelligence Agency down in San Antonio to an agency called the Defense Information Infrastructure Protection Office, which really existed only to provide cover for the joint CIA/NSA offensive information warfare project.

Someone who looks this bad must be pretty good, she thought as she followed him to the elevator. He's already made captain, and he's getting away with murder in his personal appearance. He inserted a key into the elevator, then pressed the button marked "SB3." He was taking her down to his subbasement office, off-limits even to most Agency employees, but safely hidden from electronic pulse attacks and from modern forms of wireless eavesdropping. Cisco was at least four inches taller than Sherman, but slouched forward from his shoulders so much that his face was barely higher than hers.

"I usually work alone," he said, presumably to explain the chaos of his office. He went to a chair next to his desk and cleared a heap of computer disks, wrestling magazines, hip-hop music CDs and several editions of early-twentieth-century Russian utopian novels, then invited her to sit while he briefed her on his work.

She found Cisco's toolbox kind of cool, and a little bit scary. She'd expected the usual infowar tools—port scanners, spoofers, packet grabbers, flooders, ICQ IP sniffers and so on. But she was wowed by the Agency's new quantum encryption system that put a coded message in a photon of light and shipped it through fiber-optic cables, making it almost uncrackable. Even better, as Shillingsworth had suspected, had been the Digger, which promised to be the star of the emerging offensive information weapons suite. Like a lot of IW tools, it could reach into computers and root around for old messages. It just did it to more computers, faster and more completely—and it left no tracks. Just goofing around with it, Cisco told her, he'd gone into a server at the *New York World* and paged through the e-mail of their intelligence reporter, whose work he admired. "He's a pretty good reporter, actually," Cisco said. He found one e-mail from the reporter to his editors promising to hit the CIA hard in a story. "The next day he sends an e-mail over to CIA after he's crapped all over them, saying his editors put a 'harder edge' on his story."

"That's illegal, you know," Cindy said. She was pretty sure it was.

Cisco grinned. "Lines get a bit hazy in infowar. What's public information? What's electronic eavesdropping? If I go for a walk and pick up a quarter I find in the street, am I stealing? And if I go for a stroll in cyberspace and come across information that people think is private, but isn't, am I violating any laws?"

Cisco was pure energy. She liked him.

The Pentagon
5:15 P.M.

Her elation didn't last more than a few steps back into the Pentagon. It was as if the building had been designed with antihappiness shields, she thought morosely as she sat alone at her desk in Shillingsworth's suite late that afternoon. Being stationed at the Pentagon felt like military life with most of the attractions of comradeship stripped away. It had no feeling of a platoon or even of a battalion staff. Most of the time it felt like just you alone with your career.

The workday was done. She called down to Lewis and invited him for a stroll around the emptying building. It was the first chance they'd had to compare notes on their first two days as Pentagon staff weenies.

She told him how old Captain Cisco had made her feel. "He was a kid, really. Two years out of MIT and already a captain." With his longish hair that looked like it hadn't been washed in a week, and a gleefully insubordinate attitude, he also had made her feel like an old stick-in-the-mud.

"Tracks in two?" Lewis raised his thick black eyebrows and nodded in appreciation at the achievement. In the Army, that happened only when it was fighting a war and company-grade officers were dying. "Must have been a direct commission, some kind of wonder child."

They were walking against the outgoing tide of commuters heading for the Pentagon's subway stop, and getting irritated looks from officers worn down by a busy day of writing memoranda to each other. They escaped the crowds by climbing the stairs up to the fifth floor, in what had once been the Pentagon's attic. In recent years most of this top floor had been converted from storerooms to offices, but it still felt different from the lower, busier floors of the building. Despite the remodeling, it had an anachronistic remoteness to it, as if it were a chunk of the old War

Department that had drifted loose through time and space. Its corridor around the E ring was narrower, with a lower, arched ceiling and a musty, forgotten air to it. The corridor also snaked around irregular rooms that bulged out into the neat lines of the building. Coca-Cola machines blocked the line of sight at every major bend. After it was converted to offices, the Marines had been the first to move in here, taking over much of it when General Krulak moved their headquarters down the hill from the Navy Annex. It was, noted one Navy captain who rode out the waning days of his career on the fifth floor, his service's Siberia, the attic home to functions the Navy bureaucracy didn't even pretend to care about—Western Hemisphere operations, equal opportunity advisers and war-fighting doctrine.

As Lewis listened to Sherman relate what she had learned from Cisco, he remembered how she had looked in a T-shirt at Fort Irwin. He glanced down at her.

She felt the look. It didn't bother her. Let him lust a little.

They walked past an office marked "The Commandant's Staff Group." Below that, a personnel roster listed the office's inhabitants as "Moe, Larry and Curly." Sherman found that very un-Army. She couldn't decide whether she liked it.

"What is this place?" Sherman asked Lewis.

"My new XO, an Air Force colonel named Underhill, calls it 'Marineland,' " Lewis said. "He thinks they're crazy up here." The Marines and the Air Force were the oil and water of the U.S. military. The Corps was essentially a religious institution, while the Air Force acted like a corporation. The Marines were inexpensive, interventionist and people oriented; the Air Force was costly, isolationist and technology driven.

As they walked, Lewis described his first day. Like a good Army officer, he focused on the positive: There were no problems, just challenges. He found it a pretty squared-away office, he said, with most of the staff having a real warrior spirit.

"There are lots of Special Forces guys," he said approvingly. "Even his driver, Sergeant First Class Stout, is some kind of huge SF NCO, maybe out of Delta Force. His forearms are like my legs."

Eventually he worked his way back to the toilet paper order. That was indeed a challenge. "Back at Irwin, I was, like, something hot. I mean, first I commanded a troop, then I was Ops officer. I was moving and grooving in the Mojave. Here I'm a bathroom attendant."

They walked two full rotations of the Marineland corridor. "Wasn't there some guy you were serious about when we were lieutenants?" he asked. He thought she might have been married at some point.

She stopped walking, turned and fixed her gray eyes on him. "That's over," she said. "He made a lot of assumptions about us, about me." She didn't explain. It had never quite gotten to marriage.

Lewis invited her to go find some dinner. She begged off. She had been at the Pentagon for eleven hours. She said she was going to go home and crash.

Lewis watched her as she walked down the long corridor toward the Metro exit. He couldn't figure out Sherman. She too was a challenge. A good one. He wandered idly across the quiet hallways of the Pentagon to the cafeteria. He bought a cardboard tray of salad and macaroni and cheese in the big dismal room but couldn't face eating a lonely dinner alongside a score of divorced lieutenant colonels living in the rootless land of aging singles, so he carried it back to the vice chairman's office. He liked being there alone. He e-mailed his friends on his "OPFOR buddies" distribution list. They had now transferred to a dozen posts around the world, from Germany to Macedonia to Korea, and across the U.S.

Glad you are not here, for your sakes. Wish I was back kicking Bluefor butt. My life is empty as a soldier, except for interacting with the few we have here in Ames's foxhole. The rest of the five-sided puzzle palace is chockablock with chairborne bureaucrats. They give good brief. Charts, slides and matrices are the tools we bring to the next war. Do they think we're gonna whack the bad guys with our laptops, PowerPoint them to death?

For all that, he thought as he closed the applications on his computer and then exited its security gates, Ames's shop was the place to be, if you had to be in the Pentagon. Here he could fight the good fight—and do his best for his military and his nation.

He walked the fifteen minutes home to his empty studio apartment in Crystal City, just south of I-395 from the Pentagon. It looked like most other rooms he'd lived in at Forts Knox, Stewart and Irwin since becoming an officer—closer to a motel room than a real apartment. He kind of liked that: Stay low, pack light and ride hard.

The Pentagon
Friday, May 6
9 A.M.

Shillingsworth had Sherman call the national security adviser's scheduler and say he wanted to see him that day about the Afghanistan mission.

Pitch came on the phone and asked for Shillingsworth. "Why don't you swing by around six tonight?" Pitch asked, using phrasing that disguised the fact that he was issuing an order.

"I may bring some of the other Chiefs with me," Shillingsworth said, feeling the need to be decent enough to give Pitch a heads-up.

"Sure, sure," Pitch said brusquely, then hung up without another word.

Then the general set out to line up the Chiefs to oppose the mission. He walked up to the Navy's wainscotted hallway, past glass cases holding models of submarines and aircraft carriers, to see the chief of naval operations, Admiral Warren Vane, a fourth-generation Navy officer and a second-generation carrier pilot. "Weather" Vane, as he had been known since his Annapolis days, saw it as a service issue—and ground operations in land-locked Afghanistan weren't a problem for the sea service. "I can provide intell, logistical support, even cruise missiles—but Afghanistan is kind of inland for the Navy, you know?" This entire enterprise, he said as he stood and led Shillingsworth to the door, is "just not in my threat dome," using the fighter pilot's expression for the surface-to-air missile's zone of lethality.

Shillingsworth walked the broad stairs up another flight, to the Air Force area. He walked past endless paintings of fighter aircraft in huge, pillowy, sunset-illuminated pink skies. None depicted planes flying in storms, he had once noticed. Bill Propeczki, the Air Force chief, proved amiable but distant. As Shillingsworth began to lay out his plan for the Chiefs to go to the president, he held up both hands, palms flat toward Shillingsworth: "Whoa, there, General. I'm getting G-LOC here." Shillingsworth frowned—he didn't understand the term. "Gravity-induced loss of consciousness," the Air Force chief explained. "That's blacking out in a high-gravity maneuver. When you're trying to do too much too fast and putting too much of a strain on your body."

Propeczki was the first space specialist to become head of the Air Force. The one thing he intended to do with his term of office was to hold together his service as he reoriented it toward space. "I've got enough blood on the floor internally," he said. "And I really don't have a dog in this fight."

Even though he knew by now that he didn't have the votes, Shillingsworth kept his appointment with Ricardo Blades, the Marine commandant. Despite the occasional friction between the inarticulate Army and the publicity-savvy Marines, there remained a fundamental sympathy between the services. Both were groundpounders, built around "the poor bloody infantry," the combat arm that always suffered the most. The Marines and the Army were the most human of services, because they were the ones that actually fought in the environment in which people exist. Blades was the only member of the Chiefs whom Shillingsworth considered a friend.

Talking with the Marine commandant was less a business meeting than a chat with a comrade. Blades said he agreed entirely: The Afghanistan mission was a loser. He would speak quietly to some friends on the Hill about it, he promised. But he would not join Shillingsworth in confronting a White House that wouldn't be deterred. That would be bad for the Corps, he said. And as commandant, that was pretty much his bottom line.

Shillingsworth took his time walking back down to his office. He told Miss Turley to cancel his appointment with Lieutenant General Mike "Diddle" Middleton, the director of the Joint Staff. Middleton was so consensus driven that he would never side with Shillingsworth against the Chiefs. His nickname alluded to the military's mocking shorthand for unimaginative strategy—"Hey diddle diddle / Straight up the middle."

The USS Harry S Truman
Off the Coast of Virginia
1 P.M.

The afternoon brought the quick flight for Shillingsworth and Sherman down to Norfolk and then a helicopter hop out to the USS *Harry S Truman,* the aircraft carrier that had a task force from the 101st Air Assault Division embarked upon it. The exercise scenario involved an assault on the fictional nation of Cortina, which after years of exercises had become more authentic to him than most real nations. Certainly had a better government, he thought.

It was Sherman's first flight aboard a Marine helicopter. She was taken aback by the drab, old machine, whose fuselage of radar-absorbing gray paint was blackened with exhaust fumes and oil streaks. She wondered if the Marines, knowing that they were going to be transporting the Army chief of staff, purposely had provided one of their oldest helicopters—a sort of ostentatious reminder of the Corps's spartan approach. Lifting off from the Norfolk naval air station aboard the CH-53, she looked up the side of the cabin and noticed a fat drop of transparent pink fluid—hydraulics?—oozing down an exposed green wire. She caught the eye of the old crew chief, who with his gray skin and salt-and-pepper mustache looked like he was part of the aged aircraft's machinery.

"That a problem?" she asked over the headset, pointing at the poisonous-looking pink drop.

The aging sergeant squinted up at the fluid—years of leaning out the open window of the helo into cold, salty winds and hot exhaust plumes had etched deep lines around his eyes and mouth—and grinned back at her. "Only if it stops, ma'am," he said. She wondered for a moment at his flat expression, and then caught his grim humor: If the hydraulic fluid stopped leaking, it meant there was no more—and then the helicopter went down.

Shillingsworth used the helicopter ride to think about the meeting with Pitch that night. He would tell him that these things never end. We're still in northern Iraq, a full thirteen years after the end of the Gulf War, he would say. And there is an opportunity cost here—I can't take on new missions, reorganize the Army as an expeditionary strike force and cut my budget all at the same time. What's more, there is no guarantee that the mission will go smoothly. The Afghans have already taken on two superpowers—the British in the nineteenth century and the Soviets in the twentieth. I am not sure that a few American soldiers on a half-assed "presence mission" will impress them much. We may just be making our people fat targets for anti-American factions in Afghanistan.

If he asks, I'll confess that I'm alone among the service chiefs. But only if he asks. Let him think Maddox and I have the votes in our pockets.

The CH-53's wheels clunked down on the deck of the carrier, first the back, then the front. Even though the seven blades of the rotor were swinging a good ten feet above his head, Shillingsworth still hunched down as he got out and trotted to the stairs at the edge of the flight deck. He climbed down to the 101st unit's command suite, Sherman behind him. When they walked in, Shillingsworth threw an arm over the shoulder of the brigadier, who had once commanded a company in the 82nd for him.

The unit's intelligence officer drew Sherman aside and handed her a copy of an Associated Press bulletin. "This just ran across our computer as you were coming in," he said.

She glanced at the headline and interrupted Shillingsworth's reunion: "Sir." She handed him the printout.

Shillingsworth read the story. "White House Aides: Shick to Announce U.S. Intervention in Afghan Conflict," the headline said. The unnamed aides—probably Pitch and the press secretary speaking on background, he thought—said that President Shick would soon announce that he had decided to send a small peacekeeping force to Afghanistan. The troop size would be big enough to signal U.S. resolve but not so big that it would be provocative, the aides said. Most of the troops would be relief specialists and military police, along with some water purifiers and an infantry unit for perimeter security. "The U.S. mission will be meant to reassure all parties," they told the AP. It would last only sixty days, in order to provide all sides with a "cooling-off period."

My God, Shillingsworth thought, do they think the Afghans are a labor union? What the White House really is saying is that it won't send a fighting unit.

And what they've done is cut me off before I could get in an opposing word. This is policy by preemptive leak, he thought. I've miscalculated here: Pitch thought I was coming over to tell him the Chiefs were against him, so he cut me off.

Shillingsworth was staggered. He asked Sherman for his cell phone and then walked out to the catwalk on the side of the ship. He stared at the hazy horizon. Should I resign? Put out a statement of mild disagreement? Call Pitch and try to stop this train? He remembered the conversation on the way back from the funeral in which his wife had asked why she was no longer part of his deliberations about such critical decisions. He called her at the Alexandria elementary school where she was the assistant principal. She listened to his brief outline of Pitch's sandbagging, necessarily veiled because they were on easily tapped cell phones, then asked him a one-word question: "Moab?" Was it time for him to resign and for them to pack their bags?

"No," he decided as he spoke. "I'm not one to abandon a hot LZ." In Vietnam he had watched his first platoon leader freeze up in combat, sit back against a rubber tree and stare at his bootlaces as mortar shells hit their perimeter. Men had died because of that failure—including the poor lieutenant. That year in Vietnam had taught Shillingsworth that the primary duty of the soldier is to keep going. Just put one foot in front of the other. Sounds easy, but it can get real hard.

"So what's next?" his wife asked.

"My mission now is to stand by my people." The decision had been made. What he needed to do was shape the deployment force, make sure there was at least one person in the meetings looking out for the interests of the troops. To do that, he would need to get back to Washington.

Four minutes later they were climbing back aboard the CH-53, where the crew had been shutting down the systems. Sherman saw the old crew chief grin at them insanely. As the engines began revving, the Army brigadier thrust another wire service bulletin through the still-open clamshell hatch: "Afghan Mission to Begin Within Weeks, White House Aides Say."

As the helicopter chopped through a headwind back to Norfolk, Shillingsworth stared out the small portholelike window at the cold, gray Atlantic waters. The key fact of life in Washington for a military leader, he thought, is that I play on the field of politics. It is always an away game for the military. I can't win that game. The question is how close I can make the outcome. Tugged by wind blowing through the open side door, the wire story flapped accusingly in his hand.

Office of the National Security Adviser
The White House
4:30 P.M.

General Shillingsworth entered the national security adviser's office and Admiral Maddox, the Joint Chiefs chairman, turned from staring out at the White House lawn and nodded. "John," he said remotely, in mournful greeting. He looked back out the window. *He is saying that I failed him,* Shillingsworth thought.

Pitch looked up as if he were pleasantly surprised that Shillingsworth had dropped by. "Ah, General Shillingsworth. I'm glad you're here. We were just discussing the force structure for the Afghan mission."

Shillingsworth had decided against calling Pitch on the preemptive leak. Part of being a solider was knowing when to keep your mouth shut. "Silence is a soldierly virtue," he had once read somewhere.

At any rate, it was too late for him to protest. Pitch already was dictating to Maddox, Middleton, Gates and the other Joint Staff officers the size, shape and nature of the American deployment. Shillingsworth knew that Maddox so hated and distrusted Ames that he wouldn't bring him to such meetings—which had the unintended effect of keeping Ames un-sullied in the eyes of the troops.

"I don't want a bunch of tightly wrapped Rangers or trigger-happy Marines," Pitch said, pointing his cigarette at Golden Gates, the Marine general who as J-5 was the chief planner for the Joint Staff. "That's the wrong message here." He frowned thoughtfully.

"No," he said. "I want a support unit as the core." He looked at General Shillingsworth. "I believe the Division Support Command at Tenth Mountain Division has a Forward Support Battalion in green phase." Pitch had gone around them and somehow learned that under the Army's new readiness ranking system, that mixed-gender unit of medics, cooks and mechanics had just been certified as "green"—that is, fully trained, equipped and ready to deploy overseas. "This is just a presence mission," he said. "Chapter Six, not Chapter Seven." That was ominous—going in under the United Nations' Chapter 6 rules for peacekeeping would mean far more restrictive rules of engagement, with permission to use force only as a last resort and in self-defense.

Middleton just took notes, not offering any opinions. Gates shook his head. He clearly was losing patience, both with Pitch's dictating the force structure and with his own boss's withdrawal from the conversation. "This feels to me like enough to get us into real trouble, but not enough to do anything about it," he said.

Shillingsworth seconded the thought. "You know the saying, 'If some-thing is worth doing, it's worth doing well.' I think if we're going to do this, which is something I still have problems with, then we should put in combat troops—guys ready to handle any contingency. Let's not limit our options."

Pitch sighed at this obstructionist attitude. "Look, women and children are dying on television. We are going to do something about it. And we are not going to spend weeks mucking around while you guys figure out if any combat units will deign to do this." In reviewing the readiness reports, Pitch had been taken aback to see that, due to its commitments to Korea, Bosnia, Kuwait, Rwanda, Albania, Macedonia and Montenegro, the Army had no combat units that were both ready and available for the mission.

The past week of monitoring deputies' meetings on Afghanistan had worn Pitch's patience. At some point these guys needed to understand that they worked for him. The U.S. military was going to do this mission, whether they liked it or not. "Would you all be more comfortable if I found someone else to handle this?" he asked. He was playing bureaucratic chicken, confident that Gates wouldn't take up his challenge and resign in protest.

"No, I'll do it, and you know I will," said Lieutenant General Gates. "That's why I'm the most hated man in the Pentagon. Because I dress up the shit sandwiches you guys are serving us." Only a Marine general would feel free to talk like that to the national security adviser, Shillingsworth thought and then probably only one who had been a Rhodes scholar twenty-five years earlier with both Pitch and President Shick.

Pitch snorted in appreciation at the verbal punch. "I don't recall you being like this at Oxford," he said.

Gates knew that what Pitch meant was, You weren't such a troublesome asshole back then. Well, Gates thought, that was before Algeria. I did my best for my country for twenty-five years, made sacrifices, rose to the top of my profession—only to have you clowns let Marines get killed on the USS *Kuwait City,* and put me in a position where I have to serve you.

"How would you know?" Gates slapped back. "You and all the other Ivy types wouldn't talk to me. I was beneath you—a Marine officer. The only one in that house who talked to me like I was human was Jim." He was playing the Shick card, Pitch knew: Back then, Jim Shick always had a good word for everyone, even Second Lieutenant Gates. Shick actually had seemed to enjoy conversing with the military officers in the Rhodes program. The Ivy Leaguers, by contrast, while admiring of the military, hadn't seemed particularly interested in being in it themselves or even in talking to someone who was. Gates was saying that before he resigned, he could and would go to President Shick.

The two men paused in their sparring. Maddox lifted his chin from his hand and turned back to them, as if the moment of silence had woken him from daydreaming. The other men all looked at him, but he said nothing.

Shillingsworth seized the moment of silence, uncharacteristically, to express his deepest thoughts. "My greatest fear, throughout my military service, as a company commander on up to corps commander, was not that we would go to war," he said. It was an effort for him to speak about this in personal terms, but he thought it might be the way to get through to Pitch and, through him, to the president. "I was ready for that, trained. No, what turns my guts is the thought that my soldiers would be sent into action as pawns, without a decent respect for the consequences. I worry that that is what is happening now."

Pitch stared at him for a moment, his eyes flashing with irritation. He slapped down Shillingsworth's plea. "If you'd step out of the confessional booth for a moment and work with me on this, General Shillingsworth, we could ensure there won't be any 'action.'"

The president formally announced the new U.S. mission to Afghanistan the next day in his Saturday radio address. He emphasized that this was a short-term peacekeeping mission, its intent to keep warring factions apart, and that no combat was expected.

Immediately after the president spoke, General Shillingsworth sent out an e-mail to the Army's major commands: *The decision has been made. Let's move out smartly. We will let you know if you are needed.*

The Pentagon
Sunday, May 8
9 A.M.

When Sherman arrived at the Pentagon to see if she could help out, she found its hallways seemed almost vast without their usual workweek population of overstressed, unhappy lieutenant colonels. As she went upstairs toward the Army area, she caught sight of a young sailor in his whites walking alone backward, talking to himself. She watched his back for a moment as he moved crablike toward her. "Everyone remembers Eisenhower and Marshall but forgets Bradley," she heard him say to himself. She realized he was training to be a Pentagon tourist guide, using the weekend to practice in the empty corridors.

Sherman walked into Ames's outer office and found her way blocked by the general's driver/bodyguard/factotum, Sergeant First Class Jack Stout, the big lug from Special Forces who had so impressed Lewis. He was getting ready to go for a run, and his huge muscles rippled in his black spandex shorts and black tank top.

"May I help you, ma'am?" Stout asked, more as an order to halt than a genuine question.

General Ames was standing just beyond him, talking to Underhill and Lewis. He turned with a tight grin and reached his hand out to Cindy. "Here's our Sherman, marching out of Georgia," he quipped.

The remark bothered her somehow, but she smiled back. What else did you do with a four-star? "Good to meet you, sir." Ames left for a Tank meeting on Afghanistan, Stout and the XO walking a few respectful paces behind him. She watched him leave. How did he know she had been born in Georgia?

Lewis grinned broadly, obviously pleased to see her. He explained that Ames had ordered him to join the flight down that morning from Andrews Air Force Base to Central Command headquarters in Tampa, Florida, for a major coordination meeting on the Afghan deployment. Normally, the active-duty military would conduct such a briefing by remote video teleconferencing. But there were too many reserve units involved that didn't have VTC capabilities, and as long as so many of the commanders had to travel for the brief, they figured they would do it in one place and get to know each other.

"Just sit in the back of the briefing room and be my eyes and ears," Ames had ordered. "Get a sense of the players."

Sherman liked that rationale and ten minutes later put the same argument to Shillingsworth's XO. "You're not operational," he responded. "But it would be good for the chief to have a sense of the possible taskings coming at him." Ultimately, he told her to go "space available," meaning that no chits would be called in to get her aboard the plane, but that if she could weasel her way on, fine.

They drove together in Sherman's old green Subaru to Andrews, just twenty minutes away on this quiet Sunday morning. They parked and were directed by an Air Force tech sergeant to an old Air Force 747 waiting on the tarmac. The civilian airliner had been modified in a dozen ways. Along the dorsal spine of the aircraft ran a long white bulge containing, among other things, a satellite communications system. Another bulge in the tail contained a mile-long spool of filamented copper wire that could be trailed out the back to send launch signals via extremely low frequency transmissions to ballistic missile submarines waiting under the sea, transmitting one apocalyptic letter every twenty-two seconds—the radio's five-minute-long test signal was "MENE MENE TEKEL." Behind red seals under the wings hung four round flare dispensers, the better to decoy heat-seeking missiles away from the big Pratt & Whitney engines. The aircraft was part of the old "Kneecap" fleet, the airman's bastardization of NEACP, for "Nuclear Emergency Airborne Command Post"—the post the president would take in case of a nuclear attack on the U.S. With its in-air refueling capacity, unusual for a 747, the plane could remain aloft virtually indefinitely. Now that the Cold War was over, the aging plane was being used as a bus to carry around Pentagon staffers.

Lewis bounded up the stairs and craned his neck, looking around the bizarre airplane. He picked a bottle of water from the case left by the door. In the nose he saw the president's sleeping compartment. He turned and Sherman followed him through the small conference room, dominated by a long table and a National Geographic wall map of the world, where presumably an aide could cross out cities and nations as they were obliterated by nuclear explosions. The next compartment was a small briefing theater, four rows of seats facing forward. It was followed by a command and control section, where huge old mainframes ran down the walls and big chairs faced the small blank green screens of early 1980s computers. The entire room held less computing power than a few good laptops, Sherman thought.

Finally they came to the cramped crew section at the back of the airplane, where the people actually flying the plane and serving the meals would stay while the bigwigs aboard deliberated the fate of the earth. They took the two seats jammed in the rear of the aircraft, the better to maintain Sherman's fragile claim to being aboard.

"I didn't know you were born in Georgia," Lewis said as they buckled up. "I was surprised when General Ames mentioned it. You don't have any accent."

"Yeah, I was puzzled when he brought it up," she said. "I mean, it says 'Columbus, Georgia' on my birth certificate, but my dad was moved from Benning to Dix before I turned one."

"Real Army brat, huh?"

"All the way," she said. "I went to nine schools in twelve years, including three in third grade, when the hollow Army really was landing on the shoulders of people like my dad. He was a career infantry NCO."

"Real hard-charger?"

"Not with his family," she said. "He was almost too gentle, soft-spoken, with Mom and me, especially after Vietnam, like he had to be careful or he was going to break something. But all that moving made me kind of a loner. Half my childhood memories are of sitting in the backseat of my parents' Ford Fairlane on some cross-country moving trip. And then getting to some new post where nobody knew me, except the volunteers at the base library who went out of their way to be nice to the scrawny little new girl."

Lewis passed her his bottle of water. Sharing it felt oddly like a step toward intimacy, like a high school girl borrowing a boy's jacket. "How did you get into oil painting?" he asked. "It seems so un-Army."

It was, she thought, the first time he'd ever directly asked her anything substantial. His style of conversation was Army reticent: He assumed that his comrades would tell him what they wanted to tell him and what he needed to know.

"Like a lot of things, it began with romantic attraction," she said, with the slightest undertone of flirtation, just a signal that that frequency was open and in receive mode. She felt more companionable with Lewis than she had with anyone in a long time. "In tenth grade, when we were at Fort Lewis, I had a huge crush on my art teacher, who told us all these great tales of his bohemian student days in the 1970s in New York. I lost the infatuation after he got busted for dope smoking and got fired. But that summer I took a watercolors course at Tacoma Community College, five mornings a week." But when she bicycled out to Steilacoom to do her studies, she remembered, the lightness of watercolors never seemed right for the cold, black waters of Puget Sound or the gray fog coiled among the heavy, dark-green spruce trees. She'd paint all afternoon, then wait on tables at the Tides Inn from five until midnight, then bike home. That fall she goofed around with acrylics but wasn't satisfied with that medium, either.

"I was looking for something more than watercolors," she recalled. "The intensity and richness of oil paints intrigued me, so during the winter of my senior year I took a night course in oils. I loved everything about them—well, almost everything. I hate how slow they are to dry. But when it is good, oil work has a glow in it—the live color of green in a spring leaf, as opposed to the neon feeling of acrylics.

"After that I was a confirmed oil painter, except for plebe year, when I didn't touch a brush from July to June. I especially loved the way oil could capture the nuances of light." In her favorite of the three West Point seasons paintings, *Winter,* she remembered, she'd focused on the view from Trophy Point of the black Hudson and its contending blocks of dark ice, with the heavy clouds looming above the water scumbled by the thin layer of opaque material she laid over them as if there were light trapped inside them that would never get out.

Talked out, they fell into a comfortable silence over Georgia, then landed an hour later.

The efficiency of the military, once it focused on a mission, always impressed Sherman. The big old 747 lumbered to a stop at the end of the runway at MacDill Air Force Base, just outside Tampa. Before the engines had stopped whining, a school bus painted Air Force blue parked at the bottom of the stairs. Three minutes later they walked inside Central Command's headquarters, a two-story building the size of a supermarket, perched at the edge of the base next to the tepid, shallow waters of Tampa Bay. Inside the small, windowless auditorium stood knots of officers from Centcom, from Army Forces Command in Atlanta and from Army Reserve units around the country.

Centcom's deputy director for plans, a Marine brigadier, began the briefing as soon as the Pentagoners arrived. "The NCA doesn't see this as a combat mission," he said, putting aside the personal doubts that had kept him awake in his bed long into Sunday morning. "The mission statement explicitly terms it a 'presence mission.' " So, he explained, turning to a slide of the planned force, it would be heavy on civil affairs, MPs, water purifiers. "All the usual low-density, high-demand units," he said, tapping the diagram of the planned force, showing units and their reporting chains. It was a gamble: In order to keep the size of the deployment low, the task force would have a minimum of pure combat troops. And it was unusually heavy on reservists.

"Next slide," he drove on in an even voice. Even people who knew him wouldn't have been able to tell from his even tone whether he thought this was the best mission ever or a world-class fiasco in the making. While not an assault force, he continued, the deploying task force would be fully capable of robust self-defense. It would have a small complement of AH-64D Longbow Apache attack helicopters for reconnaissance and deep strike. "If the Uzbeks got pushy, we'd pick them up out two hundred or three hundred clicks and stop them there," he said.

At the end of the briefing, the Marine said, "You got any questions, ask them now."

An Army brigadier in the front row raised one finger in front of his chest. "Counterbattery?" he asked.

"Not overwhelming but adequate for the threat," said the briefer. "Two TPQ-36 Firefinders, four 120-millimeter mortars, and two M-109 howitzers. No Q-37s—there's no reported enemy artillery within several hundred miles."

The next briefer, an Air Force colonel, walked them through all the deployment time lines, the complex samba of units, many of them reservists from Georgia and Alabama, coming together with their equipment and parent units at Fort Stewart, just outside Savannah, Georgia. It would begin in less than twenty-four hours with a company of the 3rd Mechanized Infantry Division's engineers moving out of Stewart and falling in on a set of earth-moving equipment prepositioned in the Persian Gulf. Meanwhile, an Air Force Combat Control Team and a company of the 75th Rangers would mark an airstrip in Afghanistan for C-130s and then provide perimeter security for the follow-on forces, beginning with the engineers. The camp in Afghanistan would be established three days later. Then the "air bridge" would begin, with units moving east by airlift—C-5s and C-17s to Oman, then C-130s from there for the final hop into Afghanistan. The entire camp would be in place in just nine days.

On the plane ride back to Washington the pilots dimmed the lights so planners who had been up all night preparing could catch some sleep. Their job was done. Sherman and Lewis took their seats at the very back of the plane and caught the drowsy mood. They rode in relaxed silence for a while, talked about some details for the Afghanistan mission, then fell into silence again.

Halfway back to Washington, Sherman leaned her head close to Lewis, speaking barely above a whisper in order not to waken the exhausted planners sprawled in the seats in front of them. "How did you wind up picking West Point?"

"It just seemed natural to me," he said, sitting with his eyes closed. "I grew up in Riverside, California, you know. Parents were kind of Okies who made good." His father had gone from working on a fruit farm to raising his own shrubbery for the postwar housing tracts, and wound up with a twenty-five-truck landscaping business and a Mercedes in the driveway.

Lewis had been one of those high school athletes with more enthusiasm and brains than ability, making the starting team on baseball because he played catcher, which is where smart coaches put athletes like that. In football he only made second string on the offensive line—the position for big but slow players. "No one was going to want me to play college ball. My parents could have paid to send me anywhere. But West Point appealed to me. And no one else from my congressional district was interested."

The Point fit him like a glove. " 'Duty, honor, country'—that works for me," he said comfortably, still leaning his head back with his eyes closed. "That's not a bad life. I can't imagine doing anything else."

"I can," she said. "I think about it all the time. Why do I love the Army more than it loves me?"

Lewis sat up and looked at her, surprise in his eyes, as if she had expressed disloyalty.

"I'm not disagreeing with you," she explained. "I like how you've stuck with that, 'duty, honor and country.' A lot of the people we went to the Point with have become so cynical—'Career first, mission maybe, people never.' But the Army charges a price." She said slowly, trying to be precise, " 'Duty'—well, trying to do that kind of helped split up my last serious relationship."

They flew on in silence, not quite as comfortably this time. Finally, she said, "I think constantly about doing something else. If it hadn't been for my West Point service obligation, I might have quit after my battalion XO showed up late one Saturday night at my apartment door in Killeen, Texas." She pulled a blanket up over her shoulders as the frigid air of the ionosphere seeped through the old plane's thin insulation.

"Thinking he was in love with you?" Lewis asked.

"You got it. Drunk, confused and telling me that he had fallen hard for me. With a wife and two toddlers at home across the post, angry with himself and with me for the feeling of betrayal it gave him. He knew it was wrong, and he knew that he had put his career in my hands. We talked until dawn on my porch. Nothing ever happened between us. But the next five months, until he PCS'd out, were sheer hell. When I was at battalion headquarters, he could hardly look at me. I felt like he hated me. The capacity of the Army to force imperfect people to try to be perfect and crush them if they fail scares me. I don't want to live in fear. A lot of people in the Army do. Not fear that they can destroy you—but that they can make you feel like a failure."

"But you're such a hotshot, a poster girl for gender integration," Lewis protested. "I mean, the most successful female infantry brigade S-2 ever."

"But think about it, Lewis," she said. "Being a woman working intelligence in combat arms, I'm always on thin ice. You know as well as I do that the nature of combat is failure—victory goes not to the side that does everything well, which no one ever does, but to the one that fails least, that recovers best from failure. And nothing is easier than blaming faulty intelligence. So being a female tactical intelligence officer, it is doubly easy for me to get tagged: When we win, they say it's because of how good the commanders and soldiers are. When we lose, 'That woman's intelligence sucked.' As if they lost because of equal opportunity.

"I think there is a place for me in this Army. But I worry that it tries to make me cut out parts of myself to fit into that place. If I have to lie to be part of this institution, I can live without it. Especially if they want me to lie to myself. I have to live with myself." Lewis wasn't sure what she was talking about, but didn't say so. This sort of talk, questioning the very institution, seemed vaguely insubordinate to him.

She closed her eyes. He went back to studying the printout of the deployment time line in case Ames wanted a brief on it, making sure he understood each of the moving pieces. He glanced up at her sleeping face. The thought occurred to him that she was beautiful—not in a conventional, beauty-contest way, but as a unique mature woman.

Back at Andrews, she drove him to his Crystal City apartment. Almost without discussion, they decided to eat dinner together. She changed out of her uniform in his bedroom and pulled on the jeans and black turtleneck sweater from the flight bag she kept in her car. Waiting for him in the spartan living room, its walls bare except for a Mexican rug he'd picked up while posted at Fort Irwin, she wandered over to his book-shelves.

Her gaze passed over his compact disc collection, which was dominated by popular middle-of-the-road stuff—Billy Joel, Celine Dion, Garth Brooks. A guy who buys music because it has become so familiar that he thinks he likes it, she thought to herself.

His selection of books held more promise. They were almost all about the military, but she expected that. It was a thoughtful selection of the two or three best books about most major American wars. He cared about his work. From the Civil War there was Ulysses S. Grant's *Personal Memoirs*. From World War I was Siegfried Sassoon's *Memoirs of an Infantry Officer*. There were several Vietnam books: Webb's *Fields of Fire,* McDonough's *Platoon Leader,* Sorley's biography of General Creighton Abrams, and Moore and Galloway's *We Were Soldiers Once . . . and Young.* There was Antal's *Proud Legions.* There were a few books on the Gulf War, one about Somalia, Bowden's *Black Hawk Down,* which had struck her as marvelous but almost claustrophobic, trapped at the squad and platoon level. There was a new one, *Ambush at Sea,* about the attack on the USS *Kuwait City* off Algeria.

She took down T. R. Fehrenbach's meditation on the Korean conflict, *This Kind of War,* which she'd never read. The thick volume fell open to a passage Lewis had underlined in red ink: "You may fly over a land forever; you may bomb it, atomize it, pulverize it and wipe it clean of life—but if you desire to defend it, protect it, and keep it for civilization, you must do this on the ground, the way the Roman legions did, by putting your young men in the mud." Lewis had written an emphatic red "YES!" in the margin. She agreed with him. It was a statement that accurately summarized the United States Army's view of the world, she thought.

His taste in books seemed impeccable but narrow. The books, though fine, were all personal views, memoirs and biographies, and all were by Americans and Englishmen. There were no books offering a strategic overview or a dispassionate analysis—no Clausewitz, Sun Tzu, no over-arching studies of particular wars or eras or nations, such as Samuel Huntington's *The Soldier and the State.* He's a smart guy but a bit single-minded, unaware of the world beyond the military, happy to have it that way, she thought. But that was too harsh, he told himself: He's got promise.

He came back into the living room and saw her examining his bookshelf. "I had lots of time on my hands on deployments," he said, holding his hands out palms up as if they were proof. "I bet one day there will be a book about the Afghan mission up there."

She realized that he had grown accustomed to apologizing for his love of books. She hadn't meant to put him in that position. She changed the subject. "How much are you paying a month for this place, Lewis? Around twelve hundred dollars?"

He nodded yes as they walked out.

"You're being ripped off. Why not just lease a room at the Holiday Inn? You'd save money and have just as much atmosphere."

He shrugged. "I've never been much into interior decorating."

She shook her head. "Let me take you to my favorite restaurant."

"Sure," he said. "Just know that I'm hungry."

She found what looked to be the last parking place on upper Wisconsin Avenue. They walked three blocks up a hill along a sidewalk full of weekend crowds of suburbanites, tourists and Georgetown University students. Sherman looked at their faces and eavesdropped on their conversations. She heard no indication that any of them was thinking about the Afghan mission that the president had announced just a day earlier. That wasn't part of their world.

They stopped at Bistrot Lepic. In the back of the tiny restaurant, at a tiny table flush against a lemony-yellow wall, she ordered the smoked trout salad and a pork cassoulet. "Try the onion tart as an appetizer," she recommended.

He looked up skeptically from the menu. "OK," he said, a bit reluctantly. "But for my entrée I'm sticking with the filet mignon with garlic mashed potatoes."

"Pick the wine?" she said.

"Are you kidding?" he said. She chose a rich, fruity cabernet franc from Virginia.

He didn't say much about the tart. But when his filet came he took a bite and then slowly put down his fork. "That's, um, really good," he said. "I mean, I've never had a steak that good." It's a start, she thought, and better than anything he'd had in Barstow, the town nearest to Fort Irwin, twenty-five miles away across the Mojave.

Over coffee he surprised her by asking his second big question of the day: "I'd heard, uh, that you were getting married—what happened?"

"Two cheers for armored cav subtlety, Lewis."

He grinned and raised his shoulders helplessly. "Guilty. Way I was trained, ma'am."

"I was going to marry an Apache pilot at Fort Hood but it didn't work out. When I put in for a billet at Fort Huachuca—which is my branch's home post, after all—he told me to drop it. He'd just assumed I'd leave the Army for him, follow him around to Korea and Germany. We'd never even talked about that. The engagement ended there." What she didn't disclose to Lewis was that she had been so angry about his assumption that she had broken off the relationship that night and never spoken to the man again. She'd sent a friend to pick up all the music CDs she'd lent him.

"Where is he now?"

"North Carolina, I think," she said. "He left the Army as soon as his service obligation was up. I've heard he's working for a bank in Charlotte."

"And you stayed in," he noted.

"Yeah, but after that I went looking for a psychiatrist."

He put down his coffee cup in surprise and leaned forward. "An Army shrink?"

She gave a dismissive shake of her head. "Do I look stupid? No, I went to a civilian, on my own time and my own tab, with nothing ever going into my file." For more than a thousand dollars, the psychiatrist had confirmed what she suspected: If she was going to stay in the Army, she'd have to learn to live with loneliness.

"What did he tell you?" Lewis asked.

"To learn to live with the Army," she said, slightly shading the psychiatrist's prescription. She didn't mention that the psychiatrist also told her that she had developed a tendency to dam it up and then, when she met someone she felt she could trust, to let it all flood out. As I am right now, she thought. She felt a warmth with Lewis that she hadn't felt with a man for years.

He smiled at her.

"I'm talking too much, aren't I?" she said.

"No, I like it," he said. That, he long had understood, was what you were supposed to say to women. He was surprised to find that this time he meant it.

"What about you? How come you're not married?" she asked.

"Never came close." He shrugged. "Never got engaged."

"But?"

"Don't get me wrong—I've had lots of relationships."

"No, you haven't," she said, shaking her head but still smiling. "You've gotten laid a lot."

His jaw fell a little bit. She persisted. "I know that armored cav's four basic food groups are cordite, diesel, alcohol and sex. I wonder if you've really had that many genuine relationships."

He started to protest but stopped. She might be right. He wondered if this was what it was like to have a relationship of equals. In the table's candlelight, he thought, her spikiness was softened. But not her spirit—that came through in a way he found both alluring and slightly intimidating.

"There is a difference, you know," she persisted.

"I get your point," he said. He put his hand over hers on the table. "I think I'd like to know the difference."

She smiled at him. "Smart-ass." She chuckled. But she didn't move her hand away for a full minute, until the bill came. Then she quickly pulled out her Visa card and put it on the table. "My pick, my treat."

They drove to her place in Adams-Morgan, as close as the nation's capital came to having a bohemian district. She parked outside her place on Lanier Street, across from an old firehouse, on the top floor of a three-story nineteenth-century row house rehabilitated and converted into three apartments. Inside, Lewis surveyed her big, one-room domain, the old interior walls knocked down so that there was a clear view from the old windows at the front to the big plate of glass that now formed the entire back wall. The huge rear window was curtained by strings of long hanging ivies and asparagus ferns. The plants struck him as very unmilitary—anyone in the U.S. Army these days and unmarried faces too great a chance of deploying overseas to keep those plants alive, he thought. At the back, under the plate glass and the miniature jungle of hanging plants, was a circular dining table covered with newspapers and art books. On top of the pile was Ralph Mayer's thick *Artist's Handbook* in its battered original 1940 edition, given her by her mother as a high school graduation gift, Cindy told Lewis, as an unspoken wish that she not forget this side of herself when she went to West Point. The two other walls had been stripped down to rough red brick.

Lewis nodded in approval at the green Army parachute stretched across the ceiling at the front end of the apartment, giving her low quilt-covered bed beneath it the feel of an Arab sheik's desert tent.

"I didn't realize you were jump qualified."

"Yeah, that's a souvenir of my course at Benning," she said, pleased that he was impressed.

He ran his finger along the four long rows of compact discs that stretched across the brick wall. "Who are these people?" he said, shaking his head at names like Lucinda Williams, John Prine, Joan Armatrading, Dave Alvin, Dar Williams, Greg Brown, Beth Orton, Nanci Griffith and Iris DeMent.

Cindy groaned playfully. "Let me pick." She pushed him aside with her hip and selected Fiona Apple's greatest hits CD. She closed her eyes as the strong, provocative chords of "Shadowboxer" surged into the room.

He looked down and watched her face as she swayed slightly to the bluesy music. He was no more than a foot away from her. He hesitated. He felt they were on the verge of something physical. That was an area he'd never had a problem crossing into. But this time felt different. He wouldn't be making a conquest; he would be coming together with her. He waited.

She opened her eyes and looked up at him. She leaned her face toward him and pulled him into a long, lingering kiss. He forgot his hesitation and pressed against her. They kissed again. Her breasts pushed against his chest. He nuzzled his lips down the side of her throat. She felt the small hairs at the back of her neck stand up in delight.

"I'll be back in a minute," she said, easing herself from the long embrace to go insert her diaphragm. "Why don't you get in bed?"

They made love, first on top of the quilt and then underneath it. At one point he slid out of her, then put a hand on her hip as if to roll her over, moving on to something she didn't feel comfortable with. She gently moved his hand instead between her legs and asked him to massage her there. "Softly, softly," she sighed. He began to slowly explore her, taking his time. At the same time, he took her left nipple between his lips and rolled his tongue around and around that breast, softly and steadily. She sighed again with pleasure. She still felt a bit awkward—it had been a long time. On the stereo Fiona Apple moaned "slow like honey."

"Kiss me below," she asked. He slipped his tongue down across her body. When it happened inside her it was powerful. She inadvertently shouted, which hadn't happened to her much before.

"You OK?" he asked, opening his eyes.

"I'm great," she said, flushed and grinning. "Wow. Come back inside me."

He did, and began rocking against her. She wrapped her legs around his back and pulled him even farther into her, hard. "Now, inside me," she whispered into his ear. He gasped and obliged.

When she fell asleep with her head on his chest he stared up at the parachute, riffling in the cool May breeze, and lay awake, thinking back to a female logistics captain he'd been involved with on the Montenegro deployment. It had been purely casual, "deployment sex," they both called it. For six months they met just before dawn once or twice a week in the back of a broken five-ton truck fitted with a foam mattress. He had learned about positions that he wasn't sure were possible until they tried them, like lying on their backs with their legs intertwined. His biceps and pelvic muscles had ached all day long after that one. Their encounters had been so athletic, almost competitive, that it had seemed almost like another sport: going one-on-one. When he had run into the captain a year later at a Fort Stewart planning meeting for a Kuwait rotation, she had shaken his hand and smiled blandly: "Oh, hi, Lewis, good to see you. Where do they keep the coffee here?"

He looked down at Cindy's sleeping face on his chest. There was a tranquility on it in repose that he'd never seen when she was awake. Cindy didn't strike him as a woman who would enter into a sexual relationship casually. She was too cautious, too emotionally reserved.

Cindy was right, he thought—he had gotten laid more than he'd actually had relationships.

Western Afghanistan
Wednesday, May 18
10:30 A.M.

The remains of the column once led by Obaid were among the first refugees to arrive outside the new American base. They came down from the mountains following the hillside trail along the edges of the wheat fields of the Obeh Valley until they arrived at the double rolls of concertina wire that surrounded the new American military encampment.

This was the "safe haven"—declared by the United Nations, manifested by the United States—that had become the promised end of their three-week trek.

The refugees stared at the two flags fluttering in the sharp, clear Afghan sunshine—the baby-blue banner of the United Nations and the bolder colors of the United States. The front gate of the camp was blocked by two Humvees carrying .50-caliber machine guns. The American commander had named the place Camp Noble Effort.

The knot of about one hundred Afghans didn't recognize either flag, but they had been told that here, in this narrow valley among the first hills east of Herat, were food and protection from the Uzbek forces. Here in the foreigners' camp, amid the rows of dark green tents, was medical care for the baby with shrapnel in its legs; for the teenaged mother with mud, pebbles and cloth embedded in her back from the shattering moments when she had sheltered both her children beneath her as the KA-50 cannon shells fell around her; for the village baker shot in both arms. Here was the rich camp of the well-armed foreigners. Here was protection. These people were not enlightened believers, the mullah had said, but they were at least people of a book, something called a Bible. They would help.

The Afghan refugees didn't understand much about world politics, but they knew their light weapons. And as they stared across the wire at the American troops, the first flickers of doubt crossed their minds. They could see that there were no magazines in the M-16 rifles held by the troops inside the wire. Nor were there belts of bullets in the machine guns mounted atop the Humvees. After two clumsy accidents, the troops had been told that, for force protection reasons, no rounds would be issued until a threat was perceived.

There were just 1,350 U.S. troops in the austere camp, established a week earlier. Most of those troops were support elements. *They're cooks and bottlewashers,* Lewis had commented in an e-mail to his "OPFOR buddies" distribution list. And they were operating under extremely restrictive rules of engagement. The U.S. mission was, in fact, a military bluff.

In a poplar grove just outside the front gate, the villagers set down their bags in the rocks and tied the donkeys' bridles to the tree trunks. They stared through the wire at the strange soldiers staring back at them. The

American soldiers were all wearing helmets, flak jackets and sunglasses. Some of the troops looked as dark as Hindus to the Afghans, who had seen some Indian traders at the bazaar in Mazar-i-Sharif. Even darker. Some of the smaller ones inside the camp even looked like women, but the Afghans knew that was impossible—they probably were just boys.

One of the villagers dropped and howled in shock and pain. They heard the pop of the rifle from up on the ridge behind them. Another shot, then a third, fired with leisure. It was not the shooting of a combat assault but of a political message: The Americans were neither welcome in this conflict nor able to protect the Afghans who ran to them.

From a boulder below the ridgeline came bursts of three semiautomatic rounds. With each burst, one more villager fell. The mullah leaned past his wife, trying to rouse their tired donkey. The side of his turbaned head exploded. The donkey galloped away kicking, its eyes wide in terror at its master's hot blood and brains splashed across its muzzle.

From one of the Humvees inside the gate, Walter Schultz, the *New York Financial* reporter traveling with the U.S. Army as "embedded media," watched in astonishment. The Afghans were clambering into the concertina wire, actually hurling themselves into its barbs, to try to get into the camp. One threw a baby up but its tightly wrapped bundling snagged on the top of the fence and the child dangled there.

The American troops guarding the front gate—actually the laundry detachment from the 10th Mountain's Forward Support Battalion—took cover behind the Humvees. More of the Afghans died in the outer ring of wire, raked by fire from the unseen gunmen at the top of the ridge. Finally one of the American troops slid behind the wheel of the Humvee blocking the front gate. Its engine came to life and the vehicle crept backward five feet, enough to permit the gate to be opened. The surviving Afghans rushed into the camp.

No shots were fired at the American troops, nor any of the Afghans once they were inside the U.S. perimeter. The shooters turned their attention back to the wounded among the poplars, putting additional rounds into the bodies there. When ammunition was brought up to the Humvees, the firing stopped. But the troops couldn't have responded even if they had been able to see the sniping gunmen up on the ridge: Under the UN Chapter 6 rules governing their mission, they could fire only in self-defense. And no shots had been fired at them or near them.

Schultz sat down in a corner of the Tactical Operations Center and began to write on his laptop.

The Pentagon
Thursday, May 19
9 A.M.

The next morning Schultz's story was the first item in the *Early Bird,* the Pentagon's daily compendium of news stories about the military. It ran under the headline "New U.S. Afghan Force Stands Idle as Scores of Refugees Machine-Gunned." But it was the photographs that drove the story to the top of the day's news agenda. The *New York World* carried a two-column photograph on page one of two dead refugee children sprawled across the concertina wire. The *Washington Herald* went with a close-up of the tear-streaked face of an American soldier, questioning eyes lifted to the American flag waving above him in the hot Afghan wind.

By 9 A.M., National Security Adviser Willy Pitch ordered Defense Secretary Trent Johnson to announce that the American troops would act more aggressively. "Fuck Chapter Six," he shouted over the telephone. "We look like shmucks."

"It's your party," the defense secretary responded nonchalantly. "What do you want?"

"You need to get patrols out immediately," Pitch said.

"But we don't have the right troops for that," the defense secretary noted. "You didn't want trigger-happy combat troops, remember? 'Wrong message,' you said. So we've got support folks and reservists."

"They can still walk, can't they?" Pitch argued. "Get them out there. The president doesn't want to see any more people shot while American troops watch." At any rate, he thought, all that had been fired was AK-47s, and even Army cooks could deal with that.

The defense secretary, not wanting to be publicly associated with the Afghan policy any more than was necessary, called in Admiral Maddox and told him to make the announcement in the Pentagon press room.

Maddox trudged around the E ring to the room and read the statement to a crowd of sweaty reporters relieved to now have a second-day lead for their stories. The U.S., he announced, was unilaterally declaring a three-kilometer "patrol zone" for refugees around its camp. "That area will be patrolled heavily and around the clock—starting immediately," he said, reading the words Pitch had dictated to the defense secretary. Refugees not carrying weapons would be permitted within those lines. And because the U.S. force there hadn't been structured for that mission—Jesus, it's a bunch of cooks and reserve intell weenies, he'd thought to himself—a light infantry battalion from the 1st Infantry Division and a company team of Bradley Fighting Vehicles would be flown in as soon as possible from Germany. They would land in C-17s on the old heavy-duty Soviet-built highway about one hundred kilometers southeast of Herat, then convoy to the camp. Whenever the Soviets built highways in their neighbors' countries, they had thoughtfully ensured that the roads and bridges were tough enough to carry tanks.

"Admiral, will you wait until the First ID troops are there to begin the extended patrols?" the Reuters man shouted.

"No, they start immediately," Maddox reiterated.

He stepped back from the microphone. "I think that says it all, really," he said, declining to take additional questions. He walked back to his office trailed by aides painfully aware of all the questions he had left hanging. Like what, exactly, did the U.S. intend to achieve in Afghanistan?

Maddox called Shillingsworth to apologize for not giving him advance notice on the announcement. "I watched it on CNN," Shillingsworth said.

"What do you think?" Maddox asked.

"I think Pitch is violating two basic military maxims," Shillingsworth said. "He is reinforcing failure. And having lost the initiative, he is acting in haste to try to regain it, and so is exposing our people to greater danger."

"What can we do about it?" Maddox asked.

"As far as I can tell, not a damn thing, until Congress starts asking questions," Shillingsworth said and rang off.

Shillingsworth then booted up both his computers—one open to non–Defense Department computers, the other for ".mil" addresses only. On the secure computer, the e-mail looked as banal as ever. Even on this unhappy morning, most of it was about the routine matters of his subordinates' careers.

A "new mail" notice popped up from an unusual address he didn't recognize—"SOL@Army.mil." It was titled "HONOR." Curious, Shillingsworth skipped his cursor over the other mail and opened it up.

"It isn't 'honorable service for the disabled,' " he read.

It's dishonorable service for the able. The conduct of the Afghanistan mission should make any self-respecting officer ashamed of the uniform he wears. Just as American officers don't let their troops die for no reason, American troops don't stand by as innocents die. Those who are able to protest, should! Those who feel they can't should help those who can! Afghanistan already has taken down one superpower. We have little to gain there, and much to lose. Either do it right, or don't do it at all. Stop this disaster before it happens!

It was signed, *Captain America, the Sons of Liberty, an organization of concerned active-duty patriots.*

Where the hell did this come from? he wondered. The sender's address nagged at him—"SOL@Army.mil." Such elegant simplicity was reserved for general officers. He, for example, was simply "Shillingsworth.John@Army.mil." Everyone else had lengthy addresses full of abbreviations he could never remember—like "nae@1stbde.2ndsigcmd.pop5-emhl.usareur.army.mil."

Oh, well. And the distribution list had been suppressed. Some Tom Paine in uniform, he thought—the U.S. Army harbors all types. He forwarded it to the Army inspector general and the commanding general of the Army Criminal Investigation Division, along with a note: "Dick, Bob: Who is this?" Then he settled in to compose a gentle but firm note to the lieutenant general he needed to push into retirement as part of the summer moves.

Outside Camp Noble Effort
Western Afghanistan
Sunday, May 22
8 A.M.

Two weeks earlier Sergeant Juan Jefferson had been driving a Federal Express truck under the towering oaks of wealthy northwestern Atlanta. Then came the reserve call-up for this mission. Now on this bright spring Sunday morning in May, he was on a foot patrol in western Afghanistan, one of sixteen soldiers wondering just what the hell he was doing out here beyond the safety of the camp's double ring of concertina wire.

For that matter, he wasn't really sure why he was in Afghanistan. But his thoughts on this Sunday morning weren't so much of U.S. foreign policy as they were of the behind of the female soldier in front of him—she was pretty and filled out her BDUs very nicely. The sameness of the uniform only underscored the difference of the body inside it, bringing out the female curves instead of the straight lines of the male body, he thought. He tried to take a mental photograph of her—something to meditate on in his sleeping bag that night, help a man slide off to sleep.

She was from another of the Georgia reserve units, and he knew he'd met her once at annual training, talked to her at a party one night, but he couldn't remember her name. He thought she'd been goofing on him when she said she was from "Social Circle," but later he'd checked the office map and seen there really was just such a little-bitty town southeast of Atlanta.

That was fucked up, he thought, being on patrol in a place you didn't know and with people you don't know. You don't know the rhythm of their work—and don't know who you can trust, and who falls to pieces at the first problem. His feeling was that in military operations, if you have to say it, something's wrong. The ideal military unit was one where no talking was necessary to get the job done, he thought. They were all reservists on this patrol, and the quality of their work probably varied wildly. From what he'd seen of this lieutenant so far, he wasn't sure if he would trust him to lead a patrol out of the latrine.

Jefferson was near the end of the patrol, second from the back. He badly needed to piss. He didn't want to embarrass himself or the girl from Social Circle in front of him, or get hauled up on sexual harassment charges under Army regulation DA-72-79-R, so when the patrol halted to let the lieutenant check their position against the topographical map, he took a step into the poplars and unzipped. He noticed some odd markings on the bark of one of the poplars—three horizontal lines cut with a knife through the light green underbark and into the sap wood. Have to ask the intell NCO about that in the debrief, he thought with a sigh as the pressure on his bladder eased.

As he turned back toward the patrol, the toe of his right boot brushed the top of a buried PMA-3 antipersonnel mine, delivering just the five pounds of pressure necessary to detonate the lethal little gray can. It exploded with a loud boom that felt like a huge hammer striking him on the leg, the chest and the side of his head. Dark gray smoke obscured him. He landed on his back about five feet from the mine. A black combat boot with his right foot and ankle still in it came down about ten feet behind him. A light green spring leaf from a poplar landed on the jagged red and white shards of his right shinbone.

The medic and the lieutenant scurried back down the path. The medic, another reservist who in civilian life was an EMT from the Decatur, Georgia, fire department, accustomed to dealing with people in severe pain, tied off the stump of Jefferson's leg and stuffed curlex into the hole above it in his thigh. "You like football?" he asked. "Basketball? Who's your team? Hawks?" He tried to keep Jefferson in this world. He pulled the pressure suit from his ruck. The lieutenant helped slide it over Jefferson's bloody lower torso. The medic plugged a CO_2 cartridge into the nozzle and inflated the suit.

The lieutenant high-crawled back to his radioman, Belsky. The two had met for the first time a week earlier at Fort Stewart. Belsky was a last-minute replacement for the radioman in the platoon who had been excused from the deployment. The lieutenant couldn't believe they'd given him a radioman who stuttered. What next—blind pilots? "Move off the path one hundred meters and call in the casualty," he ordered Belsky. The lanky lieutenant, a gym teacher from Gainesville, Georgia, was showing the presence of mind to remember the SOP: Where there is one mine, there are likely to be more, and some mines can be triggered by radio transmissions.

Belsky, half civilian, half Army, considered the order. He was a mouthy guy, the lieutenant thought. As they'd left the gate, the lieutenant had overheard Belsky transmitting back to a buddy in the Tactical Operations Center his opinion that this was "a f-f-fucked-up p-p-patrol on a f-f-fucked-up mission." The lieutenant had told him to stow it.

Now Belsky stared at him in disbelief. "That's n-n-nuts, LT. I'm not going to walk across a m-m-minefield."

"OK," the lieutenant said, reconsidering. "Just move back down the path about fifteen to twenty meters. Step on the footprints in the dust." The officer turned back toward the rest of the patrol. "Everyone down, in case the radio transmission detonates more mines." They lay in the sandy soil and watched the radioman reluctantly move back down the path.

Belsky kneeled and keyed the radio. "This is P-p-patrol Elvis," he called in. No explosions followed. Up the path, the rest of the patrol relaxed. "We have one WIA down. Requesting, uh, uh, uh, meh-meh-medevac."

Help would be there in fifteen minutes. There was an open area, a natural landing zone just up the path, according to the map. "We can get there by the time the medevac bird comes in," the lieutenant said. "Stay tactical and move slowly. Third squad takes Jefferson." Three men picked up the wounded man. A fourth carried his booted foot for a few steps, then looked down at the bloody boot, said, "Screw it," and flung it underhanded into the trees.

The point man stopped the patrol and called for the lieutenant. The officer scuttled forward, crouching down as if he were under fire. The point gestured toward a downed tree across the path. On a branch at waist level there was tied a dirt-darkened copper wire. It was the trip line of a booby trap. Their eyes slowly followed it to a tree about fifteen feet to their right. At the foot of the tree, held in place by two wires around the trunk, peeking out from a pile of pebbles, was an antitank mine turned sideways, about the size of a big dinner plate, but four inches thick. Its tilt rod pointed straight toward them.

"OK," the lieutenant said. He turned back toward the patrol and pointed his right index finger emphatically several times at the big mine, then at the waist-high wire, making sure everyone saw the danger. He moved carefully, with exaggerated slow movements. Like many people unaccustomed to being around mines, he did everything in morbid silence, as if speaking might detonate the mine. They would duck and roll under the wire, weapons tucked down against their chests, he mimed. Slow-ly, he thought, as the point man started.

The point went under the downed tree, focusing every bit of his energy on the dirty metal line. His body shot backward as his midsection disintegrated into a fine red mist that drizzled over his comrades. The two hidden Claymores fired seven hundred steel pellets into him, the lieutenant and the two other soldiers at the front of the patrol. In his last blinded moments of life the lieutenant realized that the dirty metal line had been a decoy intended to distract him from the real, better-hidden threat.

At the far end of the patrol, Belsky, the radioman, staggered sideways in shock and horror. He flew straight up in the air as if a giant invisible hand had yanked him skyward. When he hit the ground both his feet were gone, his shins shredded into flaps of skin and pulverized bone. His lower buttocks were raw meat. The medic, who had been with Jefferson, moved back and quickly tied off Belsky's legs, checked his arteries, then punched morphine through his uniform into his arm.

"Can you try the radio?" the medic asked through the morphine haze. Belsky did. It worked, buzzing static into his ear. The medic moved up to the front of the patrol and shouted back, "Call in one, maybe two KIAs and at least three more WIAs."

"Oh, my p-p-poor legs," Belsky said into the handset, not really sure whether he was transmitting or not. "TOC, this is Elvis Six, we need medevac, bad. We got a KIA and a bunch of WIA, not walking. Man, I'm never w-w-walking again." There was a burst of static.

"No, no, the actual's down," he responded to an officer who came on the radio. "But he said there's a natural LZ just one hundred meters up, good flat o-o-open space, just beyond the trees."

"We need help, man. . . . Oh, this is so f-f-fucked up. . . . Just get me out of here. I don't like this p-p-place anymore. Oh, my p-p-poor legs."

A Blackhawk with red crosses on white paint on its sides and belly began descending toward them through the clean, dry Afghan air. At about ten feet above the ground, the helicopter flared its nose slightly for landing. At that point the wind from its rotors shot forward and hit the small aluminum "flags" on top of plastic poles attached to a semicircle of four TMRP-6 antitank mines hidden in the bushes. The flags bent backward, triggering detonators connected to eleven pounds of TNT in each mine. A wave of flame roared out across the helicopter, knocking it sideways as it landed. Its rotors folded up as it fell on its side. The lieutenant, never having been caught in a mine trap, had been too inexperienced to question why his patrol would have been hit so hard so close to a natural landing zone.

The Blackhawk pilot felt his seat jolt forward, pinning his legs to the front of the cockpit. He realized that his Blackhawk had landed in a medevac trap. It was a trick the Afghans had learned twenty-five years earlier in dealing with the Soviets.

The mines around the LZ were connected by a "daisy chain" detonation cord to a series of other mines that paralleled the path where the bloody patrol lay. Eight more antipersonnel mines, two Claymores and one plastic antitank mine buried alongside the length of path for one hundred meters chewed up the patrol in a quick series of roaring explosions. In less than five seconds, every member of the patrol except Belsky, who was out behind it, was dead or dying. Juan Jefferson, lying on his back, was wounded again, riddled in the side with tiny bits of shrapnel. He died gazing without comprehension at the headless torso of the girl from Social Circle.

From his pinned position, the Blackhawk pilot transmitted back: "Oh, man, the whole freaking patrol looks down—too much dust to be sure."

Belsky lay amid the smoke and dust raised by the mines, his cheek pressed against a spring thornbush. He had survived the ambush's last round of explosions only because in his position twenty-five meters behind the patrol, he had been just beyond and under the killing range of the weapons. He thought he heard a siren, then realized it was just the high-pitched ringing in his ears. He wondered if he'd been deafened by the blasts. He smelled barbecue and figured the morphine must be carrying him home to Georgia. Then he realized he was sniffing the seared flesh of his comrades, inflicted by the jets of the antitank mines. He passed out.

Eight members of the patrol were dead. Another seven bled their lives into the Afghan earth while a rescue convoy of armored Humvees cautiously worked its way to them from the camp, less than a mile away. Belsky would be its sole survivor.

The White House
9 P.M.

The details released in Washington at the Pentagon were murky at first. Defense beat reporters around the city were called at home, where they were lingering over Sunday brunches or reading the weekend papers, to be told that more than ten American soldiers had been wounded on a patrol. The Pentagon press duty officers told them on background that there was more bad news to come. The death toll crept up all night. By the last deadline, Central Command was saying that there were at least twelve dead and several more wounded.

President Shick made a brief announcement that evening in the White House press room. "In bringing peace to Central Asia, a handful of dedicated young Americans have made the supreme sacrifice," he said somberly. "Their nation thanks them. They will not be forgotten." He didn't take any questions.

He walked back to the Oval Office, where he had Willy Pitch waiting for him. "You dumb SOB, what have you done to me? This was supposed to help, not hurt. I'm going to get killed on this."

Pitch, still standing because he hadn't been invited to sit, reassured his president. "It's bad, sure," he said. "But the grim fact is that you are in a better position now."

"Oh, yeah?" the president asked. "You're slick, but I don't think you can sell that to me."

Pitch laid out his private calculation. "Let the impact of this sink in for a while. Then, in a week or two, after I make the calls to the Big Eight on the Hill, you'll say we are going to stay for more than sixty days—to honor the dead and the mission they died for. Remember those bumper stickers we saw during both the New Hampshire and Iowa primaries? You go out there and say, 'These colors don't run.' Make it clear that you are taking a lonely stand on a tough issue."

"The Hill might buy that," the president said worriedly, "but the Joint Chiefs won't. They already hate the Afghan mission—you told me that yourself. It was why we rolled it out early."

"No, the Chiefs will behave," said Pitch, his jowls wagging as he shook his head. "They may be worried by your policy, but they're a hell of a lot more worried about the rest of their troops, in Kosovo, in Montenegro, in Saudi, in Korea, in Africa." He explained: "If we don't respond to this—if we cut and run, like Clinton did in Somalia a decade back—then they worry that it will become open season everywhere on U.S. troops. The one thing that terrifies the Chiefs is sending the message that our adversaries can get rid of us by killing a few of our soldiers.

"So, no, sir, they are not going to agitate for pullout." Pitch smiled. He prided himself on his nimble reactions in dynamic situations, skills honed in years of Harvard faculty battles.

The Pentagon
Monday, May 23
2 P.M.

Lewis sat at his desk in General Ames's outer office. E-mails were pouring in on his "OPFOR buddies" circuit about the Afghan mission. He was trying to hold on to his belief that his leaders would do the right thing, but he could feel that belief slipping away like a handful of sand through his fingers.

TankerDog, now in Saudi Arabia, wrote, *Buddy, what in the hell are your bosses thinking?*

Scooter, now at Fort Lewis, chimed in: *Good question.*

Lewis wrote to the group: *Stop your whining. People get killed in missions. I am sure the Army did everything it could.*

I doubt it, wrote DesertMan.

BlackhorseThree shot back: *Lewis, you are misinformed. Check out this message I got today from a friend who forwarded it from the Blackhawk pilot injured on the medevac run:*

>The pity of it was this patrol should never have been sent out.
>They were hardly trained for the mission. Our daily intell
>update had warned that some of the factions were real
>upset with the announcement that we were going to have
>this new "patrol zone." Radio Herat, "the Voice of the Western Desert,"
>even attacked us, saying the Americans never left Saudi Arabia after
>the Gulf War and that we'd never leave here unless we were kicked
>out. We also had reports of mine-emplacement activity along our likely
>routes in the new "patrol zone."
>Our brigadier commanding the task force told higher headquarters he
>planned to hold off on the patrols until he got more and better mine-
>clearing gear in place, and he was told that was the wrong answer, and

>that the White House wanted the patrols out immediately. The
>scuttlebutt is that someone from the National Security Council called
>him directly and ordered him to stop dragging his feet and get his
>people out there.

The forwarded message stopped Lewis cold. His faith and allegiance,
which were part of his oath as an officer, were being manipulated and
betrayed by this White House. The president wasn't watching the military's back.

He stared at CNN, playing on the office television, transmitting live
coverage of the dead American soldiers arriving at a military airport in
Oman. He scowled, then realized General Ames was standing next to his
desk.

He didn't know how long the general had been waiting there. Lewis
scrambled to his feet. "Sir?"

"You look bothered, son." Ames was inviting him to speak his mind.
Lewis had used the same line as a company commander.

"It's this Afghanistan thing, sir," Lewis confessed. He pointed to the
television, where coffins were being moved from a short-haul C-130
plane to a huge C-5 military cargo jet. "How can we let them down like
that?"

Ames gazed at him. His tone conveyed the sense that he understood
completely. "Steady on, Major. I know what you're thinking. But hang in
there. We are warriors. That is a tradition that precedes the republic we
defend. And sometimes the values of the warrior are at odds with the values of our political system."

That wasn't enough for Lewis. "I mean, I just don't know, sir." He
felt near tears. The other members of Ames's personal staff looked at
him. "How can we take orders from these jerks on the National Security
Council?"

"I know. We are letting our people down." Ames nodded gravely. His
low, warm tone conveyed understanding, empathy. He looked around at
his aides. "But remember what the Ames office manual says. It's basic
Sun Tzu, page thirty-six. There is more than one way to deal with this
situation." He turned and went into his inner office, closing the door behind him.

Lewis took the office copy of *The Art of War* from the bookshelf and
turned to page 36, where he saw an underlined passage: *There are occa-*

sions when the commands of the sovereign need not be obeyed. He read it again, then looked at the closed white door of Ames's office.

Upstairs a flight and four hallways over, Sherman also was struck by the somber mood in the Pentagon's offices and corridors. It felt, she thought to herself, like a death in the family. General Shillingsworth usually kept the office buzzing, asking three or four times an hour for a file or a phone call to be made. Today he stayed shuttered in his inner office. She had no taskings, not even any additional infowar documents from Cisco.

"Shillingsworth didn't come out all morning," she reported to Lewis when they met at noon at a picnic table near the Ground Zero hot dog stand in the middle of the Pentagon's inner courtyard.

Lewis told her about Ames. He didn't really get the Sun Tzu stuff, so he left that out. But he understood Ames's bottom line—and emphatically agreed with it. "He said to me, 'We are letting our people down,'" he told her, then took a big bite of his peanut butter and jelly sandwich.

Sherman shook her head slightly. "I don't think it's that simple," she said. "What are you saying—that the mission sucks, so we should just pull out?"

"That's about it," he said, folding his brown paper bag neatly.

That afternoon Lewis sent out an e-mail to the "OPFOR buddies." He titled it "Letting our people down." He also sent it to "Rocky" Gibraltar, who had been his XO and now had a company of his own at Fort Drum, in the cold barrens west of the Adirondacks in upstate New York.

Captain Diego Gibraltar, who had always idolized Lewis, took a print-out of Lewis's message over to a friend living in Drum's ratty old Bachelor Officers' Quarters, the last "temporary" housing from World War II still being used to house soldiers. They drank beer until well past midnight, arguing over the Afghan mission and what they could or should do. Some new second lieutenants joined in. Around 2 A.M. six of them went out and had a little painting party. Before going to sleep, Gibraltar sent an e-mail back to Lewis and to several other friends at the Pentagon and around the Army explaining what they had done. He signed it, *Your buddy, Rocky.*

Fort Drum, New York
Tuesday, May 24
6:15 A.M.

The morning traffic at the main gate of Fort Drum was backed up nearly a mile, Sergeant Sam Cumberbatch saw from his pickup truck. Must be some sort of terrorist threat, he thought. Because of the post's proximity to Canada, high in upstate New York, it was always seen as more vulnerable than most. The bad guys could blow off a bomb and be back across the border before the news got to Customs, he knew.

But when his truck finally crept up the one open lane to the gate, which usually wasn't manned, he saw three of the top brass—the garrison commander, the division's commanding general and a worried-looking provost marshal—all staring at the pavement and at the sign alongside it. The entrance sign normally read, "Welcome to Fort Drum/Home of the 10th Mountain Division/Climb to Victory." Today, nailed over it, was a hand-painted white poster reading, in foot-high black letters, "PRIDE IN OUR SOLDIERS/SHAME ON OUR LEADERS."

"SHAME" was also printed in five-foot-high white block letters on the asphalt. The whole area had been cordoned off with yellow and black police tape. One MP was directing traffic around it, squeezing three lanes into one, while two more prepared to erase the message with turpentine and scrub brushes.

When he finally got to his office, his computer, like every official computer at Fort Drum and every Army computer in the Pentagon, received an e-mail that explored that theme. Under the title "SHAME," it explained that:

> The painting of the entrances to Drum was done to protest those who should not have been sent unprepared in harm's way. They were the wrong people sent on the wrong mission for the wrong reasons.
>
> Some of the brass recognize this. General Ames, the vice chairman of the Joint Chiefs, had the guts to say that "we are letting our people down." But there aren't many at the top like him.
>
> It's easy to do your duty in easy times. The test is how we do our duty in difficult times. That begins with considering what your duty is. We

should all remember that part of our duty is to take care of our soldiers and to refuse unlawful orders.

Captain America
The Sons of Liberty
An organization of concerned active-duty soldiers.

At the Pentagon, several reporters looking into the Fort Drum protest were passed copies of the new e-mail, but they found it difficult to use an anonymous note, so they tended to mention it fleetingly in the final paragraphs of Afghanistan "react" stories.

Lewis used a quiet moment in the office to call the Fort Drum operator and ask for the orderly room of Bravo Company of the 2nd Battalion of the 2nd Infantry Regiment. The phone was picked up on the second ring, as per the company commander's standing orders. "Bravo Deuce Deuce may I help you sir or ma'am?" a voice said in one fast rush.

Lewis asked for the company commander. When Gibraltar answered, Lewis said hello and then asked him flat out: "Rocky, are you Captain America?"

"I guess I am today," his old XO replied. He explained that he had sent the message to a few people at the Pentagon, and had been a little surprised to see it all over Fort Drum a few hours later with his name taken off and the "Captain America" signer put on.

"So Captain America's really down here?" Lewis asked.

"No, sir," Rocky said. "I don't know that he's anywhere, sir. It's the American dream, Major—any one of us can be Captain America." Listening to Gibraltar, Lewis could envision his big sunny grin as that thought occurred to him.

In the hallway outside, General Shillingsworth took General Ames aside after the regular Wednesday morning meeting in the Tank. "Byron," he said awkwardly, his hand on Ames's right elbow. He never liked calling Ames "B.Z." But the formality of using Ames's first name was a bad way to begin an uncomfortable conversation, making it seem as if Shillingsworth were a high school teacher upbraiding a troublesome student. No one had called B. Z. Ames "Byron" since his mother died.

An awkward pause lingered in the air between the two generals. Shillingsworth had had surprisingly little contact with Ames throughout their careers. After Ames's stint in Special Forces, most of his service had been in Washington. As a general he had been the J-5, in charge of planning on the Joint Staff, then the Army deputy chief for operations, and then, after eleven months overseeing Forces Command in Atlanta—a virtual extension of the Army staff, hardly a "muddy boots" field job—he had come back to be vice chairman of the Joint Chiefs. Shillingsworth, by contrast, had dodged Pentagon billets at every chance he got, even when it appeared to damage his chances of promotion, a trait that had endeared him to many in the field Army. His only Washington experience as a general had been two years as deputy director of operations on the Joint Staff, then six months as vice chief of the Army before he took the top slot.

"About this—this thing in the goddamn papers," Shillingsworth said. "This 'letting our people down.' "

Ames stared evenly at Shillingsworth, maintaining a blank expression. He owed the Army chief nothing. He knew that Shillingsworth had opposed giving him his fourth star, only to be overruled by the defense secretary. And he knew that when Pitch had said he wanted him to be vice chairman of the Joint Chiefs, to give Maddox a strong backup, Shillingsworth had pointedly responded that he would work with whomever the president put in the job—as close as Shillingsworth could come to openly opposing the White House's choice.

B. Z. Ames didn't report to Shillingsworth, and he wasn't going to be interrogated by him.

"Johnny, I never said that," Ames said. He didn't think of this as a lie. He had never said anything official, anything to which he had intended to have his name attached.

Still, he wasn't sorry to have the comment made public. It wasn't a bad thing to get the word out to the troops that not everyone at the Pentagon was rolling over for the president on the Afghanistan mess. "I don't know where that came from, John." That was true. He didn't know how these "Sons of Liberty" had gotten wind of his comment. True, he had made no effort to find out, either. He suspected that one of his aides, most likely the new man, Major Lewis, had passed it along. No matter. He had instructed the spokesman for the Joint Chiefs to simply decline to confirm or deny what the vice chairman may or may not have said.

Shillingsworth didn't believe him. This was a novel problem for him. He didn't know what to say to a four-star Army general he didn't trust. It was outside the realm of his experience—these were his brothers, aside from B. Z. Ames, who seemed to him too smooth to be a real Army general. So he didn't say anything. He wheeled and walked away, taking the Bradley stairs two at a time, getting back to Army turf as fast as possible. Enough of Ames; time to head up to Carlisle.

Ames slowly strolled back to his suite, shaking his head, more amused than bothered. He was amazed that the U.S. Army was in the hands of John Shillingsworth— a good light colonel, fine man to run a battalion for you, but really a kind of dullard as a general. When a minor-leaguer tries to manage in the majors, it is sad but no one dies because of it, he thought. But in our line of work they do—and so, he told himself, there is a moral obligation to do something about it.

The Army War College
Carlisle, Pennsylvania
Thursday, May 26
3 P.M.

Shillingsworth went to Carlisle intending to lay down the law, to remind his people of their role as military professionals. He was worried by the Drum protest and the subsequent Ames quote. He couldn't screw B. Z. Ames's head on straight, but he could damn sure do something about the other 384,000 troops remaining in the U.S. Army after President Shick's budget cuts. At his annual War College meeting with all the Army's two-stars, three-stars and four-stars who weren't in "joint" billets, he decided, he would give his generals the message to take back home.

For two days he sat at the apex of the huge and ostentatious horseshoe-shaped table in the posh wood and steel conference facility at the Army War College, listening to PowerPoint reviews from all major Army commands. Nobody had enough people or money, but they were all confident they could do what needed to be done. Even his personnel chief, Lieutenant General Oere, insisted there were no problems, just "challenges." Like a challenge in finding about 9,500 recruits they missed on their quota last year, and on top of that a 16 percent quit rate among captains.

Then he took the floor to end the meeting. As they always did at this point in the annual meeting, the colonels and other note takers who sat in the chairs along the walls stood and left the room. This was inner-sanctum stuff, the chief of staff of the U.S. Army alone with his generals. By tradition, what the chief said stayed in the room. As the double doors closed on the last bird colonel, Shillingsworth stood, stretched to his full, lanky six feet, three inches and surveyed the room.

"Afghanistan," he began, looking around the table.

He paused. Let the word sink in. "We have fifteen soldiers dead—twelve men, three women, all of them reservists, none of them ever again to deliver a Federal Express package, teach a gym class, extinguish a house fire, make love or see their children." He paused.

"I dislike the mission. Hell, I dislike this president. My wife thinks I should quit." He saw the nods along the curve of the table. "I bet you're hearing the same thing at home." More nods, a few rueful, tight smiles.

"But not all our tests are on the battlefield," he said. "How we behave now, how we comport ourselves as military officers—this is an issue of military professionalism for me." That meant it was for them, too. What he worried about, they worried about—and so on down a thousand links in the chain of command to every last butter-bar platoon leader.

"Look, if it were me, would I have picked this man to be president?" He shook his head. "No, ladies"—there were two female generals present—"and gentlemen, I would not. But we in the military don't get to pick our president. If we did, this wouldn't be America." His look around the table made it clear that he expected agreement from all of them.

"Our Army is in Afghanistan. We are going to do the best we can by our people. But the mission, and the nation, come before them, before any of us. I would have it no other way—that is the honorable duty we owe this great nation. It sometimes requires personal sacrifice. I have served alongside many of you, and I have seen some of you make great sacri-fices." He thought in particular of "Snake" Satcheray, sitting at his right elbow. Snake's left foot had been crushed by a Bradley in a training acci-dent at the NTC when he was a captain, and running on the toeless mess the surgeons had saved was excruciating—so as a division commander Snake insisted on running ten miles a day, and then entering the base's annual marathon. Every year he took his annual leave immediately after that to recuperate, staying in his cabin in Minnesota until he could walk again without shocks of pain shooting up his left leg. More recently, Snake had lost a daughter, a West Point cadet, in a summer training heli-copter accident at Fort Campbell. Snake had paid some dues.

But the trick that military life played on you, Shillingsworth thought, was that the older you get, the more vulnerable you become physically, which distracts you and makes you watch that flank—but in fact the higher you go in the Army, the more the required sacrifices are moral. Learning to live with the ambiguity of politics sometimes could be hard for a career soldier.

He concluded with his marching orders to the generals. "So when you go home, you tell your people, 'We are going to take care of you. And we also are going to serve our nation. We will get through this.'

"And tell them to knock off this Sons of Liberty shit—and I use that word advisedly—this e-mail that challenges policy. As long as I am chief of staff of the United States Army, we will not tolerate attacks on our civilian leaders. It is a court-martial offense.

" 'Nuff said." The meeting was over.

On the drive home the Army's deputy chief of staff for logistics sat in the backseat of his sedan and tapped out on his laptop an e-mail summary for his staff of the two days of meetings.

It was a particularly good session, Lieutenant General William Still wrote. As for this fallout from Afghanistan, he concluded,

General Shillingsworth is squared away on this. He made it clear that he thinks the president is a jerk—but that we need to suck it up & soldier on. He said he & his wife have discussed retiring over the Afghan thing but that he has decided against that and we shouldn't either. Afghanistan is a mess, he said, but we've had messes before and gotten out of them. So stay low, watch out for your people and keep your mouth shut in public. Good message—let's move on it.

Outside Camp Noble Effort
Western Afghanistan
Monday, May 30
4:40 P.M.

"One-Shot" Ismail and his helper, Gulamnabi, lay hidden in their spider holes for most of a day, from well before dawn, waiting until an American patrol passed them. The patrols were random but not constant. The next one probably wouldn't pass for hours, and fifteen minutes was all Ismail needed. He was a master of the sixty-millimeter mortar, renowned among the old mujahedeen network for his ability to hit his target with his first mortar shell and then rain twenty more on the target in the next two minutes.

When the next patrol of three Humvees and a Bradley rolled by, the two men waited five minutes. When they could no longer sense any ground rumble they emerged from their holes and stiffly walked a few feet to the spot at the base of a small cliff where they had buried Ismail's aging but well-oiled Czech mortar and a box of shells.

He could do this in his sleep. While his spotter scrambled to the top of the slope to look at the American camp through binoculars, Ismail locked the barrel to the base plate, tightened the cross-level nut, checked the bubbles, then switched the selector to drop fire. He peered into the sight on the side of the barrel, flicked the wheel twice, dropped a shell into the tube, then leaned away as it fired.

The two Afghans, plainsmen from the north, had been sent to deliver the message to the Americans that they would continue to pay for intruding into Afghanistan. Their target was the knot of soldiers lining up for dinner outside the DFAC—the Army insisted on acronymizing what it used to call a mess hall. From his observation perch just over a mile north of the base, Gulamnabi could see dozens of hungry American soldiers moving toward the mess tent. What he didn't notice was that to get there, they had to navigate an S-shaped path lined by Dumpsters.

When the shell hit, not many of the Americans recognized the heavy, slamming sound, like an evil giant slowly striding the earth, as mortar fire. They threw themselves to the ground and scanned the sky for the aircraft they thought must have dropped a bomb. Most of them had never seen combat. Some were Gulf War veterans but even then hadn't been fired upon. Only two of the men in the crowd had been on the receiving end of mortar fire, in Somalia. "Incoming, take cover, mortar!" shouted one of the Mogadishu vets.

Gulamnabi scrambled down the slope to report that the first shot looked about fifty meters long. Ismail cursed himself for not accounting adequately for the slightly lower elevation of the American camp.

At the far end of the camp, the sergeant in charge of Target Acquisition Battery Bravo shouted into a microphone, "Incoming fire in the CFZ."

The three soldiers working around him would have to think hard to remember that CFZ stood for "Critical Friendly Zone," but they knew without hesitation that it meant the area they were trained to protect.

They had rehearsed this course of action a dozen times since arriving in Afghanistan and a thousand times before in their short military careers. A nineteen-year-old private flicked a switch on the Firefinder radar from "standby" to "live/acquire" mode. The Q-36's fifteen-foot-high flat black screen faced the sand hills just north of the camp that were considered the most likely sector for incoming fire.

At the same time, the mortar section cued their four 120-millimeter tubes for a wide-area shot. And at the metal apron at the rear of the camp, the ground crews of the Apaches plugged big black cables into the bottom of their helicopters' engines to wake them up. The black rotors began to swing in big, hazy circles. As the jet engines of the helicopters opened up, the flexible motors gained speed and lifted higher from the ground.

The Q-36's radar picked up Ismail's second shot before it even crested its arc. The Firefinder's computer instantly calculated the angle of fire and the speed of the shell, and from that deduced the location of the hostile mortar tube. That data passed instantly to the laptop in front of the fire support officer in the task force TOC. When the "fire solution" box on the laptop screen turned from yellow to green, she looked over questioningly at the task force's legal officer.

"Priority-one call for fire," the fire support officer said softly.

"Concur," said the JAG.

The fire support officer pressed "enter" on her laptop. Back in the mortar section, four shells simultaneously leaped from the big tubes into high arcs across the pellucid Afghan sky.

Ismail's second shot hit exactly where he intended, the area where the soldiers had been gathering for dinner. Without the maze of Dumpsters, this shot would have killed or wounded dozens of soldiers as the spray of steel fragments and flechettes shot off the ground, up into ankles, knees, thighs, genitals, intestines, lungs, necks, eyes and skulls. But as it happened the Dumpsters caught most of the exploding shell. Only three soldiers who were in the small corner of the maze where the shell impacted were hit.

When Gulamnabi signaled two thumbs up for accurate fire, Ismail grimly smiled and prepared for his third shot. He planned now to pump the whole box into that spot. But as he reached for a shell, the four American mortar shells impacted simultaneously in a bracketing box, each about three hundred meters away from him, too far away to be lethal but close enough to do their intended job of forcing him to cease fire.

Gulamnabi scrambled down the slope. Ismail left the mortar on its plate. The two men ran to their spider holes and pulled a loose covering of dirt over themselves as they heard the helicopters approach. One Apache drove directly to the spot indicated by the Firefinder while the other swung in a wide curve around it, looking not for the mortar but for anyone seeking to lure the helicopters into a "SAMbush," as the pilots called an ambush by surface-to-air missiles.

Ismail had waited out counterattacks like this twenty-five years earlier. The Soviets would fly over in their Hinds and sweep the area with fire. If you were unlucky, they hit you. Most times they didn't.

But unlike the Soviet Hinds, the American Apaches had forward-looking infrared scopes in their noses. The first Apache's UltraFLIR instantly picked up the two Afghans in their holes, their warm bodies contrasting with the desert sand and dirt cooling in the late afternoon. The Apache's M230 chain gun, slung under its nose, fired twenty-five high-explosive thirty-millimeter rounds into Ismail, then a second burst into Gulamnabi. The holes were now graves the two men had dug for themselves. The Apache gunner looked into the scope of his UltraFLIR and saw a magnified image of Ismail's prematurely aged foot poking from the end of the hole. The gunner could see quarter-inch-deep cracks reaching into the sole, cut by winter ice on bare flesh. Ismail and his helper had been out of their holes just seven minutes.

Sherman's Apartment
Washington, D.C.
11:55 P.M.

Cindy read the message from the Sons of Liberty that had come across her laptop, unsolicited. It was titled "THE WORLD."

Do our leaders understand the world out there? We just lost another
soldier, and two more wounded—for nothing! How many more will die
before we do something?

It went on, but she had had enough. She stood up and walked to the
round table at the back of her apartment, where Lewis was sipping coffee
and reading Robert Graves's *Good-Bye to All That,* which she'd given him
that day. She told him about the new SOL message. She was especially
worried, she said, by the sense she was getting that the Sons of Liberty
wanted to see some kind of action. "I know they are upset—we all are,"
she said. "But this doesn't strike me as right."

Lewis reached across the table for her hands and held them in his. "We
are so similar in so many ways," he said. She knew what he meant. They
both loved the Army, both had built their lives around it. "But," he continued after a moment, "we see this so differently. I don't know why." ·

She looked at him, puzzled.

Lewis said, "You know that I agree with a lot of what the Sons of Liberty are saying. I mean, I'd bet I know some of the guys writing this stuff.
And they're good guys."

Her objection, she said, was more to how they were saying it.

"Cindy, Cindy, Cindy," Lewis said, a bit exasperated. "People are dying
out there in Afghanistan. Our people. And you're worried about proper
form? What are you, Miss Military Manners?" He tried to smile to soften
what he was saying.

She pulled her hands out of his. She wasn't going to let it go with a put-
down and a smile. "It goes to military professionalism," she said. "Which
is all we have, really. And that is why we have to be very careful about how
we protest. We have to be trusted as being above the fray. If we start going
into the streets, we start looking like any other interest group."

Lewis stood. "I can understand that. But I still think there is a more
fundamental requirement, to take care of your people."

She realized this wasn't going to go anywhere useful. "Enough arguing,"
she said, sliding her arms around him and pulling him toward her bed.
"Let's take care of each other."

The Pentagon
Tuesday, May 31
6 A.M.

On Saturday morning Captain Robert Byrnes, the speechwriter for Lieu-tenant General Still, forwarded Still's summary of the Carlisle meeting to B. Z. Ames, along with thanks for having him for a cup of coffee with a group of other Pentagon newcomers.

That afternoon Ames read the summary, leaned back in his chair and smiled broadly. It was unusual for a new contact to pay dividends so quickly. He sent an e-mail back to Captain Byrnes inviting him to stop by again soon. And he printed out the summary and dropped it into the in box of Underhill, his executive officer. "Be a shame if this popped up in the *Washington Herald*," he said. He walked back into his inner office. The red-faced Air Force colonel knew what to do. His job, after all, was to anticipate his principal's desires.

But neither he nor Ames anticipated the spectacular play the leak would get. On Tuesday morning it appeared in the *Washington Herald*, on page 1 and above the fold: "President a 'Jerk,' Army Chief Tells Troops."

John Shillingsworth didn't know about the story during his run that Tuesday morning. He did his customary four miles among the quiet gravestones of Arlington Cemetery. He usually ran alone, without even his bodyguard. His practice was not even to try to think until the sweat reached the top of the "ARMY" lettered across the front of his gray T-shirt, which meant the hangover was burning off. Then he would begin thinking about his day. Once the sweat reached another four inches down to the bottom of the letters, he had decided, his brain would be oxygen deprived, and he would abstain from any further decisions. Between the top of the letters and the bottom he did his thinking.

At six he finished his run, showered and climbed into his service Al-phas. At 6:18 his phone rang. It was the chief of Army public affairs, telling him to read the story about him in the *Herald*. "It's bad," he said. At 6:19 the phone rang again. An aide to the defense secretary said the secretary would see him as soon as he arrived at the Pentagon. Shillings-worth walked outside to pick up the paper, but was handed it by his sedan driver, who usually retrieved it and left it on the backseat in the car. "You'll want to see the front-page story on column left, above the fold, sir," said the driver, a forty-year veteran of federal Washington, and so something of a media sophisticate.

Shillingsworth ignored the telephone ringing in his car—he could tell it was his executive officer—and instead read the *Herald* story as the black sedan carried him down the short hill from Fort Myer, past the Iwo Jima memorial and the main body of the cemetery, and to the Pentagon. "The top officer in the Army recently told his service's senior generals that 'Shick is a jerk,' according to a document circulating at the Pentagon," the story began. I never actually used that word, did I? he thought.

He read on. "At a meeting of Army generals at the Army War College in Carlisle, Pa., last week, Gen. John Shillingsworth, the Army chief of staff, also indicated that he is contemplating resigning over his dismay with the president's conduct of foreign policy." I did no such thing, he thought—except that remark about wives.

Gen. Shillingsworth's comments, which were summarized in an internal Army memorandum, mark the latest clash between the White House and the Pentagon. The president's relationship with the military has been rocky from the outset, partly because of his determination to cut the defense budget and also because of his controversial initiative to open military service to the openly gay and the partially disabled. The unhappiness between the White House and the Pentagon peaked after the unexpectedly heavy loss of life in the U.S. contingent participating in the Algerian evacuation three years ago. It subsided somewhat over the last year, but was rekindled last week after 15 U.S. soldiers were killed while on patrol in the new Afghanistan mission.

Then the story circled back to him. "But until now, most military unrest has come from lower ranks. Gen. Shillingsworth's attack on the president marks the first time a member of the Joint Chiefs has openly picked a fight with the White House." Where do I start fixing that sentence? he thought. With the fact that I wasn't attacking the president, I was doing the opposite.

"General Shillingsworth couldn't be reached for comment." Did the reporter really try?

"But another top member of the U.S. military said that he was sure that Gen. Shillingsworth's comments had been misconstrued. 'We all say things in the heat of the moment that we later regret,' this officer said last night. 'General Shillingsworth said some things behind closed doors that clearly weren't intended for civilian ears.' " That last comment was a classic Washington twist: While seeming to come to the defense of Shillingsworth, someone had confirmed the story to the *Herald*.

The sedan pulled up at the Mall entrance at 6:27. Major Sherman was standing at the bottom of the stairs waiting for him. Not a good sign, he thought. "Good morning, sir." She saluted. "I'm just here to backstop the message that SecDef is waiting for you."

He realized she didn't say why. Loyal kid—probably too painful for her to see her new boss become Washington's top clown today. He went inside the building, walked up a twisting flight and turned right toward the secretary of defense's area. Secretary Johnson's top flunky met him in the hallway and took him directly into the main office. "It's bad," he warned him in a whisper. Phrase of the day, Shillingsworth thought.

Defense Secretary Trent Johnson, a recently retired senator from West Virginia, stood behind his desk. He offered neither coffee nor a chair. His message was swift. "John, this is above me. You need to go to the White House right now."

Shillingsworth sensed the SecDef recoiling from him with the politician's instinctual fear of dead meat. Politics and espionage were the only endeavors Shillingsworth had witnessed where it was routine to shoot your own wounded. "The president wants to see you in ten minutes," the secretary said. That wasn't enough time to bring the Army chief's car back up from the basement. "My car is waiting for you right outside," he concluded. Funny how fast things happen when they want you out of their sight, Shillingsworth thought.

The SecDef's big limousine took him not to the discreet alley south of the Old Executive Office Building, but to the front gate north of the White House. This had the effect—intended by the defense secretary—of tipping off the White House press, who would understand and play it as a familiar bit of Washington political theater: the top-level official's trip to the White House woodshed.

In fact, the president didn't want to see him right away. The president thought that 8 A.M. or so would be good. So General Shillingsworth waited alone for forty-five minutes in a wing chair just outside Willy Pitch's cubbyhole. After the third pert young thing asked him, he felt like snapping, No, I don't want any of your goddamn thin Navy coffee. Finally, an officious young weenie escorted him in to see the president.

It was the first time Shillingsworth had ever met with the president alone—or nearly alone. Willy Pitch took a chair behind Shillingsworth and took notes on a yellow legal pad but didn't speak.

It looked like his day to receive rudeness. The president didn't rise to greet him. Shillingsworth stood in front of his desk, like an erring private at office hours. It was the most humiliating moment of his thirty-four years in uniform. He knew there was only one action he could take to expiate his sin. "Sir, I want to apologize, and I want to tender my resignation. I resign my commission from the U.S. Army, effective immediately."

That wasn't so hard, he thought. Moab, here we come.

The president sat expressionless and silent, ignoring the general's offer. He, not Shillingsworth, would set the tone and agenda of this meeting. He stroked his chin, gazing through Shillingsworth's chest at a point on the wall somewhere behind the general. He raised both eyebrows and seemed ready to speak, then paused again.

Finally, at his leisure, he took his hand from his mouth, slowly lifted his eyes and looked at Shillingsworth. "General, have a seat." Shillingsworth did as ordered.

"Coffee?" the president asked. Shillingsworth shook his head. This was going to be made excruciating, he saw. The president rose and strolled to a little glass table with two wheels on one end, poured himself a cup of the weak Navy mess coffee, added cream and artificial sweetener and walked back to his desk. He stirred the cup, took a sip, paused and took another. He put down the delicate blue and white cup. He was finally ready to talk with Shillingsworth.

"You know which president was really underrated?" the president asked. He didn't wait for Shillingsworth to answer. "Lyndon Johnson. Poor guy took it in the shorts from the media back then. And from you military guys ever since. But he knew this country better than either one of those outfits. And I'm going to rely on his wisdom today, in dealing with this problem."

Shillingsworth pushed down his jaw muscles, making sure he maintained a blank expression. He wasn't sure where the president was going. The only thing he could really remember about Johnson's relations with the military was what he had learned as a colonel at the War College, that the Army chief of staff had gone to the White House to resign over the president's handling of the Vietnam War, and then while at the White House gate had decided against it, a decision he came to bitterly regret, even on his deathbed. Was the president telling him he should have resigned immediately, not even bothered to come over here?

No. He realized that the president was looking at him as a problem to be defused. After thirty-four years of service, begun when this guy was fif-

teen years old, running for president of his sophomore class in high
school, this is what my military career boils down to, he thought: I'm just
a political bomb to be defused by a master at the disposal of explosive political ordnance.

"I'll tell you what President Johnson knew," the president said, leaning
forward but still speaking in the even, low-key tones of a technician. "You
don't give your enemies freebies. Letting you resign, General, would be a
freebie. They'd have a martyr. So, no, General, your resignation is explicitly not accepted."

The president sat back and said slowly, with preternatural calm, as if to
an unusually stupid and mean child, "You will continue to serve this
country and this government. You will go when I tell you to go.

"To quote the late, great Lyndon Baines Johnson, I'd rather have you inside the tent pissing out than outside pissing in. And when we go to Fort
Polk, you will be standing alongside me and smiling."

The president was seeking to minimize the problem, make it a one-day
story. OK. I can live with that, Shillingsworth thought. "Sir, in that case,
if I am to continue to serve, and to deal with you in the future, I need at
least to provide you with the context in which my comments occurred,"
he said. That was the price the president would have to pay for him staying on, to at least listen to him for two minutes. The president nodded.

Shillingsworth tried to give it to him straight. He told him, as best he
could remember, precisely what he had said at the Carlisle meeting, and
why. "More than anything," he emphasized, "I was trying to buck up the
troops, get them to shut up and soldier on. But I know it didn't look like
that in the headline today."

He then repeated his offer, having had a chance to explain the context.
The president again refused, slightly more courteously this time. "You
leave that up to me," the president said. He looked over Shillingsworth's
shoulder at his national security adviser. "Anything to add, Willy?" Pitch
shook his head.

"Then this meeting is concluded," the president said.

A staffer escorted Shillingsworth quickly out of the secured part of the
White House and left him on the north driveway—where the media,
alerted by the press secretary, awaited him in full force. There are few
things in Washington more painful than being the story of the day. It is my
turn in the barrel, Shillingsworth thought as he watched four television
cameramen hurriedly jog toward him, their faces half obscured by the

cameras on their shoulders, fuzzy-covered microphones protruding at him like wide-gauge shotguns.

It occurred to him that this was his real punishment. He had been set up. He noticed that most of the cameramen were wearing blue jeans, T-shirts and sneakers. That irked him—how could you come to work every day at the White House, the seat of the American government, and dress like a slob? It smacked of disrespect for the nation.

A large-haired woman in a red jacket of raw silk pushed through the phalanx of television cameras. He vaguely recognized her, but most female television correspondents looked the same to him, all hair and voice, except Christiane Amanpour. "General, are you going to resign?" the woman shouted at him from three feet away, as if he were on fire. "What did you tell the president, what did he say to you?"

General Shillingsworth stiffened. He had never faced the media so nakedly, so alone, in hostile territory. The public affairs officers had trained him never to say "no comment"—they claimed it just made you appear guilty.

"I had a private conversation with the president," he said finally. "Where I come from, ladies and gentlemen"—watch the sarcasm, he thought to himself, as the cameras pressed in on him—"where I come from, private conversations remain private. But apparently I was born in a different place and time. No, I am not resigning my commission. I will continue to serve at the discretion of the president. That is all I have to say. Thank you."

He stepped sideways around the human wall of reporters and walked quickly down the slightly sloping driveway to the glassed-in guardpost. When he emerged onto the Pennsylvania Avenue plaza he saw that the SecDef's car was gone. Bastard, he thought. Rubbing my nose in it.

He saw Sherman at the corner of Seventeenth and Pennsylvania, standing next to his own car and waving to him. Good aide, he thought, found out where the boss was going and got over here.

"You know I was in Somalia as a colonel in 1993, before it all began to fall apart there," he said as the car crossed Memorial Bridge. He wasn't one to tell a story for no reason, she thought, especially on a day when he already had been reamed out by the president. "The crowds of women and children would surge at the Rangers, usually shielding behind them gunmen with AK-47s. Then my guys would start taking shots from inside the crowd. So my guys near the crowd would figure out where the gunman was. They'd put the red dot of a laser designator on that guy. Then they'd have one of their snipers doing overwatch from hidden hide spots, the one who had the clearest shot, put a round into his chest.

"It didn't take long before all you had to do was put a red dot on someone's chest, just using laser pointers, like the briefers use. You didn't even have to shoot. The message we sent was, You don't know where our snipers are, but they have you in their sights."

She followed him from his car and up the Marshall staircase to his office. He was coming to the point of the story. "You could disperse a crowd really quickly that way, isolate the leader."

He walked into his office, glanced at his messages from the "Urgent" box, then stood behind his desk and looked at her. "You know what, Major? Right now I feel like I have a red dot on my chest—and I don't know who's doing it. I want you to find out." He sat down at his desk. She was dismissed.

He turned on both computers. There in his secure e-mail was one from the Sons of Liberty, titled "FINALLY":

One of the service chiefs finally speaks up! Congratulations to the Pentagon procurement department, which must have bought some backbone and issued it to the previously spineless General Shillingsworth. . . .

He stopped reading and hit the delete button. He glanced to make sure that his office door was closed. Then he put his hands over his face and let his emotions out.

He gave himself five minutes, then went into his private washroom and splashed water on his face. The primary duty of the combat soldier, he thought as he stared back at the ugly, tired face in the mirror, splotched with red and gray, is to keep going.

The Pentagon
Wednesday, June 1
4:30 P.M.

General Shillingsworth told Sherman he knew she was busy with preparations for the Fort Polk visit, her first big interagency coordinating assignment, but he wanted her to sit in next afternoon on the Criminal Investigation Division's briefing on the Sons of Liberty nonetheless.

"Bad news up front, sir," the CID colonel began, standing at parade rest at the end of General Shillingsworth's conference table. "We're still working the issue of where SOL originates."

"Working the issue" was Pentagonese for "I don't know." But by reducing the Sons of Liberty to an acronym, he was seeking unconsciously to signal that he had the problem under control. The secret of the military acronym was the implied message it sent—it meant the military mind had been brought to bear, the problem had been wrestled into something that could be addressed by the military structure.

The problem with tracing e-mail on the Internet was that the Net was so antihierarchical. It had no head, no clear structure. Messages could be forwarded as is, or pasted into a new message and so carry no history. The original Internet—DARPANET—had been designed that way by the Defense Advanced Research Projects Agency as a multiple-node communications system that could survive a nuclear attack by the Soviets. On top of that, the CID investigators kept on running into unusually impenetrable firewalls.

"At this time, I can't tell you where it is coming from," the CID colonel confessed. "But I can tell you where it is going."

He had a random sample of consumers of the SOL, done by identifying those forwarding the group's messages most frequently. The demographics were mainly white, mainly male, mostly lieutenants and captains, with a few majors. "Some ranks above that, but it is hard to sort out who is just keeping track of it and who actually is fomenting it," the colonel said.

"Fomenting"—unusual word for a cop to use, Sherman thought.

"Any variation by source of commissioning?" Shillingsworth asked.

"Really across the board, sir," the colonel said. "ROTC, academies. Lots of mustangs. Of course, a disproportionate number of Citadel, VMI grads." Shillingsworth nodded—those groups were the Jesuits of the U.S. military.

"If there is any commonality, sir, it is class and branch," the colonel continued. He was proud that he had brought the Army's Office of Military Demography in to consult on the case. "Going by the zip codes at time of accession, there are lots of middle-class or lower-middle-class backgrounds."

Shillingsworth nodded. "So far you've described about ninety percent of today's junior officers," he said. "Where's the news, Colonel?"

"The other connector is combat arms," the colonel continued. "We don't see a lot of backing for this in support and administrative branches."

"Women?" General Shillingsworth asked.

"You anticipate my facts, sir. That was a surprise to me, sir. There are more than I expected, almost all in the combat arms—Apache pilots especially, for some reason."

That's no bombshell either, thought Shillingsworth. All my Apache drivers are pissed nowadays—their lives an endless rotation of doing a stateside post like Campbell or Hood, then Korea, then the Balkans, and then do it again. They were all lonely and angry. And the budget cuts hit them disproportionately, because aviation is so expensive. None of them had the flying hours they needed to maintain their edge, especially in night combat conditions, with full loads of fuel and ammo.

"Your sense of their motivation?"

"Here I'm going by the comments they attach in forwarding SOL documents," the colonel said. "They're generally upset with the president's 'Honorable Service' initiative and the budget cuts. Lots of worry about training time, about spare parts, about micromanagement. Some talk among them about Algeria, how that went down. Lots of worry about this Afghanistan thing, with a jump the other day when we lost that kid in the mortar attack."

"Any sense of how far this reaches beyond the Army?"

"More Marines than their end-strength numbers would indicate, but you'd expect that, given their combat-heavy force structure."

"Where are their messages coming from?" General Shillingsworth asked.

"We're still working that. We've gotten as far as the servers at the National Security Agency, but the trail stops cold there. Given the power of the NSA firewalls, it is impossible to track beyond there."

"So what next, Colonel?"

"Glad you asked, sir," the CID man said. He had learned to always save the best for last in his briefings. "We have a tip just as I came over here that Captain America may be an officer based at Fort Bragg."

"Well, what are you waiting for?" General Shillingsworth said, standing up.

Rolling Knolls Apartments
Fayetteville, North Carolina
Thursday, June 2
4:30 A.M.

The takedown was flawless.

Well before dawn, while most young officers were still dreaming of sex or company command, two City of Fayetteville police cars escorted a five-man CID snatch team to a two-story apartment complex on Morgantown Road, ten minutes from the main entrance to Fort Bragg. CID managers saw this as, among other things, a high-profile chance to demonstrate that they could handle these things themselves, instead of calling in some tight-lipped Special Operations antiterrorism unit. This one was being monitored directly by the commanding general of the CID. That counted when it was time to wrestle with the snake eaters come budget time.

Most of the complexes along the road had brown walls and gray roofs. This one, for some reason, had gray walls and a brown roof. But there was no reason to notice the place unless you lived there—as Captain America did. It was a place made to be lived in for twenty-three months by junior Army officers and then never seen again. Its developer had flourished by coming up with a special "Junior Officer Real Deal," offering a two-room apartment that came fully furnished with pots, pans, a cable-connected twenty-three-inch color television and a microwave. Some officers moved in and were relaxing with ESPN in under two hours, including stocking up at the Food Lion across the road.

The snatch team's breacher, a crusty old chief warrant officer, used a universal key to unlock the front door, turned the doorknob, walked in and took the right hallway into the bedroom. He kneeled down next to the sleeping man and shook him gently with his left hand while holding at the ready in his right hand a five-pound lead-and-leather blackjack. When the man awoke, the lieutenant colonel standing at the foot of the bed said, "You'll come with us." The man looked and saw men in black jumpsuits kneeling on either side of him, ready to pounce. The two warrant officers rose when he got out of bed and followed him to the bathroom. They stood behind him in the open doorway as he brushed his teeth and shaved.

"Alphas, bravos or BDUs, sir?" Captain America asked with remarkable calm. He assumed this was some Army thing, and he knew to go with the flow.

"Bravos," the lieutenant colonel said. One of the warrants reached into a closet and handed him the polyester forest-green pants and bathroom-tile-green shirt, the basic daily office clothing that some in the Army derided as "the bus driver's uniform." In this view, simply being willing to wear this ugly, uncomfortable outfit underscored the Army's devotion to the nation.

"I wish they all were this simple," the breacher said to his door guard as they left the apartment less than five minutes after entering it.

The snatch team drove him in an unmarked blue minivan—but with federal government license plates—to a waiting C-130 at Pope. In just over two hours they were at Andrews Air Force Base south of Washington, D.C. A Blackhawk met them on the apron there and ferried them down the Potomac to the Quantico brig.

The lieutenant colonel called the CID commanding general. "Sir, we have him," he said.

"You got Captain America?" The general stood up at his desk, holding the phone.

"Yes, sir, cooling his heels in Quantico right now, not more than twenty feet from me." He looked up at the heavy door of the interrogation room.

"I'm on my way," the general said. "By the way, what are his real rank and name?"

The lieutenant colonel was puzzled by the question. "Uh, captain, sir. It checks out." This wasn't some case of fraudulent enlistment, he thought.

"And his name?" the general asked.

"Sir?" The lieutenant colonel didn't understand where this was going.

"His real name, man, what is it?"

"Sir, his name is Captain Jonathan America."

The day began to go very bad for the general. He dropped into his chair. "You arrested some poor bastard actually named Captain America? Oh, my Christ." What were the chances?

He took a deep breath and then went into damage control: *Who else knows? What did you tell him? What contact did you have with Bragg officials?*

At the end of the day, the two warrant officers deposited one very puzzled captain back at Rolling Knolls Apartments. The next day, when friends in the battalion asked him about his absence, he shrugged. "I dunno, it was some kind of Special Forces domestic threat exercise. I'm not supposed to say anything."

CIA Headquarters
Langley, Virginia
6:15 A.M.

Only in America, Sherman thought.

She'd left Lewis sleeping in her bed and hailed a cab at the corner of Eighteenth and Columbia Road. When she said, "CIA headquarters, please," the driver's eyes darted up to his rearview mirror and examined her before pulling away. Only then did she look at his hack license, encased in plastic, and see that he was Mohammed Gul Khazır—judging by that name, probably Afghan or Pashtun Pakistani, she thought, reaching back to the time of her advanced course at Huachuca when the senior foreign area officer specializing in the " 'Stans" gave an admiring, Kipling-heavy lecture on the border tribes. The FAO had recited from memory: "When you're wounded and left on Afghanistan's plains / And the women come out to cut up what remains, / Just roll to your rifle and blow out your brains / An' go to your Gawd like a soldier."

The taxi driver expertly wove his way up the high Virginia bank of the Potomac on the George Washington Parkway and exited on Route 123. But as he approached the right turn for the CIA's main entrance his hands began to shake. In the driveway he abruptly turned the wheel and stopped one hundred yards short of the guardhouse. "This is good, lady, please, you get off now," he pleaded. The odd placement of the cab in a blocking position across the driveway aroused suspicions in the guardhouse. One security guard came out to look over the cab and record its license plate number while the other called in the suspicious movement. When Sherman came inside the guardhouse, the two took down her Social Security number to check against their computer logs and skeptically scrutinized her still-fresh intelligence community badge that read "Special Access/IW."

They kept her waiting on a bench until Captain Cisco could come and personally retrieve her, which he did with a broad grin and a "How ya doing?" There was no acknowledgment in his greeting that she outranked him, she noticed with a slight twinge of envy. His stringy black hair had actually crept over the tops of his ears since they last met. He signed her in and turned to the unsmiling guards. "It's all right," he said airily. "She's my mother."

As they walked up the driveway to the main CIA building, Sherman explained the problem: General Shillingsworth worried that the Sons of Liberty wasn't so much a gumshoe problem as an infowar issue. "Booze, broads, golf, airplanes and money," Shillingsworth had said to her dismissively after the meeting yesterday. "That's what CID is good at investigating—thieving supply sergeants and generals who can't keep their pants zipped. This is way out of their lane. I need you to poke around."

And that was where Captain Cisco came in.

They signed the lobby guard's log and passed through the metal detectors. Sherman watched Cisco insert a passkey into the elevator, then press the "B3" button to take them down deep into the double subbasement. She shook her head at his long, greasy hair and overall lack of military bearing.

Historically, the hotter the pilot, the more latitude he enjoyed in the Air Force—drinking, whoring and driving too fast were SOP for decades. It was a flawed tradition, because it made it difficult for some Air Force officers to give much serious thought to leadership until one day they woke up in command of a squadron. Cisco seemed to be laying claim to this practice, Sherman thought, an infowarrior hurtling through cyberspace. His hair, his slovenly uniform, his neglect of rank—none of these would be permitted in any of the other services, but for him it was a badge of honor. Like a daredevil pilot, Cisco was sending the message that he was so adept that his commanders were willing to overlook a lot.

He had shown up for work at 3 P.M. the previous day and worked alone through the night, napping at one point while a security program gave his server its weekly scrubbing. For him the line between work and play was hazy. He had surfed a bit, looked at some new Third World revolutionary organizations' websites, sent his usual hundred or so e-mails to comrades and buddies in his line of work, composed but not sent a vaguely contemptuous e-mail to the colonel who he thought was in way over his head as program executive officer for a black infowar program, and lurked through the two best cyberwar chat rooms, including the secret one run by and for hackers at the CIA that the Agency's supervisors didn't know about.

In his suite of subterranean cubbyholes he microwaved some vegan eggplant-tomato stew and then slurped it with a plastic spoon out of its Tupperware container. She followed him from the microwave to his desk, giving him a capsule history of the Sons of Liberty. "The NSA cleanser stopped the CID investigation cold," she said.

He nodded. "It's a good machine."

"Will it talk?"

"No, NSA designed it to refuse interrogation in any form. You try and it will just knock you off its network, which is what the amateurs at CID probably found." He explained why: "The NSA cleanser was supposed to be our clean cutout in any infowar confrontation—a system that wouldn't allow the adversary a toehold. If we went offensive—say, logic-bombed Qaddafi's systems—it would be our launching pad.

"But nobody ever planned for what to do if it were turned against us. I mean, you red-team it to detect the vulnerabilities. But you don't expect a weapon that only you possess will be used against you. So you don't build your force structure toward that outcome." This stuff was real to him, she realized, just as real as tanks, helicopters and artillery pieces were to her. He lived in that world.

A reddish dot of eggplant-tomato stew landed just above his nameplate on his baby-blue uniform shirt. Sherman didn't bother to point it out to him. She handed him a folder containing printouts of all known SOL declarations.

He scanned a few, then pretended to yawn. It all read to him like a family fight in a foreign language. "You Army guys have a lot of time on your hands?"

She leaned forward. "Can you help me?"

He thought he could. "You need to understand that our rulebook is still kind of hazy, Major," he said. "Can I call you Cindy?"

What the hell, she thought. He's more like an eccentric college student than a subordinate military officer. "Sure."

"You just call me Cisco." He swiveled his chair to look at his screen. "Just checking our lines, I took the liberty of setting up a spoof program against the NSA cleanser. Kind of a friendly rivalry, you know—'Are you Fort Meade cats as hip as you think you are?'"

He assured her that he hadn't left any footprints. "All my program did was prop the door open, so when data came out of their cleanser, I could see where it was coming from."

She sat at his right shoulder and gave him the Defense Department identifying data and protocols for General Shillingsworth's secure computer. Four minutes later, he was browsing through the personal e-mail of the Army chief of staff. "Secure, my butt," Cisco sneered. "Here's one about you." He pointed at the bottom of the screen. "It's your general advising the senior Army staff that you will be participating in the investigation of the Sons of Liberty."

She leaned forward to see it. As she squinted she inadvertently brushed her left breast against his extended right arm. He smiled: "Oh, Major, I like that."

She looked at him, astounded but not angry. He was so straightforwardly pleased, so innocently unabashed. "Knock it off, Cisco," she said. "I must be eight, maybe ten years older than you. I've got some gray hairs."

"Nah, you're old, but you're not *too* old," he said. "And I like mature women. But you can be anything you want with me. You could dress up as a nurse! Or a lion tamer!" He grinned.

"This mature woman would be grateful if you'd stay on task, Cisco," she said calmly. "Explain how you do this." He was the most unmilitary officer she'd ever dealt with, she thought, and had been left alone too long in the spooks' basement.

Cisco couldn't adequately manipulate the routing data using a stale Sons of Liberty message. To do a real rollup, he'd need to lie in wait and catch a real-time transmission that was heading into the NSA cleanser—and that wasn't easy. But once he had a live transmission in hand, he could figure out which portal it had used to get into the NSA system. Then he could establish a block on that portal. The next time a message came in, it would have to slow down and search for a way around the block. With luck, he'd seize it and follow its route back to its originating computer. Then he could begin interrogating that computer's hard drive.

"That sounds like Tactical Defense 101," she said. "Drop a tree across the road, so your attacker has to detour around it, and then when he gets sufficiently backed up, mortar the hell out of his convoy."

"Pretty much," Cisco agreed. "Except for the speed with which we then go over to the offense. When I can catch him interactive with the Paragon XPS, stuck in my cleanser bypass, I'll be ready to go invasive. I'll bring in the Digger to roll up his distribution trees and ice-nine his cell lists."

"And that sounds like the classic tactic of using infantry to pin down an opponent so you can clobber him with artillery," she said, a bit eager to show that she understood.

"Could be," he said dismissively. "I really don't know much about industrial-age warfare. I'll use Crays to monitor him, Paragon to hold him and Digger to hit him. The Digger can penetrate the hard drives and interrogate them one by one. It'll take all the computing power I can get dedicated here, for a short while. But eventually I can give you the entire distribution tree—if I can catch him in the bypass and pick up his route of ingress."

He paused. "Of course, there's a danger that when I use the Digger to ice-nine our own systems, it'll trigger the suicide chips in the secure computers."

"What does that mean?" Sherman asked. The phrase "suicide chip" worried her. "Dick-and-Jane it for me."

"Only that we could crash the entire worldwide Defense Department secure network—all thirty thousand terminals." He cackled at that interesting prospect. Cindy held the bridge of her nose between her thumb and forefinger.

Ames's Study, Fort McNair
9 P.M.

Every night hundreds of thousands of e-mails rocketed around the military. Most were from buddies keeping in touch with one another, especially from units that had served in combat. But many of the messages leaped ranks. One of the reasons that the rank structure originally was devised was to control the flow of information. But now information ricocheted around the military as sergeants wrote to their old captains and captains wrote to colonels.

Many of the messages this evening dwelled on the events in Afghanistan, wondering what to do about it. The messages from the Sons of Liberty had provoked much anguished thought. How much longer could they put up with this?

Major Roland Bolton, who was now XO of a battalion at Fort Bragg, wrote to thank General Ames. *I'd heard you intervened on my behalf*, he wrote, *and so I feel obliged to tell you that I may go public with my concern about events in Afghanistan.* By intervening only halfheartedly, he worried, we might stir up the situation enough to do real harm, without really being committed to sticking it out.

Ames, typing a reply on the alternate laptop in his study at home, congratulated Bolton on his new billet. Running a battalion, he wrote, was the most rewarding job in the Army. *When the SecDef offered me this job of vice chairman of the Joint Chiefs*, he wrote, *I told him that what I really would like is to get back my old battalion.*

As for Afghanistan, Ames wrote, *I understand your feelings.* He offered to put Bolton in touch with the Sons of Liberty network, which could issue the protest anonymously.

But I understand that because of your service in Afghanistan, this is a personal issue for you, one on which you may wish to attach your name, he continued.

Ames's crucial point was that it would be a risk to go public, but a calculated one. And he was a master of measuring chances. *I doubt the SecDef will go after you*, he wrote. *The last thing they want is a public confrontation over this issue.*

Ames turned to his other e-mails. There were many more about the Afghanistan mess. It seemed to him that the president's visit the next day to Fort Polk presented a target of opportunity.

It sometimes is impossible to say when a point of no return is reached. For Ames it may have been with the next message he typed. It was to someone he had known for twenty-five years, the command sergeant major of the 49th Armored Division down in the Texas National Guard. *Are you boys going to this dog-and-pony show with the president at Polk tomorrow with shit-eating grins on your faces? Or are you going to remember the Alamo?*

Fort Polk, Louisiana
Friday, June 3
11:15 A.M.

The visit to Polk was Cindy's first major test in the routine work of an assistant aide de camp, the first time she'd handled the Shillingsworth itin-
erary entirely on her own, without being baby-sat by the XO. It grew out
of the president's campaign promise years earlier to visit every major U.S.
military base sometime during his first term. As a matter of protocol, the
Army chief of staff accompanied the president on every one of those trips
that took him to an Army post. The Polk visit had been announced a
month earlier, so it would have been embarrassing to cancel it because of
Afghanistan and the newspaper stories about Shillingsworth's remarks at
Carlisle.

The entire presidential time on the ground would be just six hours, but
in the days leading up to it, the plan was subjected by the White House
staffers to more than two hundred changes in timing, personnel and lo
gistics. Most grew out of political arcana—did the mayor of Leesville, the
town just up the road from Fort Polk, have connections to David Duke?
And on which side did General Leonidas Polk, for whom the base was
named, fight during the Civil War? The White House aides had a frantic
air to them, as if they assumed they were so overworked they had the right
to be rude, Cindy thought one day as she put down the phone after an-
swering an urgent question about the racial makeup of the children at the
Fort Polk day care center. They probably think the hardest thing you
could do in life was take the bar exam, she thought. I'd like to take a few
of them on a night march to scout OPFOR positions at Fort Irwin, when
it goes from eighty-five degrees in the afternoon to forty degrees that
night, and you're humping over the mountain, worrying about running out
of water in the Valley of Death.

She worked on the visit for several days and evenings, breaking a date
with Lewis to get ready. She reviewed the speech that Polk's commanding
general would use to introduce General Shillingsworth, and then the
chief's introduction in turn of the president, then forwarded both to the
White House aides and incorporated their nitpicking replies. She packed
extra cash, a shoe brush to touch up the general's boots and masking tape
to secure the introductory speech to the podium in case it was windy. She
made sure her counterparts in DCSOPS and JCS knew all about the

visit. She checked her minicassette recorder in order to have a record of all public comments, and threw into her attaché case an extra set of new double-A batteries. She always carried on her person two of the thin metal Cross pens he liked—one for him, and one for her as a backup. She put in the whistle she always carried for walking alone at night and always took when traveling. She double-checked all appointments, and made sure that everyone had the right time zones written down. She obtained the official biographies of all meeting participants down to the battalion level, and found out what nicknames were appropriate. Yes, the corps commander named LeRoy was really known as "Chip," and the 25th Infantry Division commander named Chester went by "Chuck." She made sure she'd memorized the general's forty most important phone numbers. She even checked cell phone coverage in the area. She was pretty proud of herself.

It never occurred to her to tell the general's wife he would be out of town until late that evening. And she didn't know it was his wedding anniversary. But by the end of the day, this sin would hardly be noticed.

The day began with Special Forces trainers putting on an exhibition of hand-to-hand combat at Warrior Field. Cindy stood just behind a knot of reporters and White House aides.

"It's easy," a Special Forces captain explained while his assistants stood at parade rest behind him. The captain had an air of easy superiority to him, almost seeming to be smirking at these plump, pasty Washingtonians. "Ignore what your adversary is doing to you, ignore the pain, get him to the ground and drive a boot heel into the skull."

Two NCOs demonstrated the point. One reached toward another to choke him, his thumbs clearly pressing into the other man's neck, cutting off the flow of air and blood to the brain. The target of the attack threw back his left foot, then hooked his right boot around his attacker's ankle. Simultaneously he jabbed the man near his eye. "In a real situation, he'd thumb his eyeball out," the SF captain explained to the visitors from Washington. The deputy White House press secretary blanched, as if close combat were simply in very bad taste.

When the attacker fell to the ground, the first NCO lifted his big black combat boot and began to drive his heel toward his assistant's face. He stopped it just inches above the forehead. "Standard SF training, ma'am," the SF captain said to Major Sherman. She knew that already. She idly wondered whether she was being condescended to because she was a woman, or because she had escorted this bunch of White House aides onto the SF captain's turf, or simply because she was regular Army. In any event, she thought, she got this snotty captain's implied message: You may be in the same military as me, but we are still in different worlds.

The president ate a lunch of chili mac at the 2nd Armored Cavalry Regiment's mess hall while a pool of four reporters stood and watched him. By the time he emerged, the weather had worsened, with low, heavy, fast-moving black thunderclouds coming in from the northwest—Oklahoma's biggest export, bad weather.

The 2,500 troops who had been assembled for him at the airfield ninety minutes earlier were dressed in full battle gear. The temperature rose to ninety-five and gray clouds lowered, threatening to rain at any minute. In the best of times, the troops wouldn't have been impressed by wasting a day waiting on the brass. Watching the weather and idly thinking about Afghanistan only made them touchier.

Most of the troops were from the 25th Infantry Division, which had just completed an intense series of exercises at Polk's light-infantry training center. "Chip," the corps commander, had filled out the crowd with reservists from the 49th Infantry Division, based just to the west in Texas. He'd figured that they probably wouldn't be as hard against this president as the active-duty guys were. He'd failed to do the additional calculation that they had less to lose than regular Army troops—they already had good jobs and established civilian lives, and they were less constrained by Army discipline, but were just as cranked off by the president's use of the military in Afghanistan.

The president climbed onto the platform as "Hail to the Chief" played and all 2,500 troops snapped to attention. Sherman watched him stand there separate from the others on the platform—the White House people had explained to her that keeping other people out of the background made for better television images.

The president stepped to the microphone. Then the captain of the company of reservists in the front rank yelled, "Company, left face," and all of his 143 troops turned ninety degrees away from the president and instead saluted the color guard's American flag, snapping in the wind at the end of the parade ground. It had all been decided by e-mail the night before: *We will salute the flag, not the man.*

Sherman had memorized the program. She knew that however crisp that movement was, it wasn't scheduled.

Just to the left of the president, one of the company commanders from the 25th ID slowly wheeled toward the flag. He didn't call out an order—Cindy realized that he was leaving it up to the individuals in his unit. For a moment his men stared at him. His first sergeant turned, and then each platoon did, as if the order indeed were being passed back silently.

The action began rippling out in waves, surprisingly quickly. Soon most of the assembled 2,500 troops, and virtually every combat soldier—infantry, armor, artillery, aviation and combat engineer—had his side turned to the president, his face lifted toward the flag. Cindy could see tears on the faces of some.

Shillingsworth, sitting next to "Chip" and "Chuck" in the steel folding chairs just to the left of the platform, fumed. What kind of general can't control his troops? Me, he thought. But he hesitated: Don't preempt the president, he decided.

"We are a force for peace and stability," the president intoned, trying to plow on, alone on the platform, speaking to a sea of silent soldiers ignoring him. "These colors don't run." He delivered that line so falteringly that it seemed almost a question. The television cameramen panned from the turned backs of the troops to the president, his hair blowing in the wind. This would be the lead story on the evening news shows. "We are the promise that this twenty-first century will be better than the bloody century in which we were born." But his words were torn away by the intensifying wind. The sky blackened, and the first fat drops of rain hit.

"So, thank you for your service," the president said, cutting short his speech. "And, hey, let's get out of here before it really rains." There was no applause.

He strode down the stairs of the platform. "Get me the hell out of here," he said to his chief of staff.

Cindy watched one of the White House pool reporters call in the troops' protest. "In an action apparently unprecedented in American history . . ." he began dictating breathlessly into his cellular phone.

Back at the Pentagon, Captain Bobby Byrnes, watching the protest on C-SPAN, decided it was time to type up his own Sons of Liberty message, instead of just forwarding notes from friends. "SALUTE," he typed into his computer.

The Pentagon
Monday, June 6
6 A.M.

General Shillingsworth had dreamed again that he was in Pickett's Charge, moving closer to the stone wall on the ridge this time. Pretty soon the Federal cannon would begin hitting them with canister. Shreds of the dream had hung on in his mind even during his morning run through the cemetery, mist rolling off the Potomac among the cheap cement grave markers.

He arrived at the Pentagon resolved to address the Fort Polk situation. He would tell Polk's commander that the Army wanted only two things from him: Clean up the mess, then send in his retirement papers.

His public affairs officer met him at his office door. "You need to read the story from Bragg in the *New York World*."

He nodded, then logged onto his secure computer again. A message from the Sons of Liberty popped up to greet him under the title "SALUTE."

A salute to the Sons of Liberty at Fort Polk who organized Friday's about-face.

The nation's warriors salute you—and join you. It is time now to move on to the next phase of the operation. It is time to stop simply disagreeing with where we are being taken—and to do something to save this military and aid our nation.

There are times when we must rise above politics. The politicians have failed. We are being misused by civilians who serve market values, not the nation. Our values run deeper than the latest polls.

We are the Army of the United States. We are not the handmaiden of the political party that happens to hold power. We swore an oath to uphold the Constitution. The president is sending us to war without consent of Congress. We now have lost sixteen soldiers in Afghanistan. Let's state it plainly: The president is violating constitutional law. He has sent us in harm's way for his own personal political reasons, to attempt to redeem his tattered reputation. But in fact he has only underscored his ineptitude as commander in chief.

We are military officers who love our nation enough to risk our careers. It is time to get our military—and the nation we serve—back on track.

1 1 4   T h o m a s   E .   R i c k s

   Keep faith with those who serve. Loyalty has to start somewhere. Let
it start now—let it start with us. Show loyalty to the troops.
   To quote Abraham Lincoln: "Let us dare to do our duty."

It was signed, as always, *Captain America, the Sons of Liberty, an organization of active-duty soldiers.*
They are moving from dissent to sedition, General Shillingsworth's judge
advocate general told him in an e-mail that forwarded the "SA-
LUTE" message.
They are becoming my enemy, Shillingsworth thought.
   I need to read that *World* article, he remembered. The weekend papers
had been full of stories about the Polk incident but had little news. The
most striking was a statement from the families of the sixteen dead
soldiers, that they would prefer neither the White House nor the Pentagon to send representatives to the upcoming funerals at Arlington National Cemetery. For the most part, the papers carried a lot of hemming
and hawing from experts about the meaning of the action and whether it
was permissible under the Uniform Code of Military Justice. Congressional reaction to the Polk action was oddly muted: Conservatives didn't
much like the Afghan mission and weren't inclined to criticize the military anyway, and liberals were uneasy with the idea of attacking people for
expressing dissent.
   "Shadowy Army Group Challenges Pentagon Brass" read the three-
column headline on the front page of the *New York World.* Always suspicious of the Pentagon, the *World* didn't seem sure whether to portray the
Sons of Liberty as a new threat from the American right—part of that vast
fascist horde beyond the Hudson River—or as a breath of fresh air in the
military establishment.
   Most of the quotations in the article were anonymous. But a Major
Roland Bolton, precisely identified as XO of the 3rd Battalion of the
504th Parachute Infantry Regiment, 82nd Airborne Division, Fort Bragg,
was quoted by name as saying that "President Shick has charted a course
in Afghanistan that is reckless and presents a danger to the military and
the nation. He has not been candid about this course of action. And he
has proven he should not be entrusted with the lives of our people."
   General Shillingsworth read the *World* article at 6:27 A.M. At 6:28 he
was on the telephone with the 82nd Airborne's commanding general. I
am going to engage this situation right now, Shillingsworth vowed.

"As a matter of fact, sir," the general responded, "I have Major Bolton here in my office right now. He's my newest battalion XO. Good man—I thought." Shillingsworth could see that office in his mind's eye—the low, two-story building, the hallway to the commander's office lined with all the framed photographs of the 82nd's commanders from Ridgway and Gavin. It would be a long day at Bragg.

"Put him on, Butch."

Bolton was standing at attention in his gray cotton "ARMY" T-shirt and black nylon running shorts. He was still dripping with sweat from the run he had been leading when the general's driver had pulled alongside him and told him to get in. He took the phone from his commanding general but remained at attention.

"Major, just what in the hell are you up to?" Shillingsworth asked him.

Bolton had rehearsed his response to that question since he had finished talking to the *New York World* reporter on Saturday afternoon. But he had expected to give it to the 82nd's commanding general, not to the chief of staff of the entire Army. "If my expression of personal opinion is construed to be an act of insubordination, sir, then I am ready to stand before any military court in the land," he slowly recited from the statement he had written in his backyard. "I will take my chances of punishment for advocating a cause which, in my opinion, sir, is dedicated to the best interests of our military, our nation and our Constitution." He paused. "Begging your pardon, sir, but beyond that, I would like to request counsel."

He's asking me to charge him, Shillingsworth thought. OK, fella, you'll get it. I will land on your chest with both feet.

But at the regular Tank meeting two hours later, the SecDef vetoed that idea. "Wrong answer, General," he ordered. "Rule one of politics: Think twice when Brer Rabbit challenges you to throw him in the briar patch. No, we are not going to give this outfit any more attention than we have to, especially with the Afghanistan funerals coming up at Arlington this Friday. Handle it quietly. No paper."

Admiral Maddox said that signals intercepts indicated the mining of the patrol had been ordered by a Taliban offshoot that seemed to be headquartered at the Bamian airport, in central Afghanistan. "If the satellite imagery is able to indicate some targets there," he warned, "Pitch and the president are going to want to hit them. Probably tactical Tomahawks, because neither Pakistan or Iran will want to clear us for manned overflights."

Back at his office, General Shillingsworth called in Cindy Sherman. "We are fighting an information war with these Sons of Liberty," he said. "And it is an insurgency, which this Army has never been good at putting down." He looked at her almost pleadingly: "Major, get me some results."

Cindy was about to call Cisco when his e-mail arrived. *We're closer, but no cigar. I saw the SOL message titled "SALUTE" when it was already in the NSA cleanser, but I don't know which entry portal it used. I'm getting a better idea of their possible routes. Still a long way from dropping your tree across their incoming path. Come sit by my computer sometime. Your pal, Cisco.*

Fort Drum, New York
12:15 P.M.

Just when the White House thought that the public and military reaction to the losses in Afghanistan was dying down, the tape of the patrol got out. Like the 1991 videotape of Los Angeles police officers beating Rodney King, it captured the public imagination and elevated the Afghanistan mission to something more than just another foreign policy problem.

The tape contained no new information, but having a human voice emerge from the fiasco of the patrol concentrated minds and emotions, especially among service members, who knew that any one of them could have been the agonized soldier on that tape.

"Oh, my p-p-poor legs." That's what hit soldiers when they listened to the tape taken off the medevac net. That poor morphine-addled radioman, his high, thin, shaky voice chopped by a stutter: "My p-p-poor legs."

Central Command, which officially owned the tape of the doomed Afghanistan patrol, classified it forty-eight hours after the incident, but by then it was too late. It already was being e-mailed around the Army and the Pentagon, passed on in an ever-larger distribution network. Within a week, many people in the reserves and in the 10th Mountain Division had received two, even three copies. *Close your office door before listening to this one,* read one introduction.

The tape bothered Sam Cumberbatch. They shouldn't put people through that type of bullshit. And classifying that—well, he thought, that was just higher headquarters doing what they do best, covering their asses: echelons above reality, miles from the truth. After the Baptist service at the base chapel, he had taken aside his battalion sergeant major. They went back fifteen years—the man had been his drill sergeant at Fort Benning and was the closest thing Sam Cumberbatch had ever had to a father. He told the older man what he was thinking of doing.

Leaning against the grille of his pickup truck in the chapel parking lot, the sergeant major folded his arms and shook his head slowly. "Sam, you are about to get your black self into a world of white trouble."

Cumberbatch politely disagreed. "No, Sergeant Major, it's soldier trouble. That's all I am, a soldier."

"Well, keep your head down, son," the sergeant major said.

Cumberbatch took that guarded response to be moral approval. At lunch the next day, he drove over to the twenty-four-hour store and used a pay phone to make a collect telephone call to Walter Schultz, the *New York Financial* reporter whose story about the patrol he'd seen in the *Early Bird,* the Pentagon's daily compendium of news articles on defense issues.

"Do I know you?" the startled reporter asked, pushing his Italian hero sandwich across his desk to make room for a notebook.

"No, sir, you don't," Cumberbatch said. "But I read your story about them refugees getting machine gunned? And I remembered your name because it's like that 'I know nothing' guy in *Hogan's Heroes*—you know, Sergeant Schultz." He had spent many long, snowy evenings at Fort Drum alone with his cable television.

Cumberbatch said he wanted to mail to the reporter an interesting tape out of the patrol in Afghanistan. But the reporter had a different idea. "I'll fly up right now," Schultz said. The fun of working for a big newspaper with deep pockets still amazed him. "I can get there tonight."

Cumberbatch told him to meet him at the enlisted club.

"How will I know you?" Schultz asked.

"Oh, I'll pick you out," Cumberbatch assured him.

The newspaper's travel office booked Schultz on the 3 P.M. to Syracuse, New York, with a puddle-jumper connection at 6:15 to Watertown. At 7 P.M. he walked out of the little terminal and asked the only cabbie there if he knew how to get to the enlisted club at Fort Drum. The driver said he knew how to get to both of them. "I drive a cab off-duty," he drawled.

"My wife and I couldn't get housing on post, and this helps pay the heat-ing bills in the big old place we rented in Black River."

"What do you mean, both of them?" Schultz asked.

"Well, there's Spinners and Pennants," the soldier-cabbie said.

They first tried Spinners, a free-standing one-story brick building in the middle of the post. Out front, Schultz peeled off a twenty-dollar bill and gave it to the driver. "I'll pay you to wait," he said. Love that expense ac-count, he thought.

Spinners was a barn of a place—dance floor on the right, billiard tables and video games on the left, divided by a big bar. The Dixie Chicks blared on big screens over the dance floor. Out on the floor, underage Canadian girls down from paper-mill towns for a weekend of fun and barracks sex danced with American soldiers. All the soldiers were white, and almost all wore tight blue jeans and loose shirts. Schultz looked around the dance floor, the bar, the billiard tables and the game machines, but no expectant face looked back at him—an overweight, middle-aged civilian in a blue blazer and rumpled Dockers was not what the Canadian girls had in mind when they crossed the St. Lawrence River.

The reporter went back out to the cab. The solider-cabbie asked if the person he was meeting was black or white.

"Black, I think, from the accent," Schultz said.

"You shoulda said so," the cabbie said. "This place is bubbaland. You want Pennants." He drove Schultz over to the other club.

As Schultz came in the front door he saw it had the same layout as the first club—dance floor on the right, bar in the middle, billiards and game machines on the left. But with his first step inside he felt the heavy pulse of hip-hop music by Outkast rattling his rib cage. In line in front of him, the pants were loose and the shirts were worn with tails out. And almost all the faces were black.

He strolled through an arched entryway, looking to see who might be expecting him. He didn't notice that the arch held a large metal detector.

A red light at the top of the arch began flashing directly over his head, and the music system automatically stopped, replaced by an alarmlike siren. On the dance floor the crowd crouched on the floor. A bright spot-light shone in his face. Two security guards were suddenly sandwiching Schultz. "Put your fucking hands up *now!*" the one in front of him shouted, his eyes bulging. Schultz obeyed. The one behind him quickly ran his hands up and down Schultz's legs, then snaked around and felt into the inside pockets of his blazer.

The security guard plucked the metal Sony minicassette tape recorder from Schultz's inside breast pocket. He smiled, turned and held up the innocuous little machine for the crowd to see, its shiny chrome reflecting the red and blue lights over the dance floor. The crowd laughed. The throbbing music resumed on the dance floor.

The security guard who had shouted in Schultz's face sagged in relief, but the adrenaline made him almost giddy. He handed the recorder back to Schultz and patted him on the shoulder. "Sorry about being hyper, man," he said. "We've had three stabbings and two shootings in here lately, and one of the guards got nailed, so we're being kind of careful. The metal detector picks up everything."

As Schultz stood absorbing this, a round-faced black man in his late thirties, almost twice the age of most of the club's patrons, tapped him on the shoulder. "I'm Cumberbatch," he said. He led the stunned newsman to a corner booth.

Nightline
Thursday, June 9
11:30 P.M.

When Schultz got back to D.C. late the next morning he played the extraordinary tape for his group editor, who immediately called a producer for *Nightline*. "I've got something for you to work with," he told the producer, who also was his next-door neighbor in Bethesda.

Schultz's story ran on page one of the *New York Financial* on Thursday. A full transcript of the tape ran with the jump of the story. But the print version could never convey the emotional impact that came with actually hearing the tape.

That night *Nightline* ran a powerful production that felt like an instant, twenty-minute-long feature film. Titled *The Lost Patrol: An American Tragedy in Asia,* it used B-roll stock footage from Camp Noble Effort shot when the troops went into Afghanistan, cutting away occasionally to painfully youthful high school yearbook photographs of the troops who were mentioned, and weaving throughout it the wounded radioman's transmissions.

"Tomorrow, fifteen young American soldiers will be buried at Arlington National Cemetery," Ted Koppel began, his slight frown and inclination of the head indicating the gravity of his subject. He knew this show was a triumph. It would win an Emmy, provoke congressional hearings, at the very least. "Another one will follow soon. It wasn't supposed to be that way.

"They were nineteen, twenty and twenty-one years old, most of them. They came from Detroit, from Los Angeles, from Atlanta and small towns across north Georgia—Dalton, Gainesville and Rabun Gap. Their lives were just beginning. Instead, those lives ended three Sundays ago in a lonely corner of western Afghanistan. It is an event that has reverberated through the U.S. military, culminating in last Friday's unprecedented shunning of the president at an event at Fort Polk, Louisiana."

Koppel paused for three beats. "Tonight, we examine how and why that happened."

His trademark frown shadowed his face. "Before we proceed, I must warn you that we will be playing a tape recording of that event that contains some unusually graphic language. It also is a moving document that provoked some tears among our staffers who listened to it here today. We have not censored it." It would be the first time the word "fuck" would be played on a broadcast network television news show.

The first shot was of the low dusty hills just outside Camp Noble Effort. Then the thin, strained tenor voice of Belsky the radioman came on. "Oh, my p-p-poor legs." The screen showed a photograph of Private Belsky grinning at his graduation from basic training, arms around two buddies. The joy of that moment contrasted sharply with the animal fear that soaked his voice on the tape.

"No, no, the actual's down," Belsky said on the tape. The narrator explained that this was a reference to the platoon leader who died that day. The screen showed a candid photo from a Gainesville high school yearbook of the reservist lieutenant who, as a gym teacher, had been assistant coach of the football team and coach of the basketball team. In the photo his Adam's apple and his eyes both protruded amazingly, making him look about fourteen years old. "But he said there's a natural LZ just one hundred meters up, good flat o-o-open space, just beyond the trees," Belsky's voice continued.

The last section of the tape played as the screen panned the treeless, rocky desert of western Afghanistan. "We need help, man. . . . Oh, this is so f-f-fucked up. . . . Just get me out of here. . . ."

Koppel then interviewed a medic from the relief column, a reservist who worked for the Gainesville fire department and who had been sent home after the disaster on compassionate leave. He haltingly described coming upon the scene of the patrol, finding body parts everywhere, troops bleeding, the arriving soldiers weeping as they saw dead buddies. He described trying to save one of the dying troops. His mouth went rubbery, and he began to weep while he spoke. "I was doing the best I could, man, and it wasn't good enough," he said. "I still dream about that day. Every night." When he hugged himself, the camera zoomed in on his fingers. His nails were ragged.

Next Koppel interviewed the father of one of the dead soldiers, who said there were too many unanswered questions about this patrol.

The chairman of the Senate Armed Services Committee, also in the studio, agreed. Koppel asked him, "That's all very well, Senator Feaver, but what precisely do you intend to do about it?"

"I am going to hold hearings that will get to the bottom of this mess," the senator vowed.

The show ended with a shot of the American flag at Camp Noble Effort, limp in an Afghan sunset, with "Taps" playing in the background.

When the show ended Lewis sat shaken in his Crystal City apartment. It was time to do something. He moved over to his laptop and typed a message titled "MURDER?" He sent it to Rocky Gibraltar at Fort Drum, who forwarded it to Captain Byrnes at the Pentagon, who made some changes and sent it to the NSA cleanser with instructions for that system to mail the message to every e-mail address it could find that ended in "pentagon.mil."

The Pentagon
Friday, June 10
10:55 A.M.

Every computer terminal at the Pentagon, classified or not, greeted its operator on Friday morning with the message titled "MURDER?"

The Sons of Liberty hear that the commander of the American task force in Afghanistan didn't want to send out that patrol because it wasn't trained or equipped for the task—and that there was intelligence that mines were being placed by Afghans opposed to the U.S. presence. But, we hear, he was directly ordered by a White House official to send out the patrol anyway. If so, someone at the White House may have committed murder. And the entire chain of command may be guilty of dereliction of duty.

The message ended somewhat mysteriously:

The Sons of Liberty call on you to listen for the shots of the funerals at 1100 today in Arlington National Cemetery. If you are disturbed by what has happened, show it.
    Do not ask who the shots are for. They are for you.

It ended, as always, *Captain America, the Sons of Liberty, an organization of active-duty soldiers.*

A gray-haired Marine colonel stood at the window of his boss's office on the north side of the Pentagon. Four stories below him was the Pentagon's helicopter pad. Across the highway was Arlington Cemetery. He could see the first of the fifteen funerals beginning but couldn't hear any of it through the soundproof and bulletproof glass.

Two Army captains waited below him on the empty helipad. Just after 11 A.M. the shots rang out over Arlington for the first interment. The captains wheeled and looked up at the colonel at the window. Both held their arms up, pointing both thumbs down at the black asphalt.

He was a "fireproof" colonel. There was nothing they could do to him—he'd put in twenty-seven years and knew he wasn't going to make general. He served at his own pleasure. He could retire at any moment on his full pension if he were given an undesirable assignment. He emerged from the office, walked down a flight, then around the E ring to the defense secretary's area. In front of the defense secretary's office he tried to sit down cross-legged, but found that he couldn't quite bend his stiff left leg, never the same since his cot was blown into a cement wall on October 23, 1983, while he was a captain on the staff of 1st Battalion, 8th Marines, on duty at the Beirut airport. So he sat with his back against the wall just outside the defense secretary's office, left leg out, right leg bent.

In the first few minutes he was joined mainly by other gray-haired colonels and junior lieutenants—people at the ends of their careers, or apprentices who really hadn't started theirs. Then the two captains who had signaled from the helipad arrived from walking around the building. At first it was all done in silence, except for a few hushed greetings as the hands of new arrivals were shaken. But as more arrived, the demonstration became less solemn and more like a high school fire drill that had broken up a particularly dreary day.

Word spread quickly. Other officers left their cubbyholes, walked up the corridors to the E ring and sat down. A few enlisted men joined them, but not many—this was officers' business, somehow. By 11:20 there were more than sixty people sitting down in the corridor. They filled the broad hallway of the E ring, with some spilling onto the top steps of the Bradley staircase. No security officers arrived. The plain brown door of the defense secretary's office remained closed.

By 11:45 the fence sitters were joining in, captains and majors who wanted to be able to tell their buddies at Camp Swampy that yes, they had been there during the great Pentagon sit-down strike of 2004. There were more than one thousand people sitting in the hallway, mostly lieutenants, captains and majors from the Army and Marine Corps, but also here and there officers from the Air Force and Navy. The entire hallway outside the defense secretary's office area was overflowing with sit-down strikers. The staircase between the first and second floors also was packed, with the spillover backing up into the area outside the offices of Admiral Maddox. Inside the offices, no one could come or go except by using the secret "escape" elevator that led down to the subbasement garage and up to the fifth floor and the roof.

Four corridors away, Cindy Sherman got word of the action. She went in to Shillingsworth to ask permission to go see what was happening, as part of her pursuit of the Sons of Liberty. He nodded and looked out the window. He felt very old. He wouldn't ask to have them arrested, he thought after she left. *I am not in control of my troops. I should be relieved of duty. I am becoming like my platoon leader in Vietnam who froze and stared at his bootlaces.*

He left the office before her, walking out the Mall entrance and taking the back path across the cemetery to Fort Myer. At home he sat and stared down on the damned city of Washington, listening to the last shots from the Afghanistan funerals ringing out down the hill in the cemetery. He had never actually sat alone on his veranda at this time of day during the workweek. It felt unnatural.

Cindy found she couldn't get past the corridor eight area, where the undersecretary for policy and the Pentagon comptroller had their offices. She craned her neck to look down the hallway, thinking that "Captain America" probably was somewhere in this crowd. But when she stood on tiptoe to look over the white shoulder of a spectating Navy captain she instead saw Lewis squatting in a knot of Joint Staff hotshots, his back turned to her as he nodded enthusiastically at something being said to the group by a particularly stunning female Air Force captain, a jolly big-hair blonde who was a gofer in J-5, plans and policy.

Sherman turned and walked back to the Army chief's offices. She wasn't happy with either her profession or her lover. She wondered about the sour feeling in her stomach—was it churning because of what her fellow officers were doing, or because of this distance she felt from Lewis? She hadn't heard from him in a week, since she had broken their date before the Polk trip. Somehow she had frightened him, she thought. But it also was her fault because she'd been focusing on this Sons of Liberty thing. She hadn't told him about her role in investigating the Sons of Liberty—she kept the infowar work compartmentalized, even with Shillingsworth's staff.

Back in her office she found an unhappy e-mail from Cisco. *The last SOL message was too short to catch, like a burst transmission,* he wrote. *I'm getting closer.* Shit, shit, shit, she thought. She got up and left the building, walking across the POAC bridge and across the north parking lot to go sit by the Potomac. Watch the light.

Defense Secretary Johnson handled the sit-down strike like a seasoned politician. He stayed inside his office and ate his regular lunch, a bowl of chicken soup and a tuna sandwich on wheat toast. He didn't give them the pleasure of walking out in the corridor to see them. As he chewed, he considered what he would say about it that afternoon at the photo opportunity at the arrival of the Slovak defense minister.

At noon the demonstration ended and the strikers returned to their offices. No one had been arrested or even confronted by authority. At 1 P.M. Slovak defense minister Januz Zizka arrived. His visit was the third by a Central European defense official this month, all of them NATO wannabes. The secretary used virtually the same patter for each meeting—professionalize your NCOs, teach English to some officers, get some radios that can operate with ours in deployments.

The less powerful the nation, the bigger the limo that ferried its visiting officials around Washington. The ferretlike defense minister emerged from the very long black limousine blinking his good eye in the harsh mid-day light of the river entrance. His sallow face was dominated by a droop-ing mustache and a black eye patch. Secretary Johnson greeted him and then turned to the waiting reporters from the Associated Press, Reuters and Agence France-Presse, the stalwarts who covered photo ops in the hope of a quote or two, anything to move more copy.

"Mr. Secretary, Mr. Secretary," shouted the Reuters man, a twenty-year veteran of the Pentagon who had seen defense secretaries come and go. "What do you make, sir, of this morning's sit-down strike in the Pentagon hallways?"

The SecDef held out his hand. He flashed his rehearsed smile and hoped it didn't come off too tight. He put on his best folksy drawl: "On the whole, Charlie, I think having people here at the Pentagon refuse to work probably *improves* the morale and efficiency of the U.S. military *es-tablishment*." He ladled out the last word a syllable at a time: "es-tab-lish-ment." Even the reporters grinned at this line as they copied it into their notebooks. It wouldn't make the lede in their stories, but it did provide a nice second graf: *Defense Secretary Johnson downplayed the impact of the unusual action, saying . . .*

The Associated Press man had another question. "Sir, what about the message this morning from the Sons of Liberty saying that the White House ordered that patrol out even though there was information saying that mines had been put out?"

The SecDef paused. "I have looked into that, and I am very confident there is no evidence of that occurring." That is, he thought to himself, Willy Pitch assures me that if such a phone call had been placed, there was no way anyone would ever find a record of it. And on that, he had de-cided, his policy was "don't ask, don't tell." He looked gravely at the AP re-porter. "I trust you gentlemen don't publish rumor and innuendo." And with luck, he thought, that is all they would ever find.

The SecDef turned and ushered the wheezing defense minister up the Bradley stairs, which had been filled with military protesters two hours earlier. An unfiltered cigarette dangled from the minister's nicotine-stained lips. No one had informed him that no smoking was allowed anywhere in the Pentagon.

Fort Leavenworth, Kansas
Wednesday, June 15
11 A.M.

An hour before they landed at Leavenworth's airstrip, General Shillings-worth leaned back in the small Gulfstream jet, closed his eyes and thought back on one of the most difficult experiences of his life, his first after-action review as a colonel commanding a brigade at the National Training Center. In the culminating exercise his attack had petered out as it emerged from Brown's Pass and onto the flatlands sloping toward Crash Hill. Even worse, most of his attack helicopters never got into the fight.

"You are one limp-dicked excuse for a colonel," he had said aloud to himself that dawn as he had sipped water and composed himself for the after-action review, a cross between a seminar and a Maoist self-criticism session. Not having slept for thirty-two hours, he was able to hold only that one thought in mind.

Later that morning he had stood under the hot desert sun before his staff and battalion and company commanders, a freshly defeated colonel struggling with confusion, humiliation and fatigue. "I failed to take the chance here," he had confessed. He explained that he had held back his attack helicopters in case OPFOR tried to flank him in the south. But that meant he lacked the punch to push through at his main point of attack. "The M-1s hit the wire and trenches, got smeared with chemicals and got bogged down," he said. "We lost the initiative."

After Polk and then the Pentagon sit-down strike he had come close to resigning. Instead he finally had decided to call this meeting of all ten of the Army's four-star generals at Leavenworth. He wanted a gut check with his peer group: Am I reading the signs wrong here? Have I taken missteps? What do you all think about Afghanistan and the Sons of Liberty? What do I say when I appear before the Senate Armed Services Committee at the end of this week?

"This situation doesn't feel right to me," he said at the beginning of the meeting. "I confess that I don't understand how we got into either mess—the external one in Afghanistan, or the internal one inside our own U.S. Army."

The ten men were gathered around a conference table in one of Leavenworth's new academic buildings. The walls had been outfitted up to chest level with the same heavy gray carpeting that covered the floor, unintentionally giving the room the feeling of a wide, shallow pit. Shillingsworth's generals stared at him, at a loss. Was this a council of war? They had all been taught at the War College that such councils invariably were worthless, producing meek recommendations. You couldn't lead by committee, they'd been taught.

B. Z. Ames, sitting near the far end of the table, just to the left of "Wimpy" Wilson, sat impassively, head bent forward, staring at the table with no expression on his face. It was almost as if Ames were there under protest. Shillingsworth wouldn't have had him at the meeting except that he felt it impossible to hold a meeting of all the other Army four-stars and not invite him.

The head of the Army Materiel Command asked whether this discussion was even proper—if charges resulted from that sit-down strike or that last Sons of Liberty message, he wondered, might not this meeting be regarded as improper command influence? The Training and Doctrine commander seconded that concern.

Shillingsworth rejected their qualms. He shook his head. "The future of this United States Army, and its relationship to our civilian leaders and to the society we protect, is more important than whether or not the JAGs can collect the scalps of a few junior officers," he said.

Perhaps we should send a letter to all commanders to read aloud to their troops, offered the head of the Southern Command. Remind them of their duties.

At the far end of the conference table "Wimpy" Wilson stirred and frowned, but this change in expression was hard to detect, because Wilson's face always looked like it had been compressed down to a series of five horizontal lines—two across his forehead; one for his squinting eyes, the eyeballs themselves barely visible; one for his frowning mouth; one across the top of his jutting chin. The only ex-sergeant among the four-stars—Shillingsworth had been enlisted, but had been plucked for OCS before becoming an NCO—Wilson had the reputation of being the meanest general in the Army, especially to officers. He now was U.S. commander in Korea, scheduled to move in a few weeks to fill the vacant post of vice chief of staff of the Army. Wilson decided that he needed to play platoon sergeant counseling the lieutenant here.

"Fuck 'em," Wilson whispered, barely opening his mouth. "Just fuck 'em."

The heads at the table swiveled to look at Wilson. Shillingsworth invited him to elaborate on that course of action.

"Look, John," Wilson said, "you can't handle this by sending out cards and letters for commanders to staple on the company bulletin board next to TRICARE and COO notices. And you're not gonna deal with it just by having a heart-to-heart with a bunch of two-stars at Carlisle. That was a good first step, but you didn't follow through. So now you're swinging from your heels."

Wilson leaned forward. "You have to regain the initiative," he growled. "To do that, you need to get personal. Track down every one of them and nail them. Get ugly. Make it clear that Sons of Liberty will be like a skull and crossbones stamped on any officer's personnel file. Like the Navy did with Tailhook."

Shillingsworth nodded. Good old Wimpy.

No one else had much worthwhile to say. Shillingsworth brought the meeting to a close with a warning: The situation is going to get worse before it gets better, he predicted. The president won't pull out of Afghanistan at the end of the cooling-off period's designated sixty days, he said. "In fact, Mr. Pitch is talking to the NATO allies and Partnership for Peace nations about their reinforcing the mission. I think they'll have several nations signed up by the time the sixty-day deadline expires next month. In my opinion we are going to be there for at least a year."

Shillingsworth thought he saw Ames roll his eyes.

The Tom Custer House
Fort Leavenworth
1 P.M.

After that session Shillingsworth needed a run to uncoil his tense back and neck. He walked alone to his second-floor suite in the old brick Tom Custer House. He had forgotten that Ames, as the second-most-senior four-star present, would be assigned to the first floor.

When Shillingsworth came back downstairs in his PT gear, Ames was standing on the porch, also dressed for a run, and already leaning against the railing, stretching his calves. Their eyes met.

Decades of Army life had finely tuned each man's sense of protocol. In a microsecond, both did the calculations and arrived at the same in-eluctable answer: There was no way out of running together. It was just not done. Spending an hour shoulder to shoulder was the last thing either wanted to do. It would be like being stuck together in a broken elevator, but somehow worse, because it would be less passive. Each would have to constantly repress the physical urge to peel off. And each also would need to summon mental restraint. Both had sensed that they had avoided a harsh confrontation only by minimizing their contact with each other. General Shillingsworth feared that in this run, his distaste for Ames's ma-nipulative ambition would pour out. General Ames, meanwhile, would have to contain his contempt for Shillingsworth's holier-than-thou stodgi-ness. He also would have to rein in his anger, which could lead him to un-consciously run the older, heavier Shillingsworth into the ground.

They started slowly on Grant Avenue, heading west toward Zais Park. They took a left at the Custer Chapel and began the loop around the Dis-ciplinary Barracks—the "Little House" at the northern end of Leaven-worth, home of the military prisoners, who in turn had built the "Big House," the heavy gray federal penitentiary bordering the southern end of the post.

They sloped down along the red-brick wall of the military prison. Ames decided to keep the conversation on as neutral and intellectual a level as possible. "Did you see Sean Naylor's piece in *Army Times* about fire ver-sus maneuver?" he asked. Don't lope out in front of him, he reminded himself.

It was the wrong question. Shillingsworth had indeed seen the column and had wondered to himself if Ames was the anonymous "one general" quoted in it who had painted Shillingsworth as a well-meaning but rather dim-witted attritionist.

"Yeah, I did," Shillingsworth said. "I thought it showed a lack of under-standing of our nation's history." He was puffing a bit already, Ames no-ticed, pausing between his sentences. "I think you should always fight based on your strengths. Maneuver needs seasoned soldiers." Pause. "Simple fact is, this nation is never going to go into the start of a war with enough adequately trained troops." The red-brick wall of the military prison cut downhill, toward the Missouri River, running swifter in its dredged channel than when Lewis and Clark had been the first Army of-ficers to lead a patrol by its bank exactly two hundred years earlier. "It does you no good to be expeditionary if you get smashed by the other guy when you get there." Pause. "I want to be able to put fires on target. Heavy fires."

Shillingsworth thought of extreme maneuverists like Ames as danger-ously romantic cavalrymen. They'd dash all over the countryside, full of sound and fury, like Jeb Stuart gone missing at Gettysburg when Lee needed him. It worried him that they'd crumble the first time they ran into heavy forces. But until that time they sounded good—the politicians and the media ate up that stuff. The press boys had admired Custer right into his grave, he thought to himself.

They hadn't discussed how long the run would be. Ames had assumed that a big guy like Shillingsworth would be a three- to five-mile man. Anyone taller than six feet seemed to peter out by five, he'd noticed, especially on a day such as this, when the late-June heat was rolling east from the prairie. Ames assumed that when they hit the riverbank, Shillingsworth would cut right for the home stretch back to the Tom Custer House. But when they came to the water's edge, Shillingsworth surprised the smaller man by turning left and taking the flat path toward the post's airstrip. This was going to be a long run.

Shillingsworth thought maneuverism was logical but best seen as a strategy of the weak—which the American military wasn't. "The well-provided rely on attrition," he said aloud, but talking to himself as much as to Ames. "Warfare—at least land warfare, which I know—isn't about Sun Tzu, his idea of winning by not killing the other guy.

"We don't get style points in our business," he lectured, taking advan-tage of the flat ground to talk more. "Mud soldiering is about pounding the shit out of the other guy. It is about the infliction of violence, pain and death. You do that with fires on target. Give me more and better tanks, self-propelled artillery and decent close air support. The other guy can run all over the countryside talking about 'augfarstrik' or whatever, and I'll still pound the crap out of him. Every time he moves, he voluntarily light-ens his load—and so lessens his firepower." He seemed to be gaining steam as he ran rather than slowing down, Ames noticed. "Overwhelming force at the crucial point, that's what I'm talking about," Shillingsworth concluded. "Find and destroy the enemy's fielded forces."

Ames considered Shillingsworth's statement. "But the way to victory may not be the shortest path," he said. "I believe modern war is more about dislocation than about killing."

"You want victory?" Shillingsworth responded. "Then destroy the enemy—however, whenever and wherever you can, as long as you can get more of him than he can get of you."

"You sound like Ulysses S. Grant," Ames said quietly, almost under his breath.

"I'll take that as a compliment," Shillingsworth said, knowing that it wasn't meant as one.

Shillingsworth would never be chosen by the current president to be chairman of the Joint Chiefs. But he might by the next. Both men knew their quiet but intense competition for the top slot in the U.S. military made the stakes in their argument far weightier than an officers' club debate. If the nation went to war in a few years, the fate of thousands of American troops could be determined by which view prevailed.

They jogged in silence back up the other side of the damp airstrip and then doubled back to the riverbank. This spot, where Fort Leavenworth met the Missouri, was Shillingsworth's favorite part of his favorite post. Just to their right, on the slope leading up the bluff to the post's buildings, the ruts of the Oregon Trail still were visible in the grass. He could see in his mind's eye the wagons straining uphill, the families heading west into the unknown, mothers and small children walking up the bluff to lighten the load on the oxen, already debating what goods to dump.

As they started up the slope, Ames began to respond. "Guderian says—"

"Guderian lost," Shillingsworth interrupted. He puffed for a second, then added, "and so did Rommel and all those other guys the maneuverists love."

"But that was an industrial advantage, not a tactical one," Ames said. "We just had more."

They reached the crest and at the French cannon turned past Bell Hall and toward the cemetery. Shillingsworth waited to respond until he had recovered from the run up the hill. "My point exactly," Shillingsworth finally said. "That is how this nation wins." Ames instantly understood the implied insult: A good general must understand his nation better than you apparently do.

Ames withdrew from the argument. I am not going to persuade this dullard of anything, he thought. They ran on in silence for miles around the cemetery and down toward the tall gray walls of the federal prison floating in the prairie's June haze. I wonder how long he intends to go. Ames realized that Shillingsworth was turning it into a ten-miler. Macho bullshit, he thought. Typical infantry move.

Had Ames better understood Shillingsworth, he would have known that the long run was actually directed more at himself than at Ames. Shillingsworth had a habit of running off his anger, not stopping until he was calmer.

Ames thought about the red-faced man chugging alongside him. He thinks maneuverism is too dangerous, the strategy of the weak? The unimaginative, uneducated military mind will always think that. Creativity and risk taking scare people like him.

They ran past the gravestones, looking like a forest of stumps. More victims of bad generals, Ames thought.

Bad generals will always choose the certainty of direct attack, despite the predictable casualties, over the indirect, with its hope of fewer casualties, Ames thought. Thus Omar Bradley questioning MacArthur's plan for Inchon. Go for the short envelopment, Bradley advised. This is the incremental approach—expand your perimeter—that appeals to the stolid, unimaginative, good soldier like Bradley or Shillingsworth. Three yards and a cloud of dust. We know now that the short envelopment was a prescription for failure, exactly what the North Koreans were preparing for.

Put a different kind of adversary in front of Shillingsworth and he is clueless, Ames thought as they came back toward Eisenhower Hall and the Buffalo Soldiers' Monument. Look at how the Sons of Liberty thing has him flummoxed. Leaving the U.S. military to the Shillingsworths would be a dereliction of duty—as obscene as letting the horse cavalry land and charge into interlocking fields of German machine-gun fire at Omaha Beach.

Shillingsworth, his face gone from red to white, finally pulled up puffing next to the man-made pond below the Buffalo Soldiers' statue. They walked slowly. Ames detected the beginnings of a stitch in his side. He sat on a cement bench under a planted sapling.

In some way, both men understood that their argument, most of it conducted in silence, had been about the Sons of Liberty and about their duty as generals. Ames pointed to the "Soldier's Oath," engraved in metal and placed on the tablet next to the bench: "I do solemnly swear that I will support and defend the Constitution against all enemies, foreign and domestic," he read aloud. He repeated the last phrase: "and domestic."

Shillingsworth looked at him. What the hell was Ames up to? He didn't know. "I prefer the Phil Sheridan quote," he said. " 'I never discussed the Constitution very much, but I have done a good deal of fighting for it.' "

When General Ames got home to Washington that night, he used the second laptop in his study, the one reserved for more sensitive communications, to send a note to Senator Feaver, chairman of the Armed Services Committee. *It is the considered private opinion of our distinguished Army chief of staff that we will be in Afghanistan at least a year, maybe longer,* he wrote. He wondered if Shillingsworth would have the guts to say in public to Armed Services what he said at Leavenworth about the duration of the Afghan mission.

The Pentagon
4:30 P.M.

With both Shillingsworth and Ames away at the Leavenworth meeting, Sherman and Lewis had a relatively quiet day. Late in the afternoon she called down to his office and got that jerk of an NCO on the line, Sergeant First Class Stout.

"Can I give him a message, ma'am?" Stout demanded. Lewis was right behind him, but he liked to take messages from outside callers.

"No, Sergeant First Class," she said, giving him the respect of using his full rank, "I want to speak to him." When Lewis picked up, she said, "Can you meet me in Marineland?"

Stout hadn't hung up his extension. He wondered what these two were up to in Marineland. He also wondered about the nature of the relationship between the two officers, both new to their staff positions. He made it his business to know these things. He considered it part of his duty in protecting Ames to track the people who enjoyed access to the general.

They met at the "Moe, Larry and Curly" sign, up on the deserted fifth-floor hallway of the Pentagon's E ring. It was still half attic. To long-legged Lewis, walking its empty stretches was like hitting the open highways of the Mojave after being trapped in Los Angeles traffic.

He always felt awkward seeing her at the Pentagon—it wasn't professional to kiss someone else in uniform in public. He stuck out his hand in greeting. She took it, looked to see that they were alone and pulled him into a kiss. She didn't notice that a Marine brigadier inside the staff office was watching them through the glass of his office door.

They began walking. Despite their kiss they kept on their game faces, walking and talking as if they were simply two more majors prepping a prebrief for their bosses. The unwritten rule of the Pentagon was that officer-officer relationships were kept quiet. You didn't want to be dropped for consideration for some choice billet because some colonel said, "Oh, she'll never take a job in Honolulu, she has a serious thing going with a guy I know here."

Also, the Pentagon wasn't a trusting place. The relationship between Sherman and Lewis would be seen in some quarters as a back channel between the offices of the Army chief of staff and the vice chairman of the Joint Chiefs. Those around the vice chairman were watched closely because that position always ran the Joint Requirements Oversight Council, which as the supreme arbiter of military equipment needs had a huge say in deciding whose pockets ultimately received the $58 billion the Pentagon spent annually on procurement. So the other services would be interested, even suspicious, to see a special relationship between aides from those two offices.

The Marines were best at tracking this sort of thing, which is odd, because with just 6 percent of the overall Pentagon budget, they weren't big enough to be threatening to the other services. But they were big enough to be a useful ally. Precisely because they had so little to offer in the way of funding trade-offs, they had learned to trade in the Pentagon's other currency, information. The Marines were very good at gathering the inside scoop and then conveying it to "friends of the Corps."

And so as Sherman and Lewis walked, Marine Brigadier General Moe told his executive assistant to start a file "on those two Army majors." The aide knew what that meant: personal records, current responsibilities, any negative information from the past.

Innocent of the attention they were receiving, Sherman and Lewis continued down the hall. She told him she was worried by how gaunt General Shillingsworth was looking, as if he were on a crash diet. "He can take the Afghanistan thing—remember, he goes back to Vietnam, when they lost five hundred soldiers a week sometimes," she said as they began walking. "I think it is this Sons of Liberty stuff that is really gnawing at him. I don't know who those guys are, but I think they are way off the reservation." For a time she had planned to give Lewis a hint about her role in the investigation of the Sons of Liberty, but after seeing him participate in the sit-down strike had decided against it.

Lewis was far more sympathetic to the insurgent group. "I mean, you talk like they're a bunch of fascists," he said. "But you know who they are. It's guys like me. People you know from the Academy, from Bragg, from Ranger School, from Irwin, from Kosovo and Montenegro, from Algeria.

"From what I know of them," he continued, "the Sons of Liberty are the real leaders in our military, the people who lead the small combat units, the ones I'd want watching my back in combat. They're the warriors." He was talking as much to himself as to her. "It isn't any big conspiracy, you know," Lewis added. "It's just a bunch of guys venting through e-mails."

She listened in silence as they marched along the small, snaking fifth-floor ring. Piles of old desks and chairs were stacked along the corridor, deposited there by a Pentagon office that was moving—there always was some Pentagon office that was moving. She was never easy when soldiers talked of "warriors," which she took as a code word for excluding women from combat roles.

" 'Warrior,' " she repeated back to him. "I hate that 'warrior' talk. Warriors only fight wars. We are soldiers, doing tough jobs in peace as well as war. If the U.S. Army is warriors, then it is a separate group, like knights of the Middle Ages, nobles doing battle in shining armor. But we are not individual fighters, and we are not a separate class. We're a team, the American Army. Americans."

She turned to look at him. "Also, I think it is kind of macho bullshit."

He tried to keep it light. "You can call it macho bullshit, but until someone figures out a better way to get scared, pimply eighteen-year-old males to stand up and charge machine-gun nests, I'm sticking with it," he said. He had heard that line in the Fort Irwin Officers' Club and had always liked it.

She was having none of it. "You don't need macho for that. Macho gets your people killed for nothing. You know that—that's why we train people not to be John Wayne. In real life, the John Wayne character frontally assaults the machine gun for no reason, instead of using one team to pin it down and another to hit its flank, and he gets gut shot and uses a colostomy bag the rest of his life—if he's lucky. You want to take a machine-gun nest, give me training, cohesion and, most of all, leadership."

They walked the hallway in silence for a few minutes, snaking around piles of filing cabinets and desks. "Exactly," Lewis finally said. "Leadership. I think the Sons of Liberty are our real leaders, the natural leaders in the officer corps. And that is the pack you've always wanted to run with. So why aren't you with us?"

She looked at him sharply, taken aback by his use of "us." They fell silent. But the question hung in the air between them: *Us?* They walked in silence for several minutes.

This had been, she thought later, the Clausewitzian point of culmination where you escalate to a new level or withdraw from the engagement. He had laid down the challenge. She had taken it. He knew her well enough to know she would.

She gave him both barrels. "I think that at some point, they—and you, if you're one of them—got way out of line. A military is only as good as its service to its nation." Her voice took on a sharper edge as the words rushed out of her. "I'm a traditionalist, a believer in traditional military values. All this Sons of Liberty stuff about doing what is right by the military, it misses the point. When the order is given, it is our duty to figure out the best way to accomplish that mission, whether we like it or not— whether it is good for us or not."

He said nothing. She considered the implied charge she was bringing against him. If it is true, then how do I fit in his life? she asked herself. The fear came to her: I am his fling, his dalliance with the Other, the bohemian he slummed with for a couple of months. After me he will revert back to his norm, find a good girl to settle down with and remember me as his last great indiscretion. His little brush with that goofy painter, she thought. It scared her.

He sensed that the conversation was simultaneously political and personal, and veering into danger in both areas. "What you mean, Major, is that we began watching out for ourselves," he said in the flat tone officers learned in the field to use in radio communications, holding on to emotional neutrality as their situation grew more threatening, as in "That's an affirmative, Sierra Six, we'll be needing more ammunition and plasma, and my left foot just got blown off." Using that empty voice in a personal conversation was his way of communicating disdain.

"Vietnam, Somalia, Algeria, Afghanistan—we were slow on the uptake, sure, but eventually we learned we had to begin watching out for ourselves." He paused, almost inserting the radio communication break between each sentence. "If we don't, who will?" Pause. "Not this White

House." Pause. "Not the other politicians." Pause. "Certainly not the media."

He walked on angrily, outpacing her slightly, his words trailing over his shoulder at her. "Do you know that the White House ordered that doomed patrol out in Afghanistan over the objection of the commander on the scene? Do you?"

"No," she said, "I didn't. That sucks, if it's true. How do you know that?"

"Yeah, it is true, and yes, it does suck. People I trust tell me it's true. The question is, what are you willing to do about it?" He turned and confronted her. "If not us, then who? If not now, then when?"

They had made a complete circuit of the fifth floor, passing only three people the entire way. Now they were back to where they had started, at the Marine "Moe, Larry and Curly" sign. They stopped and faced each other at arm's length. He was just warming up. He really is into the Sons of Liberty stuff, she thought.

"And it isn't just watching out for ourselves," he continued. "It's watching out for our troops. You have to keep an eye on presidents. They just use troops, spend them. I don't like people who use people." He looked at her accusingly, his chin lifted.

Was he veering back into the personal, saying that she'd used him? The mix was getting volatile.

She tried to move the talk back to the safer ground of military professionalism. "Even good military leaders spend their troops. Look at Gettysburg," she said. With his love of history, she knew he would know the battlefield, hour by hour, decision by decision, from the seminary to Little Round Top. "Early on day one, the Union is pulling back from Oak Hill," she said. "A company of Minnesotans is ordered to counterattack up the Mummasburg road—even as the Union line is retreating behind them. Their regimental commander knew he was likely condemning those men. They knew it too, but they went in anyway and took eighty percent casualties." She looked at him. Are you with me? she wondered.

"And that sacrifice at the northern end of the battlefield may have saved the nation," he countered. "The important thing is that the Federal colonel knew what he was doing. Sometimes you spend your troops; I understand that. But the military deal is, you are required to do it wisely. He did." He looked at her, pained. "This president doesn't. Shick squandered those fifteen troops in Afghanistan—sixteen now. He may be a tightwad with the federal budget, with his tax dollars. But he's a spendthrift with our lives."

"Don't you see," she said quickly, the words enthusiastically tumbling out. "That *is* the deal, the bigger deal, the political deal. You get some good presidents, you get some bad ones. I don't like the one we have. But he is in charge. And that isn't open to argument. We go down your route, we become a banana republic."

His mouth and flat cheekbones took on a set, harder look. He was becoming exasperated with this easy talk of spending troops. "You can't just say, 'Oh, well, I lost my people, better luck next time, that's the way things work,'" he said to her in a rush of angry words, his head bobbing from side to side as he mocked her. Then he stopped moving his head. He wanted to convey to her just how dangerous her position was. "Cindy, we go down your route," he said slowly, "we lose everything that is best about this military, about this nation. We break faith with the people we lead."

She sensed in his intensity that he was reaching out to her. Despite the huge difference that was emerging between them, he didn't want to break faith with her. But she would have to verbalize his move, she sensed. He wouldn't—he couldn't. He had been trained for years to keep his emotions out of his words, to keep his tone even when he felt terror nipping at his shoulders.

"Look, Buddy," she said. "I think that much of what you say is right. I love the Army, just like you. And I hated to see what happened to that patrol. But I think your view is incomplete. Taking care of your troops— that can't be your highest good. The military can't be governed by its own self-interest. Our ultimate duty as officers is to the nation, not to ourselves. That's selfless service. We serve—*serve*—and protect. S.L.A. Marshall says that distinction, that willingness to sacrifice ourselves, is all that elevates the soldier's claim above the civilian's. Lose that, he warned, and the nation has lost its hold on its security."

She struggled to express this without making him feel she was attacking him. "So I think there is more to it than just your right. There are other things that are right. There is more to this country than just the military."

"Yeah, right," he said dismissively. "I guess I'm just so narrow-minded that I object to throwing my life away." He looked up at the arched ceiling in exasperation. "Boy, it didn't take Cindy Sherman long to go native in Washington."

She was losing him, and she panicked. "Oh, just fuck off, Lewis." She regretted the words but couldn't help continuing. "I think you should go back to B. Z. Ames. He's the one you should be sleeping with."

Lewis's dark brown eyes searched her face, his mouth half open. "Cindy?" It was an expression of pain and contrition, not a question.

Lewis wasn't a rude man. Rather than fight her, he wheeled and left, flinging open the door to the stairway.

She stood silently, alone in the old hallway. The door hissed shut behind him. Why am I such an idiot? she asked herself.

She leaned her forehead against the corridor wall, pulling in breaths, trying to calm herself. From nowhere, it occurred to her how General Ames had known when they were introduced that "this Sherman" was from Georgia. There could only be one way: He had considered her as a possible aide and had read her personnel file. But he hadn't interviewed her—which meant she hadn't even made it into the final group. She wasn't Ames's type of officer.

A small, cheerful crew-cut man emerged from the office of the Commandant's Staff Group. "Major, you look like you could use some help," he said.

Sherman was startled to see the single star of a brigadier general on each of the man's khaki collar points. She pulled herself together, straightened up. "No, sir," she said. "I mean, thank you, sir."

"Well, I'm Brigadier General Moe," he said. "If you ever need help, you just give us a call. We Marines hate to see a pretty woman upset."

Cindy walked slowly down the stairs back to the Army corridor. Maybe she was asking too much of Buddy. She needed to withdraw a little, breathe some of the solitary air that was her natural environment.

The Old Soviet Highway
Southwestern Afghanistan
Thursday, June 16
10 P.M.

All that the commander of the 10th Mountain Division's Forward Support Battalion lived for were her battalion and her extended family—the Army.

She had given up everything else for battalion command. She had enlisted twenty-one years earlier to get away from home and had never looked back. She had stayed in touch with just one sister, and that only for the exchange of Christmas cards. When her father died she hadn't even gone back to Tennessee for the funeral.

Meanwhile the Army had detected her native intelligence and shipped her off first to get a bachelor's degree and then to become an officer. It had been a good and rewarding career.

But when she had received orders to move from Fort Lewis to Fort Drum to take over the battalion, her husband had gone morose for a month, then announced that he wouldn't be accompanying her. "I'm not going back to Drum," he said. Having retired from the Army four years earlier, he was happy with his job with General Dynamics Land Systems helping outfit the new medium-weight Brigade Combat Team at Fort Lewis. Almost as an afterthought, he said he thought their marriage was over.

She didn't fight him, nor did she ever contemplate not going. She had waited twenty years for battalion command—far longer than she had waited for him. Having a battalion was the best job in the Army, in any military. It was the first time you had a staff to help you out, to implement a variety of orders that allowed you to train and shape and lead the unit. But it was the last time you really still led in person, knew all your troops by name and face.

And it had proven to be all she expected. To her soldiers, she was a remote figure, operating echelons above the reality of their platoons. But like a good battalion commander, she saw it all. She worked with her captains and NCOs. She mentored her platoon leaders, lunching with all twelve of them on the first Tuesday of every month. "You have the hardest job in the military," she would tell them. "You are leading people who know more about your assigned tasks than you do." The challenge, she reminded them, was to learn from them while leading them.

It scared her sometimes that she cared so much about her battalion. She found taking them to Afghanistan nerve-racking, partly because her unit was split, with two of her companies up at Camp Noble Effort and the third at the airstrip sixty miles south that the U.S. was using to supply the camp. It was built on the old Soviet highway southeast of Herat, where C-17s landed once an hour. From there the goods were trucked twice weekly in fifty-vehicle convoys to Noble Effort.

. . .

Two of the commander's soldiers, both Spec 4s from the extra-duty detail—the dumping ground for sad sacks who just slowed down their regular units—walked quietly at night through a maze of containers set up alongside the runway, partly to block the line of sight to prevent potshots at aircraft. An unintended result was that most movement within the maze couldn't be observed from any of the guardposts around the area.

As the two soldiers came around the corner to the secluded spot where they had sex two or three nights a week, they were caught by their arms and knocked to the ground by wooden clubs. Two men held their arms behind them while a third blindfolded and gagged them with turban cloth. They were pushed out a hole cut in the perimeter wire and thrown over the backs of two camels.

The Afghans were surprised at how light one of the soldiers was. They only discovered at dawn that she was female. The Americans, they decided, were being truly insulting, sending women to fight against them.

The American soldiers' platoon leaders discovered their absence shortly after dawn at morning formation. The consensus of the company was that the two were such lowlifes that they just might have been stupid enough to desert into the hostile environment of the Afghan desert.

That belief was put aside a few hours later, when a handwritten notice was delivered to the front gate by a goatherd. It stated on lined paper that the two were being held as a reminder to the U.S. government that it had promised that it was only intervening in Afghanistan for sixty days—and that the deadline was coming up in a few weeks. When that promise was kept, said the Front for the Purity of Afghan Soil, the soldiers would be released unharmed.

The battalion commander was livid. She wanted to respond with everything the U.S. military had. She was left speechless when she reported to the assistant division commander and his first order was to tell her to shut down e-mail systems.

"Begging your pardon, sir, my people weren't abducted by e-mail," she said with some puzzlement.

The ADC explained: They weren't going to give their opponents in Afghanistan one more tool with which to sway American public opinion against them. Especially with an "out of Afghanistan now" demonstration outside the White House scheduled for June 26.

"Sir, I don't think we can keep this quiet," she protested.

No, the brigadier said, we can—and you will. Shut down e-mail, slow down your mails and morale phones. Tell your commanders it is a requirement of operational security, and have them tell the troops this is how we get their comrades back.

Like a good soldier, she set about her assigned task, feeling all the while like she was concealing a funeral. Just when you think you've given the Army everything you can, she thought, it comes up with something else to ask of you. Duty was often the least rewarding of the military virtues.

Subbasement 3, CIA Headquarters
6 P.M.

At chin-pulling seminars at the National Defense University, the critics said that information warfare was bullshit, Cisco recalled as he sat down alone in his basement office to launch the next, most critical phase of his project.

He turned on the laptop controlling the two big borrowed Crays—the '57 Chevys of supercomputers, he thought affectionately, low tech but with lots of horses under the hood. Using them to track every antiaircraft emplacement in the Iraqi no-fly zones was kind of an abuse of their talents, he thought. He would use them instead to monitor all incoming portals to the National Security Agency's cleansers.

Most talk about information warfare probably was just nonsense, he conceded to himself. When IW had surfaced as a nineties buzzword, there had been a lot of piling on. Everybody who did anything remotely relating to information, from electronic jamming to psychological operations, suddenly held himself out as an "infowarrior." That was natural enough—with the shrinking defense budgets of the nineties, IW was one of the few places that actually got more money. Billions of it, some of it flowing into the most classified niches of the U.S. defense establishment. In a way, all the nonsense about IW helped, because it obscured the real IW work that he and a few other people were doing.

Cisco wasn't even sure his little operation formally existed on paper. But what he was doing was real enough.

By dawn the Crays had narrowed the Sons of Liberty's possible routes into the NSA's cleansers from two thousand to twenty-five. Finding which of those twenty-five were actually live routes would be a bit harder.

A day later the Crays shook loose the answer: two lines out of the Pentagon that weren't listed on any of Cisco's charts of the national security information architecture, even the most highly classified charts. Someone was being cute, trying to hide by using those lines.

But the subterfuge also made those lines vulnerable. The off-the-books lines weren't being routinely monitored by the counterintelligence drones for intrusions.

It took him Friday and most of Saturday to set up the Paragon XPS and the Digger for his attack. Once he caught a message going in, he would send the Paragon to get into the computer sending the message. Then he would use the Digger to remotely ransack its hard drive for key words and phrases such as "Afghanistan" and "Captain America," and he would find out which computers it communicated with. Then he would go interrogate those computers. And so on, across the Defense Department network.

He was particularly impressed with the structure of interrogation he had devised. How to deal with tens of thousands of terminals? He told the Paragon to look for the rank-sensitive information embedded in computer security clearances. First it would isolate any four-star generals playing footsie with the Sons of Liberty, then three-stars, and so on down the line.

But before any of that could happen, someone would have to use one of those two lines into the NSA.

Senate Armed Services Committee Hearing Room
Hart Senate Office Building
Friday, June 17
10:25 A.M.

It was the first scorching day of the year, and the air-conditioning in the Senate hearing room had been cranked up to overdrive, dropping the room almost twenty degrees below the outside late-morning temperature of eighty-six and making the marble veneer in the room cold to the touch. Shillingsworth stood in front of the witnesses' table, making small talk with senators on the committee, most of whom had come over to inform him that in today's hearing they would be hitting him hard, but that there was nothing personal to it. He had learned that this was what was meant by "senatorial courtesy"—the mugger advised it was nothing personal before he slipped in the knife.

Sherman sat in the first row of seats behind him, the ones reserved for aides to the witnesses, reviewing his written testimony. The Army's chief legislative liaison had jovially assured her that General Shillingsworth's written statement met "the opposite test," but she wasn't quite sure what that meant. "This is your first big hearing, right?" the liaison had then correctly asked.

Senator Feaver gaveled the hearing open and curtly said that he would dispense with the usual opening statements from senators this morning. "We have a lot to hear from General Shillingsworth today, and much to say to him," he said ominously.

Reporters at the press tables looked at one another. This wasn't the usual slow-moving Senator Feaver they knew. "Who pissed in his cereal bowl this morning?" the defense reporter from *Congressional Quarterly* asked his tablemates, quietly alerting his less-seasoned colleagues that something was afoot here.

At the witness table General Shillingsworth began reading aloud his prepared statement, which had been carefully reviewed, amended and edited by staffers from legislative liaison, JAG and public affairs. The final effect, as the liaison officer had intimated to Sherman, was that almost every line of the statement said exactly the opposite of what the general really meant.

"Mr. Chairman, distinguished senators, thank you for the opportunity to appear again before this distinguished committee." (*That is, I'd rather be anywhere else than here today.*) "There have been some major developments in Central Asia, but our military stance in the region remains vigilant and essentially unchanged." (*We got our clocks cleaned, we lost sixteen people for no good reason and our policy there is a shambles.*) "We have suffered casualties, but by every standard, the performance of our troops in the field has been magnificent." (*That patrol never should have been sent out there.*) "I know the members of this committee share with me a keen appreciation for the professionalism and courage of the superb Americans who represent us in a difficult mission along the Afghan zone of separation." (*You guys don't have a clue about the kids out there, do you? They're not part of your crowd. They're small-town America, boys looking for adventure, trying the soldier's life, maybe getting some occupational training; girls looking to get out of bad situations with boyfriends or at home, maybe where somebody smacks them around or a stepfather comes into their bedroom at night. Only the old ones among you on this committee have any direct military experience. You younger ones with the blow-dried hair don't, and you don't even know anyone in the military, do you? We're just the dumb servants nowadays, doing your chores.*) "I thank you for your help in keeping America's military the world's finest, a force for peace and stability. Your leadership has been of great value and is sincerely appreciated." (*I know that you have a constitutional role to play, but you're not helping me here, especially if you're just looking to score political points on the president while American kids are dying over there. Paint him in a corner and it'll be the Army, not you, that pays the price.*) "Now, I am not at liberty to discuss our plans for Afghanistan—"

"General," the chairman interrupted, doubling the discourtesy by using only Shillingsworth's rank to address him. He hunched over the microphone. "General, I think we're gonna cut to the chase today. I thank you for your statement and we will make it part of the written record." He turned in his chair and summoned a waiting aide with a curled finger. "I'm gonna distribute to my colleagues right here a very interesting message I received this morning, which disturbed me greatly. General, I'd like to hear your comment on this document." With another wave of the hand he indicated that the waiting copies should be distributed to the fourteen senators looking at him along the curved wooden dais. General Shillingsworth remained blank-faced at this turn of events. He had no idea what "this document" was. At the long press tables the reporters looked at one another and then down at their minicassette recorders to make sure the machines were getting every word. News was being committed here. The still photographers crouched at the base of the dais below the chairman checked to make sure they had plenty of exposures left.

When all the senators had glanced at the document and frowned, Senator Feaver announced that he would read it aloud for the benefit of everyone else. " 'Johnny, like I said: You have to hold them off for me and for POTUS,' " he began. Shillingsworth shuddered inwardly but his face remained passive. He recognized it instantly. It was the e-mail he had re-

ceived last night from Defense Secretary Johnson, cc'd to the chairman
and vice chairman of the Joint Chiefs. It had come in around 9 P.M. How
the hell did Feaver get it in under twelve hours?

Feaver continued to read aloud: " 'If Feaver comes after you on troop
commitments for Afghanistan, tap-dance around it. We have to line up
the allies before we take this to the Hill. I've told NATO we will almost
certainly commit to twelve months. But that can't go public yet. I know
Feaver from years of working with him—he hates confrontation.' " Feaver
gave the piece of paper a slight rattle, underscoring his view that the defense secretary had once again misread him, just as he had so frequently
when he was in the Senate. " 'So just huff and puff and tap-dance and let
the clock run out, and he won't come after you. Tell him no decision has
been made—technically, that's true, because POTUS hasn't signed the
decision memorandum yet. SecDef/P4.' " That "P4" was Pentagon shorthand for "personal for the eyes of the recipients only." Now the entire
world was hearing it as it was used to sandbag the Army chief.

Feaver's right hand slowly laid the paper down on the dais, as if it were
a thin sheet of glass that would shatter if mishandled. "General, I'd appreciate your explaining just what that message means."

Shillingsworth tried the soft-shoe approach. "Well, sir, it is a challenging mission, especially in a resource-constrained environment," he began.
"And I am not the author of that message. . . ."

Under normal circumstances, the committee chairman might have accepted those weasel words, which basically said, *Look, you've got us
nailed, Senator.*

But the e-mail message had gotten under Feaver's skin. *Let's see who
hates this confrontation more, you or me.* The chairman leaned forward.
"Suppose you just tell me what is going on."

Shillingsworth considered that request for a moment. Where he had
grown up, in rural Pennsylvania, you didn't read other people's mail. *OK,*
he thought, *I'll tell you.* "That is an internal communication," he said
clearly and slowly, "not meant to be read by anyone but a few people at
the Pentagon."

"Be that as it may, I find it a very interesting one," Senator Feaver
drawled. "It communicates quite a lot to me. I would like your explanation of just what is going on here."

Shillingsworth looked down at the table. The legislative liaison frantically wrote a note on his long yellow legal pad and slipped it in front of

him, suggesting that he tell the chairman to ask the defense secretary about the note. Shillingsworth rejected the idea. He wasn't going to hide behind semantics. He returned the chairman's gaze. "I am unable to comment further on it, sir. I mean to say, I will not, sir."

Senator Feaver's eyes narrowed. Years of hearings with military brass had sensitized him to the subtle messages generals sent with a slight alteration in wording and tone. He sensed the double-edged meaning of the "sir" in every sentence: Shillingsworth was saying he would respect the position but not the person holding it. The senator slapped right back, with a heavy-handed and condescending "General." He leaned so far forward that his head was actually in front of his shoulders, not above it. It made Sherman think of the attack posture of an angry goose.

"General, is it your personal opinion that the United States Army, which is raised by this Congress, will be in Afghanistan more than the announced sixty days?" He glared at Shillingsworth.

General Shillingsworth sounded remote. He had made his decision. The primary duty of the soldier was to keep going. "Sir, I regret that I am not able to answer that question at this time."

Senator Feaver had him trapped. "General, I remind you that, in keeping with the agreement you expressly made during your confirmation by the United States Senate, whose commission you hold, you are required to give your personal opinion when it is demanded of you," he said with a hard edge in his voice, which conveyed the message that he was quite willing to destroy John Shillingsworth or anyone else who challenged the powers of the U.S. Senate. "I am requiring you to respond."

The still photographers wheeled in their crouches and pointed their telephoto lenses at General Shillingsworth. "I will not, sir," he said. The motor drives in the photographers' expensive cameras whirled and clicked, capturing each jerk of his facial muscles as his jaw set in anger and resolve.

The chairman spoke as if Shillingsworth were entering a guilty plea. "Do you . . . decline to testify . . . on this matter . . . before this committee?"

"Sir, with the deepest respect for this committee and for the United States Senate, I feel I have no other course."

"Then, General, there is nothing more to say here today. I must say that of all the Joint Chiefs of Staff, it was perhaps from you that I least expected this sort of political game of carrying water for the White House," Feaver said. Shillingsworth realized that Feaver thought he was refusing for political reasons rather than for reasons of honor and duty. The angry chairman continued: "But I warn you, General, this matter is not over— not by a long shot." He raised the gavel high above his right shoulder and slammed it onto the table. The report of the gavel echoed off the cold marble of the room's walls. "This hearing is suspended until further notice." He turned to his staff counsel. "Tell me what I can do to this asshole."

General Ames's Office
11:45 A.M.

Before becoming an Army officer, Bobby Byrnes had cut a wide swath at Harvard. He had been a member of the Reserve Officer Training Corps, which had bused over to MIT for its training. In the fall of 2001 the faculty stormily debated bringing ROTC back to Harvard for the first time since the Vietnam War, with the sixties-vintage senior faculty using threats about tenure to club down an insurgent effort by the more conservative junior professors. A group of students called "Campus with a Conscience," opposed to the reintroduction of ROTC, staged a protest on the steps of the library.

Byrnes had made headlines when he led a counterprotest across the Yard, with two dozen Harvard students in their ROTC military uniforms standing at parade rest and wearing black armbands of mourning. "We regret that our fellow students who come from privileged backgrounds aren't willing to open up Harvard to less wealthy students who might, with ROTC scholarships, be able to gain access to the college's unique benefits," he told the *Crimson* and *The Boston Globe,* attacking on the unexpected front of class warfare. It was a bit disingenuous, considering that his father, an avionics engineer, was a highly paid executive of a defense contractor, Northrop Grumman Corporation, outside New York City. But it was quotable, guilt-inducing and effective.

Byrnes had more in common with his classmates than he recognized. Most notably, he didn't appreciate the vast difference between being smart and being wise. Like many Harvard students, he tended to overvalue analytical intelligence and undervalue a good attitude, common sense and varied experience. Those weren't traits that won people admission to Harvard, but in them lay the essence of a good military officer.

And so when he actually went on active duty, Bobby Byrnes descended into disaffected boredom. Like many Harvard kids, he half thought that in a just world he would be in charge. In his first billet, on the staff of the separate airborne infantry brigade based in Macedonia, he had essentially been a protocol officer, memorizing the names of greasy host-nation cabinet officers as they came and went in their ill-fitting brown suits. He had done better on the headquarters staff of the 101st Airborne, where he polished the general's speeches to the local chambers of commerce, and then as a company commander. But he still felt he was moving painfully slowly. It was agony to see old classmates taking their high-tech companies public while he languished in Fort Campbell, Kentucky, double-checking bedsheet lists for the battalion inventory.

Then he had been drafted as the speechwriter for the head of the Army Logistics Command, Lieutenant General William Still, a reserved, slightly pompous black man who had attended some A & M college for the children of tobacco farmers in the North Carolina sandhills that Byrnes had never heard of. At his fifth reunion, Byrnes just told classmates that he was posted to the Pentagon and let them assume he had some snazzy job on the Joint Staff. It would have been too humiliating to confess that he was tucked away in a Pentagon backwater writing speeches about maintenance depots and base closings. To get to his obscure office he had to walk past a Dumpster.

But now he had been invited for a one-on-one with the vice chairman of the Joint Chiefs. Now he was going somewhere.

Ames waited until the young captain had settled comfortably into the wing chair in his inner office, then sat down in that chair's twin. He flashed his winning grin that said, Rank aside, we're all friends here. Byrnes relaxed.

And then Ames lunged at him verbally. "Son, are you just dicking around with these Captain America messages? Or do you want to achieve something?"

Byrnes was startled. He had expected a pep talk, maybe a little peep into the world of a senior four-star. But he hadn't expected to be tongue-lashed by the second-highest-ranking officer in the U.S. military. "Sir?" he said pleadingly. "Sir, I thought you, uh, supported my efforts?" After all, he thought, it was Ames who had given him the codes to gain access to the off-the-books connections to the NSA computers. Without the shield of the NSA cleanser, the Sons of Liberty would have been traceable in a heartbeat.

Ames sunk the hook. "You've done well," he said, giving Byrnes the re-assurance that the younger man needed. "But now you have to engage your target."

He asked if Byrnes had read Sun Tzu. Byrnes nodded. "Then you know what he says—'When the enemy presents an opportunity, speedily take advantage of it.' " Ames told Byrnes that he would be contacted soon with the name of someone from the Joint Chiefs of Staff's Crisis Action Center. "That opportunity is coming. Listen for its knock."

Pennyfield Lock
The Potomac River, West of Washington
Saturday, June 18
7 A.M.

On Saturday morning Sherman awoke alone. She stared down at the *Washington Herald* next to her bagel and decided she wouldn't go into the Pentagon. The front page of the Saturday edition was dominated by a jarring color photograph of Shillingsworth declining to testify. The image was almost Christmasy in its contrasting colors—his smooth green Army uniform and his angry red face.

The photo sat atop two accompanying stories—one news, the other analysis—about the Senate Armed Services Committee hearing. It was a brutal package. Senator Feaver vowed that action would be forthcoming, but he wasn't specific. "We are studying the remedies available to this committee and to the United States Senate," the chairman said in a prepared statement. "Counsel informs me that we have a variety of far-reaching options available." And an anonymous Senate aide had told the *Herald* that the general, "known to have a tendency toward emotionalism," appeared to be disproportionately enraged by the chairman's rather routine request.

Normally she'd use a Saturday for catch-up work, clean out the in box. But she felt she couldn't face the Pentagon. Anyway, the staff would all stand around ashen-faced and waste the day grimly gossiping about the disastrous hearing. And the Metro section's weather page promised that Friday's heat was being pushed out by a cold front that would drop the day's high down into the eighties.

She felt like leaving Washington. She went to her refrigerator and took her paint tubes from the freezer, where she kept them in a plastic food-storage bag to prevent evaporation. She leaned down and collected four Granny Smith apples from inside the refrigerator. Then she reached up into the top of her back closet and pulled down a small stretched canvas, twenty-four inches by twenty inches. She put her gear in the back of her old green Subaru Outback.

She drove up River Road for about twenty-five minutes, looking for a place near the river to paint. She saw a sign for Pennyfield Lock and followed it, parking and then walking toward the river on a dirt path lined by jewelweed, trout lilies and saxifrage. On a boulder above a pool in the middle of the river, a great blue heron stared down into the water, motionless, waiting for his lunch to appear.

The Potomac was flashing blue, throwing off sparks of light as the gusts hit it. To Sherman's eye, the river was more light than water.

So it was back to the habits of loneliness, she thought as she settled down to work.

She began by making notes on a sheet of paper on the angle, quality and intensity of light. She looked for where the shadows were, where the contrasts were greatest. The core of her work today, she realized, would be the diamonds of light on the water—how they peaked, how they rounded at the bottom and, in between them, how much the bottom shadows of the clear, shallow river were picked up by the surface. To replicate the illumination within the river, in the underpainting she would put in some Thalo and ultramarine blues from the sky. The light on the shiny tree leaves was mainly a mix of cadmium yellow and ultramarine. The sky itself was almost pure Thalo Blue, with some white overtones, and some grays mixed in along the tops of the trees along the far side of the river.

She took up her workhorse hog-bristle brush, a beautifully cupped filbert, to sketch in the outlines in the underpainting. This helped her determine the relationship of the trees to the sky and the river. Then she moved on to consider the individual shapes of those objects—the tulip poplars on her bank at ten yards; the broad river; its sandy bottom; the big dead tree snagged out in the middle at one hundred yards; the sycamores on the far bank, hazy and lighter in value even on this clear day, at two hundred yards.

Objects closest have the greatest contrasts, she remembered being taught. Like Lewis and me now, she thought unhappily. I wouldn't be pissed at him if I didn't care about him. And he wouldn't be pissed at me if we both didn't care deeply about the Army. The more intimate we've become, the sharper the contrast has grown.

It amazed her sometimes how much painting was like intelligence preparation of the battlefield. She could do an accurate call for artillery fire simply by assessing the color qualities of the trees as the slight haze of the river's surface lightened their greens along the far bank. She liked representational painting because its core task was the same as in intelligence work: to see what actually was before your eyes. Not what you think is there, not what your mind's eye tells you should be there, but what the objective reality is at that moment, the interaction of the concrete world with the transient environment. Most people usually see what they expect to see. But one enemy commander will act differently from another, just as the trunk of a pine will plunge straight into the ground, while most oaks bend and squat where they meet the soil.

She ate one of the apples as she painted. Lewis had fit into the Army without even thinking about it. He was a member of the club. Somehow, she wasn't—the "real" Army was one of those secret societies you couldn't join if you had to ask how to become a member. It was a club that minimized the emotional choices of adulthood—job location, career choices, what to wear, even where you lived, if you were lucky enough to get base housing—and maximized the emotional claim of comradeship. The big boys' club. But during their last meeting in Marineland, she had somehow challenged his membership in that club, or touched elements in himself that were questioning the club. He seemed to her to have been scrambling emotionally to stay inside it.

She worked until midafternoon, then had another apple and decided to stop. She carried the wet painting back to her car, sliding it into the flat area in the back. Above it she draped a plastic sheet so dust wouldn't drift into the sticky pigments. The same qualities that attracted her to oils also made it a very slow-drying medium.

There were three voice-mail messages on her machine when she got home. The first two began, "Cindy, it's Buddy," and she deleted them without listening further. She played one from her mother and father: "How's our big-time Pentagon major?" She rinsed her brushes in turpentine, then put dishwashing detergent on them and scrubbed each against the palm of her left hand. She wrapped the bristles of each brush in a strip of paper towel so the drying paper would pull the bristles back into shape as it contracted. She thought about the collision between Shillingsworth and the Senate Armed Services Committee, about the increasingly aggressive stance of the Sons of Liberty messages. It felt to her like they were all crashing together over her head. For the first time, a sense of foreboding came over her. This was not going to end well.

When her telephone rang she hesitated, then decided to answer it. She wasn't going to be boxed in by Lewis, afraid to pick up the phone.

It was Cisco. He was ready to update her. In a flash he invited himself over for dinner. A half hour later he appeared at the door with a six-pack of beer and a big white plastic bag of boxed take-out Chinese food from a Buddhist vegetarian place on Eighteenth Street. He hadn't had a haircut since she had seen him last, but he had changed his uniform shirt. She thought she saw the faint outline of a cleaned stain on the baby blue above his nameplate. He was wearing tan khaki shorts.

"Great uniform, Cisco," she said, pecking him on the cheek.

They pushed aside the books and newspapers on her round table. "The ambush is ready," Cisco announced, obviously pleased. He was going to explain how he'd done it whether she wanted to hear or not. "I went to the TENCAP crowd. Turns out they know you." He looked at her with new respect. TENCAP stood for "Tactical Exploitation of National Capabilities," which meant using satellite imagery to help battlefield intelligence officers such as herself.

"Yeah, I'm a woman with a past, Cisco." She smiled. "I wrote an article once about some of that stuff."

"I always suspected you were more than just a dumb soldier." He saluted her with his chopsticks. "Anyway, I borrowed two of their Crays, and that got me the two possible routes into the NSA."

She was particularly impressed by his plan to interrogate computers by the ranks of their operators. "Yeah," he said. "I didn't want to get stuck in swamps of passed-over lieutenant colonels and jerk majors." He leaned back and rested his feet on the straw seat of the third chair. "Present company excepted," he added.

Over their third beer each, she asked him how he had ever been promoted in the U.S. military with his attitudes.

He said that when he had been based down at the Air Intelligence Center, on a little hill just southwest of San Antonio, his boss had made him work at night to minimize friction with other superior officers. That had given him a lot of time to experiment, to ride the new technologies. Then the majority of officers in his branch had resigned to form a private company to do computer security for Fortune 500 corporations. Cisco had run the branch alone for several months. "I'd go up to meetings in D.C., a lieutenant filling a major's billet, and all the action officers would stare at me." Someone in Washington had figured he was a pretty hot ticket. Soon he received an order transferring him to be the liaison between R&D efforts on offensive information warfare capabilities in the military and in the intelligence agencies. "It's great," he said. "Everyone thinks I work for someone else."

Cisco said he once was changing planes at Dallas–Fort Worth and looking for a seat in the crowded airport to eat some Oreos, drink a Coke and read the newspaper. The only open seat was across from a Marine officer. "Fine, fellow military, I figured," Cisco said. When he sat down he saw that the Marine was a two-star general. "I said hello and started to read my paper. When I looked down for a second, I saw that the Marine was eating one of my Oreos. I took one. He glared at me, then took another. I figured, hey, I can't let the United States Air Force be intimidated here— I paid for these. So I took the last one. He stood up real stiffly without saying anything and marched away like he had a pickle in his butt." Only when Cisco had finished reading his paper and collected his stuff did he see that his own unopened Oreo package was underneath the folded Sports section of the newspaper. He had been eating the Marine general's cookies. "Story of my military career," he concluded.

It was one of the most enjoyable evenings Sherman had spent since she came to Washington. At her door she gave Cisco a hug. He was going back out to Langley "to run the traps."

The Pentagon
Sunday, June 19
8 A.M.

On Sunday morning General Shillingsworth took advantage of the fine weather to double his usual four-mile run. He cut through the cemetery to Memorial Bridge, then went down the Mall and looped around the Capitol, whose ribbed white dome glared in the bright morning sunlight like a polished skull.

He came back up the Mall and crossed the bridge again. He stopped for his usual breather at the western, Virginia, end of the bridge. As he paused he decided that instead of jogging right toward home, he would cut left to the Pentagon to shower and catch up on his routine work, neglected all week due to his Leavenworth meeting and Armed Services testimony.

Inside the big building's Mall entrance, empty on this almost-summer Sunday morning, he saw his photograph staring back at him, posted along with the other service chiefs below the SecDef. The images reminded him that he was the only one of the chiefs who wore that green-and-white Vietnam ribbon at the lower right corner of his fruit salad. That little ribbon had been the secret code for a generation of officers, the only open-ended ribbon ever worn by U.S. military officers. Engraved into its metal centerpiece in tiny letters were the words "Republic of Vietnam: 1963–   ." It was left blank because the awarding nation had ceased to exist. It eloquently captured the way his generation in the military — those who had stayed on through the dismal, ill-disciplined days of the late seventies—had felt: Never again.

But how to ensure that it didn't happen again without upsetting the system again? He walked up the Marshall stairs thinking that he was indeed getting too old—when even the other chiefs didn't share that experience, didn't carry that lesson in their guts. He wondered: Have I stayed too long?

Outside his office, a middle-aged but trim black man in a black suit stood like a sentry. "General Shillingsworth," he said crisply, almost coming to attention, straightening his back and bringing together his heels. He clearly was former military. "Sir, I am the deputy sergeant at arms of the United States Senate. This is a subpoena for you." He thrust it at the general.

It hadn't occurred to Shillingsworth that they could compel him to give his personal views of the Afghan mission. Forcing the testimony of a service chief on an operational issue had never come up before.

He was ordered to appear before the committee at its next meeting at 9 A.M. on the next business day—Monday. "Yes," his judge advocate general told him over the phone a few minutes later, "you're a member of the executive branch, in the eyes of Congress. So I'd say, yes, they can."

His chief legislative liaison proposed a "slow-rolling" response. "We can do the big stall, argue that you can't comment on executive branch work product."

Shillingsworth thanked both men for their time and hung up. He strode about his office on his long legs, considering his career, half gazing at the trophies on the walls as he contemplated possible courses of action. There was the engraved 155-millimeter brass shell casing from his old division staff. His old brigade flag. An Iraqi mortar plate, engraved with the thanks of the now-defunct Third Armored Division. A photograph of him with the current SecDef, another of him with the previous one. Another, wider shot of him and the other chiefs stiffly posed with President Shick. The guidon from the first company he commanded during the "hollow military" days of the midseventies.

His advisers were proposing the Washington approach. But Shillingsworth instinctively felt that was the wrong way to go. It was playing the adversary's game—and so letting the other guy make the rules.

Shillingsworth thought it better to act as a soldier, to keep the home-field advantage. He would give them both barrels. He would stop this questioning of his honor. It would feel good.

But as he stared at the artifacts of his career, another thought emerged: That wasn't the soldier's way. Laying it all out would undermine the president and could even damage the nation. And refusing to testify could poison the Army's relations with Congress for years to come.

The Army and the nation come before my own needs, he decided. Duty comes before honor. Where did duty lie? In being a good soldier. In putting your head down and keeping on moving.

His duty, he concluded, was to mask his personal views, to not be honest with the Senate. He hated the idea—it ran against all his values. But that was irrelevant. You didn't get to pick the orders you obeyed. You couldn't turn duty on and off like tapwater. And the Army couldn't be used by the Congress to torpedo the president.

He tapped out his testimony. "I fully support the president's policy on Afghanistan. In my personal opinion, it is a good mission." (*The president is enormously vulnerable on this. I am not going to lead a military revolt against him.*) "I believe we can do it." (*I took my best shot, but the president has thought differently. In this country, when that happens, we salute smartly and move out and do our best.*) "As this committee has indicated, we have considered additional options for the Afghan mission. We always examine all options in our military planning process. To not do so would be unprofessional. In this case, one possibility is to extend the mission. Thus far we have received no order to do so." (*Yes, I said some things at Leavenworth to a group of people I should have been able to trust. But at least I know it is one of those ten, probably Ames.*) "I further believe that any officer who cannot join me in making this statement ought to resign his commission." (*That ought to make it clear where I stand on this Sons of Liberty crap.*) "This is my sworn testimony. John Shillingsworth, Chief of Staff, U.S. Army." (*You can take this and stuff it, Senator Feaver.*)

He e-mailed the statement out to several members of his staff and walked slowly home on the shortcut through the cemetery. He sat on the veranda and watched the shadows stretch across the lawn until the sun set behind his back. He didn't eat. His wife finally came out and handed him a glass of ice water. She sat down in the rocking chair next to his. He said nothing.

After five minutes, she finally said, "John?"

He looked at her bleakly. "This is what Maddox must have felt like after Algeria," he said remotely. He felt as if he were physically plunging through deep space, alone and cold, millions of miles from human contact. He felt he had made a huge and unexpected sacrifice: He was compromising his integrity for the good of his Army and his nation. He didn't know how to tell her that he had chosen to diminish himself, even to betray himself, because he felt he had to. He fell back into silence.

When he went inside he found his wife packing an old suitcase. She was going to move in with her friend Patsy, the principal of the elementary school where she worked.

His eyes asked why.

"John, I think you're on a combat deployment right now, right here," she said, looking over the lid of the old Samsonite. She came around the bed and embraced him. "My soul is with you—you know that. And I'll be back in a heartbeat when you say so. But right now you need to be in the fight, not with me."

He said that probably was the best thing. He went back outside and poured himself a tall whiskey.

He dreamed again that night of Pickett's Charge. This time he dreamed he was drunk as he fast-stepped up the humid slope toward the stone wall.

Across the river, in her apartment in Adams-Morgan, Sherman read General Shillingsworth's statement. She knew that he didn't believe those words. She walked around the apartment, watered the plants, then went back to her computer and read the statement several more times. Slowly, unwillingly, she settled on the unhappy thought that General Shillingsworth was giving up his honor in order to do what he understood to be his duty.

PART

TWO

SUMMER

Late on Sunday night Julia reported hot news that kicked off alarms, first at the National Reconnaissance Agency, then at its parent, the Defense Intelligence Agency, next at the Pentagon and finally at the White House.

In 1962 the designer of the first satellite made to intercept signals communications had ruefully named it Marilyn, after his ex-wife, as a way of apologizing for years of neglect. But subsequent designers had assumed it was in honor of America's reigning sex symbol, and so had continued what they thought was a tradition by sending Raquel to spy on the Soviet Union in the late 1960s, and Farrah a decade later.

And on Sunday a descendant of those satellites, a KH-13(ER) nicknamed Julia, captured and relayed microwave audio signals from northern Afghanistan indicating that the Front for the Purity of Afghan Soil, which had kidnapped two American soldiers, would hold a meeting of its leadership on Monday night, local time, in the central Afghanistan mountain town of Bamian, probably to discuss how to dispose of those two American hostages, still being held somewhere out in the desert. That would be at 9 A.M. Monday in Washington. At that time, the CIA analysts predicted, they probably would promise to free the two soldiers in exchange for the U.S. simply keeping its pledge to leave Afghanistan after sixty days.

The president wanted Operation Plan 9827-04 executed before they issued any such statement, Willy Pitch told the Joint Chiefs at a meeting at 7 A.M. Monday in the Tank.

"Centcom is handling it, but Afghanistan is an Army-oriented mission, so he wants you in the Crisis Action Center," Pitch said to General Shillingsworth. "We'll have real-time monitoring from here, both of the strike and of initial bomb-damage assessment, using the Vultures." Those were two long-loiter unmanned aerial vehicles that were already on station, circling undetected miles above the peaks of the Hindu Kush. Developed by the Air Force in a black program, the stealthy long-dwell drones specialized in sniffing out chemical and biological weapons, but their sensors also proved handy at the simpler task of beaming video and infrared imagery from airstrikes.

Shillingsworth thought to himself that Pitch was using him for political cover: They wanted him in the room because he was the last general officer with time in Vietnam and so the last one able to bring to their operation the moral authority of having undergone sustained ground combat. He brushed aside the thought and told Pitch that he had been subpoenaed to reappear before the Senate Armed Services Committee at that time. Pitch waved away that concern. "I'll tell Feaver you were unavoidably detained on the president's orders," he said airily.

True to his word, Pitch a few minutes later called the senator and advised him that, in the president's view, it was "inappropriate" to resume the Shillingsworth hearing at this time. Pitch loved the word "inappropriate"—it was the essence of official Washington, an insiders' password that had the beauty of meaning whatever the bearer wanted it to mean. In this case, it meant that if Feaver went forward with the hearing, he would be vulnerable to being portrayed as interfering in a military operation. He agreed to postpone the hearing.

At 8 A.M. General Shillingsworth walked down to the Crisis Action Center, directly across from the SecDef's corridor. He thought of the sit-down strike just ten days earlier and snorted as he recalled the SecDef's dismissive line, ". . . probably *improves* the morale and efficiency of the U.S. military *establishment*." Got to hand it to the old bastard, Shillingsworth thought, logging in with the guard and moving through the double-doored airlock.

The more serious a situation is, the quieter the Crisis Action Center becomes. There were forty computer terminals, twenty along each side of the long room, with one officer at each screen, another at that officer's elbow. In each corner of the large, cool room there hung a television set displaying a torrent of weather and entertainment news on CNN, the usual fare on a summer Monday morning in America—no hint of an impending military action. The far end of the room opened onto the secure conference room where the brass sat and harassed the worker bees during crises. Shillingsworth saw the eighty officers, mainly captains and majors overseen by team leaders with the rank of lieutenant colonel, beginning to enter the complex series of six levels of passwords required to tie their terminals into various command and control networks involved in the operation—logistics, imagery, signals, even global weather. The first password was to enter the Pentagon's piece of the secure military intranet. The second was the next level up, their personal profile of security clearances. The third and fourth were for the Joint Chiefs of Staff operations network and for the Central Command operations intranet.

At screen 36 sat Marine Captain Dewayne Decamp, whose operations buddy had just headed to the men's room. Decamp slipped into his A drive the floppy disk handed to him that morning by a Captain Byrnes from Army logistics, who said he had been sent by a "senior mutual friend," whatever that was. Decamp at first declined, partly because Joint Staff officers were expressly forbidden by written order to introduce any data from outside the classified network. But Byrnes had insisted, saying it was an important, one-time-only request from the Sons of Liberty. "All it needs from you is to open up the only file on the disk and hit 'enter,' " the Army captain had told him as they spoke in the hallway. "The disk will do the rest."

Decamp decided it wasn't that big a thing and did as he was asked. He opened the only document he found and pressed the "enter" button. When he did, the self-executing document followed its own embedded instructions and sent itself through an off-the-map dedicated fiber-optic line that led to the NSA complex at Fort Meade. The message rocketed over to NSA—but didn't come out of the NSA as fast as usual. In all the world, only one person noticed that extraordinary five-minute delay—the man who caused it, Cisco, watching intently at his basement post ten miles up the Potomac River from the Pentagon.

General Shillingsworth strode to the exact center of the room and looked around. The action officers swiveled in their chairs and looked at him expectantly. They were not about to get the usual preoperation pep talk.

"Good morning. There may be some people in this room who think that what we are about to do is the wrong course," General Shillingsworth began. "I might know some of those people." They sensed he indeed was one—and they also sensed that he wouldn't say it. "But we've had a chance to express our views. And our democracy has decided on a different course of action. Now we are embarking upon that course. Our nation is committed."

He had thought long and hard that morning about how to express his sense that duty sometimes requires military professionals to execute orders with which they disagree. He reached back to the speech that an Air Force general had given in August 1995 as the U.S. began to launch airstrikes against the Bosnian Serbs. The general had argued against those strikes, and then, after losing the argument, had led the planning for them.

"Our democracy has said that these people we are targeting are the enemies of our nation," Shillingsworth said, quoting the general precisely. "Now, whether or not you personally believe that to be true, I think we can all agree that it would be a terrible thing if people around the world started thinking you could be the declared enemy of our nation and nothing would happen to you. It could damage our nation. And it would be dangerous for our troops the next time we send them in harm's way." That was something he knew they could all understand. "So we will execute this mission with all the skills and weaponry our nation has given us.

"We are going to hit them high and low, hard and harder," he said. He had reviewed the ordnance load and had seen that it was heavy with cluster-munition warheads. They were going to rain cruise missiles down on this remote corner of Afghanistan that had been all but silent since Genghis Khan's malevolence descended eight hundred years earlier and killed everyone in the valley. The president and Pitch wanted these people ripped up. "We will be as savage as the laws of war will allow us to be."

But now for the real threat, he thought, swinging his gaze from one side of the room to the other. "We are here today, in this room, in these uniforms, because we are military professionals." He tried to catch the eyes of the officers as he surveyed them. "But we are people of conscience. If yours won't permit you to continue to be here, you may leave."

They looked at him wide-eyed. Where was he going with this? "But there will be consequences. No charges will be brought against you. I promise you that. But I promise you also that my opinion, which will be expressed in a letter in your personnel folder, is that you probably should not continue as a member of the United States military."

He looked around. An Army captain in the signals section got up and walked out in silence. He was young enough to start a new career tomorrow morning, probably at double the salary, Shillingsworth thought. You could open up the back of *Army Times* and find pages of advertisements trolling for technically adept people able to follow orders and govern themselves. The departing captain's operations buddy moved to the main chair at the computer and began entering his security profiles. It is amazing how military forces can dress their ranks, Shillingsworth thought. He thought of the way the Federal cannon had punched holes in Pickett's and Pettigrew's lines, only to have gore-splattered soldiers close in to fill the holes, hardly losing a step as they marched toward their doom.

Shillingsworth waited until the door swung closed behind the captain. "The rest of you, boot up to operations level." On that order, the lieutenant colonel overseeing information security opened the secure gate, and the other officers looked at their SecurID readouts and tapped in the fifth and sixth passwords—double algorithms that changed constantly— that allowed them to enter the CACNET.

But this time, as each finally got to an operational screen, he or she saw a "Flash Override" message—military terminology for a message of the highest priority, claiming precedence over all other traffic. Within a minute all were staring at identical screens.

Good morning, each screen read.

The Sons of Liberty have taken action to prevent the further needless shedding of the blood of American soldiers. Please refrain from using this computer. Shut it down now. Any further action on the CACNET related to the monitoring of the execution of Op Plan 9827-04 will trigger an inner program that will transmit the entire plan to several media outlets, foreign and domestic, by facsimile and e-mail. To avoid this problem, do not enter any additional commands into the CAC system. We apologize for this inconvenience, and regret that this action has become necessary.

We appreciate your understanding. Bring our boys home now.

With faith in the nation,

The Sons of Liberty

An organization of concerned active-duty patriots

Shillingsworth read the message over a major's shoulder. The threat to divulge the plan could be a hoax. Probably was, in fact. Yet it was clear that operational security had been violated massively. The Sons of Liberty were inside the system—a closed system that communicated only with secure computers within the national security establishment. One of the officers sitting in front of him could be part of it. Or more than one. He surveyed the Crisis Action Center. They were all looking back at him. What now?

"Tell Central Command operations center to cancel the execution," he said. "Immediately." The forty screens began closing down. "I'll call the CinC."

Shillingsworth looked over to the information security officer, who was nervously working on the free-standing security network. The officer was staring incredulously at his computer. "The message appears to have come out of the NSA," the worried officer said, squinting at the screen. "That means it probably is untraceable, sir." Shillingsworth nodded and walked out the double doors and directly across the corridor to the SecDef's office. The man needed to understand that they had a higher priority than pummeling some medieval guerrillas in a forgotten valley of the Hindu Kush. The U.S. military establishment was being threatened from within.

With Shillingsworth in the room, the SecDef called the national security adviser and told him what had happened in the Crisis Action Center. Pitch didn't even threaten them. He just said, "You two better get to the bottom of this pretty fast." Later, Pitch told the SecDef that he'd heard Shillingsworth hadn't seemed too broken up about canceling the operation. Had Shillingsworth checked with anyone before ordering it terminated?

Subbasement 3, CIA Headquarters
8:45 A.M.

"Yes!" Cisco exulted, leaping from his chair in his basement office ten miles to the north. "Got you!"

Before him his computer screen flashed in orange, "USER ID CAPTURED."

He reached for the phone and called his boss upstairs, who in return for securing the Crays and Paragon had asked to be kept informed of Cisco's progress. Cisco told him that he forced the originating server to give up the user identification information on the latest Sons of Liberty message. It had come from the heart of the heart of the Pentagon, a terminal inside the Joint Chiefs' Crisis Action Center. What puzzled him was that it had been sent back to the same location.

Cisco read the message to his boss, who paused, then asked him, "The CAC terminated its own operation?"

Cisco unwrapped the message's history. "Sort of." He explained: It had been forwarded by CACNET terminal 36, at that point operated by a Marine captain named Dewayne Decamp. But every computer message carried the DNA of its origins. And the "Flash Override" message from the Sons of Liberty had been stamped as originating on a computer in Army logistics. To be specific, it was U.S. Army terminal "PNT/DOA-C/ODCS4/26"—that is, Pentagon/Department of the Army—Classified/Office of the Deputy Chief of Staff for Logistics/Terminal 26.

Cisco's boss thanked him for the good work and said he would notify Vice Admiral Bugby, the military liaison to the intelligence community, with the information. Nothing justified next year's budget request like this year's flashy results.

Cisco sent the Paragon after Army logistics terminal 26. Once it was in, the Digger began to work it over, and terminal 26 began to talk.

Brookmont, Maryland
Wednesday, June 22
5 P.M.

Cisco was more subdued than Cindy had ever seen him, mainly because he hadn't slept much for the previous forty-eight hours. "Right after the Sons of Liberty shut down the Afghanistan missile strike on Monday morning, this whole mob of Dick Tracy types descended on me," he said sorrowfully over a cup of bitter-smelling Lapsang souchong tea.

But he had something for her, he said, sitting in the front room of his red cottage, which in the nineteenth century had been a two-room schoolhouse. He slept and lived in the front room and used the back room as his kitchen, shop and study, with three computers lined up next to one another on a table made of sawhorses. He actually had twice as many phone and DSL lines as he did rooms in the house.

The house was on the Maryland side of the Potomac, directly across the river from the CIA's headquarters on the southern, Virginia, bank. Some of his neighbors commuted by canoe, but they were analysts, not operators. His hours were too erratic for that luxury.

"There were guys from CID, FBI, the Naval Criminal Investigative Service, even someone from something called the Office of Special Collections and Assessments, which I'd never heard of, and I'm an intell guy. They showed up in my office late Monday morning. My Paragon was midway through limning the Sons of Liberty distribution tree"—creating an accurate history of all computers involved in primary passes—"while the Digger interrogated individual computers." The visitors had tried to follow his work by watching over his shoulder.

While the painstaking process of computer interrogation occurred, there was little the humans could do, so they had elbowed each other for jurisdiction. The J-383 information warfare cell had sent a representative who didn't say anything. The FBI representative tried to get him ejected on the grounds that this was a law-enforcement matter and that the presence of a representative of the Joint Chiefs violated posse comitatus, which generally barred the U.S. military from participating in domestic law enforcement matters. But the man from J-383 refused on the ground that this was in fact a military affair. "All the while, no one seemed to notice that it was an Air Force officer that they were getting their information from," Cisco said.

"I wonder why," Sherman said sarcastically, glancing at his stubbly chin, khaki shorts and dirty T-shirt, which advertised a concert by something called "Insane Clown Posse."

Cisco had told the Digger to work at half speed—partly out of fear of crashing the Defense Department system, partly so he could think about just how much data he was going to turn over to this crowd of kibitzers. "To get them off my back, I gave them all printouts of the whole distribution tree, which is about seven thousand names," he said, holding his cup of smoky tea under his nose. "It's the entire distribution tree, but in alphabetical order, which is kind of useless. It's a mix of everybody who ever got a primary pass of a Sons of Liberty message. I figured that ought to keep them busy for a while."

When the government gumshoes had tumbled out his door, hot on the trail, each agency determined to be the first to find the starting point in the tree, he had settled down to the real investigative work. "On the second pass, I had the Paragon re-sort the findings chronologically. And this tubby little guy from CID comes back—"

"Guy named Ojeda?" Cindy interrupted.

"Yeah, how did you know?"

"He called me today to make an urgent appointment for tomorrow morning," she said.

"Anyway, he comes back and starts looking over my shoulder," Cisco said. "He says as if it just occurred to him, could I give him an ordering, by frequency of appearance, which terminals and user IDs appeared most often? I did, and he left. But when he collates those, he should have a pretty good idea of who the Sons of Liberty are and how they work."

After the CID man finally left that night, Cisco had initiated the crucial task of rank ordering. "That was interesting. I began by asking for all four-star security clearances that imprinted on the tree by passing as well as receiving."

"How many were there?" Cindy asked.

"You're going to be disappointed, I think," Cisco said. "I thought there would be a lot more. There was only one, this General Ames guy. I think he's on the Joint Staff."

"Oh, shit," Cindy said.

"Friend of yours?" Cisco asked in genuine innocence.

"Not quite," Cindy said. "But a, uh, buddy of mine works for him."

"So I sent the Digger after him, and I had another disappointment: It comes back empty-handed about fifteen minutes later. There was almost nothing relating to the Sons of Liberty on Ames's office computers. So then I checked for his home PC, and again there was almost nothing."

He smiled. "This is the good part. I was thinking, this doesn't compute—literally. I mean, the Paragon finds his fingerprints all over the Sons of Liberty transmissions, but the Digger can't find anything that's making those fingerprints? I drove home to take a rest, eat some food. I'm cooking in my kitchen when I look at my computers and it occurs to me: He's got more than one computer in his home.

"So I went back to the office and asked the Paragon where it had found his fingerprints—the security imprint he makes when he uses his IDs to sign on. It was on a laptop that wasn't issued to Ames at all, but to some Air Force colonel named Underhill. Then I found the number of the phone line that laptop had been using. I cross-traced that line, and it turned out that the laptop had been dialing on an unpublished number out of Ames's home address.

"That made me real suspicious, because he clearly was making an effort to cover his tracks—disguising the laptop use, using an unlisted phone line."

"So what was in it?" Cindy asked.

"Don't know yet. Haven't gotten in yet. His secret little laptop won't be accessible until he dials into the Defense Department network. The Paragon is monitoring that line. When he uses it, the Digger will go in and get him."

"Let's go," she said, standing.

"It's kind of boring, just watching the Paragon," Cisco protested, still sitting. "You know, I could think of something we could do that would be a lot more fun." He gave her an exaggerated leer.

Cindy ignored the Groucho Marx–like innuendo. "I'll drive. Come on."

"There's nothing like a strong-willed woman," Cisco said, sighing and standing.

"Or the fact that I outrank you," Cindy said.

"Yeah, but let's not let rank come between us," Cisco said, following Cindy to her Subaru.

For five hours Cisco fiddled with the computer while Cindy paged through the intelligence manuals he left lying around. Just past 11 P.M. the Paragon signaled to Cisco that the secret laptop had dialed into the Defense Department network. Cisco waited for Ames to type in his security ID, which opened the gate both ways, then sent in the Digger to ransack the laptop.

"The Digger says there are dozens of folders, each with lots of files," he said, looking up from his screen. "What do we want first?" He answered his own question, clicking on an icon labeled "Lewis and Sons of Liberty." Documents from that file began to move.

"No, that one," Cindy said, pointing instead at an icon just below it labeled "Ames P4." "That's what the general really doesn't want anyone else to see."

Cisco instructed the Digger to stop with the other folder and grab that one. He had been inside Ames's laptop about twenty seconds and had moved a total of thirty-two documents. Then his computer screen hiccuped, flashing twice as if its internal power had been interrupted. Finally all the icons on the screen disappeared, leaving Cisco's screen a blank sea of blue.

"Holy shit," Cisco shouted, his hands flying across the keyboard as he verified what he had just witnessed. "I'd heard about this but I hadn't seen it before."

"What?" Sherman said.

"Hara-kiri. Ames's laptop just did a total meltdown." Cisco was talking at twice his usual high speed, even as he typed. "As soon as it saw what I was doing, it killed all its remaining documents, then blew out its own operating programs. A total hard-drive meltdown. Ugly. Leaves you nothing but a keyboard and a blank screen."

"What had you heard about?"

"Suicide chips in DoD laptops," Cisco said with some awe. "Mess with a four-star and you learn a lot of new stuff."

He reached behind his terminal and unscrewed the cable connecting it to the Paragon. "I don't know what else Ames has got up his laptop. The Paragon can protect itself, but my terminal can't. I'm going to disconnect before I get counterattacked."

"Won't General Ames know that someone has been inside his computer?" Sherman asked.

"Probably." Cisco shrugged. "But he won't know for sure. The Digger doesn't leave a trail. He might just figure an electrical surge fried him out, or the suicide chip misfired. Generals usually aren't very computer savvy."

Cisco paged through the part of the "Ames P4" file that he had captured, Cindy sitting at his shoulder. "I don't understand any of this," he said.

"I do," she said. "I need to get it to the Pentagon. Make me some copies, would you? Put them in secure read-only mode—I don't want people to be able to fiddle with these." She'd heard the rumor that a record of a phone call from the White House to the commander of the U.S. task force in Afghanistan had been deleted from all databases.

She quickly skimmed the first three documents in the "P4" file. It was clear that General Ames knew "Captain America" and had encouraged the Sons of Liberty all along the way.

"I'll create them in 'lock/protect' mode so people can't even make a copy of them," he said. "These will be the only four copies in the world." He labeled the disks, put "Ames 1 of 4 only" in the canvas PBS tote bag he used as a briefcase and gave her the other three.

She stood to leave.

"What about this other file, labeled 'Lewis and Sons of Liberty'?" he asked, looking up at her and pointing to his screen. "I got a few from that file, too. It seems kind of relevant."

She thought for a moment about loyalty to people and duty to institutions. The thought of destroying Buddy sickened her. But so did the thought that he was a leader of the Sons of Liberty. She had what she needed. She didn't need to ruin a good man. But she needed to see what was in that file. "Make me just one copy of that one, will you?" she asked.

"It's your investigation." Cisco shrugged.

She leaned over, slipped an arm behind his neck and kissed him on the lips. "Thanks, Cisco—for everything."

He grinned up at her. "Gee, if I get that for a couple of disks, what would I get if I gave you a whole computer?"

The Pentagon
Thursday, June 23
12:15 A.M.

Sherman drove down the dark parkway along the Virginia bank of the Potomac and walked into the deserted Pentagon fifteen minutes later. Just after midnight she slipped "Lewis" into her computer. She was relieved to see that it was pretty much what Lewis had said to her in Marineland the day they broke up: He was sympathetic to the views of the Sons of Liberty, and had forwarded the Sons of Liberty messages to his "OPFOR buddies" distribution list, but wasn't one of its leaders.

A chill hit her: The most worrisome thing about this file was that it existed. The only way it could have been created, she realized, was that Ames secretly monitored his subordinates' e-mail traffic. It was as if Ames used Lewis as a kind of laboratory animal, watching the young officer's reactions to events.

What had she written to Lewis that Ames had seen? she wondered. She was glad she'd never mentioned her role in pursuing the Sons of Liberty to him. But had she ever mentioned anything about the existence of the investigation? Had she begged off a lunch because she had to go out to CIA to see how Cisco was doing? She couldn't remember.

She put the "Lewis" disk at the back of the bottom drawer in her desk and turned to the disk labeled "Ames 2 of 4 only." She began with the older "P4" documents. Since he had become vice chairman of the Joint Chiefs, she saw, Ames had routinely sandbagged his adversaries on defense policy. When Maddox and the service chiefs testified before the

Senate Armed Services Committee, she saw, he had supplied Senator Feaver with pointed questions to pose. This was sneaky and underhanded, she thought as she read the messages, but not unheard of in Washington, and hardly requiring the elaborate security measures that Ames appeared to have taken with this file.

She shook her head at the note that Ames had sent just after the Leavenworth meeting. Shillingsworth had thought administration policy wrongheaded but had been determined not to undermine the president— and Ames had clobbered him with that contradiction: *It is the considered private opinion of our distinguished Army chief of staff that we will be in Afghanistan at least a year, maybe longer,* Ames had reported to the senator. The cost those twenty-five words had imposed on Shillingsworth, forcing him to give up his integrity in order to do what he perceived as his duty—it took her breath away.

Before the *New York World* article appeared, Ames had sent an e-mail to Major Bolton down at Fort Bragg reassuring him that Defense Secretary Johnson was reluctant to charge anyone. Ames also had been in steady contact with Byrnes, first giving him pats on the back, then spurring the younger officer to move from simple protest to mutinous action.

There were two notes that she thought would finish Ames. The White House would be most antagonized by his behind-the-scenes encouragement of the turnaround at Fort Polk. She wondered what the president would do when he saw the welcome that General Ames had helped set up for him at Polk: *Are you boys going to this dog-and-pony show with the president at Polk tomorrow with shit-eating grins on your faces? Or are you going to remember the Alamo?*

But the military would be even more provoked by Ames's note to Byrnes, which would come to be known in certain national security circles as "the access note." If there was anything that was chargeable in this file, she thought, it was this note. Just the previous week, she saw, Ames had written to Byrnes: *As you know, access codes for the CACNET are restricted to UMBRA and above. We always must keep in mind operational security. I suggest you contact a Marine captain named Decamp who is CAC staff. He isn't aware of my interest in this matter, and you will leave my name out of it, but I have reason to believe through my staff that he would be willing to aid you in your important work.*

That was the last piece in the puzzle: It was Ames who connected Byrnes to Decamp.

She wondered why. Did Ames really object so deeply to the president's foreign policy that he would violate the key tenet of American military professionalism and cross over into political action? Did he just think he knew better? Or was he just so determined to become chairman of the Joint Chiefs that he would do anything to push all competition, even damaged goods like General Shillingsworth, completely out of the way?

No matter now, she thought; they are going to have to court-martial the vice chairman of the Joint Chiefs. It will be the biggest military trial in U.S. history. And this rich catalog of manipulation, betrayal and intrigue is the evidence that will do him in.

There were just four disks. Cisco had the first. She locked "Ames 2" in her briefcase. She slipped "Ames 3" into the lower pocket of her uniform jacket. The fourth she would give to the chief.

It was 3 A.M. She slept on the office couch for two hours, then, after the rising sun awoke her, washed up at the POAC and donned the spare uniform she kept in the locker there.

At 6:30, she met General Shillingsworth as he arrived at the office door. "Remember that red dot on your chest?" she said enthusiastically. "I think we have the spotter."

Shillingsworth nodded mournfully and took the disk. He didn't thank her—indeed, he didn't say a word. Sherman realized that he had probably hoped against hope that there was no conspiracy in the ranks. He closed the door to his inner office and stayed behind it for several hours, reading every word on the "Ames 4 of 4" disk. Then he dropped the disk into the "Infowar" file of his secure cabinet and locked the drawer. His right hand trembled as he slipped his keychain back into his uniform pocket. Ames would have to be crushed, of course. He would stamp out this sedition, tear it our root and branch and plow salt into the soil that fed it. All his life, all his military experience, all his knowledge of top command demanded it.

But not yet. Before he brought agonizing scandal down on this Army, before he threw it into the arena of uninformed public scrutiny, he would damn well think through his course of action. Lashing out was no way to regain the initiative. He would need to assess the threat, review his resources and then develop a plan. Only then would he move out—the Army way. There was plenty of time. He shook his head over Ames. There was time to deal with him—and it would take time to do everything that needed to be done, and also to reassure the public that the Army was in good hands. Yes. He stared down at his shoes. There was plenty of time.

The Pentagon
7:30 A.M.

B. Z. Ames strode into his inner office and picked up the phone. He was still furious over what had happened to his laptop at home the previous evening, but he kept all of that anger out of his voice as he called the military liaison to the director of Central Intelligence.

"Jack, it's been too damn long," he purred to the three-star admiral who answered the phone out at CIA headquarters. He asked Jack to come by his office that morning for a cup of coffee.

When Jack Bugby arrived forty-eight minutes later, Ames first asked him about his plans. Did he have any interest in taking over NSA? That was a three-star billet, the premier job in the military intelligence community. Or was he more interested in a CinCdom?

Bugby shook his head. "The Navy would never support an intell guy for Pacific Command," he said.

Ames sipped his iced tea. "No, they wouldn't," he agreed. "But wouldn't the Navy love to pick up Southcom?"

The admiral grinned unabashedly at the possibility. What a coup it would be. And it made sense: Most of the activity in the Southern Command's area of responsibility—the Caribbean and South America—was now naval. And much more than conventional operations, the drug war rested on a foundation of intelligence gathering. So why not have a top naval intelligence officer take that command? "That could make real sense," Vice Admiral Bugby said, grinning. "Especially with a good word from someone like you wearing an Army suit and four stars on each shoulder."

"Well, let's think on that," Ames said, rising. As Ames walked Bugby to the door, he turned to the real issue weighing on his mind. "Hey, I hear your basement boys have been poking around inside my CACNET," he said conversationally. "What's with that?"

Eager to please the vice chairman, this unexpected ally, Bugby told him what he knew. "According to our executive brief this morning, one of our information operations specialists kind of stumbled across some sort of leakage in the Crisis Action Center system."

Ames wondered aloud what someone from Langley was doing inside a Pentagon system. Bugby told him the operator was actually a loaner from the military. "Kid named Cisco," Bugby said. "Crazy as a loon, but good. Comes out of the Air Force's Air Intelligence Agency, information security division."

"I'm glad he's playing little Dutch boy," Ames said. "But the stray voltage is driving our systems haywire. Can you ask him to back off for a few days? I don't want our systems knocked down because some info ops gumshoe wants to read everyone's e-mail."

Bugby said he'd ask them to keep it down.

After the admiral left, Ames called the chief of the Office of Special Collections and Assessments and said he'd need a file on this Cisco, including current home address. And, he added as an afterthought, "check to see what weapons he has registered there."

The Pentagon
9 A.M.

Augustino Ojeda, the chubby CID investigator out of Fort Belvoir, came through the door for his appointment with Cindy Sherman right on time at 9 A.M. "We're going to bust this Captain Byrnes," he announced. "General Shillingsworth insisted that I bring you along."

"What about General Ames?" she asked. Ojeda hadn't seen the contents of the secret laptop, but there was enough evidence just in the distribution tree to point toward Ames.

"Out of my lane, ma'am," Ojeda said. "I was ordered to go after the unknown parties originating the Sons of Liberty messages. And the evidence indicates that General Ames didn't send a single one." He was invoking a favorite Army metaphor, "staying in your lane." It promised that if you did what you were supposed to do, when you were supposed to do it, you wouldn't be hit by friendly fire, or have the tread of a seventy-ton M-1 main battle tank jellify your foot.

"I'm not sure there are any lanes on this one," Cindy said. "I think we're breaking trail across unknown country."

To Ojeda the regulations represented the distilled wisdom of generations who had gone before him. "Well, ma'am, I'm a by-the-book kind of investigator."

To that end, Ojeda said that first they were going to pay a "courtesy call" on Lieutenant General Still. "Partly to make sure that Byrnes is my man, partly to see if the general is involved in the Sons of Liberty," he said. "Mainly to give him a heads-up."

He only gets away with his weight because in CID he can wear civilian clothes, Sherman thought. "You must not know General Still," she said. "He wouldn't be into the Sons of Liberty."

She had watched Still interact with Shillingsworth. They were two Old Army types, deeply sympathetic to each other in an inarticulate way. They seemed able to hold entire decision meetings in which they spoke only in a mélange of acronyms, slang, tactical terms and the nicknames of old friends. In her first week on the job, Cindy had witnessed them resolve a minor issue in which artillery doctrine was potentially at odds with mobility requirements. Still said, "OK, I'll rub this down with the redleg side at TRADOC, you'll fire H and I to keep OSD PA and E off my back, and my XO will lash it up with Sly's schoolhouse at Sill?" Shillingsworth had responded with a muted "Hoo-ah," the catch-all Army response that in this case meant "I'm with you; next issue."

Ojeda and Sherman walked around the E ring to the office of the deputy chief of staff for logistics, Still's official title. Listening to the CID's suspicions, General Still wove his hands together under his chin, occasionally nodding his bald, mahogany-colored head, but keeping his face expressionless. Cindy noticed how the light reflected off his buttery skin—he was almost shiny, not just his hairless pate, but his smooth face as well.

When Ojeda finished laying out the evidence against Byrnes, the general had his conclusions ready. "That's your man," he said in his back-of-the-mouth Carolina accent, born and shaped on a sandy tobacco farm near Kinston. It was a reserved, even parsimonious form of speech. "Little rich kid. Never had any appreciation for logistics, anyway. Didn't understand that what we do is the heart and soul of military operations.

Always gave me these snotty little answers, 'Yes, sir, right away, sir, just as soon as I finish sending this e-mail.' Now I know what those e-mails were about."

Cindy thanked the general for his time. The CID man said he thought he would go arrest Captain Byrnes right away. General Still announced that he would go with him. "Can I put the handcuffs on the little fucker?" he asked.

"Sorry, sir, you shouldn't accompany us," Ojeda said, uneasily. "You might be recommending the disposition of this case."

Still escorted them to his door and watched them walk away from the E ring into the less-desirable middle rings of the Pentagon, the low-rent land of the depressed midcareer drones. Ojeda and Sherman descended two flights and then walked past a Dumpster into 1B530, the DCSLOG's staff suite. The female sergeant with the desk by the door, effectively the staff receptionist and gatekeeper, looked up in boredom to see who had found her dusty lair. Behind her was the typical Pentagon office, a room meant during World War II for two or three people that had been chopped up into ten cubicles separated by chest-high dividers covered in neutral gray fabric. There were five cubicles on each side of a passageway not much wider than a big man's shoulders.

"Byrnes?" Ojeda asked.

The staff sergeant nodded leftward. "Last cubicle on the right," she said, and went back to her book. Byrnes's corner was the low spot on this suite's totem pole, all the way down and away from the window, which at any rate only looked onto the well of an airshaft and other opaque windows a few feet away.

The two walked in single file along the passageway, the only way it was possible to move in it. At the end, under a nameplate that read "Captain Byrnes," an officer was writing on his computer keyboard, his back to them.

Byrnes looked over his shoulder, saw them and stood up. Sherman and Ojeda effectively formed a fourth wall to Byrnes's cubicle. Sherman saw thumbtacked up in the fabric some cartoons lampooning the president, a clipping of a column by William Safire and a bumper sticker that simply read, "Afghanistan?"

Byrnes didn't seem entirely surprised to be read his rights or even to be told that he would be restricted to quarters. But he flinched when Ojeda added a new twist: From this moment, he would not be allowed to use or interact in any fashion with government computers. His PC here would be impounded as would the government-issued IBM ThinkPad laptop he had at home. Should he need a computer to help prepare his defense, one would be issued upon request.

The Pentagon
Friday, June 24
10 A.M.

"Scores May Be Charged in Military Dissent Probe," the *Washington Telegraph*'s front page reported on Friday morning, quoting "senior Pentagon sources."

The leak provoked the defense secretary to convene a meeting the same morning in his conference room of all the lead investigative agencies. The CID chief told the SecDef that he was honored to be there but unable to discuss a pending investigation in that venue. The SecDef dropped his usual glad-handing demeanor. "Stop dicking around, General. You tell me what you have right now, or start thinking about which state police force you're gonna work for. And I can assure you it isn't going to be West Virginia or anywhere else I have a say, you keep up that goddamned attitude."

The FBI man was more cooperative. He told the defense secretary that he was confident his agents could soon identify at least five more "ringleaders" in addition to Byrnes and Decamp. And depending on what sort of cooperation they got, they could nail two dozen or so additional participants, probably one from most major Army bases.

Defense Secretary Johnson nodded throughout as if in pleased agreement. He thanked the FBI man for the "thoughtful and comprehensive" brief. Then, maintaining this genial posture, he emphatically reversed the investigators' entire approach.

"Now, as you know, this is a matter of national security, which means that I call the shots, and this is how we're gonna do it," he drawled easily. "We're not gonna hold any mass trials of United States military officers."

He looked down one side of the table, then up the other. "You go to those boys on the bases that are mixed up in this Sons of Liberty crap, tell them they can resign quietly or get real familiar with back-to-back unaccompanied tours in northern Greenland until they are gray-haired. Tell them they'll never get laid again. They'll get out. If they don't, just tell their CGs to harass the shit out of them—make them base VD officers and such."

Maddox's legal counsel, a smart, independent-minded Air Force colonel, cleared his throat. "With respect, sir, I don't think you want to improperly interfere in the disposition of this matter."

The defense secretary glared at him. "That's a question above your pay grade, well above it," he said. "This is a question for political leadership, not for lawyers. And I am telling you that we are not going to give troublemakers on each post of the United States Army a rallying point."

He again surveyed the table. "That leaves you Byrnes and Decamp. You get those cases in the hands of the right authorities, tell them to use discretion, move them along quietly and swiftly.

"As for Senator Feaver, I will inform him that we are willing to quietly drop our investigation of his consorting with the seditious targets of the investigation, as long as he stops trying to subpoena my chiefs."

Pennsylvania Avenue Plaza
Outside the White House
Sunday, June 26
9:30 A.M.

Lewis thought long and hard on Sunday morning before deciding to go to the White House demonstration. He could think of good reasons not to go, but somehow they felt more like intellectual excuses. His heart and gut told him he should be there—and, ultimately, he felt, those were the impulses you had to obey. He could explain to other people why he couldn't go—but he wasn't sure he could look himself in the mirror.

It came down to duty. He saw his duty mainly as flowing downward, given to the soldiers he led in exchange for them trusting him with their lives. Break that bargain, he thought to himself, and you aren't a leader, you're just a murderous bureaucrat, unworthy of the uniform.

And so he went to the closet and took out his newest set of Alphas, reserved usually for official functions of the vice chairman's office. He would wear his best, remembering the teaching of his old OPFOR commander: "If you are going to go, go all the way." Half measures were what killed soldiers. Half an hour later he stood outside the northern gates of the White House.

Inside, Willy Pitch looked out the window at the gathering crowd. Until Friday, he had thought the demonstration would fizzle. No Americans had died in Afghanistan since May 30, and the sixty-day deadline on the mission didn't come up until July. They could finesse that when it came, maybe get the two hostages out before then. "Sure, there are some remaining problems, but the Afghan situation is settling back in the lingerie pages, the way these things always do—look at Bosnia, Kosovo, Haiti, Iraq," he told the president. "Ironically, the Sons of Liberty action to prevent the cruise missile strike probably helped us."

"Make sure the defense secretary understands I don't need any more of that kind of help," the president responded.

But then at the last moment the news broke that more than twenty serving military officers could be charged, and that two officers already had been taken into custody. That was unprecedented. The sense that the administration was going to play legal hardball with the military transformed a routine protest march into something far greater. Vets riding Honda 750s and Harley-Davidsons with huge American flags flying from plastic poles on their backseats sent noisy delegations from as far away as Illinois and Missouri. Men wearing the uniforms of officers lay down in body bags at each White House entrance, leaving only their faces visible at the top of each bag's zipper.

Lewis, in the main body of the crowd, watched the body baggers be interviewed by reporters. He suspected that these men actually were military wannabes. But he saw in the crowd at least half a dozen faces he recognized from the Pentagon, some in uniform, most not.

The main body of the crowd, about fifteen hundred people, stayed immobile on the plaza, listened to speeches and chanted. A retired Army sergeant led the protesters in a call-and-response imitation of a boot camp jody: "I don't know, but I been told / President Shick is mighty cold."

The national security adviser came in for special attention in the speeches. It was Pitch, much more than even President Shick, who was seen as the villain of the Afghanistan mission. At the end of a speech by a fighter pilot turned talk-show host turned congressman from San Diego, the crowd took up a new chant: "Pitch and Shick / Shuck and jive / Bring our troops / Home alive!"

After the last "Out of Afghanistan now!" speech, the crowd suddenly hushed and heads turned toward the White House lawn. Taking a page from Richard Nixon's book, the national security adviser had emerged from his office to invite the leaders of the demonstration to come in and meet with him. He stood at the Pennsylvania Avenue guardhouse, just behind the black steel bars of the gate. Pitch was telling one of the organizers that he thought there was "common ground to be explored" when the body bagger just outside the gate stood up—he looked to Lewis to be wearing a first lieutenant's single silver bar—and lobbed a fat plastic bag of cow's blood at him. The thin plastic of the bag broke open on the black metal bar, splashing blood across Pitch's face and rumpled gray Brooks Brothers suit. Pitch reached for his cheek, felt the distinctive slimy feel of blood—this wasn't colored water, he could tell with one touch—and his jowls turned ashen with fear. He stumbled backward from the fence, thinking of the possibility of AIDS. Three Secret Service uniformed officers surrounded him and hustled him back up the driveway into the White House.

Lewis watched from the main body of the crowd, fifty yards away. He felt confused. *Where are we going with this?* He still wasn't sure that the body bagger really was an active-duty military officer. But he knew that there were plenty in the crowd. The American system's civilian control of the military suddenly seemed a delicate arrangement to him. If soldiers started making up their own rules, they would be a mob, he thought as he watched the excitement over the attack on Pitch send a ripple across the crowd.

A wedge of D.C. police officers who had been standing on the sidelines of the demonstration pushed into the crowd, aiming for the blood-throwing body bagger. The crowd pushed back. More cops came to the aid of the first group, and the crowd responded again. Two more bags of blood came flying over the crowd and splashed around the police. Some of the Harleys roared to life, as if to ride at the police lines. From the police command and control van parked at the corner came the signal: Arrest them all.

The District of Columbia Jail
1 P.M.

Jailers are never in a hurry. Time is what they charge other people. The guards running the D.C. jail in the basement of the federal courthouse were absolutely leisurely as they went about the task of separating the demonstrators as they arrived, meeting the buses at a loading dock and directing the seventy-one wearing military uniforms toward a chain-link cage lit by long fluorescent lights high overhead.

Seven hours later an assistant U.S. attorney came down to address the seventy-one uniformed demonstrators. She was an angry-looking woman in her late thirties wearing an expensive-looking but wrinkled black linen two-piece suit and white Nike sneakers. She looked overworked, Lewis thought, watching her through the chain links. "Active-duty military, those of you that aren't phonies, will be transferred in the morning to military authority and transported to Quantico, Virginia, to face processing and possible charges there. Could be a while, it being a weekend." She wheeled and left. "Show your military IDs as you board."

It suddenly came home to Lewis that for him and the other officers, a conviction and sentence of more than a month could mean time in the "Little House" at Fort Leavenworth's disciplinary barracks, the only place in which the Army, Air Force and Marines imprisoned officers. Mainly it was military dentists who raped their anesthetized patients, he'd heard, along with the occasional jealous-lover murderer and drug-peddling cokehead.

He looked for space in the cell to lie down. If the pissed-off prosecutor was right, this was a good time to grab some sleep. In the field, always be ready to go twenty-four hours, his first tactical officer at West Point had taught him. He loosened his plain black uniform tie and lay down in a corner, trying to ignore the buzz of instant-replay talk among knots of arrested protesters. It was more comfortable than trying to fall asleep in the turret of a Bradley. He dozed off quickly.

He awoke to see a man leaning over him—a U.S. marshal, by the badge and uniform. The man was studying Lewis's face with a puzzled, uncomprehending look. "Lieutenant?" the marshal said. "Lieutenant Lewis?"

Lewis focused on the face and searched his memory. Then it clicked: The man was "X Files," one of his troops from when he had an OPFOR weapons platoon, about seven years back. He was a trooper who ran into more than his share of trouble—it just seemed to happen—but who was always willing to hump the .50-cal or the mortar plate. Like a lot of Lewis's best soldiers, he had more heart than brains. Lewis had once driven thirty-five miles to Barstow at 2 A.M. to bail X Files out of jail after the kid had waded into a bar fight to save another OPFOR trooper he didn't even know. It turned out later that the other trooper actually was a dirtbag who thought he had been burned on a mescaline deal.

Looking up, Lewis remembered what a scrapper X Files had been. Beaten as a kid by his mother's boyfriend, he had fraudulently joined the Army at age seventeen, aided by a recruiter desperate to make quota who had forged the signature giving the required parental permission for the underaged recruit to enlist. He had slowly turned his life around in the Army. His tour at Fort Irwin, deep in the empty black and brown hills of the Mojave Desert, had suited him: "Further away I am from the city and my so-called dad, the better off I am," he had concluded. He had always maintained that he was going to use his Montgomery GI benefits to go to school and become an "FBI man," so his squadmates had hung him with the nickname "X Files," after the television reruns they watched incessantly about two government investigators. He apparently hadn't made it into the Bureau, but his trajectory had carried him close, to the U.S. Marshals Service. He now was on its lowest rung, as a guard in the subbasement of the D.C. court complex.

"X Files, you old pain in the butt, how are you?"

"Lieutenant Lewis, I mean, Major Lewis," he said, crouching next to him and nodding at the golden oak leaves on Lewis's shoulders. "Anyone else here I know, sir?"

Lewis gazed around the cell at the scores of men in uniform. "Not that I know of."

"Better class of folk than what we usually get in here," the marshal said.

"X, you know that Webb book I had the platoon read, *Fields of Fire*? Remember how he said they're the best we have? These men here are the ones who really care."

"I know what you mean, sir." A wave of worry clouded X Files's face. "I'll be back in five."

He returned in exactly that time, accompanied by three other marshals—the Army and Marine veterans' contingent in the subbasement night shift. Lewis stood to greet them.

"No way I'm locking up my old LT," X Files said. "I remember you getting me out of the Barstow jail on your Visa card, sir."

X Files stepped back in deference to a black Marine vet who was senior to him in the marshals' service. "I understand you're pretty squared away for a doggie," the marshal said by way of introduction. His deep voice was made unnaturally hard by the knowledge of what he was about to do. "We talked"—he nodded at his three subordinates—"and we figured it ain't a crime for officers to look out for their troops. Crime when they don't—like this foul-up with that patrol in Afghanistan." So, the marshal explained, they had come up with a plan. "Happens that we're close to break time. All of us are going upstairs for coffee. Wouldn't be surprised if them doors out back was unlocked. There's no paper on anyone here yet, so it'll just be like it never happened." He gestured toward the big chain-link gate at the back of the holding area. "You might find that corridor there goes out to Pennsylvania Avenue. Man can get a cab there."

"Thanks," Lewis said.

X Files nodded in understanding of the plan. "If you're not here when break's over—well, that's the way things go, sir." He extended his right hand and shook Lewis's in farewell.

All in all, sixty-three men in the holding tank walked out. Another eight stayed, wanting to make a statement by going through the legal process. The leavers departed in good order, a quiet, grinning group. At the Pennsylvania Avenue exit they waited at the base of a big ramp and departed at intervals, strolling up to street level, spacing it out over fifteen minutes, careful not to call attention to themselves.

Lewis was one of the last left at the base of the ramp. As he waited in the shadows near the wall he stared up at the evening sky and felt a pang of worry. This is wrong, he thought. This is a jailbreak. Are we protecting this system or undermining it?

He thought about going back but felt that would be a betrayal of the personal loyalty just shown him by X Files. The personal always won out over the theoretical with Lewis. So instead he walked up out of the subbasement, feeling like he was pulling with him a small piece of the foundation of the government. He hailed a Statue of Liberty taxi on Pennsylvania. Once in the backseat, he realized that he hadn't considered where to go. Home seemed like a bad idea for someone escaping from jail, but the Pentagon was a big safe place. He could go to his office and collect his thoughts. He asked the driver to take him to the Pentagon's river entrance.

He swiped his pass at the door and walked in the building just after 10 P.M. Surprisingly, the door to the vice chairman's office was unlocked.

He pushed it open and found Stout at the front desk and Ames and Underhill deep in conversation behind him. They looked a bit startled when he walked in. There was a laptop on Underhill's desk, its screen open but blank. The colonel looked at Lewis in an oddly challenging way, as if to say, What could possibly be strange about us meeting here in a deserted Pentagon on a Sunday night?

Ames recovered first. He looked up and down Lewis's wrinkled, dirty uniform but didn't comment on it. "We are going through what the Chinese lament as 'interesting times,' Major Lewis," Ames said softly. "So it is important for me to know: Are you with me, with us, on this?" He didn't say what "this" was.

Lewis looked him in the eye. "Sir, I promise you, you can count on me. I will do the right thing." Ames weighed that response and half smiled. It was the type of answer he would have given—and he didn't trust it.

After Lewis left for a shower in the POAC, Ames asked Stout to make sure that he kept an eye on "our young major's wanderings."

Ames sat for half an hour at his desk, considering his dilemma. How far was he willing to go? All his life, there had been one answer: as far as necessary to achieve victory. The winners write the history, he'd always said.

And now the SOBs were invading his computer, conspiring to set up a case against him, undermining his effort to save the Army from dinosaurs like Shillingsworth. American soldiers will die if Shillingsworth and his type prevail, he worried. He wasn't going to give up twenty-five years of effort so easily. He thought of his father, bitter and legless in his wheelchair for forty years after being sent into Korea with bazookas that couldn't stop a North Korean tank.

He walked back out to the desks where Underhill and Stout awaited his orders. "We need to think now of the good of the Army," he said. "In many ways John Shillingsworth is a good man, a loyal soldier. But he isn't the man for our Army right now. We all have to make sacrifices."

Stout nodded. For the good of the Army.

"There are people trying to destroy us," Ames said. "And all we've worked for."

Stout nodded again.

Brookmont, Maryland
Monday, June 27
8:30 P.M.

As the moon rose over the Potomac, Sherman drove out MacArthur Boulevard to Cisco's little red house in Brookmont. Unusually, she had lingered while figuring out what to wear—she wanted to look appealing but not dressy. She wound up picking a sleeveless white cotton blouse and tight black jeans. Both showed off her figure well, she thought, without being flashy. She had decided that after she and Cisco finished wrapping up his pursuit, she would take him to a celebratory dinner at the Indian restaurant in Georgetown near the Key Bridge. They'd have lots of vegetarian dishes for him.

She wondered as she drove if she intended to sleep with Cisco. She hadn't figured that out yet. But the idea appealed to her. She liked him. They were kindred spirits. And she could use some company—after he'd washed his hair.

Parked on the street outside Cisco's cottage were three Montgomery County police cruisers and two unmarked blue Crown Victoria sedans. Neighbors gathered in the street parted to let her car through, craning down unabashedly to look at her. In the driveway there was an ambulance. Two medical technicians worked at its open back doors, lethargically assembling equipment. As she drove past them, she heard them chatting about the Redskins' first exhibition game, coming up in just two weeks. Their sluggishness, it occurred to her as she braked the Subaru, was a very bad sign.

At the front door she showed her military ID card to a uniformed policeman and identified herself as a colleague of Captain Cisco. At that a black man in a suit came out of the front room and identified himself as being from "Montgomery Homicide, lead investigator on this case." He asked her to come in and "pos ID the body for us."

He turned, kneeled beside the bed and lifted a corner of the gray plastic sheet covering a body on the floor. "That's enough," she said. She closed her eyes. She knew it was Cisco as soon as she saw the long black hair. She began to weep.

The detective led her to a chair. "Looks like a burglary gone bad," he said conversationally. She only half heard the words as the mellow voice washed over her. The detective seemed to be miles away.

"Every homicide has a surprise somewhere," he continued, "and the one here seemed to be that the blow to the head didn't come from a blunt object but from a shoe or boot—but not from the toe. Usually in a fight, someone kicks someone when they're down; they hit with the toe. Here it looks like a heel of a shoe or boot, right into the side of the head. Just crushed it in."

Sherman stood up again and wandered aimlessly around the front room. Cisco was here, now he's gone, she kept thinking. She walked to the doorway between the cottage's two rooms. Something was different, she thought. Something was wrong here. She looked around the back room again. The three personal computers were missing, and the floppy disk holders between them had been emptied.

She walked back into the front room and sat on the bed, trying to collect her thoughts. Finally she asked if she could go. The detective took her phone numbers and said yes. As she walked out, a tense female lawyer from the CIA arrived. She signed for custody of the body and of the house. The CIA actually ran its own funeral home business, a captive private firm in McLean that most years turned a small profit that was forwarded to the Agency's widows and orphans fund.

Sherman drove home and sipped a cup of green tea as she took in Cisco's death. She felt very alone. She called her parents but didn't share her news and took small consolation from their chat. She didn't feel safe in her own apartment—"Ames 2 of 4" sat in her briefcase, and "Ames 3 of 4" was still in the uniform jacket she had worn on Thursday.

It's my fault, she thought.

She packed her briefcase and her uniform into her car, drove for ninety-five minutes out I-66 and checked into a motel in Front Royal, Virginia. But she felt even lonelier the next morning when she read the *Herald* over coffee at a McDonald's on the interstate and saw that there wasn't one word about Cisco's death in the newspaper, not even an obituary among all those aged colonels. She drove back to the Pentagon.

Headquarters Building, Fort McNair
Washington, D.C.
Tuesday, July 5
9 A.M.

The court-martial of Captain Bobby Byrnes began one week later.

Sherman was surprised that it happened at all. The scuttlebutt had been that the SecDef had sought to avoid it. Decamp, the Marine captain who had loaded the Sons of Liberty message into the Crisis Action Center's intranet, had pleaded out on one charge, dereliction of duty, under Article 92 of the Uniform Code of Military Justice.

In exchange for agreeing to testify against Byrnes, Decamp was quickly sentenced to thirty days in the Quantico brig, followed by confinement to home and place of employment for the subsequent five months. After six months, he would be dismissed. Decamp left the Marine sticker on the rear window of his pickup truck.

Following the SecDef's nudges, and over the angry objections of Augie Ojeda and others at CID, Captain Byrnes was offered only a slightly harsher deal: just six months in Leavenworth, followed by a dismissal. "What does flat-out treason get you nowadays?" Ojeda had disgustedly asked. "Maybe a year with time off for good behavior?"

Byrnes had staggered them all by refusing the lenient offer. He insisted on pleading not guilty and exercising his right to have a full scale trial. Then his lawyers waived the Article 32 preliminary hearing and asked to proceed directly to trial — all the evidence was against him, they figured, so there was no reason to have it introduced in a forum where he couldn't fight back.

Before the trial began he pursued what military lawyers call "the Kelly Flinn defense." It was high-risk, but it was the best course when they had you nailed on the facts and they had you nailed on the law. You pled the injustice of the military law itself. Flinn was an Air Force bomber pilot who had slept with the husband of an enlisted woman, then been charged with lying to an investigating officer and disobeying a direct order, as well as adultery. Her lawyer took the case to the newspapers, saying that his client was being victimized by a puritanical adultery law. After all, didn't a woman have the right in this day and age to choose her sexual partners? Likewise, Byrnes argued that he hadn't given up the right to free speech when he chose to serve his country.

So while his lawyers prepared for the court-martial, Byrnes worked the media. He began with talk radio the day after his arrest but in seventy-two hours was getting nibbles from television. Larry King's booking people called him after the White House demonstration got their attention. They were intrigued by his argument and liked his looks—the curly hair, the lopsided grin, the boyish charm, the articulate manner. He was a still youthful Harvard man who wore the Army uniform but who spoke the language of the times. He also skipped his weekly haircut, letting his hair lengthen to soften his appearance and so make him less threatening to an American public now unfamiliar with military life.

"A disgrace to be court-martialed?" Captain Byrnes said on the July 4 show to King, who leaned forward in rapt attention, head thrust forward from his shoulders. "No, by God. It would be a disgrace not to speak out. I consider it an honor to have my statements examined. I welcome the judgment of my peers." He also privately relished the telephone calls and e-mails from old Harvard classmates who had wondered what had become of him.

The trial took place in a surprisingly small room on the third floor of the headquarters building of Fort McNair, directly across the Potomac from the Pentagon, not more than one hundred yards from Ames's house. Aside from the Walter Reed Hospital complex, Fort McNair was the only Army installation actually within the borders of Washington, D.C. In one of his few light moments, General Shillingsworth told Cindy that he thought it was appropriate to hold this particular court-martial at a post named after a general killed by friendly fire. General Lesley McNair, he explained, had been killed by U.S. bombers that dropped their load short in Normandy in World War II.

Behind the wooden railing in the tiny courtroom there were just two lines of chairs offering only eighteen places for spectators, with the place for the last two seats taken up by a television camera brought in for the occasion. The trial would be carried via closed circuit to the auditorium of the National Defense University at the other end of the post.

Sherman took a seat in the back of that big room, where members of the Army staff were congregating. Down in front there was a special diplomatic section, in which all sixty seats were filled. After fifteen years of overweening behavior by the world's greatest military power, there was an ill-concealed glee among the diplomatic corps at the U.S. military's dirty laundry being washed in public. "I am here to see if our North

American friends can learn as enthusiastically as they teach," said the Paraguayan defense attaché, resplendent in his gold-braided uniform and ready for payback after enduring years of well-intentioned lectures about the role of a military in a democracy. He knew very well how a democracy worked, he just didn't want to be part of one.

The four representatives from the British embassy—two from the defense attaché's office, one from the political affairs section and one intelligence officer from the agricultural section—were more discreet in public but still pointed in their private conversations. "In Cromwell's time we had our own set-to with our army," the political officer told a friend from the Turkish embassy. "That's why we have a Royal Navy and a Royal Air Force, you know, but not a royal army. They chopped off the king's head."

Captain Byrnes was represented by two defense lawyers, one military, one civilian. Lead defense counsel was a captain from Fort Meade named E. C. Walker. He was assisted by a conservative Republican congressman named Casper Casmiro from Long Island, New York, who was friendly with Byrnes's father and had been an astute litigator before running for federal office.

As they waited for the military judge to appear, the bald congressman made his biggest single contribution to the defense of Bobby Byrnes. Worried that Byrnes would strike the jury as smart-alecky, he leaned over and whispered, "Keep your fingers crossed. People forget that at the Nuremberg war crimes trials, three of the twenty-one defendants were acquitted." Byrnes looked at him sharply: Were those the chances here? Representative Casmiro drove the point home: "Of course, most of those found guilty were hanged." Byrnes appeared properly sobered, almost meek. Good, Casmiro thought, knock off that prime-time posturing.

At the bailiff's "All rise," Judge Homer Trice and the military panel entered the courtroom at the same time. As in a civilian courtroom, everybody stood. But it was striking that here every military person in the room—the prosecutor, the defense counsel, the defendant and the soldiers in the spectators' seats—came to attention and remained rigidly in that position, staring straight forward, until the judge and the eight members of the military panel were seated. Judge Trice, a thin-faced military lawyer from Vermont, wore a black robe, but the shirt and tie of his Army uniform were visible in the open V of the robe below his chin. Under his robe were the eagles of a full colonel.

Walker now had his first opportunity to address the members of the military panel, which essentially was the jury, but enjoying more power and respect than a jury had in civilian jurisprudence. Walker's advantage was that military officers, unlike civilians, wore their résumés on their uniforms, in the form of insignias and ribbons.

The makeup of the military panel was key in court-martials, far more so than in civilian trials. The bailiff had assigned the higher-ranking officers, four colonels, to the front row of the jury box, with the four lieutenant colonels seated in the second row. All the officers were male. One of the colonels was black, as was the lieutenant colonel sitting directly behind him. But race meant far less to the members of the panel than did their branches in the Army—that was the real divider. The senior colonel, who by virtue of his seniority would be president of the military panel, was a career acquisition specialist named Shufflebarger. He would be tolerated but not much respected by the officers from the combat arms. The rap on guys like him was that they did their twenty-five and then got out and made a killing in the defense industry selling overpriced weapons to their former subordinates—or to the nation's foes, on occasion.

The key to the defense strategy, Walker suspected, might be the juror in the middle of the back row, Lieutenant Colonel Jimmy Ryan. By time in grade he was the most junior member of the panel, but judging by his uniform insignia he was likely to be counted one of its most respected members. There were two forms of military deference—official and personal. Colonel Shufflebarger would receive the first, Walker calculated, and Lieutenant Colonel Ryan the second.

Ryan's military credentials were impressive, Walker saw. On Ryan's lapel were the crossed muskets denoting membership in the infantry branch. Above his chest ribbons he wore both the little silver "ice cream cone" badge of the paratrooper and the combat infantryman's badge, a long rifle on a blue backing framed by a wreath. He was far too young for Vietnam, Walker knew, so that badge commemorated service in either Panama or the Gulf War.

Walker's eye looked over to Ryan's right shoulder, where Army personnel were allowed to wear the patch of any division in which they had served in combat. Ryan was wearing the distinctive red and green of the 24th Mechanized Infantry Division. Walker knew the 24th ID did the Gulf War but not Panama. He confirmed this by looking at the fruit salad of ribbons on Ryan's chest. There, at the lower right-hand corner, he saw the red, black and green of the Kuwait liberation medal. One of the top ribbons denoted the receipt of a Silver Star—not many of those awarded for the Gulf War, Walker knew. Finally, the lawyer noted that below Ryan's other shoulder was the little yellow-and-black curved "Ranger" tab.

This Lieutenant Colonel Ryan, Walker concluded, was a lifetime member of the insiders' club. Walker would focus his arguments on Ryan and hope that the young hotshot could bring along a few other members of the jury—all that Walker needed to get a hung jury, his only hope of avoiding a finding of guilty.

The prosecutor, a smart young major from South Carolina named Winston Bray, stood and addressed the judge. "The prosecution is ready to proceed with the trial in the case of the United States against Captain Robert Byrnes," he said.

Judge Trice nodded. "The members of the court will now be sworn," he responded. "All persons in the courtroom, please rise."

Bray approached the jury box and asked the eight officers to raise their right hands. The judge gave them his standard opening talk, but its emphasis on the importance of conscience and the permanent secrecy of their deliberations resonated unusually with this panel. He asked them all to "swear that you will faithfully and impartially try, according to the evidence, your conscience and the laws applicable to trials by court-martial, the case of the accused now before this court." And he reminded them that Captain Byrnes was presumed to be innocent. "The government has the burden of proving the accused's guilt by legal and competent evidence beyond a reasonable doubt. A reasonable doubt is an honest, conscientious doubt, suggested by the material evidence, or lack of it, in the case. It is an honest misgiving generated by insufficiency of proof of guilt."

In the second row of the jury box, Lieutenant Colonel Ryan jotted his first note of the trial: "honest misgiving." He liked that phrase.

The judge then made explicit the basic ground rule of balancing rank against each member of the jury's voice. "The senior member of the panel will act as your presiding officer in your closed-session deliberations, and he will speak for the court in announcing the results," he said. Colonel Shufflebarger nodded. He was in charge.

The judge continued: "However, each of you has an equal voice and vote with the other members in discussing and deciding all issues submitted to you." At this Lieutenant Colonel Ryan nodded.

Major Bray stood to announce the government's charges. What he wouldn't disclose was that those charges had been the subject of a protracted fight inside the Pentagon over the previous two weeks. Augie Ojeda had shown Sherman the CID memorandum recommending six major charges, each carrying possible sentences of at least two years, and some of five or more.

Sherman knew there had been an argument but hadn't realized how much those proposed charges had been stripped down to the bare minimum. Article 90—willful disobedience of a superior commissioned officer—had been dropped, because prosecutors couldn't point to any order Byrnes had explicitly disobeyed. Gone too was Article 92, failure to obey a lawful order. It was more that he had encouraged others to do so.

Finally there were just three charges remaining. There even had been some argument over one of those, the Article 81 specification—conspiracy to solicit desertion or mutiny.

The other two were standard charges that could be brought against anyone who stepped out of line: Article 133, conduct unbecoming an officer, and 134, behavior prejudicial to the good order and discipline of the armed forces or of a nature to bring discredit upon them. The latter was known among military prosecutors as "the Billy Mitchell charge," in memory of the 1925 court-martial of the insubordinate Army flier. It was the military equivalent of nailing Al Capone for income-tax evasion—that is, weak but better than nothing.

Next in the trial came voir dire, the chance for the lawyers to knock people off the panel. Bray asked the members if each of them could vote for a finding of guilty if convinced of the accused's guilt beyond a reasonable doubt. Ryan considered this, then decided yes, he could—but noted to himself that he had a lot of reasonable doubts about whether anyone should be punished for opposing a mission as ill-considered and poorly executed as the one in Afghanistan.

Bray had noticed the crossed arrows on the lapel of one of the lieutenant colonels, indicating membership in the Special Forces branch. Like many military prosecutors he had learned to be wary of Special Forces officers, who tended much more than regular Army personnel to be individualistic and skeptical of authority, and so inclined to go along with defense counsel arguments that, hey, things got a little out of hand, but it happens to everyone. He used his one peremptory challenge to dismiss the Special Forces officer from the panel.

Representative Casmiro wanted to use the defense's sole peremptory challenge to remove the old colonel, Shufflebarger, whose sour expression worried him. But Walker said that with just six people on the panel, the prosecution under military law needed only four votes to convict. But with seven, it would need five to get the two-thirds of the panel required for a conviction. "I win with three for 'not guilty' in either case," Walker explained. "So I like the percentages better with seven members." Casmiro nodded—the numbers game was different in a military courtroom, where trials are permitted to end with a hung jury. In civilian law, by contrast, a hung jury simply means a retrial.

Headquarters Building, Fort McNair
Wednesday, July 6
9 A.M.

Bray, the prosecutor, made his major mistake at the beginning of the second day of the court-martial. And he did it without even opening his mouth.

As he stood to make the opening statement that would begin the trial on the merits, he smiled at the task before him. His expression of nervous glee would be repeated in lesser ways by the lead defense counsel, but it would cost Bray more because the burden of proof lay on his side.

The problem was that Bray and the defense counsel loved being assigned to the case of *United States v. Captain Byrnes*. For years both had slogged through the legal scut work thrown off by everyday life in the military—unauthorized absences and desertions, sexual harassment allegations and, most of all, Article 112a for the wrongful manufacture, possession, distribution and use of narcotics. For them, *U.S. v. Byrnes* was bliss, a beautiful snowy mountain peak rising above a vast swamp of mundane charges against undereducated enlisted men. And so they arrived at Fort McNair each morning full of unconscious good cheer.

The members of the military panel, by contrast, hated it. None had joined the Army in order to sit on court-martials. They did it because it was their duty. But it felt to them like they were being dragged away from their real work to deal with an ugly family fight that should have been handled quietly rather than in a public spectacle that could only diminish the Army in the eyes of an ignorant public.

Bray laid out the evidence of Byrnes's guilt. He was unemotional. "There are certain elements we must prove in order for you to find the accused guilty," he said. "We will." He said he would give them what they needed—not just the live testimony of the coconspirator, but also Byrnes's e-mails to people at Forts Polk, Drum, Bragg and elsewhere. He could demonstrate the planning to stop the Afghanistan operation and the clear intent to do so.

"The whole idea of disclosing an operation plan in the middle of that operation—that is breathtaking irresponsibility," he concluded. "This is an offense that could have resulted in lives being lost."

Walker objected to the assertion as "crossing the line into speculation." The comment was struck.

Walker's opening statement was shorter. "I'll make it easy on you," he said, almost sighing as he turned toward the prosecutor. "Captain Byrnes did many of the things of which he is accused."

He swung back toward the panel. "But his conduct wasn't unbecoming. I will seek to demonstrate that whatever he did, he did not disgrace his uniform."

The first witness for the prosecution was Lieutenant General Still, who expressed the Army's disappointment in Captain Byrnes's performance.

Then Bray led the jury through the government's investigation. He began with the CID information systems investigator, who mapped out the Sons of Liberty e-mail trail, showing how most of the activity was directly traceable to Byrnes's computer at the Pentagon—the first message titled "HONOR," the second one titled "SHAME," then "THE WORLD" and "FINALLY," then the follow-up to Fort Polk titled "SALUTE," then the "MURDER?" message the day of the sit-down strike inside the Pentagon the day of the Afghanistan funerals, and ultimately the shut-down of the Afghanistan operation.

Then came Augie Ojeda, who offered a highly selective account of the government's subsequent investigation. Sherman, watching on the auditorium monitor, thought he made it seem like the Pentagon had one day decided to put a stop to the Sons of Liberty and the next had slapped the cuffs on Byrnes. There was no mention of that poor captain they'd mistakenly arrested down at Fort Bragg, or of the role played by the National Security Agency's supercomputers. Most striking of all, she thought, was the complete omission of Cisco's efforts. It was as if the dead Air Force captain had become a nonperson, she thought as she walked alone to the Metro that night.

And eventually, she thought as she walked the quiet street, the court-martial would have to get to the central role played by General Ames. He was the spider in the middle of the web. But when?

Headquarters Building, Fort McNair
Thursday, July 7
9 A.M.

Most of the third day was taken up by the final government witness—Decamp, the Marine who had entered the Sons of Liberty message into the CACNET. His captain's uniform hung on him—he had lost about twenty pounds in three weeks. The shattered officer gave a depressed, mumbling account of his actions on the morning of the aborted cruise missile strike on Afghanistan. There really wasn't much to say. He had ruined his life with four clicks of his mouse, he said. Byrnes had given him a disk, he had put it in his CAC terminal, opened up the document and hit "enter."

Bray asked, "Do you feel you have been punished for your offense?"

Decamp looked up at the prosecutor, almost bug-eyed with puzzlement. "I'm confined to an eight-by-six cell pretty much twenty-three hours a day. There's no air-conditioning. We sleep in sheets on top of sleeping bags on steel racks."

The prosecutor never asked how Decamp had come to know Byrnes, Sherman noticed as she watched in the auditorium. She was incredulous: Would Ames get away without being touched? Neither she nor Shillingsworth had told anyone about what was on the four disks labeled "Ames." Three disks now, she thought, now that the one Cisco had kept probably had been destroyed.

The judge looked at Walker and Casmiro. "Defense counsel—cross-examination?"

"Yes, thank you, sir," said Walker, standing. He could have called the judge either "Your Honor" or "sir," but chose the military usage to emphasize that the judge, like the jury, like himself and like many members of the audience, was an officer—but that this hostile witness no longer fully enjoyed that status.

"Speaking of your new assignment aboard Quantico," Walker began, "are you addressed as 'sir'?"

"No, they called me 'detainee' from the minute I got there. After the plea took effect they changed that to 'prisoner.'"

Walker acted as though that were news to him, though he knew this was true from dozens of previous cases. He paused as if to absorb that information. His purpose was to convey to the jury the unspoken message that this man was no longer really an officer—*no longer one of you, one of us.*

"Prisoner Decamp, I have just two final questions for you," he said.

The prosecutor objected to his addressing Decamp that way. The judge sustained it. "In this courtroom he remains entitled to his military rank," he ruled.

Walker asked the question again, using no form of address at all. "Did you understand what you were doing when you did it?"

"Yes, I think I had an idea," Decamp said.

"And did Captain Byrnes ask you to do it?" Getting the damage out of the way as fast as possible was what Walker had planned.

"Yes, he did."

"That's all. Thank you."

Memorial Bridge
Friday, July 8
5:43 A.M.

The U.S. military is headquartered in Washington, but it is not of Washington, in cultural terms. Its heart lies a thousand miles away or more—for the Army, at the edge of the Great Plains at Fort Leavenworth; for the Air Force, along a dozen different desert runways; for the Navy, in the languid harbors of Norfolk, San Diego and Pearl Harbor.

For the rest of official Washington, Congress is the engine that drives daily life. When Congress is in session, there is an extra energy in Washington's downtown. For every possible bit of legislation, a hundred government officials are kept hopping, and every official is attended by at least a dozen lobbyists, lawyers and reporters. When Congress is in session, people work later hours; having a spouse be absent from a dinner party is a badge of power. As a result, the pace of the politically engaged part of the city is that of Congress—rising late and not engaging the world until about ten in the morning.

But the military sticks to its own timetable in Washington, hearing a rhythm that predates democracy. It follows a schedule set on thousands of battlefields, where the most dangerous time of day is just before sunrise, when there is enough light to attack but still enough dark to cloak many movements. Even in Washington, members of the military rise in darkness most of the year and are at work by dawn. The effect of this is that the military has the capital largely to itself around sunrise.

B. Z. Ames jogged alone, westward past the Lincoln Memorial, in the half-light of the predawn. He was peering through the mist for one runner as he came to the Memorial Bridge. He knew John Shillingsworth's habits. He saw the old general lumbering along two hundred yards ahead of him, barely visible in the mist rolling off the river. Ames nodded to himself and stepped up his own pace a notch. He watched as Shillingsworth stopped on the grass at the Virginia end of the bridge and collected himself, leaning over and putting his hands on his knees, catching his breath before the final push past the Iwo Jima memorial and up the steep hill to his house.

Ames ran as softly as a cat, but Shillingsworth still had the ears and instincts of a seasoned infantryman. The chief of staff, red-faced and sweating, turned and straightened as Ames glided up behind him.

"You shouldn't have done it, Byron," Shillingsworth said, expressing exactly what was on his mind, his disgust evident in every syllable. "You went too damn far." He shook his head mournfully.

This was what Ames had come to learn. He understood: Shillingsworth had been mediating on the disk, and might actually charge him. The older man had that prerogative—even though Ames was in the Joint world, as vice chairman of the Joint Chiefs, he still was subject, in terms of military justice, to his service's chief of staff. Shillingsworth could make him a modern Benedict Arnold, the first four-star general ever to be court-martialed.

"John, I know we've had some disagreements," Ames said, standing between Shillingsworth and the river. "But I was doing what I thought best for our Army. What I saw as my duty."

Shillingsworth reddened. "Don't tell me that. I've read the disk," he said. "I know exactly what you did."

Ames said nothing. He knew now that there was no alternative. He shot a glance leftward to check that the car he expected was coming. Then he took one long stride toward Shillingsworth, planted both hands flat on the larger man's chest and pushed with all his strength.

Shillingsworth stumbled backward onto the empty cobblestoned roadway, fighting to keep his balance. The rented blue Ford Taurus coming across the bridge accelerated. Shillingsworth was falling backward when the black rubber bumper caught him in the kneecaps and flung him to the stones, smashing his skull. Sergeant First Class Stout expertly jerked the wheel to the left, ensuring that the right rear wheel crossed Shillingsworth's torso.

The car braked one hundred feet on. Stout got out as if to look for help, his body language conveying the message that he was acting responsibly. He actually was surveying the area to ensure that there were no passersby watching. Ames jogged up to the stopped car. "Clean it before you return it," he reminded Stout.

The car pulled away. Ames looked back at Shillingsworth's still body in the roadway. If the old guy wasn't dead, he was close to it. "Alpha Mike Foxtrot," Ames said quietly to himself, using the U.S. military code for "Adios, motherfucker." He turned and resumed his morning jog up the west bank of the Potomac.

John Shillingsworth's consciousness was ebbing away.

I am dying, the thought came to him. The caisson won't have to go far. Just up the hill. Wouldn't want to cause trouble for the Army. Low gray clouds, coming lower.

Haze everywhere. The dream again. Gettysburg. Clouds got inside head. Hot. Smoke everywhere. Fire from those trees on the right flank. A stone wall not twenty yards away. They are firing canister. Blown sideways. Belly full of shot. Lying in the grass, looking up across the rocks of the wall, see the Federal cannoneer's face: It is Byron Ames, grinning down at me. I have failed.

No one was aware of the attack on General Shillingsworth as the first defense witness took the stand four hours later.

The witness for the defense was Captain Byrnes himself. Walker wanted to introduce the accused as soon as possible, to make him real and to convey the point to the military panel that he was not afraid to speak in court. Walker took him through his career and assignments, seeking to emphasize that Byrnes was an officer just like the members of the panel. Shufflebarger, the old colonel who by virtue of his rank and seniority was the president of the military panel, was having none of that. He gazed straight ahead, not looking at Byrnes the entire time he testified.

Major Bray began the cross-examination of Captain Byrnes. This was the maximum point of danger in the trial. It was a calculated risk that Walker had taken, putting Byrnes on the stand. Bray could go almost anywhere he wanted with Byrnes.

The prosecutor's intent in his line of questioning was to drive a wedge between Byrnes and the military panel, to make Byrnes seem an aberration whose continued membership in the officer corps shouldn't be tolerated. "Now, Captain, your Sons of Liberty outfit put out a statement a few short months ago that said, 'The conduct of the Afghanistan mission should make any self-respecting officer ashamed of the uniform he wears.' This harsh opinion was originally transmitted from your laptop. Did you write it?"

"Yes, sir, I did," Byrnes said.

"Did you mean that to be taken literally?" The prosecutor's eyebrows shot up and stayed there, the lines of wrinkles across his forehead giving physical manifestation to his deep skepticism.

Byrnes sat erect in the witness box. He was careful to be earnest rather than slick. "Yes, I did, and I do," he said, turning to look at the military panel. "I think professional military officers who are subjected to the command of people who do not seem to have the welfare of officers and troops in mind, who put American soldiers in morally untenable positions—I think it is repugnant to ask a man to give up his life in such a situation. It goes against everything that we are taught to believe about this nation."

He had stepped into Bray's trap. "Ah, giving up lives." The prosecutor seized on the phrase. "Giving up lives," he repeated, letting the phrase roll around the courtroom like a live hand grenade. He asked the witness if he had ever been wounded in combat.

"No, sir, I have not," Byrnes said.

"Led troops into battle?"

"No, sir, I have not had that privilege," Byrnes said.

"Been in combat in any role or capacity whatsoever?"

"No," Byrnes said, a bit testily.

"Heard a shot fired in anger?"

Walker objected: "Asked and answered."

The judge nodded. "Let's move along here."

Zing. "The prosecution has no further questions for the witness," Bray said, turning his back on Byrnes.

Judge Trice took a note from the bailiff, then shook his head. He announced that the Army chief of staff had been critically injured. He asked the military panel if it wished to continue. Shufflebarger conferred with the others for a moment, then asked that the proceedings be recessed for the remainder of the day.

Sherman called the chief's office. A weeping Miss Turley told her that Shillingsworth was in surgery at Walter Reed but that it didn't look good.

Headquarters Building, Fort McNair
Monday, July 11
9:15 A.M.

The second week of the court-martial began with the president's national security adviser, Willy Pitch, being called to the stand by the defense. Bray had played the combat card; Walker was responding by putting the Afghan mission on trial.

Still red-faced and sweating from his brief exposure to Washington's summer heat between his limousine and the front door of the McNair headquarters building, Pitch approached the stand with confidence. He used a cane, as he frequently did when the stress of his work seeped into his joints.

Luckily, the big man thought as he waddled across the courtroom, the Afghan situation had stayed off the front pages for weeks, since the demonstration. And news of the hostage taking had never leaked.

Yet for all that good fortune Pitch was unable to disguise his fundamental irritation with this court-martial taking place. He had been shocked when Byrnes had refused the sweet plea deal he had been offered.

"Professor Pitch, did you know Robert Byrnes when he was an undergraduate at Harvard?" Walker began, partly as a relatively neutral way of gauging Pitch's mood. He had counted on Pitch's irritation and hoped to use it to undermine the government's case.

"Unfortunately, I did not make his acquaintance," the national security adviser huffed. "Had he taken one of my classes, he likely would have come away with a better understanding of the proper role the American military plays in this society."

Perfect, Walker thought. He resents our taking time out of his schedule, he is irritated that this came to trial and he blames the entire U.S. military for embarrassing him. Let it all hang out, Professor, he thought. The more he indulges his emotions, the more he will alienate the jury.

Walker asked "Professor Pitch" to recount when he had first encountered the Sons of Liberty, and his reaction thereto.

Pivoting on the head of his cane, Pitch turned his huge frame in the witness box to face the military panel. "Members of the U.S. military bent on inflaming opinion for the purpose of forcing or preventing government action engage in an exceedingly dangerous and unpredictable undertaking," he lectured. "Any American is welcome to challenge government policy—as a private citizen. A serving military officer is not a private citizen."

Take all the rope you need, Walker thought as he listened. Then the defense counsel moved on to the Afghanistan mission: What did Professor Pitch think of Byrnes's criticism of that? Bray objected to the question; Judge Trice allowed it.

"Afghanistan was a good mission," Pitch intoned. "We have prevented the possible breakup of nations, with the untold deaths that might cause through starvation and war. Now all the Pakistani nuclear warheads are believed to be accounted for and in responsible hands. As for the unfortunate patrol, who could have seen that that would happen? This was the price of doing business.

"I regret to report that among the tools issued me by the General Services Administration, there is no crystal ball," he said, patronizing the entire courtroom. "We are all fallible. We should try to do our jobs the best we can. That works better than telling other people, well above you in rank, what their jobs are."

The old colonel on the jury agreed. The rest listened respectfully but remained unpersuaded.

Lieutenant Colonel Ryan asked permission to ask "Professor Pitch" a question or two. The judge told him to write them down, then excused the panel and held an Article 39a discussion with counsel on whether to permit it. The penciled questions were: "Were you aware that the patrol sent out in Afghanistan wasn't made up of front-line combat troops? And did someone in the White House order out the patrol over the objections of the commander on the ground?" With the panel out of the room, Bray argued successfully that this was beyond the reach of the trial. But Walker privately celebrated the fact that the panel was thinking along those lines. He might be able to pull this off.

Walter Reed Army Medical Center
Washington, D.C.
3:30 P.M.

Cindy parked her Subaru outside the Heaton Pavilion, the main hospital building in the Walter Reed Army Medical Center. She looked up at the inverted cement pyramid of seven stories that dominated the smaller, older brick buildings around it in the Walter Reed complex. It was as if the Army, an institution focused on death and destruction, had been at a loss when required to erect a building dedicated to health and healing—and so had erected it upside-down. The result, Cindy thought as she passed through the sliding doors into the huge lobby, was that Heaton, with its heavy top layers pressing down on the smaller three stories, wound up as a kind of monument to power—which perhaps was what the Army was after all this time. You can hurt us, the building said, but we are strong, and we will take care of our own and send them back out again.

Miss Turley had set up shop in the living room of the chief's suite on the top floor of Heaton, turning it into a reception and screening area. It was the first time a serving Army chief had been hospitalized at the Army's premier hospital, a military outpost in a tree-drenched neighborhood of upper northwest Washington, since General Creighton Abrams's losing fight with lung cancer in 1974.

Shillingsworth's wife was sitting alongside Miss Turley. She looked up at Cindy and with quiet dignity handed her the "Special Interest Casualty Report." It read, "Progress—not expected. Morale—NA, patient unconscious. Diet—IVs. Ambulatory—No. DNR."

That grim summary still didn't prepare Cindy for the sight of her broken chief, his skull fractured, shoulder bones broken, internal organs bleeding, his entire left side deeply abraded, a tangle of tubes running into his bruised and cut flesh. The huge main room, half the size of a full ward, was dark, the curtains pulled tight against the heat of the afternoon sun. She opened her mouth but didn't say anything when she saw him.

"There aren't a lot of reserves there," a low voice rumbled out of a dark corner of the room. She turned to see General "Wimpy" Wilson sitting alone in an old cracked red leather armchair.

"Sir?" she said.

"The infantry life gave him an old man's body at fifty," Wilson explained in his low, slow voice. "What I mean is, the chief's dying." Cindy peered into the shadows and saw that Wilson's cheeks were wet.

He knuckled away a tear and told her to sit on the sofa next to him. "What we need to do now is think about how to help the Army," he said. He told her he knew about her work on the Sons of Liberty, and he understood that someone out at the Agency had traced some of that back to Ames.

"Now tell me what you know about B. Z. Ames," he ordered. She did tell him most of what she knew. But until she knew where Wilson was going, she wasn't going to mention the fourth disk, tucked away in a corner of the chief's desk.

Headquarters Building, Fort McNair
Tuesday, July 12
9:15 A.M.

The sixth day of the court-martial began with the last defense witness, Specialist Fourth Class Belsky, the radioman from the doomed patrol. He rolled himself into the courtroom, the forest-green cloth of his uniform pants folded back at the knees and tucked under the stumps of his legs. He had spent the last three months at Walter Reed Hospital. His face was pasty white, and he had lost weight.

His wheelchair didn't fit into the witness box, so he testified from just to the left of it, which placed him that much closer to the jury box than other witnesses. The bailiff clipped a wire microphone to his uniform lapel. When he was sworn in, he responded, "I d-d-do," in that high, reedy voice that sent every mind in the courtroom racing back to the tape that had been played on *Nightline*: "Oh, my p-p-poor legs." His voice was still chopped by stutter, but without the radio static it was even more distinct. And it was somehow hollow. He clearly had left part of his spirit that day among the poplars and pebbles of Afghanistan's plains.

"Now," Walker began, "Professor Pitch told us this was a good mission, well considered, but subject to unpredictability. In order to give the court a sense of what it actually was like on the ground, would you recount the first thing you said on your last patrol, as you passed out of the camp gate?"

Bray objected on the grounds of relevancy. Walker said they would establish that quickly.

Belsky answered remotely. His head dropped down slightly and he crossed his arms over his chest. "I really can't recall what I said, sir," he mumbled. "It wasn't important. I was just j-j-jiving with the duty man in the Three shop—that's the ops section—about that day's mission." His body language conveyed the underlying message that this court-martial was some kind of officers' fight and he was really not going to get involved here.

Walker pushed him. "I believe your exact remarks were transcribed. We can have them read to you." At the defense counsel's table, Congressman Casmiro reached for a folder.

Belsky shrugged his shoulders: *OK, I give up.* He gave it to Walker straight: "I said it was f-f-fucked-up to be here, that this was the most f-f-fucked-up patrol on the most f-f-fucked-up deployment I'd ever been on."

"And then, when you were reminded you were transmitting on the command net?"

"When s-s-someone from the TOC called and t-t-told me to identify myself, I said I was f-f-fucked-up, but I wasn't *that* f-f-fucked-up." In the back row of the jury box, the lieutenant colonels allowed themselves to grin a bit. This was the way soldiers talked. After days of Washington-style testimony, the radioman carried the credibility of the field Army. It was almost as if he had brought the aromas of diesel fumes and mud wafting into the cramped courtroom. The jury seemed to come awake: This is what the Army was really about, troops in the field. This soldier had lost his legs and his buddies.

Walker then delved into the structure of the mission. "Did you know the other soldiers with whom you were sent out to patrol potentially hostile territory?"

"Of the fifteen, sir, I knew t-t-two, both from my reserve unit. One, Pasquarette, I'd been to b-b-basic with, too—we were in the same DEP stick, you know, going into b-b-boot camp. The other was Zebrowski, who dated my little s-s-sister awhile in high school." The remaining thirteen, he said, were "pretty much s-s-strangers, sir."

Bray stood and objected again, "Your Honor, I do not believe this is a trial of the Army's personnel policies."

The judge looked at the defense lawyer. "Counsel?"

"No," Walker responded. "It is a trial of Captain Byrnes and statements he has made. This testimony goes to some of those statements about the structure of the Afghanistan mission." Judge Trice ordered Walker to move along. But the panel had gotten the point: The brass hadn't cared enough to send a cohesive unit in harm's way.

Walker asked Belsky if he was "familiar with this electronic organization that calls itself the Sons of Liberty?"

"I never sent any of that st-st-stuff but saw it sometimes," Belsky said. "Sir, with respect, that was kind of o-o-officers' turf," he added. "But I knew where they were c-c-coming from. I agreed with a la-la-lot of it."

His testimony finished, Belsky pushed the left wheel of his wheelchair and saluted the judge, then the right wheel and saluted the colonels in the front row of the jury box. Then he rolled himself to the wooden gate held open by the bailiff and left the courtroom.

Major Walker turned to the judge. "Sir, the defense rests."

When Cindy got to the office that evening, Miss Turley was there, her vigil at Walter Reed ended. She solemnly handed Cindy a piece of paper titled "General Order." Even as she took it, she had a good idea of what it would say: "The death of General John Clark Shillingsworth, Chief of Staff, United States Army, which occurred this afternoon at 1205, is announced with deep regret." She plunged into helping make calls inviting the chief's old comrades to the funeral on Thursday.

In between calling retired generals she looked out the window and realized she could see Fort McNair across the river, including the headquarters building, where the court-martial was being conducted. A chill crept across her: Ames's name wasn't going to be raised in the proceedings. And that meant he would stay in power. He wasn't the prey. She was.

Headquarters Building, Fort McNair
Wednesday, July 13
9 A.M.

Judge Trice began by announcing that the trial would suspend the next day in honor of the late chief of staff and to permit attendance at the memorial service. Then he nodded to Bray.

"Please the court," Bray said, standing. He looked about the room— first at the judge, then at the military panel, then at the audience. His slow gaze encompassed them all.

"We are a nation of laws, not of people," the prosecutor said. "This junior officer cannot be permitted to decide which laws are good for this country. Nor should he be allowed to judge which rules are good for this military. Most of all, he cannot decide which orders or policies he will follow.

"Think of the foolishness of letting this young man, who has never led men in battle, never been wounded—indeed, never heard a shot fired in anger—think of the *effect* of letting this man decide what is wise for a vast military organization. All military regulation, accumulated painfully over the centuries, is built upon one abiding goal: holding troops together in combat. It is not the place of this untested junior officer to overturn that body of wisdom."

Bray took two steps toward the military panel and looked directly at them. "Nor is it yours. Your duty here is to uphold the law. To do otherwise—that is, to disregard the law and judge the policy—would strike at the very heart of this democracy.

"And it would be doubly troubling in a military context, where we obey the laws of our nation and also the lawful orders of our superiors. This young man"—he held out his hand, palm open and rising up, as if measuring the very moral lightness of Captain Byrnes—"obeyed neither."

"Who is he, then? He is a familiar type in other nations, but thankfully not in our own. He would be the man on the white horse, who wants to do away with all the messiness of democracy and replace it with the bright lines that he somehow sees more clearly than do the rest of us. He is a danger. While telling us that he is protecting our system, he in fact undercuts it. Permit him to go unpunished, and you will be joining in his works." In the front row of the jury box, one of the colonels raised his chin, as if he were being accused.

"What message would be sent by leaving this man in the Army? The message would be: Do your own thing. Duty would be whatever each man decided it was that day. Discipline would be undermined across the breadth of the service.

"Every drill sergeant, every squad leader, every company commander would shudder. Don't do it to them. Don't do it to yourselves."

Bray paused for a moment as he fixed his eyes briefly on each of the seven members of the panel. "You have dedicated most of your adult lives to the United States Army. Together, you have given more than one hundred fifty years of honorable service to the nation. If you love the Army as much as I hope and think you do, you must help it by convicting this man. Now is the time to come to the aid of the Army.

"I trust you will do your duty.

"Thank you."

Walker now rose and threw off the cordial reserve he had maintained throughout the trial. Having sat and taken notes throughout Bray's stately denunciation of his client, he appeared outraged. He stood and theatrically paged through a fat red paperback edition of the *Manual for Courts-Martial,* as if vainly searching for a citation. He turned and bellowed at the audience, "Is patriotism a court-martial offense? I think not." He turned back and slammed shut the manual. "No, it is not. I have searched the law low and high, and nowhere does it say such a thing."

Red-faced, he looked straight at the front row of the jury. "This trial is really about our military." He raised his eyes to the three lieutenant colonels in the back row. "Who are you? And what role do you play in our society?"

He strode back to the audience and spoke again to the two rows of spectators—and to the television camera behind them. His left arm pointed at the military panel, his palm open, as if pleading not for Captain Byrnes but for them. "Are these men mercenaries, well paid but without a voice in the affairs of our society? Are they dumb servants whose services are expected—indeed, required—but whose views aren't welcome? Have they somehow, when none of us were looking, become a lesser class of citizen, welcome to die for the nation, but not to participate fully in its life?

"I think not." He trembled for a moment. "And I most sincerely hope not."

It was a risky gambit, putting the jury on trial. It appeared to backfire, at least with Colonel Shufflebarger, who stiffened and appeared about to ask the judge if he had to put up with this. But the tactic went over better with the lieutenant colonels sitting behind the colonel—and those three younger officers were all Walker needed to win for a no-conviction vote. The defense counsel came back across the courtroom and spoke directly to the lieutenant colonels in a lower, easier, conversational tone.

"We as a nation have not really come to grips with what should be the proper role of uniformed officers in debates about issues that affect the armed services. It is especially problematic in an era of deference to expertise of all sorts in many areas. At a time when fewer and fewer members of government and the electorate have any military experience, how should military officers bring their expertise to public discussions of national security issues? If military officers are made to sit on the sidelines, how can the debate be truly an informed one? And how can we, in our great democracy, ask American men and women to go out and die if we haven't held an informed debate? In this key sense, the quality of the political debate boosts our military efficiency, our promise to the troops that they will be used wisely and well.

"I guess what I am saying here is that it is very difficult to draw the line or, more relevant to this case, rein in the troops on any particular issue. Captain Byrnes is young. He acted impetuously, in a way that neither you nor I likely would. He committed an offense in doing so. There is no question of that."

The defense counsel paused. He balled his fists as if imploring them to heed the key point. "But at least he acted! I submit that his offense is small—forgivable, if you will, much as the surgeon's scalpel is pardoned, even appreciated, for the cut it inflicts on the flesh in excising a cancer. And by acting, he improved the quality of debate.

"His small transgression came in reaction to a far greater threat to the republic. Consider the ominous potential posed by a military force alienated from participation in democratic processes. I think we need to be very cautious about telling the kind of professional military we have today that they are expected to lay down their lives for a country that, by the way, wants to deprive them of the same rights the rest of the unserving population want to enjoy. Imprinting such a force with the notion that they are little more than mercenaries is, to my way of thinking, very worrisome." Walker stared at the three lieutenant colonels. He knew now that the outcome rested with them and them only.

"Is there a grave offense here? Yes, there is. But I submit to you that it is not the one of which the captain is accused." Now he turned away from the military panel and again paused to look around the courtroom, repeating the slow, long gaze he had used at the beginning of his summation. "It is the one committed by me, and by you—by every one of us," he said mournfully. "We, as a nation, have committed it. We have placed this man in an impossible situation, where his duty to his superiors could not be reconciled with his duty to his subordinates. It is we who have done the wrong. Captain Byrnes and his peers have simply tried to right the wrong done to them. That is the lesser sin."

He spoke to the audience, as if explaining how the military would have to make good this wrong. "Here the military panel must think upon its own duty. Sometimes a situation is so unjust, so vile, so repugnant to our sense of ourselves as officers and Americans that it is necessary to violate lesser laws in order to obey higher ones. There lies wisdom, there lies the hard duty of the commander. I submit to you that anyone who has never felt the need to violate standard operating procedure isn't fit to lead American troops."

He turned back to the jury. "Under our system, when a significant clash

occurs between law and conscience, we put the question of that justifi-
cation to our fellow citizens, a jury of our peers. When that clash takes
the military form of conflicting duty, we put it to our fellow officers. That
is the issue that we all, as members of this court, face today.

"You"—he nodded to the rear row of the jury box and lowered his voice,
as if speaking only to them—"you, for whatever reason, have been chosen
and brought here today by Providence to be the conscience of the entire
officer corps. A corps torn by conflicting duties. It may be the most awe-
some mission you ever perform during your entire service to the nation.

"Captain Byrnes was faced with two conflicting imperatives. There is a
notion of subordination of the military to civilian authority—I say 'notion'
because I cannot find it in the Constitution, and believe me, I am a military lawyer, and I have looked. And there is the equally unwritten and
equally powerful claim that you must take care of the people you lead. In
a military of, by and for the people, it is your implicit promise to your
troops, and to their spouses, parents and children, that you will not spend
their lives casually.

"The government brought only three charges against this officer. What
each boils down to is the phrase 'conduct unbecoming an officer.' You
must ask yourself, did Captain Byrnes discredit our military? Or did he
somehow redeem it?

"As you weigh this fellow officer, consider his duty. And as you consider
that, can you ignore what happened in Afghanistan? And if you do ignore
that, God save this military and these United States. Major Bray talked
of the necessity of good discipline. I ask you to consider that there are
not enough jails, not enough courts, to enforce obedience to a policy
that would destroy this military." This last sentence was the culmination of Walker's risky strategy of appealing to at least three members of
the military panel to move toward the court-martial equivalent of "jury
nullification"—to disregard the overwhelming factual evidence and find
the defendant not guilty.

"I submit to this honorable court that Captain Robert Byrnes is a
citizen-soldier. And this citizen-soldier"—he violently jabbed a finger at
his client—"this officer whom some seek to vilify and pillory as a rene-
gade, this officer fulfilled his highest duty: looking out for the welfare of
his comrades and of his nation.

"And has our government thanked him? Has it? Yes, I say, it has: It has
shone its powerful and unblinking spotlight on his acts. You can see that

he has done nothing that requires you to break him. Rather, we should thank him. He and his comrades are"—his eyes swept across the courtroom, taking in the jury, the audience and finally the defendant—"like you, the best we have.

"Thank you," Walker concluded and sat down.

In the auditorium around Sherman, applause erupted, even among some of the defense attachés down in front.

Arlington National Cemetery
Thursday, July 14
10 A.M.

John Shillingsworth's will requested that he be buried in Arlington National Cemetery in a plot adjacent to the area occupied by the 1st Independent Pennsylvania Rangers, a Civil War outfit drawn from the Alleghenies. They were his mother's people, Scots borderers, kicked out three times—first from the borderlands, then from Ireland, finally from Philadelphia. They fought the Indians in western Pennsylvania, feuded with each other, then headed south as a scout unit during the Civil War.

Wimpy Wilson, the acting chief of staff, delivered the eulogy in the little ivy-covered chapel in Fort Myer, just a two-minute stroll from his house and almost as close to the Penn Rangers' ground. Wilson stood in the pulpit and began in a low, clear voice that somehow rang across the chapel. "He cared," Wilson said, taking off his reading glasses. "He did his best. He led a full and generous life. We will miss him."

Wilson looked at the other chiefs sitting in the front row. They knew he was saying that John Shillingsworth somehow had tried and died a failure—and that he would pick up where his friend had left off. "And we will profit from his example. The time has come to prove that we can learn from the lessons he provided."

Ames felt Wilson's eyes rest on him. A flash of suspicion struck him: Did Wilson know what was on those disks?

"None of us is bigger than the Army," Wilson concluded. "The Army matters most of all—the Army and the nation."

Sitting at the back of the chapel, Cindy wondered where Wilson was going. Did he mean to go after Ames? Or was he saying that the interests of the Army required them to keep it all quiet? The Army's instincts were always to veil its internal disputes.

Following Shillingsworth's written request, the service concluded with his three favorite songs—"Amazing Grace," "The Battle Hymn of the Republic" and the Irish lament "Carrickfergus." Then the pallbearers rose. None were from the Joint Chiefs, and all were Army generals and colonels.

Wilson and Shillingsworth's widow led the three hundred people who had squeezed into the chapel out its front doors and behind the casket, draped in an American flag and mounted on a black artillery caisson. It was drawn by seven huge black horses. Behind the caisson walked a color bearer, carrying the flag of the chief of staff of the U.S. Army. After him came an eighth horse, even larger and blacker, cavalry boots reversed in the stirrups.

The mourners arranged themselves around the open grave. Sherman stood respectfully at the far edge of the group, letting Shillingsworth's old Vietnam buddies, some of them his former commanders there, now bent and gray, stand at the lip of the hole. One poured in a cup of dirt saved from Danang. She saw Ames file by the casket, followed by Lewis.

On the hillside below them, four cannons—actually World War II anti-tank guns—fired four times and then one fired a final time, giving Shillingsworth his full seventeen. Finally "Taps," written by another Army general, drifted across the hot hillside.

With the ceremony over, Sherman looked up and saw Ames's factotum, Sergeant First Class Stout, standing apart from the mourners in the trees forty yards away. She turned in the opposite direction. She walked away. She sensed someone hurrying to catch up with her and turned to see who it was, bracing herself to confront Stout.

It was Lewis. She greeted him stiffly, just flatly saying his name. "Buddy."

"Cindy, you look like you've seen a ghost," he said.

Cindy hesitated, then asked Lewis to walk with her to the reception at Shillingsworth's house. They went together slowly back past the chapel and down Lee Avenue toward the chief's residence.

"Look, Buddy, I don't think it was an accident," she finally said as they turned right onto Jackson.

"You're being paranoid," Lewis said. "He probably just tripped and fell into traffic in the dark."

At the house Shillingsworth's widow sat in an armchair in her living room, toughing it out, just like her husband had.

Cindy saw Ames holding court on the side porch, where the refreshments were set out on tables. Youngish lieutenant colonels riding fast-track careers flocked around him. "It's our turn now," she heard one say to another at the punch bowl. "Wilson's a place holder—he'll be gone soon."

Ames noticed Cindy watching him and his group. He cut through his admirers and walked over to her. He extended his sympathies for "your fallen chief."

He was your chief too, Cindy thought. But she held her tongue.

He lowered his voice. "Do you have something for me, Major Sherman?" he asked in an even, almost friendly voice. "Something for a computer?"

Cindy looked him in the eye. "No, sir, I do not."

Ames straightened and stiffened as if he had been slapped. "I see," he said, and wheeled away from her.

Lewis absorbed the exchange for a moment. "Cindy, we need to talk," he said. "I'm worried."

"It's a little late for that, Major," she said, and walked away to her car. She wasn't going to be pimped by Lewis for that disk, either.

Headquarters Building, Fort McNair
Friday, July 15
9:45 A.M.

Cindy sat in her usual seat at the rear of the National Defense University auditorium, watching Judge Trice on the big screen give a final set of instructions to the jury. He reminded them of the presumption of innocence until guilt was established "beyond a reasonable doubt."

Colonel Shufflebarger handed the bailiff a note. There was another query from Lieutenant Colonel Ryan. The judge read it aloud: "Could you explain what you mean by 'reasonable doubt'?"

Major Bray, the prosecutor, put his hand to his mouth. This was a very bad sign. "By 'reasonable doubt,' " Judge Trice said, "I mean an honest, conscientious misgiving." Lieutenant Colonel Ryan nodded with evident satisfaction.

The judge continued. He looked over the panel. "Each of you must impartially decide whether the accused is guilty or not in accordance with the law I have given you, the evidence admitted in court and your own conscience." Ryan nodded again.

The bailiff said, "All rise." Bray, Walker and other officers in the courtroom audience stood at attention as the members of the panel walked into a conference room behind their jury box.

Colonel Shufflebarger began the jury's discussion. He gave a summation of the facts of the matter as he understood them, and asked if they all agreed. They did, with a few amendments and quibbles.

"Fine, then," he said. "Look, this is pretty cut and dried. I think I have sat on about one hundred court-martials in my career—in Korea I once had court-martial duty for four straight months. And our Captain Byrnes here is one of the guiltiest people I've seen. Even if they didn't charge him with treason, which they should have.

"Even his lawyer said he committed an offense. Decamp testified that Byrnes asked him to put the disk in. So that gets him on the conspiracy charge—and remember that it was a conspiracy to impede a properly ordered attack by U.S. forces on an enemy. And all those e-mails he sent encouraging stuff such as the turnaround at Polk and the sign painting at Drum mean that under General Article 134, his conduct has been prejudicial to good order and discipline."

"Amen to that," said one of the other colonels.

Shufflebarger nodded, then looked to the lower-ranking officers at the other end of the table. "I mean, this captain has been pretty busy the last three months undermining administration policy."

Lieutenant Colonel Ryan cleared his throat. "Sir, I have some problems with your last there," he said. The other six men looked at him, somewhat puzzled.

"For me, this is about the Constitution," Ryan said. "Our oath as officers is to support the Constitution, not to support the president or his policies. The best way to support the Constitution, when the president is abusing his power, damaging the military, hurting the nation, is not to

convict Captain Byrnes. Show that the military is above this, that it is
loyal to the nation.

"I would say that these Sons of Liberty officers were doing their best to
fulfill their oaths. They were fulfilling their most fundamental, basic duties. And we shouldn't convict officers for doing their duty. At least I know
that I cannot."

The two other lieutenant colonels followed him. They said they were
not so sure as Ryan. But they had some doubts about whether to convict.

The old colonel began to speak, but Ryan cut him off. "Begging your
pardon, sir," he said. He reminded them of Judge Trice's closing instructions. "The last thing the judge said to us was you must decide according
to your own conscience." He flipped back in his notepad to find the
phrase. "If you have an 'honest misgiving' about finding the man guilty,
you shouldn't."

The black lieutenant colonel, an infantryman who was deputy commander of the Old Guard, spoke up for the first time. "I'm not so sure I
go along with you on that, Ryan," he said in a soft Alabama drawl. He
looked around the table. "Yeah, I think the captain actually followed the
dictates of duty," he continued. "But I stop there. I still think the evidence
indicates that he is guilty. I mean, Dr. King practiced civil disobedience,
but he was willing to do the time too. So why not salute the man as we
send him to prison?"

Colonel Shufflebarger seized on this. "Byrnes practically pleaded
guilty—how can you not find him guilty?" he asked.

Ryan ignored him and spoke to his fellow lieutenant colonels. "Remember that the judge said we have to meet all three standards—the law,
the evidence and our conscience. Two out of three isn't good enough.
Can you in good conscience find this man guilty of what you would have
done—or at least what you and I hope we would have done?"

The old colonel at the end of the table was losing his patience with this
line of thinking. "I sure as hell can," he shouted. "He fucking stopped an
operation ordered by the commander in chief!" He slapped his hand
down flat on the table. In his chambers next door, Judge Trice heard the
noise and prepared to call the bailiff if the panel got any rowdier.

"I wasn't asking you, sir," Ryan said coolly. He turned back to the two
men at his end of the table. "Can you—in good conscience?"

The two undecided lieutenant colonels looked at each other. Neither
spoke for a full minute.

"No," the Old Guard officer finally said, trying to picture how he would have acted as a member of a jury weighing the fate of Martin Luther King. "I guess I can't."

Ryan nodded in thanks and turned to the other, a bald air-defense officer. "And you?"

"No, I can't either."

That was it. The indication was four votes for guilty, three for not—the government wouldn't get the two-thirds vote required for a guilty verdict. If that stuck, Byrnes would be found not guilty on all specifications. Under military law, he couldn't be tried again.

The rules governing military panels permitted only one formal vote to be taken. Colonel Shufflebarger declined to poll the panel that night. Instead, he decided in his capacity as president of the panel to inform the judge that the panel needed to go home and take the weekend to think on it.

Headquarters Building, Fort McNair
Monday, July 18
9:08 A.M.

On Saturday morning as he golfed thirty-six holes at the Army-Navy Country Club, Colonel Shufflebarger's mood shifted from anger to puzzlement. By Sunday night it had boiled down to resignation. On Monday morning he walked into the jury room and said, "Are you three still where you were Friday?"

"Yes, sir, I am," said Ryan. The other two nodded.

"OK," the colonel said. "Write down your votes—this is up or down, on all counts." He looked at Ryan. "Junior member collects and counts them."

Ryan walked around the table with his uniform cap. Each member dropped in a slip of paper. He counted. As he expected, it was 4–3, all the colonels for conviction, all the lieutenant colonels against it. Seniority didn't rule. Neither did the majority, for that matter.

Shufflebarger shook his head and wearily stood up. This wasn't his military anymore. He had come in as an ROTC lieutenant in 1979, when it was the enlisted you didn't trust, not your fellow officers. First thing he had done on the day he reported to Fort Benjamin Harrison was bust a sergeant he found selling marijuana in the parking lot. "Let's inform the judge," he said. And then let's put in my retirement papers, he thought.

In the courtroom, the trial counsel and the defense lawyers were preparing their sentencing arguments for the session that under military law must immediately follow the finding of the jury—which both sides had presumed would be guilty.

The jury filed back into the courtroom. "Has the panel reached a verdict?" the judge asked.

Colonel Shufflebarger stood. He paused. "It has." He pointedly did not say "we."

"Accused and counsel, please rise," the judge said.

Captain Byrnes, following military custom, rose from the defense table and marched to stand in front of the jury box. He saluted Colonel Shufflebarger.

Slowly, unhappily, Shufflebarger read the verdict. "Captain Robert Byrnes, it is my solemn *duty* as the president of this court to advise you that this court, in closed session, finds you on charge one and its specification, not guilty. On charge two and its specification, not guilty. On charge three and its specification, not guilty."

Byrnes looked back over at Walker and Casmiro, who didn't immediately react. It was only when he saw Bray, the prosecutor, drop his head into his left hand that he realized he had gotten off.

Well, I'll be damned, Judge Trice thought, a nullification jury. He picked up his gavel and shook it but didn't strike it.

The extraordinary verdict made his last instruction more significant than usual. He looked back at the panel and the old colonel, who still stood, almost dazed at the outcome. "Colonel Shufflebarger, you may be seated," he began.

"Members of the court," the judge continued, "before I excuse you, let me remind you of the oath you took. You are barred from discussing your deliberations with anyone. Nor may you disclose any member's vote." That was it. His gavel still hovered.

"Thank you for your attendance and service," he said. "You are excused. This court-martial is adjourned." He brought down the gavel smartly, but just once.

In the auditorium where Cindy and about 450 other officers were watching, the monitors in the auditorium went blank almost the moment the gavel fell. The British officers looked shocked; the Paraguayan looked pleased. Cindy squeezed around some high-fiving U.S. Army lieutenants and walked up the post, across the ground where Lincoln's assassins were hanged, to the headquarters building.

Byrnes already was being interviewed by CNN's Pentagon correspondent on the front steps. It was the first time she had seen him in person since the day Ojeda arrested him.

"I intend to form an exploratory committee immediately," Byrnes was saying with a grin. "Yes, as a resident of Virginia." Representative Casmiro stood behind him, beaming like a proud father. Cindy stood at the back of the crowd and watched with amazement as she realized that Byrnes was announcing that he was resigning his commission and declaring his intention to run for Congress. It made sense, she thought—with a high-profile court-martial on his record, his Army career was shot.

Even so, she hated him for it. The smug little bastard saw himself not at the end of a military career but at the beginning of a political one. He wasn't showing any of the sorrow she would feel at leaving the Army. He was throwing it away. She suspected that he never really had wanted to be an officer. Yet from all appearances he had been accepted fully into the officer corps of the United States Army. *Why was he taken in wholeheartedly, but not me?*

She turned and walked out the post gate up to the Yellow Line Metro station. It was on the edge of a rough neighborhood and she was glad she had her little steel whistle.

Men are accepted in the Army until they prove themselves unacceptably weak, she thought as she waited for the subway train back to the Pentagon, while women are held suspect until they prove themselves acceptably strong. Then, of course, they're labeled lesbians.

At his tiny office in the White House, Willy Pitch watched the Byrnes interview on CNN with growing irritation. He stubbed out one cigarette and lit another. For all his pompousness, his seeming insensitivity to those around him, especially subordinates, he had a finely tuned sense of how the American government worked—and how fragile the system actually was at times. In theory, he had taught in his senior seminars, the American system shouldn't have worked. It was designed as an adversarial system based on the consent of all those governed. Problems arose when some of those tried to withdraw their consent, as the Southern states once had done.

With this court-martial, he sensed, part of the officer corps seemed to be withdrawing some of their consent. A few of the thousands of gossamer strands that made up the American system had been swept away by that jury. It was just a handful. In itself, that wouldn't threaten the nation. But it was a trend that should be countered. If not, what would be the next operation that someone in the military refused to permit?

He stepped out of his small West Wing office and asked the staff secretary for fifteen minutes with the president later that day. He would tell the president, "These guys are out of control." Clearly Maddox was adrift. They needed a new chairman. Also, part of the military had been off the reservation ever since Shillingsworth inexplicably had gone up to the Army War College in May and denounced the president to his generals. For all his protests, Shillingsworth's action had seemed to Pitch to have breathed life into this Sons of Liberty nonsense, which had led first to that embarrassment at Polk and then had stymied the execution of the Afghanistan cruise-missile strike. Sure, in retrospect, that probably was for the best—but having junior officers counter the commands of the White House couldn't be tolerated. And now a court-martial jury had refused to convict on clear evidence. We need new leadership, Pitch thought. Someone who can whip the military into shape, who knows how to push the hidden levers of bureaucratic power. Who?

To Willy Pitch, the answer was clear: B. Z. Ames.

The POAC Pedestrian Bridge
Outside the Pentagon
9:15 P.M.

Cindy Sherman stayed late at her desk at the Pentagon that night, puzzling out her situation. The court-martial had come and gone without Ames ever being mentioned. Could General Wilson have ensured that his name was kept out of it—"for the good of the Army"?

She was at her wit's end. She had done her duty with the three disks Cisco had given her. She had obtained them in executing a mission General Shillingsworth had assigned her. She had completed that mission and given him the "Ames 4" disk. It was up to the new chief to decide how to deal with Ames, she thought, not me, a lowly major on the Army staff. So she simply left the two disks where she had put them, one in her uniform jacket and the other in her briefcase.

What more could she do? It was unclear to her where her duty lay.

At 9:30, she finally left the office and walked the deserted E ring down to the long bridge to the POAC entrance. She looked across the bridge to the huge north parking lot, which had been almost empty for four hours. She was reassured to see her green Subaru waiting under a lamppost in the distance, her incomplete study of the Potomac River at Pennyfield Lock still under a plastic shroud in the back. It was parked where Norman Mailer and thousands of others had protested the Vietnam War in October 1967, college kids ostentatiously placing daisies into the bulletless rifle barrels of M-16s held by working-class kids. Now the sixties had come home to roost inside the Pentagon.

As she reached the far end of the bridge and took a step down the white concrete ramp, a hand gloved in black leather, the kind of tight working glove machine gunners wore so they could quickly change out an overheated barrel, reached out from the cedar bushes and grabbed her windpipe from behind, lifting her backward onto the flat area at the end of the bridge.

Her first reaction was that of an intelligence analyst: What a strange place for a mugger to operate! Then a memory drifted up into her fading consciousness: *It's easy. Just knock your opponent to the ground, and grind a boot heel into his skull.*

She didn't fight being thrown to the ground. When it came she tried to roll with it, hitting the ground as she had when parachuting at Benning. She gasped air back into her lungs. She looked up at a shoe. It was shiny black, plain in style. Military, she thought. It was plunging toward her forehead. She tried to jerk her head away to the right but wasn't quite fast enough. Her left eyeball turned into a ball of dazzling light. The shoe heel smashed into the left side of her jaw, ripping her skin and fracturing the upper cheekbone just below her eye.

Amid all the blood she thought her left eyeball had been crushed. With her unbloodied eye she could see her attacker's hand reach down and rip open her uniform jacket, two brass buttons bouncing away down the ramp. His targeting intelligence was good but not precise: He first rummaged around the inside pockets, pulling out her metal pen and dropping it next to her head, then the little steel whistle and dropping that too. The gloved hand reached into the left lower pocket. It snapped back closed around the black floppy disk labeled "Ames 3 of 4."

Pain hit her in a blinding wave. Another phrase from that day at Fort Polk drifted up into her brain: *Ignore the pain and concentrate on your adversary.*

In the half moment her attacker took to ensure that he had the correct disk, Sherman picked up the Cross pen next to her head and jabbed it as hard as she could crosswise through his black sock and into the back of his left ankle, just in front of his Achilles tendon. He stood straight up and then his back arched in pain. "Son of a bitch," he muttered in a soft but pained voice, still maintaining his combat discipline. He knelt, his back to her, to pull the pen from his ankle. She picked up her little steel whistle and blew an urgent, screaming series. The sound echoed across the parking lot.

"Bitch," he grunted. He stood and lifted the shoe of his unwounded foot over her forehead. He moved it down toward her, but the wounded ankle couldn't carry all his weight. He stumbled back three awkward steps to catch his balance. She blew the whistle urgently again. He looked around to see if anyone was responding. Then he picked up her briefcase and swung its end down at her, hammering her shoulder. She blew the whistle one more time, a long screech.

A door flew open at the far end of the POAC bridge, seventy-five yards away, and light streamed halfway down the white cement toward them. She puffed into the whistle again but it just burbled, filled with blood from three holes her own teeth had punched into the left side of her tongue. Her attacker was spooked by the open door. His wound would limit his ability to elude a pursuer. And he had what he had come for. He hobbled down the ramp toward the huge parking lot that stretched to the river, her briefcase bobbing up and down in his right hand. The door at the end of the bridge closed.

Black was rushing in on both sides of her vision like double doors closing. Her unwounded right cheek pressed against the ground, blood running from her left cheek and open mouth across the white cement and down the top of the ramp.

She woke alone in the quiet dark. The odd thing about being knocked unconscious was the loss of the sense of the passage of time—she had no idea whether she'd been out thirty seconds or six hours. She brought her watch up to her good, right eye. Blood dripped off her nose and onto the watch face. It had been maybe five minutes or so. She lay on her back and took an inventory of herself and her situation before trying to move. Used her swelling tongue to try to feel the inside of her mouth. The teeth on the top of the left side were loose. Her left cheek was bad. She wiped around her eye with her hand. The eyeball seemed to be functioning. She rolled onto her right side and rose to one knee. She waited until the wooziness passed. She took a few steps, then had to kneel again. She began to move slowly back across the bridge, toward the security guard who would be just inside the Pentagon entrance—and who probably had scared off her attacker by opening the door. She took another four steps.

Who was the attacker? She stopped. It probably was Stout or someone like him, sent by Ames—and that meant the Pentagon wasn't necessarily safe. He probably had come from there. Might have doubled back in. *Go somewhere else.* She turned around and pulled herself together for the journey to her car, which now seemed almost infinitely far.

But he might be waiting near her car in the deserted parking lot. She stopped again.

Finally she decided to walk down the ramp, cut back under the POAC bridge and slide over the low fence to the edge of the highway. There she sat under a streetlight. A woman in a passing car pointed at her and picked up a cellular phone. A few minutes later a Virginia state trooper flashed his light on her. He picked her up and took her to the emergency room at the Alexandria Memorial Hospital.

"You need to be more careful walking alone at night," he chided. She tried to nod.

The Pentagon
Thursday, July 21
10:30 A.M.

It was Sherman's first day back at the Pentagon since being attacked. Her left cheek looked as if it had a huge tobacco chaw tucked inside it. The bulge was purple and black, with angry red bruises reaching down her neck and curving behind her ear. Her attacker's fingers had left four other long bruises across her neck where his hand had closed around her windpipe. Tiny bright green stitches held together a ragged four-inch-long cut from the corner of her left eye to her scalp—the emergency room doctor had said the impact of the shoe heel had yanked apart the soft skin. The white of her left eye had turned bloodred. But it was no longer swollen shut. The aches in her left shoulder and hip from being hurled to the ground had been eased by the painkillers the doctors had prescribed.

She felt like she was falling apart. *What else is there to lose?* Sherman thought. *Cisco is dead, murdered. My chief is dead too, probably the same way. Lewis abandoned me and went over to a group of people I despise who are eroding the Army I love. He may be in league with an officer who slithered out of a court-martial. I have lost my friend, my mentor and my lover. And I think I nearly lost my life. For what? A duty that only I seem to see here.*

Being in the office hadn't helped. Miss Turley was efficiently handling all the calls. The XO was rearranging the schedule for the new chief. The telephones rang incessantly—the Army conducted most of its business by e-mail but still needed to convey condolences for its leader by voice. She was in no condition to answer phones—her voice could hardly be understood. As the phones burred all she could think of was the phrase, *What do I do?* It hammered at her. She knew she wasn't thinking clearly. *What do I do?*

She thought of the last surviving disk, "Ames 4 of 4," still locked in Shillingsworth's secure file in the inner office, and shuddered. Those disks were killing people. She considered walking in there, taking it out and cutting it up with scissors. But it occurred to her that even if she did that, she'd never convince the disks' pursuers that it was gone, was no longer a threat. They would just ransack her home, her car. They would keep coming after her until they had it—and until she was somehow neutralized.

So she slowly made her way down to the Pentagon Officers' Athletic Club. She needed to be somewhere where she could calm down, she figured. A steam bath might ease the ache in her face, seep some soothing warmth into the bruised bones. At the spot where she'd been attacked, just outside the front door of the club, she saw that the concrete at the top of the ramp had been scrubbed clean of her blood and was now whiter than the surrounding area.

No one else wanted to take a steam bath in midsummer in Washington, so Sherman had the place to herself. Alone in the white ceramic steam room, she sat under a towel, watching the billows of steam that occasionally puffed from pipes along the base of the walls. "What do I do?" she said aloud.

Get a grip, Major Sherman, she thought. You've done this kind of work before. You're under attack. So you assess the situation. Get your intell staff to do the analysis and recommend a course of action. Get the S-2 in here.

What is the problem? she thought. Assess the situation.

The problem, ma'am, she said to herself, is that I have a situation in which the best course of action isn't apparent to me. I am aware of an object that is dangerous to me and those around me, but that also contains information that could shape the future of the U.S. military. I also am aware that any attempt to act in this situation likely will terminate my career in the U.S. military. And probably my life.

What might you do with this object?

That's a good one, ma'am. I am contemplating trying to convey it to someone who could and would act upon the information it contains.

List those persons who might act upon it in a fashion that would bring this situation to a satisfactory resolution.

Tough one, ma'am. We're still working that issue. Maddox? No. The defense secretary? Probably not—he isn't a boat rocker. Likely to sweep it under a rug. Wilson? It isn't clear where he intends to go with this.

Possible recipients outside the building?

Well, ma'am, I hate to say it, but there is Mr. Pitch.

Pitch?

Yes, ma'am. I could get to him, probably. I know his people from the Polk trip.

What would the consequences of this action be?

Well, I would have ratted out a senior Army general to a White House that is despised by many if not most of my comrades and commanders.

Which is to say?

I would be toast. A pariah. If I got away with it without being charged, I certainly would never be trusted again by this Army. A female staff aide who tattletaled on an Army problem to the White House? Give me a break. I'd rather be Oliver North.

Where is the Army on this, ma'am?

Good question, she thought. I am alone out here. I need to stop this and get back to my Army. It won't come to me.

So your course of action is?

She sat and thought for several minutes.

Ma'am, we're waiting on your orders. Ma'am?

Go away.

She sat alone sweating for another fifteen minutes. She wasn't going to do it. She wasn't going to take them on anymore. Know when to stop, she remembered her oil painting instructor saying. It seemed to be time.

This is what giving up feels like, she realized. It didn't feel that bad—it was better than what preceded it. Knowing was better than not.

The Army was all she had. It was her real family. Maybe a bit dysfunctional, but what family wasn't? She was committed to staying in it. For all her brave talk of leaving the Army, she knew she wouldn't. It was her life. Steam blew up around her.

She slowly stood up and walked into the shower room. There, under the cold water, she leaned her forehead against the side of the shower stall and let herself weep. You couldn't fight the Army forever. The primary duty of the good soldier, she'd heard General Shillingsworth say, was to keep on going. She would do what she had to do. Shillingsworth had given up some of himself when he decided to lie about how long the Afghanistan mission would last. She would give up some of herself now.

But she would keep going. If you didn't know what else duty told you to do, you could always keep going.

She tried to apply some makeup in the locker room but abandoned the effort as ridiculous. Her face already had enough color, she thought grimly.

She trudged back to the office. It was lunchtime, and the operation was manned only by the buck sergeant at the front desk. She asked him to take the brigadiers' promotion board file down to GOMO, the General Officer Management Office, an errand that would take at least five minutes. Then she went into Shillingsworth's inner office, twirled the combination lock on the secure file and removed "Ames 4 of 4."

She went back to her desk and sent an e-mail downstairs to Lewis. "Meet me in Marineland. Please. It won't take long. I have a disk for you."

Down in the vice chairman's office, Lewis read the message. If she had a disk, he'd want another. He took one out of his laptop, stood up and strolled out the door. A moment later General Ames came out of his inner office, pleased that Sherman had come around. "Sergeant First Class Stout, are you keeping an eye on our major?" he said.

Stout, his left foot in a cast—"Pulled my Achilles running, sir, it's a bitch"—said he was on the case.

"Why don't you use my elevator?" Ames said.

Stout arrived in Marineland before Lewis and tucked himself alongside the Coke machine at the bend in the corridor.

Sherman climbed the three flights of stairs slowly—the climbing jarred her fractured cheekbone. When she came out the stairwell door on the fifth floor, Lewis was waiting for her. He hadn't seen her since the funeral a week earlier.

He winced at the sight of her bruises and stitches, then reached out to her. "Oh, Cindy," he said softly.

She stepped back from him. She didn't want to be touched. His people already had done that. She leaned against the wall, fatigued from the journey up the stairs.

It was hard for her to talk. She tried to do it moving only the right side of her jaw. "Tell Ames"—it came out "Ame-th"—"that I am giving up," she said in a hoarse whisper. "You guyth win." She spoke with her teeth almost clenched together, making her sound angrier than she felt. In fact, she was more tired than anything else.

Lewis leaned close to hear her. He studied her mournful gray eyes. His own face began to break up. This is a good person, he thought with a chill, and something evil has been done to her. "Oh, Cindy, I am so sorry for this. I really didn't know about this." He looked desolate, as if he'd been punched in the gut and had the wind knocked out of him. She sensed that he really hadn't known anything about the attack on her.

She handed him the black disk. "Tell them thith is the latht one. There were only four. There are no copieth—can't be."

She moved slowly, not turning her neck at all. He looked at the disk: The label read "Ames 4 of 4 only." At the next bend in the corridor fifty yards away, Stout slid backward from his hiding place and moved off quietly to find a telephone.

Lewis slipped the disk into his inside left jacket pocket, over his heart. "Can I help you? I'd like to help you," he said. He reached out again.

She held up both hands flat in front of her in the universal signal to stop. "No, no," she said. She was tearing up.

Lewis persisted. "Cindy, I want to help."

She shook her head. "Good-bye, Lewith," she said. "Pleath." She turned and walked down the hall away from him.

He opened the door, then turned back and said to her, "Cindy, be careful."

She didn't have the energy for sarcasm. She shook her head very slightly. When she heard his footsteps going down the stairs, she leaned her forehead against the corridor wall and closed her eyes. Her tears stung when they ran into the small red gaps between the stitches in her wound.

Lewis assessed the situation and considered his course of action as he walked down the stairs. Until now, Cindy's concerns about Ames and the Sons of Liberty had seemed theoretical to him. Seeing her wounded physically and damaged spiritually had transformed his sense of the matter. It was now personal. He had never expected her to give up.

He had been trained to take over when a comrade faltered. By the time he was three flights down, he was sure he was going to do something but not sure what that would be.

Underhill was standing just inside the office door when Lewis walked in. He quickly closed the door behind Lewis. Before being asked, Lewis reached his left hand into his uniform jacket and took a disk from his inside right pocket. The XO put a hand out for it.

General Ames came out of his office expectantly, gliding in his catlike way. "Thanks for getting this," he said brightly, the tension evident in his liquid eyes. "I was wondering about you, amigo—I'm glad to see you're with us."

Ames wanted Lewis out of the office. Check the last of these troublesome disks in private, he thought, and then the way will be clear to the chairmanship. By prearrangement with Ames, Underhill handed Lewis a sealed classified file. "These are the background papers for the general's nomination package for the chairmanship," he said. "SecDef's chief of staff needs them immediately. We're fast-tracking this. They want to announce the nomination this week."

Lewis figured he had about two minutes before Ames and Underhill punched in all the security passwords necessary to open the unlabeled disk he had turned over, which contained nothing more than his daily record of pending work. The major document on it, labeled "REDTEAM," they would soon see, was simply the planning he had been asked to do for the nomination celebration party Ames had scheduled for the coming weekend. Colonel Underhill had ordered Lewis to "red team" the dinner party to look for possible vulnerabilities. Willy Pitch, Senator Feaver and others would be attending. Pitch would sit on Ames's left, Feaver on his right. Who would be across from Pitch? How to explain the absence of all other top Army generals, who weren't being invited because none of them was likely to celebrate Ames's elevation? Lewis had been told to game out those questions using the dossiers on the guests kept by Underhill.

Lewis walked out the door with no idea of what to do and conscious that he had about one hundred seconds remaining in which to do it. For lack of an idea, he began by doing as he'd been told and started up the Bradley staircase toward the SecDef's suite. As his shoe touched the first step, someone plucked his sleeve at the elbow.

He turned and saw that it was a Marine officer wearing on each collar point the solitary star of a brigadier general. The crew-cut officer took him by the elbow and steered him into corridor 8, where a crowd of about fifty Pentagon tourists was following a backward-walking sailor through the last part of a Pentagon tour. At the end of the corridor the sailor would take them left and deposit them back at the building's Metro entrance, where they had begun.

"Seen you up in our area with that woman major," the Marine officer said, using a gender term peculiar to the Corps. Sherman had once complained to Lewis about it, noting that no one ever referred to him as a "man major."

"I'm Brigadier General Moe, head of the commandant's staff group," the officer continued, propelling Lewis to the center of the group, where they were almost completely obscured by the tourists. The sailor had noticed them—it was part of his job to watch his group—but he wasn't about to question a Marine general. They bite, he'd heard.

The brigadier leaned his head close to Lewis. "You know, the Marine Corps has the reputation of being a bunch of knuckle draggers, but we're actually pretty well plugged into the intell community. We think we know what Ames is up to. And we believe we have a pretty good idea of who stomped your girlfriend—and why." They walked along inside the fast-moving tour group.

"I think I do, too, now," Lewis confessed.

"Good," Moe said briskly. "You might also guess that Ames is using that file to track you." He pointed at Lewis's right hand.

Lewis looked down at the package as if it were radioactive. He'd forgotten that the new classified files had transmitters to enable security officers to track them. He walked over to a trash can.

"No, don't," Moe said. "Take it with you. This is what you do: Walk downstairs, get on the Metro. Leave it on the train when you get off. They're so in love with their technology, they'll confuse the icon with reality."

The general told Lewis to get himself out to the Shenandoah Valley somehow. "I don't want to know how," he said, holding up a flat hand. Once there, he said, walk on the Appalachian Trail to Desch's Gap. "You'll see two red ribbons on a tree. Take the path there down toward the valley. Just past halfway down the slope, in Lewis Cove, like your name, you'll see some evergreens and a gate. Wait there."

"Wait for who?" Lewis asked. A train was coming into the station. He needed to get on it.

"Whom," the Marine coolly corrected. "For 'Pistol' Pete Petrosky. He's an old friend." He was also a Corps legend, a warrior-intellectual who had won the Navy Cross working for Al Gray during the evacuation of Saigon and then had been General Blades's CO in the Gulf War. "We use him for unusual problems like this, when someone needs to go to ground fast." The subway train door opened.

"Thank you, sir," Lewis said, and slipped into the Blue Line train. South on the Trail to Lewis Cove, he repeated to himself.

Tucked under a seat at the rear of the Metro car, the plastic classified file remained unnoticed by other riders on the Blue/Orange Line as it made its way under the Potomac River, across the District of Columbia and into Maryland. A half hour later it sat in the Metro railyard in New Carrollton. The two duty officers in the Defense Security Office tracked the little purple dot the entire way. They only raised an alarm forty-five minutes later, when the dot stopped moving.

Lewis had exited the train at Roslyn. As the train plunged into the tunnel he was mounting the station's long escalator. He rode it up, then back down, then up again and turned left toward Key Bridge. He stood in the middle of the bridge for several minutes, looking down at the sturgeon holes in this, the deepest spot on the Potomac, then upriver at Fort Marcy. Finally he was confident that he wasn't being followed.

Wearing his Army uniform would make him a bit conspicuous on the canal path. At the Georgetown end of the bridge, he walked two blocks to a sportswear shop on M Street and bought a plain blue running outfit—shorts, T-shirt, socks, sneakers and a thin nylon warm-up jacket. He changed in the store, rolled his service Bravos in a ball and stuffed them into the plastic bag. Then he remembered the "Ames 4" disk in his left inside breast pocket. He took out the disk and slipped it into the nylon jacket pocket, carefully zippering the pocket closed. He tossed the bag into the curry-scented Dumpster of an Indian restaurant. Then he turned toward the Chesapeake and Ohio Canal towpath and began walking at his usual tactical pace of 4.5 miles per hour.

Ames was furious: "He shouldn't have been allowed to leave the building." It was time, he told Underhill, to call in OSCA—the Office of Special Collections and Assessments. Underhill wasn't familiar with that agency, but he could guess what it was just by the studied neutrality of its name—which to anyone who knew the military was very threatening. In keeping with U.S. military usage, the more violent the name, the blander the product—and vice versa. So "the Warrior DFAC" turned out to be a mess hall, and the "Army War College" studied anything but war—it had evolved into a chance to golf for a year and read up on foreign policy while recovering from the stress of battalion command and preparing for staff duty as a new colonel. By contrast, the bland term "collateral damage" meant cluster bombs sending thousands of steel ball bearings ripping through hundreds of lives, inflicting unimaginable pain and suffering that would last for decades. And "special studies" connoted sneaking into Vietnamese villages late at night and slitting the throats of suspected Communist leaders.

The colonel sensed that the Office of Special Collections and Assessments must be unusually vicious if its members flew so low that they had never crossed the radar screen of the XO of the vice chairman of the Joint Chiefs of Staff.

An hour later, a man introduced himself to Underhill as "Oscar" from OSCA. He didn't say whether it was a first name or last name, and Underhill didn't ask, assuming that in either case it was a pseudonym. The man explained that OSCA was a tiny office dedicated to dealing with "special problems." The "collections" part was for recovering assets—"that is, officers and agents"—who had gone bad. The "assessments" part was evaluating the impact of turncoats and other security violations at intelligence agencies and in the military. "Oscar" had been assigned to respond to the urgent call from General Ames's office because he was the agency's specialist for "collecting" military problems.

"We're the Alcoholics Anonymous organization of the intell world, the folks you go to when you finally confess to yourself that you have a problem you can't handle," the razor-thin man from OSCA said jauntily. "And that's good, because that means you're on the road to recovery from your counterintelligence problem."

Oscar said he came out of the Army MP community, but he didn't have the cop's tendency to dress in matching shades of the same color. Rather, he was a man of stylish contrasts, wearing a shirt of sky-blue Egyptian cotton, a black silk knit tie, a brown checked blazer of summer-weight wool, sharply creased black pants and hand-tooled black Church shoes.

Underhill told Oscar the problem was an Army officer.

"That's good, for the predictability factor," Oscar said. He then quizzed Underhill about Lewis's habits, friends, use of alcohol and sexual orientation.

That afternoon OSCA placed a GPS tactical broadcaster inside the gas tank of Lewis's Pontiac Fiero. At Underhill's request, and to Oscar's evident disappointment, the little black box didn't include the optional remote detonator. OSCA also queried all local connections of SABRE, the universal travel agency computer system, to monitor all reservations made in the area for airline travel and car rentals. It also assigned low-ranking street officers from the Defense Security Agency to watch Union Station and the interstate bus station just up the street from there.

By the time the OSCA dragnet was in place, Major Lewis already was twelve miles outside it, striding up the C&O Canal towpath. With the flat terrain and unlimited potable water, he figured he could make the Shenandoah Valley easily in two days of walking. He'd stop each day, buy a newspaper. *Until I see the headline saying that the vice chairman of the Joint Chiefs has been fired*, he thought as he walked, *I'm keeping my head down.*

Just past the canal's milepost 19 he came to Pennyfield Lock. He walked down to the riverbank and rested. *Sherman stood up for the rule of law*, he thought, *and got kicked in the face as thanks. I'm next if they catch me, and a kick will be the least of it.*

By running with the disk he was doing the right thing. But he was also betraying his commander. He skipped a flat rock across the water, running clear and slow at its midsummer low. He counted six jumps. I've jumped too, he thought. I have broken faith with General Ames. Lewis didn't know what he was anymore. He no longer felt like a soldier. He was becoming something else.

Under the light of the moon he walked along the deserted pathway, listening to the croaking of frogs in the canal. When he came to a sandy beach exposed by the low water of the river, he settled down for the night, pulling a pile of dry tulip poplar leaves over himself as the night cooled. He fell asleep looking at the stars and thinking of Cindy, especially their first day and night together. He woke in the middle of the night when he heard a nearby rustling, but it was only a small, shadowy animal emerging from the water—probably a beaver, he thought.

On his second day of walking he came to the outskirts of Harpers Ferry, where the Shenandoah flowed into the Potomac. He was wary of the narrow railroad bridge that led across the Potomac, which looked too much like a potential tactical ambush, so he walked down to the river, put his clothes inside a blue plastic barrel he found caught in the bushes, and swam across the deep pools just below the rapids at the confluence, pushing the barrel before him. On the Virginia bank he dressed and then bushwhacked up the scree until he picked up the Appalachian Trail at the top of the ridge.

Lewis Cove
Shenandoah Valley
Friday, July 22
7 P.M.

Two red ribbons on an oak tree fluttered in greeting just north of Desch's Gap. Lewis followed the path descending into the Shenandoah Valley. A half hour down the slope he left the national parkland and came upon a grove of spruce with a little metal gate blocking a side trail. I SHOOT TRESPASSERS, proclaimed a hand-painted red sign on the gate. Below that opening it added, THIS MEANS <u>YOU</u>. The last word was underlined. He decided to sit and wait there, outside the gate.

The rest felt good on his legs, but he had the eerie sense that he was being watched. He sniffed in the air an odor he couldn't place but that something in the back of his mind told him wasn't right. The hair on his arms stood on end. He was very vulnerable—he was unarmed, he had come to this lonely spot on the recommendation of a stranger who had grabbed him in a Pentagon hallway, and he had in his possession a disk that probably placed him in violation of national security laws. Three strikes, he thought glumly. He stood and looked around.

"Major Lewis?" a gruff male voice somewhere behind him said. He turned warily, half expecting a crushing blow to the face. He didn't see anyone. He looked again and finally noticed, sitting against the base of a big spruce tree about fifty yards beyond the gate, half hidden among its low-hanging branches, a man who looked like a Blue Ridge version of Rip Van Winkle—a gray beard, a gray ponytail running down the back of his black Harley T-shirt, blue jeans, work boots and what appeared to be a joint in the corner of his mouth. A lot of hard living in that creased face. The man rose and strolled down to the gate, taking his sweet time. Lewis noticed now that the man wore a pistol in a black nylon holster—by the looks of it, the nine-millimeter Beretta that was standard issue for U.S. military officers.

He looked Lewis up and down. "I heard you were coming," he said, his right eye squinting through the curl of blue smoke from the joint.

Lewis felt goose bumps of fear rise on the back of his neck. He glanced over his shoulder to see if he had been trapped. No one except a few Marines should know where he was. This cracker hippie seemed to know way too much. Stay cool, he thought.

"I'm looking for a Colonel Petrosky," he said. "You know where I can find him?"

"You got him," the man said evenly.

"Marine Colonel Petrosky?" Lewis asked skeptically. Give me a break, he thought.

"That's me." The man grinned. "*Semper fi,* mac." He pulled up the left sleeve of his black T-shirt to show him a sinewy upper arm. On the bicep was a black tattoo of a toothy, cartoonish bulldog wearing a saucer-like World War I helmet and a spiked collar. Above it curved the word "DEVILDOG" in bright red capitals. He leaned the tattooed upper arm over the top of the gate, as if showing his identity card. With his other hand he pointed the joint at Lewis reprovingly. "I could hear you a mile off—that's why I was here to meet you at my gate."

"I wasn't being tactical." Lewis shrugged.

"From what I hear out of the fifth floor at the Pentagon, maybe you should be."

Petrosky opened the little metal gate and invited Lewis to step in. Lewis followed him along the forest path, which followed the contour of the slope. He asked how a Marine combat-arms colonel could retire and smoke marijuana—a violation of the UCMJ.

Petrosky glanced back over his shoulder with a grin. "Well, I tried one life, now I'm trying another. Three decades of looking like Ricky Nelson, maybe three more of looking like Willie Nelson."

"Aren't you worried about getting busted?" Lewis asked.

"Nah, not so long as it's just for personal use," Petrosky said, following the smooth dirt of the trail down into a small glen that had a tiny stream running through it. "Local sheriff is a Marine vet and so are most of his deputies," he added—as if that explained it all. On the far side of the rivulet was another blood-red sign: STOP NOW/LAST NOTICE/You Could Be DEAD Now.

Rather than stay among the clear ground of the big trees, mainly mature, high-limbed beeches, tulip poplars and oaks, Petrosky's trail wound unnecessarily into a patch of alder bushes. He motioned for Lewis to stop, then had him step around a spiked booby trap, constructed so that it would hit about five feet above the ground, whizzing harmlessly over most animals but puncturing the chest or face of most adult human intruders. "Be careful—when I heard you were coming and might have someone on your tail, I activated all my traps," he said.

Finally the trail crested a small ridge and came down into a two-acre opening in the woods, big enough to pasture a few goats, a horse or a cow. In this case, the clearing held a plot of prime Blue Ridge marijuana, the eight-foot-high plants swaying dark green in the summer breeze. A spartan but modern one-room cabin tucked into the trees at the top of the meadow overlooked it all. "You should taste the meat from the deer that nibble on my patch," Petrosky said over his shoulder. "They die laughing."

Over a dinner of smoked venison, hand-picked Jerusalem artichokes and home-preserved fiddlehead ferns, all served with a Stag's Leap cabernet at a homemade table on the cabin's stone front porch, Petrosky explained his relationship with marijuana. "I'm an old soldier. I find it reminds me of going into battle—when the adrenaline starts pumping, and you see every blade of grass, every leaf. With dope, I get the hyperalertness, but without the freaking muscle tension of combat. My neck and back are too old for that."

He stirred the fire in the cooking pit just below the porch. "It's like in *The Iliad,* when the Trojans are camped on the plain waiting to attack the Greeks at dawn." He lifted his chin, looked up at the night sky, and recited: " 'And so their spirits soared, and down from the high heavens / Bursts the boundless bright air, and all the stars shine clear.' " He looked at Lewis. "That's what it makes me feel like—'all the stars shine clear.' "

The citation was lost on Lewis. What was this *Iliad* shit? he thought.

Petrosky's Cabin
Saturday, July 23
8:30 A.M.

The next morning Colonel Petrosky opened his laptop on the front-porch table and read the entire "Ames 4" disk. He exclaimed occasionally, then gave a long, slow whistle of disapproval when he read Ames's "access" note to Captain Byrnes. He showed the note to Lewis, who until then had only guessed at what was on the disk Sherman had handed him two days earlier in Marineland.

When he finished reading every document he looked up at the waiting Lewis. "This guy's a piece of work," he said, shaking his head at the laptop. He stood from the table and told Lewis to come for his morning walk with him—"walking the perimeter," Petrosky said.

"Tell me about this General Ames," Petrosky commanded as he climbed up the slope. Lewis began with his first meeting with the general at Fort Irwin, then through his three months as his assistant aide de camp. They clambered through a huge, steep barren field of black boulders called Devil's Alley. Threading between the car-sized rocks, Lewis recounted the events of the last month, beginning with when he came back from the jail to find Ames, Underhill and Stout all in the office.

The skinny old guy was in surprisingly good shape, the heavier-built Lewis thought as he followed him and tried to catch his breath. Some "walk," Lewis thought. At the top of the ridge they hit the Appalachian

Trail and turned south. They stopped and rested at Rattlesnake Point, an outcropping atop a small cliff that offered a commanding view of the entire valley.

Lewis finished by recounting his agony at encountering Sherman's battered face in Marineland.

"Not too analytical, are you, son?" Petrosky drawled, not unkindly. "You had to see it to believe it."

Lewis considered that comment. Petrosky pointed out features of the valley below them, the river winding around the neat fields laid out three centuries earlier by conscientious German farmers moving down from Pennsylvania. He pointed out the dirt road that came up from the valley highway to the edge of his property. As if drawn by his index finger, a shiny black pickup truck bounced up the road over the tracks of the Virginia Central Railroad and slowly edged up to Petrosky's parking spot at the base of the slope.

"That's no one I know," the colonel said, peering at the truck in the hazy valley below them. "How about you?"

Lewis worriedly shook his head. "No one should know I'm here," he said.

Petrosky asked if Lewis had brought the "Ames 4" disk.

"No," Lewis said.

"Let's move out," Petrosky said, jumping to his feet. Lewis was impressed by how fast the retired Marine could move. When Petrosky got back to Devil's Alley, instead of picking his way through it, he jumped from boulder to boulder like a mountain goat, recklessly crossing the rock field in five minutes, compared with twenty minutes on their ascent between the boulders. A misstep would have meant a smashed shin or worse.

Lewis caught up with Petrosky only because the older man stopped and crouched at the border of his land, signaling back to Lewis with his hand flat and facing downward. The pickup truck's driver was somewhere on his property. Petrosky unholstered his pistol, thumbed the safety off and held it next to his boot, barrel pointed at the ground.

They waited in silence for several minutes. They heard a slapping sound, then a brief whistling like an arrow and then a thud. "That's one of my booby traps, and it wasn't a deer," Petrosky murmured. He scampered down to the trail.

It was, or had been, Sergeant First Class Stout, who had been doggedly pursuing Lewis, the cast on his left ankle dirty from walking in the woods.

He looked like he had sat down in great astonishment, his hands open on either side of him, as if questioning this sudden fate. His eyes were frozen open. An iron railroad spike was embedded two inches deep in the middle of his forehead, flung there at the end of a limber branch, catching him in his low, wide-footed, stalking crouch.

"You're good at this, aren't you?" Lewis said. Fashioning lethal traps from rusty railroad spikes was outside the realm of his military experience.

"Yeah, I guess I am." Petrosky shrugged, kneeling to lift the black computer disk labeled "Ames 4 of 4 only" from the dead man's open right hand. "Probably too good. There's a price to be paid for learning it."

Lewis told Petrosky the identity of the corpse. "I think he works alone," Lewis said.

"Worked," Petrosky said, sharing Brigadier General Moe's penchant for correcting Lewis's grammar. He looked Stout over carefully, pushing him into a mental file that already was overflowing. This wasn't the first person he had killed, or even the tenth, which was one reason he spent most of his nights awake on his porch, alone with the marijuana, the stars and his ghosts. His dead comrades were more real to him than most live people he met.

"Virginia law frowns on trespassing," Petrosky informed the dead man. They walked to the cabin. "I'll take care of the body," he said, putting the disk back on his table and picking up a spade from the side of the woodshed. "You wait on my porch."

Lewis watched Petrosky amble into the trees, then sat in the chair next to the laptop, looking out over the beautiful valley.

He never saw the hand, just the four-inch-long blade of a hunting knife that snaked under his chin. He reached up and grabbed the blade with both hands, feeling his palms sliced open as he pushed it away. Then the blow to the back of his head knocked him clear off the porch.

He woke facedown in the dirt in front of the house. He looked around. The disk was gone. He was alone, which meant that his attacker was off trailing Petrosky.

He crept back up the path. Through the bushes he saw Petrosky on his back, next to the grave he had been digging, and another man, dressed similarly to Stout, lying dead next to him. Petrosky looked up at Lewis. "I guess sometimes they don't work alone," he said dryly as he lay on the forest floor, still catching his breath after this latest attack.

Back at the cabin, Petrosky cleaned and bandaged the gashes in Lewis's hands, then left to finish his burial detail. When he returned and stripped and showered on a stone terrace outside the cabin, using a hand pump and a bucket, Lewis asked him what he intended to do about the Ames disk.

"Still thinking," the naked colonel said.

Aftershocks of adrenaline made Lewis uncharacteristically talkative. Petrosky lathered and rinsed and let Lewis recount the entire episode, from seeing Stout's pickup to Petrosky lying in the leaves. The old Marine dried himself, then dressed in black jeans and a faded black T-shirt that said, "I liberated Kuwait and all I got was this lousy T-shirt."

"Funny," Lewis concluded, suddenly contemplative, "after thirteen years as a professional military officer, I'm involved in killing for the first time—and I don't feel like a soldier at all."

Petrosky cocked an eyebrow at him. "You may not be a military officer in your soul anymore. You need to think about that—who you are and where you are going."

Lewis nodded. He was all talked out.

The old Marine picked up his cellular phone and dialed a number at the White House.

"Yes, I'll hold," he said to the person who answered at the National Security Council. Petrosky looked over the phone at Lewis. "I was a jarhead at Harvard," he said. "Did my Ph.D. dissertation under Professor Pitch: 'Siege Warfare and the American Military Ethos.' "

He looked back down. "Professor Pitch? Pete Petrosky here." He paused. "Well, not quite a hermit. I keep getting uninvited visitors from Washington.

"Got a few minutes? I need to talk to you about your boy Ames. Gotta tell ya, bud, shit like this is why I moved my own self outside the Beltway." He sighed. "You need to call in General Ames and ask him a few questions." But first, he said, he wanted to read some excerpts from General Ames's e-mails to him. "He's played you fellows like a Stradivarius."

When he was finished, Lewis called Sherman. They talked for an hour.

Petrosky's Cabin
Sunday, July 24
9:30 A.M.

The next morning Lewis hiked down to the railroad tracks to meet Cindy and guide her back to the cabin.

Her face looked almost worse, he thought. The bruises were turning a sickly yellow at the fringe, but had ripened to black at the middle. Her tongue was still swollen, and her left upper teeth sported a shiny steel brace.

"What happened to your hands?" she asked, her thick tongue making the last word come out as "handth."

"Oh, an accident with a knife," he said. She looked at him skeptically but he didn't offer any further explanation.

Sherman in turn thought Lewis looked drawn, even a bit anxious. His black eyebrows were a bit furrowed, as if he was wondering just what the hell had happened to him in the last three days. There were circles under his eyes. She liked the change. It gave him some ballast, some gravity, she thought. He may not have stared into the abyss, but at least he had found out there was one.

"I owe you an apology," she said softly, standing outside Petrosky's gate. "I broke it off with you too quickly."

"You also underestimated me," he said. "Bad move for an intell officer."

"Lesson learned," she said, the word coming out as "lethon." "I apologize for that too," she said, her gray eyes looking straight into his.

"Accepted," he said, opening the gate.

But she wasn't finished. She stood her ground outside the open gate. "I also covered for you, you know," she said, alluding to Ames's file on "Lewis and the Sons of Liberty."

"I thought you might have," he said. "Thanks for watching my back." He stepped back to let her in.

She still didn't move. "And I was right about the Sons of Liberty too," she said.

"I don't know about that," Lewis said, determined to show her the respect of being honest. "I still agree with a lot of the Sons of Liberty messages. But I think they went too far with it, encouraging the demonstrations. And I think General Ames used it all for his own purposes."

They sat on the front porch while Petrosky swayed back and forth in his rocking chair and placidly puffed on a huge spliff of his homegrown, king of all he surveyed.

She told them the news: Ames was out. Pitch and Wimpy Wilson had called Ames in and informed him that the Pentagon was announcing at that very moment that General Ames had decided to retire. If he went without a fuss he would still get a nomination—but as ambassador to Portugal, she said.

At Pitch's behest, Maddox had ordered a wholesale cleaning of Ames's office. Colonel Underhill was being transferred to be the public affairs officer for the X band radar station in Thule, Greenland. Under interrogation by the flexible Oscar, who could handle problems from any perspective, the XO had insisted that Stout had overzealously interpreted his instructions when he attacked Sherman. "Quite frankly, I never told him to do anything like that," Underhill had protested. At any rate, Sherman said, word was that Special Forces, which had a reputation of preferring to take care of its own problems and excesses, already had transferred Stout to Fort Huachuca. At this Lewis and Petrosky looked at their feet and nodded gravely. Lewis's candor didn't extend to making her an accessory to two homicides.

Maddox would step down as chairman of the Joint Chiefs as scheduled in eight weeks. It wasn't clear who his successor would be.

They walked down the hill to the old Subaru. "Can you drive with your handth like that?"

"Sure, I'll hold the wheel mainly with my fingers, not my palms."

"Then you drive, pleathe," she said, passing him the keys. He saw the plastic draped over the back area under the hatch. Curious, he craned back to lift the plastic and saw the half-finished painting that had been there since late June.

"It looks like Pennyfield on the Potomac," he said. "It's good."

"It ith," she said, watching him. "It'th your Chrithmath prethent." She gave him a wan smile, only the right side of her mouth moving. She got in the passenger seat and rested her good cheek against the window. Before they were on the interstate she was raggedly snoring as the air struggled through her smashed left nasal cavity. He drove east through the rolling pastures of northern Virginia and glanced over occasionally to watch the sun play on her wounded face as she slept.

The Pentagon
3 P.M.

At Ames's old office they were greeted by a Special Forces warrant officer working behind Stout's desk, packing the contents into a cardboard box. "May I help you, sir and ma'am?" he challenged. The office was being cleaned out—there were no signs of Ames, Underhill or Stout, nor, Lewis realized, of himself. All plaques, photographs, even personal computers had been removed. Lewis realized the warrant didn't know who he was.

Ames emerged from his inner office carrying a box of personal effects. He was dressed in civilian clothes—sharply pressed khaki pants, blue polo shirt and loafers. He looked smaller somehow, Sherman thought. Ames stopped when he saw Lewis.

"Made out all right for yourself, didn't you, Sunny Jim?" Ames said bitterly.

He thinks I acted out of ambition, Lewis realized. "Just doing my duty, sir," Lewis said evenly.

"Your duty was to me, not her," Ames snarled as he brushed by Lewis.

Lewis and Sherman walked up to Marineland to thank Brigadier General Moe for his timely help. As they strolled around the fifth-floor E ring toward the commandant's staff office, the newly self-conscious Lewis commented that this probably was the last time he would walk these halls as an officer. He said he thought he would go to law school.

He would need to give up that big expensive empty apartment in Crystal City, she said. Maybe he should move in with her in Adams-Morgan.

At the "Moe, Larry and Curly" sign, Lewis knocked on the door. A cueball-bald Marine gunnery sergeant opened it to find Sherman sliding her arms around Lewis and giving him a lopsided kiss with the right side of her mouth. He shook his head in dismay. Like all good Marines, he long had contended that the Army was going to hell in a handbasket.

Ames's Study
Fort McNair, Washington
11:40 P.M.

B. Z. Ames sat in his study, looking out into the dark waters of the Potomac. *Am I to be judged by the Shillingsworths and Wilsons of the world, treated as a problem to be disposed of?* The thought appalled him.

He went upstairs and changed into his swimming trunks. He walked outside, sat on the riverbank just under his study window and pushed off into the warm dark water of the river. The river and the swampy air above it were close in temperature and in humidity. At age fifty-four he was still lithe and slim, a powerful swimmer. He settled into an easy Australian crawl, heading down the channel and out into the broad, main section of the river.

On the far side of the river the last flights of the night were hurrying to land at National Airport before the midnight curfew. They came in so low above him that he could feel the heat of their exhaust settle on his head. He swam even harder, heading south down the river.

I won't have Wimpy Wilson put me on hold in Portugal while he decides whether to put me on trial. I have done only what my duty demanded. I will go on my own terms.

The weak, warm tide was with him, adding an extra knot to his speed. He swam another five miles down the river, passing under the decaying cement of the Wilson Bridge, the cars and trucks whining just fifteen feet above his head. The river broadened and turned brackish, tasting more like the Chesapeake than a freshwater river. The lights on either side were at least a mile away. He stopped, treading water and looking up at the sky. No stars penetrated the humid cover of the Washington summer.

Twice Ames thought he had defeated Shillingsworth. The first was on June 15, during that run around Leavenworth. He had thought he had beaten Shillingsworth then, but the old man had kept on going. And today, six weeks later, was the second time. He had thought Shillingsworth was gone, but the people Shillingsworth had set in motion had completed their mission, executed their duty, even after their leader was dead. It had turned into Shillingsworth's game, attrition warfare, and Shillingsworth had won.

Ames could swim no more. He thought of a baby dying in its crib in Indonesia nine years earlier. His legs were rubbery, numb, losing their ability to tread water. He slipped a little lower into the river, the soupy water slipping up to the bottom of his jaw. He looked at the quarter moon on the horizon. "Alpha Mike Foxtrot," he said in final salute to the world. He allowed his exhausted body to slide under the surface.

The newspapers were told General Ames had drowned in a boating accident while fishing at night. Two days later, General Ricardo Blades, the commandant of the Marine Corps, became the first Marine ever to be nominated to serve as chairman of the Joint Chiefs of Staff. He was unanimously confirmed by the Senate just before its August recess.

Glossary

AAR. After Action Review. A discussion after any military event of what happened and the lessons to be learned from it.

actual: In military radio communications, the term for the real commander of a unit, as opposed to the radio operator using that commander's call sign.

ADC: Can mean either an aide de camp or, in a division command structure, the assistant division commander—usually a brigadier general.

Alphas: Military uniform resembling civilian business attire, with a jacket and tie. Less formal than a dress uniform.

BDU: Battle dress uniform, the current term for combat fatigues.

black program: A classified program not disclosed in the Pentagon's budget documents and supposedly not known to the public.

BLUEFOR: Short for the Blue Force, which represents U.S. forces in exercises against the OPFOR.

Bravos: Military uniform less formal than Class A officewear, or Alphas, but more formal than BDUs.

C-17: Military cargo aircraft capable of flying long distances but able to land on short or undeveloped airfields.

Cat Four: Short for Category 4, the lowest mental category of recruit accepted into the U.S. military.

Centcom: Central Command, the headquarters overseeing U.S. military operations in the Mideast and Persian Gulf regions, including Afghanistan.

CG: Commanding general of a post or unit.

CH-53: Transport helicopter used mainly by the Marine Corps.

CIC: Combat Information Center, which coordinates combat operations aboard modern U.S. Navy ships.

CID: Criminal Investigation Division. Army's organization for internal investigations of service personnel.

CinC: A commander in chief of a given U.S. military region of operations, such as the Mideast, Europe, the Pacific, Korea or South America.

Claymore: Antipersonnel mine that explodes, sending hundreds of small steel balls horizontally in one direction, inflicting wounds for up to about one hundred meters.

click (or "klick"): U.S. military slang for "kilometer."

COO: The Army's Consideration of Others program, intended to increase sensitivity toward women and minorities.

CoS: Pentagon shorthand for "chief of staff."

DASD: A deputy assistant secretary of defense. A fairly high-ranking civilian position at the Pentagon, usually filled by political appointees rather than civil servants.

DCSOPS: Deputy chief of staff for operations. One of the most prestigious posts on the Army staff.

DEP: Delayed Entry Pool, for recruits who enlist but aren't immediately shipped to basic training.

DoD: Department of Defense.

Early Bird: The Pentagon's daily compendium of newspaper clippings about defense issues.

Humvee: The modern version of the military jeep.

IW: Information warfare.

J-5: The chief planning officer on the staff of the Joint Chiefs. Other positions are J-1 (personnel), J-2 (intelligence), J-3 (operations), J-4 (logistics), J-6 (communications). In other units, these would be designated by a *G* or an *S*.

JAG: Judge advocate general. The abbreviation has come to be used loosely to mean any military lawyer.

JCS: Joint Chiefs of Staff. In the Pentagon, frequently used to mean the staff people who work for the chairman of the Joint Chiefs.

KIA: Killed in action.

LT: Soldier slang for "lieutenant." Pronounced as two separate letters.

LZ: Landing zone.

medevac: Short for "medical evacuation."

MOPP: Mission Oriented Protective Posture, the bizarre name for the protective suit worn in combat when there is a possibility of being attacked by chemical weapons. Probably the single most obscure acronym in U.S. military usage.

MP: Military police

NCA: National Command Authority. Pentagonese for the president and those who represent him to subordinates.

NCO: Noncommissioned officer. Usually a sergeant.

NSA: National Security Agency. Large U.S. intelligence organization headquartered at Fort Meade, Maryland, and dedicated to intercepting foreign communications and electronic emissions.

NSC: National Security Council, the president's top national security advisers. Often used to mean the staff of the national security adviser.

NTC: National Training Center, located in the Mojave Desert in California. The Army's premier facility for realistic combat exercises. Home of the prestigious OPFOR.

OCS: Officer Candidate School.

OPFOR: The "Opposition Force" at U.S. Army training centers. Originally modeled after the Soviet military, the OPFOR now uses a wider range of weapons and tactics.

OPS: Short for "operations" section on a military headquarters staff. Also known as "the Three."

PCS: For "permanent change of station"—that is, a transfer to another post.

POAC: Pentagon Officers' Athletic Club. Exercise facility located just north of the Pentagon building and connected to it by a pedestrian bridge.

POTUS: Washingtonese for "president of the United States."

POV: Privately owned vehicle. Military term for "unofficial automobile."

S-2: Staff officer responsible for intelligence. At higher echelons, referred to as G-2 or J-2. Informally sometimes just called "the Two."

S-3: Staff officer responsible for operations, the most prestigious of the staff positions. At higher levels, G-3 or J-3. Informally sometimes just called "the Three."

SAP: Special Access Program.

SecDef: Pentagonese for "secretary of defense."

SF: Special Forces.

SOP: Standard operating procedure.

Spec 4: Army rank similar to corporal but without the status of a noncommissioned officer.

STU: Secure Telephone Unit. U.S. military telephone system for conducting classified
conversations.

Tank: In Pentagonese, the room where the Joint Chiefs of Staff meet.

TRICARE: Military medical care plan, referred to by some soldiers as "try to get some
care."

UAV: Unmanned aerial vehicle. A drone aircraft, generally used nowadays for reconnaissance.

VTC: Video teleconference. The means by which senior military officials are able to micro-
manage distant subordinates.

WIA: Wounded in action.

XO: Executive officer. Usually the number two person or the top assistant in a military
unit.

ABOUT THE TYPE

This book was set in Fairfield, the first typeface from the hand of the distinguished American artist and engraver Rudolph Ruzicka (1883–1978). Ruzicka was born in Bohemia and came to America in 1894. He set up his own shop, devoted to wood engraving and printing, in New York in 1913 after a varied career working as a wood engraver, in photoengraving and banknote printing plants, and as an art director and freelance artist. He designed and illustrated many books, and was the creator of a considerable list of individual prints—wood engravings, line engravings on copper and aquatints.